**I made my way slowly toward the window,
wishing I had a weapon,**

or any idea how to use one. I would have felt better. There were probably lots of things that could be used as improvised weapons in the kitchen and living room, but I didn't know what would work, and so I didn't reach for anything. I wasn't a fighter. I did, however, have a pane of glass between me and whatever was in the side yard. I held that thought firmly at the front of my mind as I inched around the couch and peered out the window.

Three of my neighbors were standing in the side yard, their hands down at their sides, staring at the fence. I recognized them all, even if I only knew one—Mr. Carson from next door—by name. None of them were moving. One of them, a woman, was wearing a bathrobe a little newer than mine. Her socks were soaked and grass stained. The other woman was wearing one shoe, and her hair looked like it was halfway-combed. I bit my lip. They were just *standing* there.

Then Mr. Carson turned and looked at me.

I let out a little scream and stumbled backward, falling over the couch in my retreat. His eyes were like Chave's had been: totally empty of anything resembling humanity or life. Dead eyes. He looked at me like a man who had crawled out of his own grave.

PARASITE

PARASITOLOGY VOLUME 1

MIRA GRANT

www.orbitbooks.net

Orbit
Hachette Book Group
237 Park Avenue, New York, NY 10017
HachetteBookGroup.com

First Edition: October 2013

Orbit is an imprint of Hachette Book Group, Inc. The Orbit name and logo are trademarks of Little, Brown Book Group Limited.

The Hachette Speakers Bureau provides a wide range of authors for speaking events. To find out more, go to www.hachettespeakersbureau .com or call (866) 376-6591.

The publisher is not responsible for websites (or their content) that are not owned by the publisher.

The characters and events in this book are fictitious. Any similarity to real persons, living or dead, is coincidental and not intended by the author.

Library of Congress Cataloging-in-Publication Data
Grant, Mira.
    Parasite / Mira Grant. — First edition.
       pages cm. — (The broken doors ; v. 1)
    ISBN 978-0-316-21895-5 (hardcover) — ISBN 978-1-61969-675-4
(audio download) — ISBN 978-0-316-21893-1 (ebook)
    I. Title.
    PS3607.R36395P38 2013
    813'.6—dc23
                                        2013005713

10 9 8 7 6 5 4 3 2 1

RRD-H

Printed in the United States of America

For Melissa and Rachel.
You are very good sisters.

INTERLUDE 0: GENESIS

My darling ones, be careful now, and don't go out alone.
—SIMONE KIMBERLEY,
DON'T GO OUT ALONE

Here there be monsters.
—DR. SHANTI CALE

August 17, 2015: Time stamp 15:06.

[The recording is crisp enough to look like a Hollywood film, too polished to be real. The lab is something out of a science fiction movie, all pristine white walls and gleaming glass and steel equipment. Only one thing in this scene is fully believable: the woman standing in front of the mass spectrometer, her wavy blonde hair pulled into a ponytail, a broad smile on her face. She is pretty, with a classic English bone structure and the sort of pale complexion that speaks less to genetics and more to being the type of person who virtually never goes outside. There is a petri dish in her blue-gloved hand.]

DR. CALE: Doctor Shanti Cale, *Diphyllobothrium symbogenesis* viability test thirty-seven. We have successfully matured eggs in a growth medium consisting of seventy percent human cells, thirty percent biological slurry. A full breakdown of the slurry can be found in the appendix to my latest progress report. The eggs appear to be viable, but we have not yet successfully induced hatching in any of the provided growth mediums. Upon consultation with Doctor Banks, I received permission to pursue other tissue sources.

[She walks to the back of the room, where a large, airlock-style door has been installed. The camera follows her through the airlock, and into what looks very much like an operating theater. Two men are waiting there, faces covered by surgical masks. Dr. Cale pauses long enough to put down her petri dish and put on a mask of her own.]

DR. CALE: The subject was donated to our lab by his wife, following the accident which left him legally brain-dead. For confirmation that the subject was obtained legally, please see the medical power of attorney attached to my latest progress report.

[The movement of her mask indicates a smile.]

DR. CALE: Well. Quasi-legally.

[Dr. Cale crosses to the body. Its midsection has been surrounded by a sterile curtain; the face is obscured by life support equipment, and by the angle of the shot. She pulls back the curtain to reveal the gleaming interior of the man's sliced-open abdomen. The skin has been peeled back, and the blood has been suctioned away, revealing a wide array of colors. Liver brown, intestinal green and glistening white, and the smooth pink sac of the stomach. Calmly, she reaches into the man's body, pushing organs aside until the surface of the small intestine is revealed.]

DR. CALE: Scalpel.

[One of the masked men passes her the requested tool. She takes it, pressing down against the man's intestine. He does not move. Her hand does not tremble.]

DR. CALE: I am not following strict sterile protocol, in part because infection is not a risk. The subject's immune system has been supplemented. *D. symbogenesis* eggs were introduced to the subject's system six days ago, fed into his body along with the nutrient paste we have been using to preserve basic biological functions.

[The surface of the intestine splits, spilling a thin film of brownish liquid over the surrounding organs. Dr. Cale ignores it as she sets the scalpel aside and thrusts her hand into the man's body. He still does not move as she digs through his small intestine. When she finally retracts her hand, she is clutching something. She pulls down her mask with her free hand and directs a beatific smile toward the camera.]

DR. CALE: I am pleased to report that we have multiple fully-formed proglottids present in the subject's body, as well as some partial strobila.

[She holds out her hand. The camera zooms in on the white specks writhing against her gloved fingers.]

DR. CALE: *D. symbogenesis* is capable of maturing when cultured inside a living human host. Ladies and gentlemen... at long last, it's alive.

[The film ends there. There are no notes in Dr. Cale's progress reports relating to the eventual fate, or original identity, of the first human subject used to culture *D. symbogenesis*. The medical power of attorney referenced in the recording has never come to light.]

[End report.]

June 23, 2021: Time stamp, 13:17.

   This is not the first thing I remember.
   This is the first thing that I was told to remember; this is the memory that has been created for me by the hands and eyes and words of others. The first thing I remember has no need for hands, or eyes, or words. It has no need for others. It only needs the dark and the warm and the distant, constant sound of drums. The first thing I remember is paradise.
   This is not the first thing I remember. But this is the first thing you will need to know.

Sally Mitchell was dying.
   She was up against an army—an army that had begun with paramedics, moved on to doctors, and finally, to complicated life support machines that performed their function with passionless efficiency—but none of that seemed to make any difference. She had always been determined, and now, she was determined to die. Silently, and despite everyone's best efforts, she was slipping further and further away.
   It was not a swift process. Every cell in her body, damaged

and undamaged alike, fought to retain cohesion. They struggled to pull in oxygen and force out the toxins that continued to build in her tissues and bloodstream. Her kidney function had been severely impaired in the accident, and waste chemicals had ceased to be automatically eliminated. She no longer responded in any meaningful way to external stimuli. Once she was removed from the machines that labored to keep her body functional, her life would come to an end in very short order.

Sally Mitchell existed in a state of living death, sustained by technology, but slipping away all the same.

Her hospital room was crowded—unusually so, for a woman standing in death's doorway, but her doctor had hoped that by bringing her family to see her, he could better plead his case for taking her off life support. The damage from the accident had been too great. Tests had shown that Sally herself—the thinking, acting girl they remembered—was gone. "Clinical brain death" was the term he used, over and over again, trying to make them understand. Sally was gone. Sally was not coming back. And if they kept her on artificial life support for much longer, more of her organs would begin to shut down, until there was nothing left. If her family approved the procedures to harvest her organs now, her death could mean life for others. By pairing her organs with splices taken from her SymboGen implant, the risks of rejection could be reduced to virtually nothing. Dozens of lives could be saved, and all her family had to do was approve. All her family had to do was let her go.

All they had to do was admit that she was never waking up.

Sally Mitchell opened her eyes.

The ceiling was so white it burned, making her eyes begin to water in a parody of tears. She stared up at it for almost a minute, unable to process the message she was getting from her nerves. The message wanted her to close her eyes. Another part of her brain awakened, explaining what the burning sensation in her retinas meant.

Sally closed her eyes.

The doctor was still pleading with her family, cajoling and comforting them in turn as he explained what would happen next if they agreed to have Sally declared legally dead. His voice was no more or less compelling than the buzz of the machines around her. None of his words meant anything to her, and so she dismissed them as unimportant stimuli in a world that was suddenly full of unimportant stimuli. She focused instead on getting her eyes to open again. She wanted to see the white ceiling. It was…interesting.

The second time Sally opened her eyes, it was easier. Blinking came after that, and then the realization that she could breathe—her body reminded her of breathing, of the movement that it required, the pulling in of air through the nose, the expelling of air through the mouth. The respirator that was supposed to be handling the breathing process began beeping shrilly, confused in its mechanical way by her sudden involvement. The stimulus from the man in the ceiling-colored coat became more important as it grew louder, hurting her ears.

Sally sat up.

More machines started to beep. Sally winced, and then blinked, surprised by her own automatic reaction. She winced again, this time on purpose. The man in the ceiling-colored coat stared at her and said something she didn't understand. She looked blankly back at him. Then the other people in the room started making noise, as shrill and confused as the machines around her, and one of them flung herself onto the bed, putting her arms around Sally and making a strange sound in her throat, like she was choking.

More people came into the room. The machines stopped making noise, but the people kept on doing it, making sounds she would learn were called "words," asking questions she didn't have answers for, and meanwhile, the body lived. The cells began to heal as the organs, one by one, resumed the jobs they had tried to abandon.

Sally Mitchell was going to live. Everything else was secondary.

STAGE 0: EXPOSURE

Your health is too important to trust to just anyone.
Choose SymboGen. Choose freedom.

—EARLY SYMBOGEN
ADVERTISING SLOGAN

Where am I?

—SALLY MITCHELL

When the hygiene hypothesis was proposed in the late 1980s, most people laughed it off as fringe science. It was based around the idea that more people were developing life-threatening allergies and autoimmune conditions because they weren't getting enough early-life exposure to infectious agents. Not just viruses—everyone gets exposed to viruses, unless they live inside a bubble—but allergens, bacteria, even parasites. We weren't living in literal bubbles, but we were sterilizing our environments more every year, and we were starting to see the effects. Children were getting sick because we refused to let them play in the dirt. It was a ludicrous idea. Pure scientific comedy.

Except that by the beginning of the 21st century, no one was laughing. More and more, the human race was being faced with a choice: find a way to keep our systems in the equilibrium they had evolved to maintain, or accept a future of chronic illness, increasing biological and neurological disorder, and potentially, eventually, extinction.

That's where we came in.

—FROM "KING OF THE WORMS," AN INTERVIEW WITH DR. STEVEN BANKS, CO-FOUNDER OF SYMBOGEN. ORIGINALLY PUBLISHED IN *ROLLING STONE*, FEBRUARY 2027.

...traffic cameras captured images of the driver's hands beginning to shake uncontrollably in the middle of the intersection before she apparently experienced a massive seizure, losing control of her vehicle and causing a dramatic sheer to the right. Witnesses reported that Sally Mitchell, age 20, appeared unaware of her surroundings as she drove straight into the path of an oncoming crosstown bus.

In his deposition, the bus driver (David Alexander, 37) claimed he had been unable to either hit the brakes or swerve to avoid Mitchell's car. The two vehicles collided without slowing, sending Mitchell slamming into the wall of a nearby bank. One pedestrian was hit, Anthony Thomas, 28. Mr. Thomas was hospitalized for a broken leg and several minor contusions, and was released two days later. At the time of this writing, Sally Mitchell remains under hospital care, and has not yet regained consciousness...

—FROM *THE CONTRA COSTA TIMES*, JUNE 13, 2021.

Chapter 1

JULY 2027

Dark.

Always the dark, warm, hot warm, the hot warm dark, and the distant sound of drumming. Always the hot warm dark and the drums, the comforting drums, the drums that define the world. It is comfortable here. I am comfortable here. I do not want to leave again.

Dr. Morrison looked up from my journal and smiled. He always showed too many teeth when he was trying to be reassuring, stretching his lips so wide that he looked like he was getting ready to lean over and take a bite of my throat.

"I wish you wouldn't smile at me like that," I said. My skin was knotting itself into lumps of gooseflesh. I forced myself to sit still, refusing to give him the pleasure of seeing just how uncomfortable he made me.

For a professional therapist, Dr. Morrison seemed to take an unhealthy amount of joy in making me twitch. "Like what, Sally?"

"With the teeth," I said, and shuddered. I don't like teeth. I liked Dr. Morrison's teeth less than most. If he smiled too much, I was going to wind up having another one of those nightmares, the ones where his smile spread all the way around his head and met at the back of his neck. Once that happened, his skull would spread open like a flower, and the mouth hidden behind his smile—his *real* mouth—would finally be revealed.

Crazy dreams, right? It was only appropriate, I guess. I was seeing him because I was a crazy, crazy girl. At least, that's what the people who would know kept telling me, and it wasn't like I could tell them any different. They were the ones who went to college and got degrees in are-you-crazy. I was just a girl who had to be reminded of her own name.

"We've discussed your odontophobia before, Sally. There's no clinical reason for you to be afraid of teeth."

"I'm not afraid of teeth," I snapped. "I just don't want to look at them."

Dr. Morrison stopped smiling and shook his head, leaning over to jot something on his ever-present notepad. He didn't bother hiding it from me anymore. He knew I couldn't read it without taking a lot more time than I had. "You understand what this dream is telling us, don't you?" His tone was as poisonously warm as his too-wide smile had been.

"I don't know, Dr. Morrison," I answered. "Why don't you tell me, and we'll see if we can come to a mutual conclusion?"

"Now, Sally, you know that dream interpretation doesn't work that way," he said, voice turning lightly chiding. I was being a smart-ass. Again. Dr. Morrison didn't like that, which was fine by me, since I didn't like Dr. Morrison. "Why don't you tell me what the dream means to *you*?"

"It means I shouldn't eat leftover spaghetti after midnight," I

PARASITE   17

said. "It means I feel guilty about forgetting to save yesterday's bread for the ducks. It means I still don't understand what irony is, even though I keep asking people to explain it. It means—"

He cut me off. "You're dreaming about the coma," he said. "Your mind is trying to cope with the blank places that remain part of your inner landscape. To some degree, you may even be longing to go back to that blankness, to a time when Sally Mitchell could be anything."

The implication that the person Sally Mitchell became—namely, me—wasn't good enough for my subconscious mind stung, but I wasn't going to let him see that. "Wow. You really think that's what the dream's about?"

"Don't you?"

I didn't answer.

This was my last visit before my six-month check-in with the staff at SymboGen. Dr. Morrison would be turning in his recommendations before that, and the last thing I wanted to do was give him an excuse to recommend we go back to meeting twice a week, or even three times a week, like we had when I first started seeing him. I didn't want to be adjusted to fit some model of the "psychiatric norm" drawn up by doctors who'd never met me and didn't know my situation. I was tired of putting up with Dr. Morrison's clumsy attempts to force me into that mold. We both knew he was only doing it because he hoped to write a book once SymboGen's media blackout on my life was finally lifted. *The Curing of Sally Mitchell.* He'd make a mint.

Even more, I was tired of the way he always looked at me out of the corner of his eye, like I was going to flip out and start stabbing people. Then again, maybe he was right about that, on some level. There was no time when I felt more like stabbing people than immediately after one of our sessions.

"The imagery is crude, even childish. Clearly, you're regressing in your sleep, returning to a time before you had so many things to worry about. I know it's been hard on you, relearning everything about yourself. So much has changed in the last six years." Dr. Morrison flipped to the next page in my journal, smiling again. It looked more artificial, and more dangerous, than ever. "How are your headaches, Sally? Are they getting any better?"

I bared my own teeth at him as I lied smoothly, saying, "I haven't had a headache in weeks." It helped if I reminded myself that I wasn't totally lying. I wasn't having the real banger migraines anymore, the ones that made me feel like it would have been a blessing if I'd died in the accident. All I got anymore were the little gnawing aches at my temples, the ones where it felt like my skull was shrinking. Those went away if I spent a few hours lying down in a dark room. They were nothing the doctor needed to be concerned about.

"You know, Sally, I can't help you if you won't let me."

He kept using my name because it was supposed to help us build rapport. It was having the opposite effect. "It's Sal now, Doctor," I said, keeping my voice as neutral as I could. "I've been going by Sal for more than three years."

"Ah, yes. Your continued efforts to distance yourself from your pre-coma identity." He flipped to another page in my journal, quickly enough that I could tell he'd been waiting for the opportunity to drop this little bomb into the conversation. I braced myself, and he read:

Had another fight with parents last night. Want to move out, have own space, maybe find out if ready to move in with Nathan. They said wasn't ready. Why not? Because Sally wasn't ready? I am not her. I am me.
I will never be her again.

He lowered the book, looking at me expectantly. I looked back, and for almost a minute the two of us were locked in a battle of wills that had no possible winner, only a different order of losing. He wanted me to ask for his help. He wanted to heal me and turn me back into a woman I had no memory of being. I wanted him to let me be who I was, no matter how different I had become. Neither of us was getting what we wanted.

Finally, he broke. "This shows a worrisome trend toward disassociation, Sally. I'm concerned that—"

"Sal," I said.

Dr. Morrison stopped, frowning at me. "What did you say?"

"I said, Sal, as in, 'my name is.' I'm not Sally anymore. It's not disassociation if I say I'm not her, because I don't remember her at all. I don't even know who she is. No one will tell me the whole story. Everyone tries so hard not to say anything bad about her to me, even though I know better. It's like they're all afraid I'm pretending, like this is some big trick to catch them out."

"Is it?" Dr. Morrison leaned forward. His smile was suddenly gone, replaced by an expression of predatory interest. "We've discussed your amnesia before, *Sally*. No one can deny that you sustained extensive trauma in the accident, but amnesia as extensive and prolonged as yours is extremely rare. I'm concerned there may be a mental block preventing your accessing your own memories. When this block inevitably degrades—if you've been feigning amnesia this whole time, it would be a great relief in some ways. It would indicate much better chances for your future mental stability."

"Wouldn't faking total memory loss for six years count as a sort of pathological lying, and prove I needed to stay in your care until I stopped doing it?" I asked.

Dr. Morrison frowned, leaning back again. "So you continue to insist that you have no memory prior to the accident."

I shrugged. "We've been over this before. I have no memory of the accident itself. The first thing I remember is waking up in the hospital, surrounded by strangers."

One of them had screamed and fainted when I sat up. I didn't learn until later that she was my mother, or that she had been there—along with my father, my younger sister, and my boyfriend—to talk to my doctors about unplugging the life support systems keeping my body alive. My sister, Joyce, had just stared at me and started to cry. I didn't understand what she was doing. I couldn't remember ever having seen someone cry before. I couldn't remember ever having seen a *person* before. I was a blank slate.

Then Joyce was throwing herself across me, and the feeling of pressure had been surprising enough that I hadn't pushed her away. My father helped my mother off the floor, and they both joined my sister on the bed, all of them crying and talking at once.

It would be months before I understood English well enough to know what they were saying, much less to answer them. By the time I managed my first sentence—"Who I?"—the boyfriend was long gone, having chosen to run rather than spend the rest of his life with a potentially brain-damaged girlfriend. The fact that I still hadn't recovered my memory six years later implied that he'd made the right decision. Even if he'd decided to stick around, there was no guarantee we'd have liked each other, much less loved each other. Leaving me was the best thing he could have done, for either one of us.

After all, I was a whole new person now.

"We were discussing your family. How are things going?"

"We've been working through some things," I said. Things like their overprotectiveness, and the way they refused to treat me like a normal human being. "I think we're doing pretty good. But thanks for asking."

My mother thought I was a gift from God, since she hadn't expected me to wake up. She also thought I would turn back into Sally any day, and was perpetually, politely confused when I didn't. My father didn't invoke God nearly as much, but he did like to say, frequently, that everything happens for a reason. Apparently, he and Sally hadn't had a very good relationship. He and I were doing substantially better. It helped that we were both trying as hard as we could, because we both knew that things were tenuous.

Joyce was the only one who'd been willing to speak to me candidly, although she only did it when she was drunk. She didn't drink often; I didn't drink at all. "You were a real bitch, Sal," she'd said. "I like you a lot better now. If you start turning into a bitch again, I'll cut your brake lines."

It was totally honest. It was totally sincere. The night she said that to me was the night I realized that I might not remember my sister, but I definitely loved her. On the balance of things, maybe I'd gotten off lightly. Maybe losing my memory was a blessing.

Dr. Morrison's disappointment visibly deepened. Clearing his throat, he flipped to another point in my journal, and read:

Last night I dreamt I was swimming through the hot warm dark, just me and the sound of drums, and there was nothing in the world that could frighten me or hurt me or change the way things were.

Then there was a tearing, ripping sound, and the drums went quiet, and everything was pain, pain, PAIN. I never felt pain like that before, and I tried to scream, but I couldn't scream—something stopped me from screaming. I fled from the pain, and the pain followed me, and the hot warm dark was turning cold and crushing, until it wasn't comfort, it was death. I was going to die. I had to run as fast as I could, had to find a new way to run, and the sound of drums was fading out, fading into silence.

If I didn't get to safety before the drums stopped, I was never going to get to safety at all. I had to save the drums. The drums were everything.

He looked up. "That's an odd amount of importance to place on a sound, don't you think? What do the drums represent to you, Sally?"

"I don't know. It was just a dream I had." It was a dream I had almost every night. I only wrote it down because Nathan said that maybe Dr. Morrison would stop pushing quite so hard if he felt like he had something to interpret. Well, he had something to interpret, and it wasn't making him back off. If anything, it was doing the opposite. I made a mental note to smack my boyfriend next time I saw him.

"Dreams mean things. They're our subconscious trying to communicate with us."

The smug look on his face was too much. "You're about to tell me I'm dreaming about being in the womb, aren't you? That's what you always say when you want to sound impressive."

His smug expression didn't waver.

"Look, I can't be dreaming about being in the womb, since that would require *remembering* anything before the accident, and I don't." I struggled to keep my tone level. "I'm having nightmares based on the things people have told me about my accident, that's all. Everything is great, and then suddenly everything goes to hell? It doesn't take a genius to guess that the drums are my heart beating. I know they lost me twice in the ambulance, and that the head trauma was so bad they thought I was actually brain-dead. If I hadn't woken up when I did, they would have pulled the plug. I mean, maybe I don't like the girl they say I was, but at least she didn't have to go through physical therapy, or relearn the English language, or relearn *everything* about living a normal life. Do I feel isolated from her? You bet I do. Lucky bitch died that day, at least as long as her memories stay gone. I'm just the one who has to deal with all the paperwork."

Dr. Morrison raised an eyebrow, looking nonplussed. Then he reached for his notepad. "Interesting," he said.

Somehow I managed not to groan.

＊   ＊   ＊

The rest of the session was as smooth as any of them ever were. Dr. Morrison asked questions geared to make me blow up again; I dodged them as best as I could, and bit the inside of my lip every time I felt like I might lose my cool. At the end of the hour, we were both disappointed. He was disappointed because I hadn't done more yelling, and I was disappointed because I'd yelled in the first place. I hate losing my temper. Even more, I hate losing it in front of people like Dr. Morrison. Being Sally Mitchell sucks sometimes. There's always another doctor who wants a question answered and thinks the best way to do it is to poke a stick through the bars of my metaphorical cage. I didn't volunteer to be the first person whose life was saved by a tapeworm. It just happened.

I have to remind myself of that whenever things get too ridiculous: I am alive because of a genetically engineered tapeworm. Not a miracle; God was not involved in my survival. They can call it an "implant" or an "Intestinal Bodyguard," with or without that damn trademark, but the fact remains that we're talking about a tapeworm. A big, ugly, blind, parasitic invertebrate that lives in my small intestine, where it naturally secretes a variety of useful chemicals, including—as it turns out—some that both stimulate brain activity and clean toxic byproducts out of blood.

The doctors were as surprised by that as I was. They're still investigating whether the tapeworm's miracle drugs are connected to my memory loss. Frankly, I neither care nor particularly want to know. I'm happy with who I've become since the accident.

Dr. Morrison's receptionist smiled blandly as I signed out. SymboGen required physically-witnessed time stamps for my sessions. I smiled just as blandly back. It was the safest thing to do. I'd tried being friendly during my first six months of sessions, until I learned that I was basically under review from the time I stepped through the door. Anything I did while inside the office could be entered into my file. Since those first six months included more than a few crying jags in the lobby, they were enough to buy me even more therapy.

"Have a nice day, Miss Mitchell," said the receptionist, taking back her clipboard. "See you next week."

I smiled at her again, sincerely this time. "Only if my doctors agree with whatever assessment Dr. Morrison comes up with, instead of agreeing with me. If there is any justice in this world, you'll never be seeing me again."

Maybe the comment was ill-advised, but it still felt good to see her perfectly made-up eyes widen in shock. She was still gaping at me as I turned back to the door and made my way quickly out of the office, into the sweet freedom of the afternoon air.

One good thing about being the first—and thus far, only—person to be saved from certain death by the SymboGen Intestinal Bodyguard: I wasn't paying for a penny of my medical care, and neither were my parents. Instead, the corporation paid for everything, and got running updates from my various doctors, all of whom had release forms on file making it legal for them to give my medical information to SymboGen. It sucked from a privacy standpoint, but it was better than dying.

SymboGen developed the Intestinal Bodyguard. My father works for the government, but even they don't know enough about what the implants can do to manage my care. So everything went on SymboGen's bill, and the corporation kept learning about what their tapeworms can do, while I kept getting the care I needed if I wanted to keep breathing. Breathing was nice. It was one of the first things I remembered discovering on my own, and I wanted to keep doing it for as long as possible.

Even with SymboGen looking out for me, we'd had our share of close calls. Since my accident I'd gone into full anaphylactic shock multiple times, for reasons I still didn't fully understand.

The first time had corresponded with a course of antiparasitics provided by SymboGen. They were intended to help me pass my old implant—a pretty way of saying "they were supposed to kill my tapeworm and force it out of my body"—and they'd nearly killed me, too. The second and third attacks had come out of nowhere, and the attack after that had corresponded with another course of antiparasitics, different ones.

What mattered to me was that I'd nearly died each time. Without SymboGen, I *would* have died. I needed to remember that. No matter how much I hated the therapists and the tests and everything else, I owed my life to SymboGen.

I looked back at Dr. Morrison's office before walking down the street to the empty bus stop. I sat down on the bench and settled in to wait. I'm patient. I'm rarely in a hurry. And I don't drive.

Patience may be something I have in abundance, but punctuality is not. My shift at the Cause for Paws animal center was supposed to start at four o'clock. Thanks to my missing the bus—again—and having to wait for the next one—again—it was already almost five when I came charging through the door.

"I'm sorry!" I called. I shrugged off my brown leather messenger bag and hung it next to the door, where it looked dull and out of place next to Tasha's rainbow crochet purse and Will's electric red backpack. In an organization made up of eccentrics and chronic do-gooders, the girl with the unique medical history is the boring one.

The door slammed behind me. I flinched.

"I'm sorry," I repeated more quietly to Tasha, who was standing next to the coffee machine with an amused expression on her face.

"You're sorry?" she asked. "Really? You're late, and you're sorry about it? Truly this is unprecedented in the annals of our humble shelter. I'll mark the calendars."

I stuck my tongue out at her.

"Did the bad psychologist try to tell you that you were crazy again?" asked Tasha, seemingly unperturbed. Perturbing Tasha was practically impossible. She was the kind of girl who would probably greet Godzilla while he was attacking downtown by asking whether he'd ever considered adopting a kitten to help him with his obvious stress disorder. "You can tell your Auntie Tasha about it. I swear I'm not a SymboGen plant reporting all your actions back to the corporation."

"You're a jerk," I said mildly, and grabbed my apron. "Come on. Scale of one to murder, how mad is Will over the whole 'late' thing?"

"Will isn't mad at all, because you just volunteered to clean all the cat boxes," said Will. I turned to see the shelter's owner standing in the doorway of the kitten room, a seemingly bone-less cat draped across his forearm. "Thanks, Sal!"

I rolled my eyes. "Lateness is not a legally binding promise to scoop shit."

"No, but keeping your job sometimes means doing things you don't want to do. Now go forth and scoop." Will stepped out of the doorway. "Look at it this way. You spent the afternoon feeding metaphorical shit to your therapist, and now you can clean up some literal shit. It'll be symbolically cleansing."

"You just don't want to do the boxes."

"That, too," Will agreed.

I rolled my eyes again and walked past him to the supply cabinet. Will was making a bigger deal of punishing me than was strictly necessary—I had a disability clearance excusing me for all my mandatory medical appointments, and since Symbo-Gen made healthy donations to the shelter in exchange for keeping me on the staff, it wasn't like he was going to argue with them needing a little of my time. I was also making a bigger deal of disliking my punishment than I had to. He was right. I needed a little normal after the day I'd had. I didn't like dwelling on the reality of my situation, or the fact that SymboGen essentially controlled my future, at least for now. They paid for everything. The medical care, the lab work, the classes…everything. Until I was perfectly healthy and finished relearning the world, they held the strings.

The cats chirped, meowed, and hissed their greetings as I came into the room and shut the door behind me. I smiled at them, ignoring the paws that reached for me between the bars of their cages. "Okay, guys," I said. "Let's get to work."

There's one more good thing about being the girl who lived because her genetically engineered tapeworm refused to let her die: I lived. That made everything else possible. Everything else in the world.

I was wondering when you'd get around to asking about the Mitchell case. She's a remarkable girl, young Sally. There are some people who think SymboGen saved her life. Well, I don't feel that I'm bragging when I say that they're probably right. We were nowhere near the accident, of course, we didn't find out about it until later, but the presence of her implant made it possible for her body to survive the amount of trauma she experienced. The machines can only do so much, they're on the outside. An implant, on the other hand...that can work from the inside, *it can tailor its response faster than any doctor. It helps that the Mitchell family was able to get a really good, top-of-the-line model for Sally. Colonel Mitchell made sure his entire family was equipped with tailored Intestinal Bodyguards™. That must be what saved her.*

SymboGen saves lives. Don't let anyone try to convince you differently. If you think I'm wrong, well. Why don't you try asking Sally Mitchell?

—FROM "KING OF THE WORMS," AN INTERVIEW WITH
DR. STEVEN BANKS, CO-FOUNDER OF SYMBOGEN. ORIGINALLY
PUBLISHED IN *ROLLING STONE*, FEBRUARY 2027.

...the core genetic material for the SymboGen Intestinal Bodyguard™ was taken not from T. solium, *as many would*

naturally assume, but from a subspecies of Diphyllobothrium— *specifically* D. yonagoensis. *Many other genetic sources were utilized in the development of the Intestinal Bodyguard™; however,* D. yonagoensis *provided fully 63% of the initial genome.*

By using a species not known for parasitizing humans as a primary host, SymboGen was able to control the life cycle of the Intestinal Bodyguard™ to an unprecedented degree. Their guarantees of sterility and planned obsolescence have thus far been borne out by all independent and internal testing. Their tailored species of Diphyllobothrium, D. symbogenesis, *is stable, and genetically distinct enough not to be confused with any naturally occurring genotype, yet is incapable of reproducing itself outside the laboratory environment...*

—FROM "THE DEVELOPMENT AND LIFE CYCLE OF
DIPHYLLOBOTHRIUM SYMBOGENESIS," ORIGINALLY
PUBLISHED IN *THE STANFORD SCIENCE REVIEW*, JUNE 2017.

Chapter 2

JULY 2027

It took half an hour to do the litter boxes, and another hour to feed and medicate the kittens in the isolation room. They would be kept away from the rest of the cats until their blood tests came back negative for any infections or parasites; then they would be integrated into the rest of the shelter's population, to await their "forever homes." The irony of an organization where every human was a proud parasite-carrier working diligently to cure animals of parasites was not lost on me. Nathan liked to say that SymboGen wouldn't rest until they'd perfected the Intestinal Bodyguard for use in every animal in America. Then he'd laugh like he was joking, even though we both knew he wasn't.

I didn't get the chance to check my phone until I was done with the last cage. There were two messages waiting for me. The first was from my sister, demanding—in her usual, strident

Joyce way—to know how therapy had gone, and whether she got to keep treating me like the crazy one. There was a note of genuine concern under her nagging. She knew how much I hated seeing Dr. Morrison.

Nathan had left the second message only a few minutes before. It was substantially shorter than Joyce's had been:

"Look outside."

I lowered the phone as I crossed to the window. Nathan's car was parked across the street. He was sitting on the hood in an easy cross-legged position, elbows resting on his knees as he smiled at the shelter, like he was waiting for me to appear.

I swiped my thumb across his name on my contact list before raising my phone to my ear. He dug out his own phone a few seconds later. "Hello?" he said.

"This is stalker behavior, you know," I said sweetly. "Only stalkers park outside women's places of employment and sit there waiting to see if they're going to come out."

"I prefer to think of it as being a compassionate, concerned boyfriend who didn't want to make you take the bus," said Nathan. "Stalker behavior would have me hiding in the supply closet."

"What if I was looking forward to riding that bus?" I asked. "What if I'm playing a game of guess-that-smell with the driver, and I don't want to let him pull ahead of me as we approach the championship round?"

"I suppose I'd just have to slink sadly back to my empty apartment, no girlfriend in my car, no one to go out to dinner with me," said Nathan, and sighed theatrically. "I'll just sit there in the dark, all alone..."

I laughed. "You're a ham. You're an absolute ham."

"Probably true, and good use of the word 'ham,'" Nathan replied, the faux mournfulness gone in an instant. "Come down, Sal. I'll give you a ride home, and you can tell me how your appointment with Dr. Morrison went."

"Do I have to?"

"Come down? Sure, unless you want to live at the shelter—a valid lifestyle choice, I admit, but probably boring in the long run." Nathan paused before adding, "We don't have to talk about Dr. Morrison if you don't want to. I just thought you might."

As soon as he said it, I realized that he was right: I did want to talk about it. I didn't want to go home and try to sleep with all that rattling around my brain. "I'll be right down," I said, and hung up.

Tasha was gone when I emerged from the back. Will was still there, sitting at the front desk. The cat from before was sitting next to the computer, nonchalantly washing a paw. It looked up when I entered the room, flicking its tail once. The tail landed across the keyboard, and Will looked up.

"Taking off?" he asked.

"Yeah. Nathan's here to get me." I retrieved my bag from the hook by the door. "The kittens in the isolation room are fed, and all the boxes are scooped in all five rooms. You going to be okay without me for the rest of tonight?"

"Yes, and for the rest of the week. See you Saturday." Will smiled, making a waving gesture toward the door. "Go on, Sal. You need to spend some time with your boyfriend. Do normal things before your review. I worry when you let yourself get this stressed out."

"You, Tasha, and everybody else," I said. "Goodnight, Will."

"Goodnight, Sal."

It was a warm night, and the streetlights cast just enough light to make walking down the steps feel like something out of a movie: darkness that wasn't really dark, more...cosmetic. Nathan slid off the hood of the car when he saw me coming.

He was in the driver's seat by the time I reached the passenger side door—which was, naturally, locked. I tugged the handle and glared at him through the glass. He smiled without showing his teeth. I made a downward gesture with my free hand, and he hit a button on the steering wheel, causing the window to drop.

"Yes, miss?"

"You're a dork," I informed him. "A giant dork."

"That's a new word." He pressed another button. The door unlocked. "Where'd you learn that one?"

"Eric—the kid next door. He said it was less offensive than calling someone a dick, but that it came from the same family of words." I slid into the seat, glancing toward Nathan and quirking an eyebrow. "Why? Did I use it wrong?"

"No, you seem to have grasped my essential dorky nature." Nathan leaned over to kiss me slowly. "Missed you today."

"I missed you, too." I returned his kiss before sinking deeper into the seat, trying to let my shoulders relax. Nathan adjusted the environmental controls. My seat warmed up and began rubbing my back in slow, rhythmic motions. "Mmm. Thanks."

"You're more fun when you're not so tense that I can see the whites all the way around your eyes," he said, and started the car. I tensed again, and relaxed as Nathan pulled smoothly onto the mostly empty street. Cars make me nervous. But Nathan was a good, safe driver who let me read his insurance statements when I asked him to confirm that he'd never been in an accident. He also kept both hands on the wheel when he had me in the car with him. "How did it go with Morrison?"

"He thinks I'm crazy."

"Yes, he does."

Nathan's honesty was usually one of the things I appreciated most about him. At the moment, I wasn't feeling much like embracing my inner truth. I glared at him. "You could be a little slower to agree there, you know."

"I didn't say I thought you were crazy, I said that he thinks you're crazy. Or at least he's convinced himself to think that you're crazy."

I frowned. "Support your thesis."

"Normal people don't say 'support your thesis' in casual conversation, honey."

"Right." I sighed. English is not an easy language to learn, and it was no better the second time. Basic sentence structure was mostly okay, but I had trouble with colloquialisms—the slang, the shading of the words, the reason that some things were more appropriate than others. English is a language full of words and syntax and phrases. It was a good reason for not talking much around strangers. "Can you explain?"

"Look, to Morrison, you're a unique case that needs to be studied, and he figures that he might as well be the one doing the studying. Most people don't come back from what you experienced."

"I know that," I said peevishly. "Why does that give him the right to act like I'm insane?"

"It doesn't. It just gives him the motivation he needs to convince himself that you need his help more than you need anything else in the world, and so he keeps looking for excuses." Nathan glanced at me, then back at the road. "He thinks I'm doing the same thing, you know."

I blinked. "What?"

"Morrison. He thinks I'm dating you because it's the best way to keep track of what's going on with your metabolism."

"That's…wow. If you were doing that, you'd be an idiot. I'm peeing in so many cups and giving so many blood samples every week that you wouldn't need to buy me dinner to keep track of my condition." Nathan was a doctor—a parasitologist, to be exact—at San Francisco City Hospital. We'd met when Joyce had to go to the hospital to have the health of her implant checked. He'd given her some basic nutritional supplements and asked me out to dinner. It was the first time someone had shown interest in *me* like that, and I'd been delighted. I still was.

Nathan laughed. I loved that sound. "I know. Add the fact that SymboGen handles everything having to do with your Intestinal Bodyguard internally, and there's a media blackout that means I couldn't get your medical records if you asked me to, and I'd be a specialist without a subject."

"That's why I adore you," I said. "You're willing to waste time on me even when I don't advance your career."

"Right now, I'm more interested in advancing dinner," he said.

"Good plan," I said. "How do you feel about Mexican?"

"Excellent," he said, and we drove on into the night.

In less than twenty minutes, we were seated at a white Formica table with a basket of chips and salsa, watching the waitress weave her way through the crowd to put our orders in. Nathan had ordered iced tea; I had ordered watermelon agua fresca, which I was intending to doctor liberally with Tabasco sauce. We'd discussed the relative merits of one another's drinks a dozen times before—he thought mine was disgusting, I thought the same of his—and so we were able to skip that exchange in favor of a brief, companionable silence.

Nathan looked toward the window, watching someone walk past. I watched him. It was an activity I'd learned to like a lot since we met. I'd been surprised when I first realized that I found him attractive; that hadn't happened to me before. The fact that he turned out to be handsome to other people was irrelevant.

He wasn't tall as men went, only an inch or so taller than me, and having a Korean father and an English mother meant that he was always tanner than me, no matter how much time I spent in the sun. Both my parents were Irish, and the Irish word for "suntan" is "burn." Of the two of us, he was still better about remembering to put on sunscreen, since he was much more aware of the dangers of cancer than I was. He wore wire-framed glasses in front of his dark brown eyes, citing a dislike of sticking things into his body as a reason to avoid either contacts or retinal implants.

That was another thing: Nathan was the best parasitologist I knew, and knew more about the SymboGen Intestinal Bodyguard than almost anyone who hadn't helped to develop it, but he didn't have one of his own. In a world where most people managed their medication automatically via tapeworm, he still took pills, because he said that it was less disturbing than the alternative.

The pause, and the introspection, couldn't last. Nathan turned to look at me. I bit back a sigh. I knew that look. It was the "I'm about to ask you how therapy went" look, and it never ended well, for either of us.

"Did you tell him about the dreams?"

Yup: this was going to suck. "What about them?" I asked lightly. "The red part, the red part, or the red part?"

"Sal..."

"Yes, I told him about the dreams. He thinks I'm dreaming about being in the womb. I think he's wrong. He's probably going to tell SymboGen I'm repressing, or regressing, or something, and I'm going to wind up with another year of therapy." I stabbed a tortilla chip viciously into the salsa. "*He's* the one who needs therapy."

"Unfortunately, he's not the one getting it. You are."

"Nathan, I'm *fine*." Sure, I woke up screaming three or four times a week, but that was normal for me. It was what I had been doing for all six years of my remembered life.

Nathan frowned, starting to say something. He was interrupted by the return of the waitress with our drinks. Once she was gone, he said, "You didn't know who I was yesterday morning."

I stopped in the middle of reaching for my agua fresca. "Excuse me?" My mouth was dry. I grabbed my drink and took a gulp, trying to rinse the dryness away. It didn't work.

"Yesterday morning, you screamed and sat up in bed. I asked you what was wrong. You looked at me like you'd never seen me before. Then you looked at your hands and screamed again. I was honestly waiting for my neighbors to call the police and report that I was beating you, you screamed so much."

My head was spinning. It felt like all the blood had drained out of it, heading for safer climes elsewhere in my body. "What happened after that?" I didn't remember any of this, I didn't remember *any* of it. Was Nathan lying to me? Worse, was Nathan telling me the truth?

"You stopped."

The words were so simple that they didn't quite make sense. I blinked at him. "What?"

"You stopped screaming. You didn't wake up, you didn't react when I touched you, you just collapsed back onto your pillow like you'd never moved at all. When you sat up again, about ten minutes later, you didn't remember any of it."

I *did* remember Nathan being oddly concerned about how I'd slept, and asking three times whether I was going to keep my appointment with Dr. Morrison. I bit my lip before asking, "Why didn't you say anything? You know I don't like it when people keep things from me."

"You also don't like it when I upset you right before you have to see Dr. Morrison, and I'm saying something now," Nathan countered. "If it weren't for your medical history, I'd think you were having night terrors—they're rare in people in their twenties, but they're not unheard of. But with your amnesia…"

"There goes my medical history, complicating everything again," I said bitterly.

"I love you, medical history and all, but it scared me. It should scare you, too. That's why I wanted you to tell Dr. Morrison about the dreams. I know you don't like him, but you don't have another psychiatrist you can discuss this stuff with, and it's better if this is psychological."

I caught his meaning immediately. If this was psychological, it meant I was still recovering from that first big knock to the head. If it was physical, it could mean almost anything—and very little that was good. "I know. I'll tell you what: we'll keep a record of how I'm sleeping for the next few weeks, okay? If it happens again, I'll tell SymboGen."

"You promise?"

I solemnly drew a cross across my left breast with my right index finger. "Cross my heart and hope to die, stick a needle in my eye."

He actually laughed. "When did you learn *that*?"

"Yesterday, from a little girl who came into the shelter to pick out her new kitten." I grinned. "I am full of surprises."

"Yes, you certainly are," he said, and leaned across the table to kiss me.

I returned the gesture, although my mind was only half on the moment. I might not understand the gruesome details of my medical history the way he did, but I knew enough to understand that my problems didn't end with any of the nasty physical side effects that I was being tested and monitored for on a regular basis. My implant had kept me alive. We still didn't know what that meant, but it did involve waiting, every day, for the other shoe to drop.

Talking to SymboGen about the night terrors—if that was what they were—meant resigning myself to even more therapy, and possibly another sleep study at SymboGen. I could deal with that. If Nathan was worried, I'd be a fool not to be.

When I pulled away, Nathan smiled. "Love you."

"I love you, too," I said. "And I'll talk to SymboGen. I just won't be happy about it."

"If you were, *I'd* start worrying about your sanity."

"I don't trust Dr. Morrison."

"You shouldn't," Nathan said, with a wry smile. "He works for SymboGen."

I laughed, and then the food arrived, and we had better things to talk about.

Nathan didn't ask me anything else important until the waitress came back to pick up the check. Then he asked, "You sleeping over tonight?"

There was only one good answer to that question. So I smiled back, and said, "I was just waiting for you to ask."

Nathan's apartment was in a gated complex near the Ferry Building. He had almost a quarter of the ninth floor, complete with a balcony on the wall that faced the Bay. He had it decorated in what he assured me was an utterly forgettable mishmash of Ikea and bachelor pad chic. It didn't look like either the sleekly sterile halls of the hospital or like Sally Mitchell's room, haunted by the ghost of a girl I didn't remember being, and so I loved it.

But I loved him more. We were barely inside before I grabbed his hand and pulled him toward the bedroom, where the big black bed was waiting for us. Nathan went willingly. I'd been the one to first take our relationship sexual; he was always trying to go slowly, trying to let me be sure of what I wanted. *This* was what I wanted. This room, this place, this time, and a man who'd never met Sally Mitchell, but who loved me for me.

By the time we fell asleep, tangled in the sheets and in each other, it felt like things would be better. And I dreamt...

When I listened to books about dream imagery—which I did more than I was willing to admit, because I wanted to understand my dreams as much as Nathan did, if only because I was worried about Sally rising from below and fracturing my fragile psyche with her own, older memories—they always seemed to focus on things happening to bodies. Bodies flying. Bodies getting older, or losing teeth, or being seen in public without their clothes on. Bodies everywhere, doing *things*.

I never dreamt about bodies.

Instead, I dreamt about the dark—the hot warm dark, which was always those three distinct things. It was hot the way a summer night was hot, when the air trapped moisture like a sponge, even in San Francisco, all humidity and untaken breaths. It was warm the way Nathan's arms were warm, comfortable and close and safe, and the two states weren't antithetical at all. They were two parts of the same whole. When I dreamt, it was absolutely natural that hotness and warmth would be different things, capable of existing simultaneously. It was only when I was awake that it seemed like a contradiction. And the dark...

The dark wasn't like the dark in the apartment when the lights were off, or the dark in the street when the sun went down. It wasn't even like the dark inside my eyelids, although that came closer than anything else did. The dark *was*. It was entire and eternal, without question, and it didn't need to be anything else, because there was nothing else that the dark could possibly be. It was just the dark, the hot warm dark, and it was perfect. I didn't need anything but the hot warm dark, and the feeling of the world's arms closed around me.

That night was one of the good dreaming nights, where it was just me and the hot warm dark, and part of me was still dimly aware of the apartment where my body lay sleeping in its own cocoon of hot warm dark, the space created where my skin pressed against Nathan's. We encompassed a world between us. Anything outside that world wasn't worth worrying about.

Somewhere across the Bay, a boat horn blew a long, mournful note. Everything else was still, and I slipped deeper down into dreams and the safety of the hot warm darkness inside me.

The early success of the SymboGen Intestinal Bodyguard™ line of products can be partially ascribed to canny advertising. Their marketing department hired an actress best known for her work in a series of horror movies featuring a monster modeled off a species of parasitic wasp. Her first infomercial began with her in her original costume smiling her A-list smile and saying, "I know a bad parasite when I see one. Now it's time for you to learn about a good parasite—one that wants to help you, not hurt you."

While SymboGen would quickly move away from use of the word "parasite" in advertising material, the early groundwork had been laid, and people were beginning to trust the concept behind the Intestinal Bodyguard™. After that, all that remained was to sell the idea to the world.

—FROM *SELLING THE UNSELLABLE: AMERICAN ADVERTISING THROUGH THE YEARS*, BY MORGAN DEMPSEY, PUBLISHED 2026.

Little boy with faith so thin,
Little girl so strong within,
I said I'd never leave you, and I'm sorry, but I lied.
If you're set to pay the price,
Learn the ways of sacrifice,

Leave this world to grieve you, take a breath, and step outside.

The broken doors are waiting, down the path you've always known.
My darling ones, be careful now, and don't go out alone.

—FROM *DON'T GO OUT ALONE*, BY SIMONE KIMBERLEY, PUBLISHED 2006 BY LIGHTHOUSE PRESS. CURRENTLY OUT OF PRINT.

Chapter 3

AUGUST 2027

I glared at the sheet of paper in front of me. The words that were printed there swam in and out of focus, seeming to actively evade my attempts to understand them. Joyce placed a steadying hand on my shoulder. "Deep breaths, Sal," she said. "Let them come to you."

"Yeah, because *that's* going to happen," I muttered, and kept glaring at the paper.

Learning to read again had been more difficult than learning to talk, and I still wasn't comfortable with it. Apparently, I hadn't been dyslexic before the accident. The old Sally Mitchell was a voracious reader. I preferred audiobooks, which didn't change themselves around when I was tense or tired.

After several minutes of continued glaring, the recalcitrant letters began to obey me, assembling themselves into tidy sentences, which read:

THE PRESENCE OF PATIENT SALLY R. MITCHELL
IS HEREBY REQUESTED AT SYMBOGEN INC. ON THE
MORNING OF FRIDAY, AUGUST 20TH, TO DISCUSS
ONGOING TREATMENT. PLEASE BRING ALL RECEIPTS
RELATING TO HEALTHCARE EXPENSES INCURRED
SINCE FEBRUARY 2027, INCLUDING BUT NOT
LIMITED TO HOSPITAL STAYS, TRANSPORTATION TO
AND FROM APPOINTMENTS, APPROVED SPECIALISTS
(SEE APPENDED LIST) . . .

The words started scrambling themselves again. I stopped trying to read them. There was only so much SymboGen doublespeak I could take at any one time, and "requests" from the corporation were never really requests. They were commandments wearing their best Sunday clothes, and that didn't make me like them any better. "I think I have everything they've asked for," I said, and thrust the paper at her. "Can you please check the list? I can't read this anymore."

"You tried, and that's what matters," said Joyce, taking the paper and glancing down it. "It looks like we have everything. Now come on, Sal, it's going to be fine. This is just your six-month review. They're not trying to pull a fast one. They're making sure they have all their paperwork in order and that you haven't started hiding symptoms from them. This is totally normal, and that means it's *fine*."

"You know, I don't mind so much when our parents talk to me like I'm six, but you need to cut it out," I said. "You're not the one who has to go to SymboGen and get poked at by their scientists for an entire day."

"I'm also not the one who decided to play chicken with a bus," said Joyce. "See, this is how a single bad decision can shape your whole life. I'm the good daughter, and you're a cautionary tale."

Despite myself, I laughed. Unrepentant to the end, Joyce grinned.

Joyce and I looked alike enough for our relationship to be obvious: we had the same pale Irish skin, the same round faces, and the same lanky frames. We even both had brown hair and eyes. But my hair was a middling chestnut, while hers was a dark red-brown that looked like it belonged in a shampoo commercial. Her eyes were light enough to be almost hazel, while mine basically matched my hair. We both burned in any kind of strong light, but my skin freckled, while hers eventually tanned. It didn't take me long to realize that of the two of us, she was "the pretty one"—something I'm sure I resented when I was Sally and had to deal with growing up shadowed by a prettier, smarter, genuinely nicer younger sister. Now that I didn't have any of that baggage, I could appreciate Joyce for what she was. That was nice. If I was going to have a sister, I wanted her to be someone I could like.

She was also a biologist, working with our father in his lab. I'd been going to college for a general Liberal Arts degree—something everyone I met assured me was useless—when I had my accident. Now I seemed destined for a long, productive life as a lab rat. So I guess we were in the same general profession, at opposite ends of the food chain.

"Now come on." Joyce dropped the paper on the kitchen table and grabbed my hand. "You promised me an afternoon of mindless shopping at the mall, followed by a brainless summer blockbuster and all the popcorn I could consume. This is our sisterly bonding time, and I won't let you out of it again."

"But Joyce—"

"Nope, no buts. I was promised commerce and togetherness, and commerce and togetherness I shall have." She gave my hand a tug. "Come on, Sal. Live a little. Buy uncomfortable shoes and makeup that you'll never wear in a million years."

I sighed. "You really want me to go shopping with you."

"You'd think that would have been obvious, from the way I've been saying 'hey, let's go shopping like you promised' since you got out of bed, but yes, I want to go shopping. It'll help you relax before your review." Joyce dropped my hand. "Come on. We'll go to the big mall in San Bruno. They have an Orange Julius!"

"Why didn't you say so before?" I stood, stretching slowly just so I could watch the impatience blossoming in her expression. Joyce glowered at me. I smiled. "What? Am I not fast enough for you?"

"Stop messing around with me, or I'm making you drive."

My smile died. "Not funny, Joyce."

"Oh, shit, Sal, I'm sorry," said Joyce, immediately seeing that she had gone too far. She leaned over to touch my shoulder, adding, "I just keep thinking it's been long enough. I'm sorry."

"I'll tell you when it's been long enough, okay? Just...for right now, please, no more jokes about making me drive."

Joyce nodded, biting her lip.

I somehow forced myself to smile. "It's not that bad. Don't American social norms mean that younger siblings are normally fighting to be the ones behind the wheel?" Not that I was that comfortable having Joyce drive me anywhere. According to her driving history, she'd been in six minor accidents and received eleven speeding tickets since she got her license. It wasn't the sort of thing that inspired confidence. But if I was going to be a good sister, I was going to let her drive me to the mall.

"Every time I think you're halfway back to normal, you go and say something like that." Joyce rolled her eyes, distress forgotten in favor of making sure I realized how weird I was. That had been the idea. "You get your coat. I'll get the keys."

"I'm on it," I said, turning toward my room. Dwelling on my upcoming appointment wasn't doing me any good, and maybe Joyce was right. Maybe commerce would do the trick.

*   *   *

After an hour at the mall, I was absolutely certain of one thing: Joyce was wrong. My feet hurt, my shoulders ached from carrying Joyce's bags—something I hadn't volunteered to do, but seemed to be doing all the same—and I was starting to think longingly of the isolation room back at the shelter. It was hot and snug and always smelled like cats, and it would have been paradise compared to the food court at the San Bruno Mall.

Worst of all, the outing wasn't doing anything to take my mind off my upcoming visit to SymboGen. If anything, it was making me dwell on it *more*, since the mall wasn't giving me anything better to think about. Except for maybe going home.

I'd been sitting by myself for almost fifteen minutes, ostensibly guarding Joyce's many purchases, when she came flouncing back through the crowd and placed an Orange Julius cup in front of me with a grand flourish. "Ta-da!"

I raised an eyebrow.

"What?" She frowned. "You're supposed to be overcome with gratitude. I hunted and killed that smoothie for you."

"My hero," I deadpanned.

"I think you mean 'heroine.' Heroes are male."

"Whatever." I shook my head. "I'm sorry, Joyce. I'm not trying to be a spoilsport."

"Yet somehow, you're still managing to do an excellent job." Joyce flopped into a plastic chair, propping her chin on her knuckles. "You wanna tell me why *this* SymboGen trip has you all fucked in the head, as opposed to all the other ones?"

I sighed, taking the lid off my smoothie and swirling my straw through the thick orange goo. "I had another fight with Mom."

Out of the corner of my eye, I saw Joyce wince. "The moving out thing?"

"The moving out thing," I confirmed. "Until SymboGen says I'm both healthy and mentally stable, she's not going to let me move out." For most adults, "let" wouldn't matter. For me...there had been a period following my accident when I wasn't expected ever to recover the ability to make my own decisions. My parents had been granted conservatorship over me until such time as my doctors judged me fully recovered. Until SymboGen signed the papers to certify that I was both healthy and sane, "let" was the only word that mattered. I couldn't do anything my parents didn't want to *let* me do.

"It could be worse," Joyce said.

"Sure. They could decide not to *let* me go to work anymore. Or maybe they'll decide not to *let* me see Nathan." I shoved my smoothie aside. "I wouldn't be alive if it weren't for them. I know that. And I know that I have to let SymboGen keep studying me, because we need to understand why I didn't die. But sometimes I'm just tired of feeling like this is my life, you know? Like this is all I get, and it's all because of our parents, and *SymboGen*."

I stopped, startled by the venom in my own voice. Even Joyce was staring at me, briefly shocked out of her normal too-cool-for-this attitude.

"I..." She stopped, reaching for the words, and tried again: "I didn't know you felt that way."

"Yeah, well." I shrugged halfheartedly. "It feels like there's no way out sometimes."

"You've been so much better these last few years. It's like you're...it's like you're happy for the first time in your life. I thought that meant...I mean, you seemed happy, so I thought you had to *be* happy."

"I *am* happy," I said. "I'm happy that we're friends. I know from what you've said, and from what everyone who knew me before the accident won't say, that you and I didn't always get along. I like my job. I like working with animals."

"And Nathan?" asked Joyce, a trace of her normal insouciance creeping back.

"And Nathan," I allowed. "I like him, too. I love him, even. So it's not that I'm not happy. It's just that I don't like feeling trapped."

"I get that," said Joyce. "Sometimes—" She cut herself off, blinking at something behind me. "What the hell is going on over there?"

There was a new air of confusion to the general chatter in the mall. I'd been too busy focusing on Joyce to notice it before. I twisted in my seat, following her gaze to a little girl outside the boundaries of the food court. She was too young to be on her own—no more than six or seven—and she was half-walking, half-staggering toward the exit. From the way she was moving, she'd hurt her foot recently. If she'd been older, I would have suspected her of having had a stroke. And yet her gait managed not to be the strangest thing about her, possibly because the sight of a little girl towing a fully grown woman bodily along was weird enough to make everything else seem incidental.

"Helen, sweetie, come on, stop playing this bad game," said the woman—her mother, judging by the resemblance between them. There were tears running down her cheeks. Her obvious dismay just called the utter slackness of the little girl's expression into sharper relief. "Let's go back to Daddy, okay? Okay, sweetie? Please?"

The little girl—Helen, her name was Helen, and that seemed suddenly very important, although I couldn't have said exactly why—gave no indication that she'd heard a word her mother said. She just kept plodding forward, moving surprisingly fast considering that she was barely lifting her right foot off the floor. Her mother was dragged along in her wake, unable to stop the girl's forward motion.

I heard Joyce gasp. "There's another one," she whispered loudly. Her hand stabbed past my face, pointing into the crowd. I turned to look where she was pointing, and saw a man shamble through the gathered bodies, moving with the same unsteady speed as the little girl. Like the little girl, his expression was slack, eyes focusing on nothing in this world...and like her, he was heading straight for the exit.

"What the hell...?" I stood, taking a step back, so that I was standing next to Joyce. She scrambled to her feet, latching onto my arm with surprising strength. "What's wrong with them?"

"I don't know. Food poisoning maybe?" Joyce gave me a pleading look. "It's not something contagious, is it? There's not something in the air vents?"

"You're the one who works in a lab," I said, keeping most of my attention on the man and the little girl. "Shouldn't you know what causes this sort of symptomology?" Helen's mother wasn't stopping her, but she was slowing her down, and the man was starting to catch up. I wanted to see what would happen if they saw each other. I wanted to see what they would do.

"Helen!" wailed the mother.

Helen plodded ceaselessly on. The man's longer legs were rapidly shortening the distance between them. He was walking better than she was, although his balance didn't seem to be as good; several times, I was sure he was going to topple over. But he didn't.

And then they were next to each other, and with no more ceremony than a step, they stopped. The little girl turned to face the man, tilting her chin up as she stared into his eyes. Their expressions remained slack, neither showing any emotion as they considered each other. The entire mall seemed to have gone quiet; the only sounds were the music playing softly through the speakers overhead and the pleas of Helen's mother.

Unsteadily, Helen extended her free hand toward the man. Just as unsteadily, he reached out and took it, mashing his fingers around hers with so much force that it had to hurt her. She didn't react. Now hand-in-hand, the pair turned and resumed their trek toward the door, dragging Helen's wailing mother in their wake.

They had almost reached the doors when the mall EMTs descended, summoned by someone who reacted better in a crisis than the rest of us. They had no trouble separating the man from the little girl—when they pulled on their joined hands, the pair just let go. They had more trouble getting Helen's mother to let her go. I think they may have finally threatened to sedate her, because she dropped Helen's hand and stepped away, pleas fading into sobs.

Joyce and I watched as both man and little girl were strapped to gurneys and wheeled away, vanishing through an EMPLOYEES ONLY door into the back corridors of the mall. A stunned silence hung over everyone who had witnessed the scene. Several people had their phones out and were snapping pictures of the crowd, like the disoriented faces of the witnesses would somehow provide the answers that none of us had on our own.

"I think we should go home now," said Joyce, in a very small voice.

"Yeah," I said. "I think you're right."

Joyce switched the radio from station to station as she drove, taking her eyes off the road so many times that I was afraid I was going to start hyperventilating. "Traffic, weather, stupid comedy show, traffic, traffic— God!" She slammed her fists against the wheel. "Doesn't anybody talk about anything *important* around here?"

"Do we need to pull over so you can calm down?" I asked the question as calmly as I could, but my hands were pressed against the dashboard so hard the skin on my fingers was bleached bloodless white. My stomach felt like it was turning backflips. The only thing stopping me from giving in to the urge to throw up was the knowledge that it probably wouldn't improve her driving.

"No! I'm fine." She stabbed the search button with her index finger, sending the radio skipping to the next station.

"—doctors are baffled by a spate of what appears to be a new form of viral sleepwalking. Five victims of this 'sleeping sickness' have already been admitted to Bay Area hospitals. While the experts insist there is no evidence that this illness is contagious, it seems fairly obvious that something must be causing it, as none of the known victims have any history of narcolepsy or somnambulism—that's falling asleep without warning, and walking around while you're sleeping, for those of us without a medical degree. There is no word yet on whether the Centers for Disease Control—"

I leaned forward and turned the radio off. Joyce yelped.

"I was listening to that!"

"You were getting upset by that," I corrected. "Let's get home and talk to Dad. He'll know if something is really going on, and you won't wind up scaring yourself half to death before we fully understand the situation."

Joyce glared. I looked impassively back, trying not to twitch at the fact that she wasn't paying enough attention to the road. Finally, as I expected, she relented.

"I hate it when you're reasonable," she grumbled. "You should be freaking out."

"You're freaking out enough for both of us," I said. "I just want to know what I'm going to be freaking out about before I waste energy freaking out about the wrong things. Conservation of panic is important."

"Pretty sure we're not having a panic shortage, Sal."

"I don't care. You're still not turning that back on until we're home. If you kill us both because you're too busy being upset at the radio to keep your eyes on the road, I'm never going to speak to you again."

Joyce glared again before turning and looking resolutely out at the road. I closed my eyes, pressing myself back in my seat, and tried not to think about the cars around us. We passed the rest of the drive that way. I relaxed when I felt the car take the familiar turn into our driveway, and opened my eyes when Joyce turned the engine off.

"I'm sorry," she said quietly.

"You should be," I said, before I thought better of it.

"What?" Joyce turned to me, eyes wide. "What did you say?"

"You know I'm not okay with that sort of stuff."

"I said I was sorry! Don't freak out on me."

Somehow, her sheer wounded indignation was the final straw. "Believe me, I'm not freaking out. If I start freaking out, you'll have to sedate me to get me to stop," I snapped, and opened the door, barely remembering to undo my seat belt before I stormed away. Joyce could carry her own damn bags. I was done being the helpful big sister for the day.

Mom and Dad were in the living room. They both looked up at the sound of the front door slamming, and for a moment, I saw that flicker of wary unhappiness that I thought of as the tracks of the old Sally—the one whose moods apparently made my panic attacks look like a fair trade in terms of "daughter we can live with."

"Sal?" said Mom carefully, standing. "Honey, are you okay?"

Somehow, making her look at me like that just made the day worse. I shook my head and walked over to embrace her, pressing my face into her shoulder. Alarmed, she closed her arms around me.

"Honey, where's Joyce? Was there an accident?"

I shook my head, not lifting it from her shoulder. I heard Dad stand and walk over to us. He didn't say anything. That was probably for the best. At the moment, I wouldn't have been able to answer him.

The door banged open again as Joyce came stomping in, dropping her bags with a series of rustles and thuds before she demanded, "Turn on the news!"

"Joyce, what's going on?" asked Mom. "Why is your sister so upset?"

"There were these people at the mall, I think they were sick."
I lifted my head to see Joyce grabbing the remote off the coffee
table. She clicked the TV on, flipping channels until she landed
on CNN. They were airing a story about reality-star salaries.
She snarled. "Why aren't they saying anything? I'm going to
my room. Maybe the Internet will have a clue." She whirled and
went stomping out of the room. Her bedroom door slammed a
few seconds later.

I pulled away from Mom. "So what was that you were saying last week, about how I used to be the dramatic one? Can we
have a re-vote on that title?"

"I think that might be a good idea." Mom looked down the
hall toward Joyce's room. "What happened? Did you two have
a fight?"

"If they'd had a fight bad enough that Joyce would be looking for it on CNN, I think we'd be down a daughter, Gail,"
said my father reasonably. He was usually the reasonable one.
Mom was a lot more like Joyce, only older and slightly less
inclined to drag me to the mall when I didn't want to go. "What
happened, Sal?"

I sighed. "I wanted to talk to you about this anyway. See,
there was this little girl..."

It didn't take me long to explain what we'd seen at the mall.
Mom and Dad listened without comment until I was done. I
shrugged, spreading my hands. "That's everything. It was
weird, and sort of scary, but it really upset Joyce. The way she
was driving scared the hell out of me, and it was like she didn't
even care. All she wanted to do was get home and find out what
was going on. We were supposed to talk to you, but she didn't
even wait. I don't get it."

"She was probably worried about a biochemical attack on
the mall," said my father.

I blinked. Joyce had mentioned something in the air
vents... "Dad? Is there something I should know?"

My father—Colonel Alfred Mitchell, United States Army, former director at USAMRIID and current director-slash-lab manager of their San Francisco research center, which is how my entire family wound up with the earliest specialized versions of the SymboGen implant—looked at me for a long moment without saying anything. Finally, he sighed, and said, "We didn't want to worry you."

"You know, that's one of the most worrying things anyone ever says."

"I know." He paused before saying, "There have been a few isolated events recently. Unique pathogens showing up in inhabited areas. Nothing we can solidly say points to terrorist activity, but…"

"Enough that when we see people sleepwalking in broad daylight, you jump to bad conclusions," I said. "How long have you known about this?" I paused, and added, "How long has *Joyce* known?"

"Sal—"

"Didn't you think this might be something I'd want to know about, too?"

"It's not public knowledge, and given your current condition, it seemed best not to upset you," Dad said.

I stared at him. "It's been six years since the accident. How long does this get to be my 'current condition' before it becomes just the way I *am*? I mean, really, I'd like to know, since I guess I'm going to have to wait until we hit that day before you're going to start treating me like an adult, instead of like a child you have to protect."

"Sal, that isn't fair," said Mom.

"I didn't mean your memory loss, Sal," said my father. I frowned. He shook his head. "I meant SymboGen."

Understanding came suddenly. It did not come kindly. "You think SymboGen is involved in this?"

"Honey, I don't know what I think. What I do know is that

it's a big, scary world out there, and I can't protect you from it."
He looked toward Joyce's room. "I need to go check on your
sister."

"Yeah," I said. "You do that."

Mom took my arm as Dad walked down the hall. "Let's go
make some tea."

I thought about shaking off her hand, but experience told me
that would be a bad idea. If I started acting like a child, she'd
just work harder to treat me like one. "I'm not so delicate that
you have to hide things from me," I said.

"I know. It's just your father's way. You were used to it
before...before." She stumbled a little, sidestepping the issue
of my memory loss with her usual awkwardness. Even after six
years, it hadn't gotten any easier. "He needs to be sure of the
facts before he really starts frightening people."

"He told Joyce."

"Joyce works in his lab. I'm not sure he could avoid telling her."

"She's just an intern."

"Even interns have to understand what they're doing." Mom
let go of my arm, pushing me gently toward the kitchen table. I
sat down. "I'm pretty sure we have some rosemary shortbread
left over from last night. It's always better on the second day,
don't you think?"

That was her way of saying that the conversation was over.
I wasn't quite ready to let it go. "Mom, should I be scared
right now?"

"I don't think it would do any good, and that means it's not
worth wasting the energy." Mom got down the cookie jar and a
tin of loose-leaf tea. "Now why don't you tell me how the trip
to the mall went, up until those people showed up?"

I sighed. There was no way I was getting anything else out of
her. "Well, first Joyce dragged me through every shoe store in
the place..." I began.

Reciting the minutiae of our trip to the mall took very little of my attention. Mom fixed tea, and I kept talking. I couldn't stop thinking about the look on that little girl's face, the dead-eyed blankness that still projected a type of unwavering determination, like all that mattered in the world was getting to that door. The man had looked the same way, and they'd known each other through the fog.

Whatever was going on, it was bigger than Dad was admitting, maybe big enough to justify Joyce's panic. It was definitely a hell of a lot more important than shoe stores and shopping. Mom put the shortbread in front of me, and the summer afternoon ticked inexorably by, like so many others before it, like so many more that hadn't arrived yet.

I don't remember what we talked about. None of it mattered, and I couldn't stop thinking about the little girl.

It wasn't until I went to bed that night that I realized I'd been hearing the drums all day.

...in biotech news, a patent for a lab-created organism has been filed by genetic research leader SymboGen. The patented organism, dubbed "Diphyllobothrium symbogenesis," is a form of modified tapeworm hybrid. The representatives from SymboGen, led by Dr. Steven Banks, have successfully demonstrated that this hybrid cannot arise in nature, and more, that the modifications to its genome have resulted in several medically and scientifically useful changes to the overall organism.

Rumors that SymboGen is already petitioning the FDA for permission to begin human testing of the D. symbogenesis *organism have yet to be confirmed. This would represent a dramatic escalation of the normal timeline for research of this type. Sources inside the company say...*

—FROM *THE AMERICAN JOURNAL OF PARASITOLOGY*,
PUBLISHED SEPTEMBER 2015.

San Bruno officials have as yet made no statement relating to the strange events at the downtown San Bruno Mall, although one mall employee has reported a strange smell in the area of the second-floor public restrooms. Sources indicate that a gas leak of some kind may have triggered the strange behavior in the five individuals affected by what locals have begun calling "the Sleeping Sickness."

All five of the victims of this strange outbreak have been hospitalized, and are being held in quarantine pending further updates on their condition…

—FROM *THE CONTRA COSTA TIMES*, AUGUST 19, 2027.

Chapter 4

AUGUST 2027

The morning dawned bright, early, and awkward. Joyce was sullen and refused to talk during breakfast; Mom was already gone by the time I got up. I had an e-mail from Nathan apologizing for not calling me the night before; there had been a sudden surge of patients at the ER, bad enough that it overwhelmed the normal doctors and caused them to call as many specialists as they could lure out of their labs. As a staff parasitologist, Nathan was accustomed to doing ER rounds—there were medical conditions that could be alleviated by making adjustments to the patient's SymboGen implant, and others that could kill the implants, requiring them to be extracted immediately, before decomposition could set in. There were very few medical emergencies that could be improved by having two and a half pounds of dead tapeworm decaying in the patient's gut.

I might have thought that the influx of patients was somehow related to what Joyce and I saw at the mall, but he was using the code words that meant "accident." I didn't like to think about car crashes, and so he avoided discussing them with me in any specific terms. He invited me to come to the hospital for lunch. Since I didn't have to be at the shelter that day, I wrote back saying I'd be there. Anything to get out of the house.

Dad and Joyce were leaving for work at ten: unusually late, but a concession they were sometimes able to make when I needed a ride. They dropped me off six blocks from the hospital, at a little florist's shop I'd discovered during my outpatient physical therapy. The shop always had terrible roses. They made up for it by having some of the most beautiful orchids I'd ever seen—but that wasn't their specialty: McNally's Flowers specialized in carnivorous plants.

The bell over the door rang as I stepped into the warm, moist confines of the shop. There was no one in sight. "Hello?" I called. The store's orange tabby came strolling out from a rack of vases, his tail held in a high, relaxed position. I knelt to offer him my hand. "Hey, Tumbleweeds. How are you today? Where are your people?"

Tumbleweeds deigned to walk over and sniff my fingers before butting his head against the back of my hand. Then he turned and walked away again, having accomplished his duty as store greeter.

"You're lucky," said a voice. I lifted my head. The owner, Marya, was standing near the cooler where she kept the substandard but seemingly obligatory roses. She was a tall, solid woman with long black hair and a narrow waist that she kept cinched in a wide leather belt at all times. I sometimes found myself wondering whether she would explode if the belt was removed.

She kept smiling as she strolled toward the front of the store, adding, "Tumbles has been standoffish lately. People come in, and he snubs them. He even hissed at a poor woman yesterday.

She'd come in to buy flowers for her husband, and here's my cat, hissing at her."

"Did you sell her flowers anyway?" I asked, straightening up.

"Four dozen of the long-stemmed red roses." Marya clucked her tongue. "I tried to steer her toward something worth giving to a person who doesn't feel his best—who wants my roses when they're already unwell?—but eh, can't steer a person who won't be steered, now, can we? She seemed happy enough."

I laughed. "You can't save everyone," I said.

"No, I suppose I can't," Marya mildly agreed. "What can I get for you today? Something sweet and covered in pretty blossoms?"

"I was hoping you had some new sundews, actually," I said. "Nathan had a hard night last night. I wanted to bring him something pretty."

"Ah! A discerning customer is the joy of a retailer's heart." Marya waved for me to follow her to the back of the store, where another glass door stood between the common flowers and the more exotic climate-controlled carnivorous plants. She held the door open for me, waiting until I was past her before closing it tight and flicking on the overhead lights. "Browse as you like, I've nothing better to do."

Marya's attitude wasn't as odd as it seemed, despite the fact that she was the only one currently working. The bell over the door would ring if anybody else came in, and her true joy was selling her carnivorous babies. Having someone who actually wanted to look at sundews was worth any number of missed opportunities to sell bad roses to tourists.

"I have some gorgeous King Sundews," she said, guiding me toward one of the trays of plants resting under their heat lamps, sticky petals spread toward the absent sun. The largest of the King Sundews was bigger than my palm, with beads of delicate pink "dew" clinging to the cilia of its long, green and orange fronds. "They just came in day before yesterday; you're the first one who's come in to see them."

From her proprietary tone, I could tell what she wanted to hear, and I was happy to give it to her: "Oh, Marya, they're *gorgeous*," I breathed, crouching down to study the sundews with a careful eye. They were no less impressive up close. "What are the care notes?"

"Dormancy isn't required, but it's a good idea if you want your King to flower; they can handle pretty good-sized prey, even up to moths and large beetles. You still want to be careful with feeding, don't feed live if you can avoid it—just don't worry too much if your King snatches a few snacks without your approval. They actually wrap their leaves around the things that they're digesting. Hard to grow, intermediate to care for." Marya smiled slyly. "Your boy would love one."

"You're probably right." I straightened. "How much are they?"

"For you, my darling, thirty dollars even, and you bring me a picture next time you come in, let me see how the new beauty is rooting into the office."

"You've got a deal." I looked over the tray again before pointing to a sundew near the back. "I'll take that one."

"A wonderful selection. Come now, you sweet thing, time to move to a new home…" She cooed to the sundew as she plucked its pot from the tray, mixing endearments in English and Ukrainian. I smothered a smile, following her out of the room.

Marya was a botanist before she moved to the United States. She probably could have continued working in the field, but instead, she'd chosen to do what she loved best: spend all her time with plants, and occasionally foist them off on people who promised to keep them alive. The cut flowers and cheap stuffed toys with "Get Well Soon" slogans were a sideline, another way of meeting expectations.

"Everything is well with you and your boy?" Marya asked, as she rang up my new sundew. "No more headaches, no more bad dreams?"

"Lots of headaches, lots of bad dreams," I admitted. "Symbo-Gen still has me under observation. I have to check in tomorrow for another review."

"Such a shame. They should find something else to spend their time on." Marya handed me the bag containing the sundew. "There's a care sheet inside, and don't hesitate to call if either of you has any questions. There are no bad questions in horticulture. There are only bad people who kill their babies through overwatering."

"Thank you, Marya." I took the bag, smiling.

"Now go on, see your boy," she said, and made a shooing gesture with her hands. "He'll be excited by what you have to give him."

"If he's not, he can't have it."

"Never 'it,' never 'it,'" Marya chided. "None of God's creatures is an 'it,' even if they're not a boy or a girl or a mammal or a pretty bird. Call them 'he' or she' and be a little wrong, but never take away their individuality like that."

"Sorry, Marya," I said, and waved as I left the store. Tumbleweeds followed me to the door and sat there, staring at me through the glass with his tail wrapped around his legs, as I walked toward the hospital. Nathan would be waiting for me.

The nice thing about spending most of my remembered life in hospitals is that it's become virtually impossible for them to make me uncomfortable. They're more like home than home is. I'd been awake for almost a year before I realized that normal people aren't supposed to find the smell of bleach and floor wax comforting. I walked through the main doors of the San Francisco City Hospital, made my way to the elevator, and pressed the button for Nathan's floor. All business as usual.

A few orderlies nodded to me as I passed. I nodded back, and kept going. Nathan's lunch hour was never as long as we wanted it to be, and I'd already spent too much time at the florist's to spend more in being social. I looked down at the brown paper bag in my hand. It was worth it.

Nathan's research assistant wasn't at her desk when I reached the ninth floor. I kept walking until I came to Nathan's office. The door was open. I stopped, knocking on the doorframe. He raised his head and smiled.

"Hey there," he said. "Come on in, babe. I'll be done with this in just a second."

"Babe, darling...this is one of those days where I don't get to have an actual name, isn't it?" I crossed to the chair in front of his desk and sat, making sure to hold the bag where he could see it. "Doctor, I've got a pain."

Nathan ignored my joking attempt at a come-on, eyes going to the bag. "Someone called you 'darling'?" he asked, in a carefully casual tone. "Was that someone by any chance black-haired, wearing a leather belt, and originally from the Ukraine?"

"Funnily enough, that's a very good description of that someone," I said. "How did you guess?"

"Experience and greed," he said, and held up a finger as he turned back to his screen. "Just let me finish this before I get distracted by trying to convince you to let me look inside that bag."

"Paperwork?" I ventured.

"Oceans of it," he said. "Sometimes I think that's the downside of going green—you can't look in and see how buried I am by measuring the piles on my desk. Now I look exactly the same whether I'm busy or not, and so people feel like they're doing me a favor by giving me something to do. Some of them also—not you, you have a free pass at all times—feel like they're allowed to intrude without asking whether I have time to deal with them." He typed as he spoke, making quick notes on what had to be a seemingly endless succession of reports.

I quieted, settling in the chair and waiting for him to finish. He would answer if I talked to him—I knew that from previous attacks of unfiled paperwork—and so I didn't need to verify it by bothering him. I'd have his undivided attention faster if I let him take care of work.

About five minutes slipped by in the sound of typing and the reassuring chill of the air conditioning. Finally, Nathan turned in his chair to face me across the desk, extending both hands in a palms-up "gimme" gesture.

"I beg you, be merciful, for I have just filed fifty-seven patient reports," he said. "Let me see inside the bag of wonders."

"I don't know," I began. "I mean, you *did* say that people kept interrupting you…"

"You are never an interruption, a distraction, or anything else of the sort," he said, hands still outstretched. "Please. Be the most wonderful girlfriend in the world, and let me look inside the bag."

"You're lucky I'm soft-hearted," I said, and passed the bag over to him.

Nathan placed the bag on his desk with proper reverence before reaching inside and pulling out the King Sundew. The light from his desk lamp glinted off the tiny beads of sticky sap coating its fronds, making them look like jewels. Nathan's eyes lit up.

"You found a King Sundew," he breathed. "Sal, it's beautiful."

"I *bought* a King Sundew," I said. "Marya sold it to me."

"You found Marya's shop, something I hadn't managed in eight years of working here. Ergo, you found the King Sundew, and you should get the credit. Let me give you the credit. Please." Nathan stood, the sundew cradled lovingly in his hands. "This is an incredible plant. I mean, really remarkable."

I smiled. "You like it?"

"I love it." He paused. "And I'm being stupidly presumptuous again. Is this for me?"

My smile grew. I liked carnivorous plants as much as Nathan did—enough that I had a small terrarium filled with thriving flytraps and a few pitcher plants that were suitable for a gardener with more enthusiasm than actual skill. They were one of the things we'd bonded over. I'd come to meet him for lunch carrying a flytrap from Marya, and suddenly we had all these things to talk about. The walk we'd taken so I could show him Marya's store was one of our first dates. He was a lot further along in our mutual hobby than I was; there was no way I could keep a King Sundew alive. And yet the fact that he even felt the need to ask somehow made the gift all that much sweeter to give.

"All yours," I said. "I figured you needed a new friend to make up for the night you'd had. There's a care sheet in the bag, if you need it."

"Best girlfriend." He stepped around the desk, pausing to bend and kiss me quickly on the lips before he crossed the office to the terrarium where he kept the majority of his sundews— the ones pretty enough to pass muster for work. There were no pitcher plants, since the administration frowned on keeping dead bugs in your office, even if they *were* in the process of being digested. There were no flytraps, either. Thanks to hundreds of horror movies, everyone knew that flytraps ate meat. But the sundews, with their bright colors and glittering leaves, were just fine—never mind that they were, in some ways, the most vicious killers of them all. An insect that got stuck to a sundew could live for hours before it died, being slowly digested the whole time.

Carefully, so as not to jostle the plant in his hand, Nathan removed the lid from the terrarium and shifted the heating lamps to the side. Then he moved a few pots around, all one-handed, before lowering the King Sundew lovingly into the center of the display. Its fronds were still clumped together from their time in the bag. He picked up a long skewer—the kind people use for barbecues—and used it to gently tease the sticky leaves apart. Then he replaced the lid on the terrarium and stepped back, looking proudly at his modified display.

"Beautiful," he said, and turned to walk back to me, bending to pull me to my feet.

"Me or the sundew?" I asked.

"Yes," he said, and kissed me.

Being kissed by Nathan was one of my favorite hobbies, and I was more than happy to stand, put my arms loosely around his neck, and kiss him enthusiastically back. We passed several pleasant minutes that way. Finally, Nathan pulled away, cheeks flushed and eyes a little overly bright behind his glasses.

"You are amazing, and I am *starving*," he said. "Lunch?"

"Lunch," I agreed. "Indian?"

Nathan grinned. "It's like you read my mind. Let me get my coat."

He left me in the office while he took care of the last few details required before he could leave the hospital. I walked over to the terrarium, bending to study the King Sundew. It was already relaxing into its new environment, fronds fully extending as it mapped out the limits of its space. It would have insects stuck to those leaves by the next morning, using the nutrients in their bodies to feed its own.

"You're beautiful," I murmured.

"Sal?" said Nathan, from the office doorway. "You ready?"

"I'm coming." I straightened, smiling again. "Let's eat."

Nathan clicked the office lights off as he stepped out to the hall. The lights in the terrarium stayed on, casting a bloody red glow over everything. I grabbed my bag from the chair and followed him into the hall, leaving the silently growing plants behind.

The Indian restaurant we wound up in was half a mile from the hospital, tucked into one of those odd warrens of half-residential, half-commercial streets that seemed to spring up all over San Francisco. Every neighborhood had its own character, a mixture of city natives, transplants, and people who thought of themselves as just passing through, even though they'd been living there for longer than I'd been alive. On such blends are cities built.

Nathan took a sip of his mango lassi as he looked thoughtfully at his goat curry. I leaned over and poked him in the arm with my fork. He looked up, startled.

"What?"

"We're supposed to be having lunch together, but I don't know where you are," I said. "What's on your mind?"

An odd look crossed his face. Putting down his lassi, he reached up and adjusted his glasses—a sure sign that he was uncomfortable. "Did you know that curry powder is a natural antiparasitic? That's probably part of why it was originally so popular in Indian cuisine. India has a warm, moist climate. That encourages high levels of parasitism, and the more parasites you have, the more ways you'll need to keep them out of your population. Assuming you want to have a healthy population, that is."

"And it's not until recently that we've been put into the position of needing to *add* parasites for the sake of our health, rather than getting rid of them," I said. "I know. You tell me things like that every time you don't want to talk about what's really on your mind. It's a good thing I was never enthusiastic about developing a taste for sushi. I think you'd get us kicked out of any sushi restaurant worth visiting."

"Just because people don't want to consider the risks inherent in their food choices—"

"Nathan, what's *wrong*? You don't usually try to change the subject twice in one meal."

He paused before sighing heavily. "If I say you really don't want to know, Sal, will you believe me?"

"Yes, but I won't stop asking." I poked him with my fork

again. This time the action earned me a brief smile. "I would be a terrible girlfriend if I didn't make you tell me what was on your mind. You listen to me whine about dealing with Symbo-Gen enough. I can listen to you."

"It's about what happened last night."

The words were simple, but still sent a thread of unease into my guts, where it curled and twisted like a parasite in its own right. Last night he'd been dealing with an accident. I hated hearing about accidents . . . but this was Nathan, and he deserved better than me shutting him out because I was uncomfortable. "I'm a big girl," I said. "I can handle it."

He sighed again. This time he took off his glasses, polishing them on the tail of his shirt as he said, "It was a nine-car pile-up on the Bay Bridge. The people who made it as far as the hospital said they had no warning at all. One minute, traffic was moving normally. The next, a big rig was jackknifing to block all four lanes of traffic, and cars were slamming into it before they had a chance to realize what was about to happen to them. Eleven people died before emergency services could even get to the scene."

"That's horrible," I breathed, feeling the unease twist harder in my stomach. It was horrible, yes, and it involved a car crash, which was normally enough to make Nathan reluctant to discuss his work with me. But was it horrible enough for him to be *this* reluctant?

I didn't think so.

Nathan heard my confusion. He looked up, putting his glasses back on, and said, "You said you were going to the mall with your sister yesterday. In San Bruno. Where those people started sleepwalking."

"Yes. Joyce and I were both there. But what does that have to do with anything?"

"The driver of the big rig survived. So did the driver of the bus that capped off the accident. His passengers—the ones who lived—said he hit the gas when he came around the curve on the bridge and saw the wreckage. Not the brakes. The gas."

The similarity to my own accident made me go cold. "What are you—"

"Both drivers are showing the same symptoms as the people from the mall. They're walking in their sleep. And apparently, causing multi-car pile-ups in their sleep, too. The trucker had no passengers, but the people on the bus said that their driver was perfectly normal when they first got on. He took their fares, said hello, asked about their families...some of them had been riding with that driver for years. They said he seemed perfectly normal, right up until he stopped responding to questions. The accident happened a little bit after that."

I didn't know what to say, and so I didn't say anything at all. I just stared at him, trying to formulate the words that came next. I couldn't find them.

Nathan nodded, seeming to understand my silence. "More than half the people who were in the accident didn't make it out of the ER. Some of the others will never be the same. That doesn't even go into the ones who won't wake up."

"There's more than just the drivers?" The question came out in a whisper.

"Two from the bus, a few passengers from the cars—it's hard to tell 'sleepwalking, won't wake up' from 'genuine coma' right now. You were in a coma. You came out of it." Nathan paused, wincing. "Oh, hell. Sal, I didn't mean to..."

"It's okay. I asked, remember? And I know my coma didn't end the way the original Sally might have wanted. I wanted to be supportive." My stomach was still rolling. I pressed my hand flat against the skin above my navel, grimacing. "Maybe I was a little *too* supportive. I'll have to remember that for next time."

"Thank you for trying." He reached across the table to take my free hand. "Even a little supportive is good enough for me."

"Don't say that. I'm still learning social norms, remember?

You tell me I don't have to support you to the best of my ability, next thing you know, I'm not showing up for dates anymore, and I keep asking you to do my laundry."

A small smile creased the corners of his mouth. "I think that's kids coming home from college."

"Or working as biotech interns. I have just described my sister, only substitute 'dinner' for 'dates.' "

"Good, because I don't want to date your sister, and I don't want to think about you dating your sister, either."

I burst out laughing, earning myself a startled glance from the people at the next table over. "Now that would *definitely* be going against social norms."

"Very true." Nathan released my hand and looked at the remains of our lunch. Neither of us had cleaned our plates. "Are you going to eat anything else?"

With how upset my stomach was, I wasn't sure I was going to keep down what I'd already eaten. "No," I said. "Can we go for a walk?"

"Sure," he said, and signaled for the check.

I leaned back in my chair and tried to smile, despite the fact that I really felt like I was going to throw up at any moment. The check came quickly, and Nathan paid. Pushing the feeling of roiling unease aside, I took Nathan's hand, and we walked together out into the early afternoon sun.

Every six months or so, some conspiracy nut starts in with "what they aren't telling you" and "these are the things they don't want you to know," and you know what? Not one of them has produced verifiable scientific evidence that the Intestinal Bodyguard™ is harmful in humans. Not one! Don't you think that if there were some kind of negative side effect, we'd have seen it by now? I don't mean to sound like I'm claiming nothing can ever go wrong—we're all human at SymboGen, we make mistakes—but even if you're into conspiracy theories, you've got to admit that it's pretty far-fetched to believe that we could somehow suppress every possible bad effect of the Intestinal Bodyguard™. Millions of people have our implants. Millions. That's not a small number, and those people talk. We couldn't keep them all quiet if we wanted to.

And why would we want to? Look at the blogs, look at the social media updates! No more allergies, no more missed medication—heck, some people even claim their Intestinal Bodyguards™ guard against hangovers. Now, that's not a feature that we were necessarily aiming for, and it's not in the brochure, but if your implant wants to help you have a little more fun, I say go right ahead. What's the harm?

—FROM "KING OF THE WORMS," AN INTERVIEW WITH
DR. STEVEN BANKS, CO-FOUNDER OF SYMBOGEN. ORIGINALLY
PUBLISHED IN *ROLLING STONE*, FEBRUARY 2027.

Steve's initial proposal was as fascinating as it was flawed. He wanted to take D. yonagoensis—*a type of tapeworm that parasitizes fish in its natural environment, using small crustaceans as a secondary host—and use it to design a sort of "super tapeworm," a specially crafted hybrid that would enhance the human immune system, protect against allergies and autoimmune conditions, and die every two years. That way, it would be the perfect pharmaceutical tool, but it wouldn't put the entire pharmaceutical industry out of business. I won't pretend that he wasn't thinking about the profits. We all were. Money makes the world go 'round.*

It's a pity, really, that the design for his D. yonagoensis *was never going to be viable. He used too many genetic strains, blending them without a cohesive core. The entire plan was flawed from the start. It couldn't have worked.*

That's where I came in.

—FROM *CAN OF WORMS: THE AUTOBIOGRAPHY OF SHANTI CALE, PHD.* AS YET UNPUBLISHED.

Chapter 5

AUGUST 2027

The Embarcadero encompasses a series of grassy lawns and jogging paths along the San Francisco Bay. It's one of the most scenic places in an already beautiful city, and even on a workday afternoon, it was decently crowded with a mix of tourists and natives. The sky was a flawless blue, the color of surgical gloves, which probably had something to do with the size of the crowd. There's something about a beautiful day that just encourages trips to the seaside, even when the seaside is only a few blocks from your office. Maybe especially when the seaside is something you can see from your window while you're pretending to care about work.

Nathan and I walked along a stretch of grass near the street, close enough to each other that we didn't feel like we were in danger of getting separated by random joggers, far enough apart that we could enjoy the day on our own terms. Nathan

liked to look at the ground as he walked, watching for interesting plants and examples of the increasingly rare local wildlife. I
preferred looking at the sky. Somehow, the endless blueness of
it all never stopped amazing me.

A man jogged by with a black Lab at the end of a nylon leash.
The dog looked miserable, dragging her feet and carrying her
tail tucked low between her legs. I stopped walking to watch
them go by. "That's weird..."

"What?" Nathan stopped in turn, turning to face me. "Sal?"

"Did you see that dog? The black Lab?" I pointed after the
man and his dog. Well, presumably his dog. A dognapping
could explain the animal's distress, which was only growing
as the pair moved on. Now she was visibly pulling against the
leash, trying to get away. "You never see a Lab that unhappy.
They're the best-natured dogs in the world. That's why they
wind up being used as service animals so often."

"You can't save every animal you think might not be optimally happy, you know." Nathan squeezed my shoulder. "I
wish you could, but you'd run out of room at the shelter before
you ran out of animals that needed help. I run into something
similar with patients. I want to help them all. I can't."

"Time and insurance are cruel masters," I said automatically.
I still couldn't take my eyes off the dog. The jogger had stopped
and was scolding his pet now, although they were too far away
for me to hear what he was saying. The dog pulled harder on
her leash, and barked, once. *That* sound was loud enough to
carry, and several other heads turned toward it. Dogs barking
in the city wasn't anything unusual. Dogs barking in that much
evident distress was.

Maybe we weren't the first ones to witness what happened
next; maybe other people saw it happen before we did. But
those people didn't tell anyone what they'd seen—maybe didn't
understand what they'd seen—and we did. That made all the
difference in the world.

First the jogger dropped the leash. It fell to the grass, and the dog ran several yards before turning back to face her master, barking again. She was a good dog. I could tell she was a good dog, even without knowing her name or why she was so unhappy. A bad dog would have run as soon as she had the chance. This dog looked back to her master, waiting for whatever was wrong to go away and leave things the way they were supposed to be. I abandoned all thoughts of a dognapping when I saw the look the dog was giving to that man, to *her* man, as she waited for things to fix themselves.

The man didn't move. For several seconds, he didn't move at all. Then all the tension went out of his shoulders and neck, leaving his head to loll limply forward. Several more seconds passed. Nathan's hand tightened on my shoulder.

"I don't like this, Sal," he said. "Whatever this is, I don't like it. We should get out of here."

"But the dog—"

"Will be fine."

"What if he's having a seizure or something? Shouldn't you see if you can help?"

Nathan shook his head. "This doesn't look like the start of a seizure. I don't know what it is, but it could be viral, and it's not something I'm equipped to deal with."

The man raised his head.

The dog immediately started barking again, her ears going flat against her head and her posture going rigid, something I recognized from the shelter as a sign that she was about to attack. Without thinking about it, I put two fingers in my mouth and whistled. Her head whipped around, ears going back up, and she broke into a sudden run, heading straight for us.

"Oh, crap, she's going to attack!" said Nathan, and pulled me backward, seeming set on physically removing me from the scene if that was what it took to keep me from getting savaged.

I pulled my shoulder out of his grasp. "No, she's not," I said, and dropped into a crouch just as the dog reached us. She practically flung herself into my arms, whining frantically. She stank of urine, a hot, acrid smell. At some point during the confrontation with her master, she must have pissed herself.

"What did he *do* to you?" I muttered, and raised my head, intending to give the dog's owner a piece of my mind. Then I froze, arms tightening around the still-whimpering dog. She plastered herself hard against me, like she thought she could somehow protect us both by cowering just a little more thoroughly.

The man—her master—was walking toward us with his arms held out for balance, a blank look on his utterly slack face. He looked like the people Joyce and I had seen at the mall; he looked like he was sleepwalking. All around us, people were shouting and pointing at him. Many of them were filming his shambling approach with their phones. The footage would be all over the Internet before the news crews even showed up.

This time, when Nathan pulled on my shoulder, I didn't pull away. Instead, I scrambled to my feet, grabbing the dog's leash at the same time. She whined, but she came willingly as the three of us turned and ran, as fast as we could, away from the Embarcadero.

We arrived back at the hospital winded and sweaty, having run the first two blocks and walked the rest. Only the dog seemed unaffected, probably because she belonged to a jogger—keeping up with me and Nathan had to seem like a walk in the park to her.

Just thinking the word "park" made that uneasy feeling in my gut reappear. I staggered to a stop just inside the lobby, catching myself against the wall with my free hand as I gasped for air. The dog sat down by my feet, assuming the patient waiting posture that has been the characteristic of the Labrador retriever since the breed was born.

Nathan stared at the closed door, and then turned to stare

at me. "Did you see that?" he asked needlessly. I looked at him without saying a word. He grimaced. "I'm sorry, I know you saw that, of *course* you saw that, but that was—he was perfectly normal, and then he was just…"

"Gone," I whispered. I pushed away from the wall and knelt next to the dog. She had a full set of tags. I dug through them until I found the one with her name. "He was gone, and Beverly here was all alone. Weren't you, Beverly?"

The dog—Beverly—looked up at me with warm, trusting brown eyes. I was a human. I had her leash, and I knew her name. Clearly, I was going to make everything okay. It must be nice to be a dog.

"I have to notify the ER. They need to send someone to pick him up…" Nathan raked a hand through his hair before whipping around to look at me. "Can you wait in my office for a few minutes? I promise, I'll be there as fast as I can."

"Right now, I'm not going anywhere that isn't in this hospital, and neither is Beverly," I said, and straightened.

Any protest Nathan might have been considering died when he saw the way I was holding the leash. He nodded. "Okay. I'll be right there. I love you." He kissed my cheek, and he was gone, speed walking toward the nearest set of doors.

The nearest security guard frowned in my direction as soon as Nathan was out of sight. I was disheveled, and I was with a dog who didn't have a service jacket on. I offered the woman a wavering smile and turned to walk quickly toward the nearest bank of elevators, hoping that she'd let me go off and become someone else's problem.

Luck, or maybe laziness, was with me; the guard kept glaring until I was safely in the elevator and bound for Nathan's floor. Beverly walked easily on her leash, with none of the pulling or foot-dragging that I'd witnessed when she was being walked by her owner; she even heeled naturally, settling against my leg like she'd been born there.

"You're a good dog, aren't you, Beverly?" I asked her. "You're a good, good dog. A good dog like you shouldn't be treated like that. I'll make sure it doesn't happen again. You have my word on that."

Beverly turned her big brown eyes on me and believed every word I said. I could see it in her face, and belief is in the nature of dogs.

The elevator let us out on Nathan's floor, where everyone was much more familiar with me, and hence more inclined to be forgiving. Nathan's research assistant, Devi, still raised an eyebrow at the sight of my new black shadow. "Sal, I don't mean to sound like I'm prying here, but...is that a dog?"

"She's a dog," I confirmed needlessly. "Beverly, I want you to meet Devi. Devi, this is Beverly. She joined us in the park."

"It's nice to meet you, Beverly," said Devi to the dog, as politely as if she were addressing a human. Her eyes flicked back to me. "Still not trying to pry, but you look a little flushed. Can I get you a glass of water or something?"

The unspoken *Are you okay?* in her words was loud enough that she might as well have said it. I mustered a smile and said, "A glass of water would be good." A fainting couch would be better, but if I asked for that, I was going to find myself getting more medical attention than I wanted—and there was no telling what would happen to Beverly, who really wasn't supposed to be in the hospital.

"Uh-huh." Devi rose, still watching me. "Are you going to tell me why you look so tired, or are you going to let me spin wild stories to amuse myself? You're secretly an international spy who's been faking amnesia while you waited for your contact to meet you with the goods."

"'The goods'?" I echoed.

"You know. Information that can be used to prevent the next World War." Devi walked into the small nurse's closet behind the desk as she spoke, and called back, "It's probably on a thumb drive hidden inside the dog. That's why you have her, right?"

I'd seen enough bad spy movies to know where Devi was going with this, and decided to play along. It would make us both feel better. "Yes, but I've decided to abandon my mission," I deadpanned. "I just can't bring myself to cut open a dog to get to the secret plans."

"That's what makes you a better person than your government masters." Devi emerged with a bottle of red Gatorade. I wasn't sure whether it was the red kind that supposedly tasted like fruit punch or the red kind that supposedly tasted like cherry. I also wasn't sure it mattered. I was thirsty enough that the first half of the bottle didn't taste like anything but sweetness. By the time the first traces of artificial fruit came creeping in, the dryness in my throat was mostly gone, and Devi was no longer watching me like she was afraid I'd keel over at any moment.

"Thank you," I half-said, half-gasped, and replaced the lid on the bottle. "I think I needed that pretty bad. We saw—"

The image of the man in the park—Beverly's real master, even if she had abandoned him for me—as the animation drained from his face rose behind my eyes. My stomach gave a lurch, objecting to the memory more than to the Gatorade. The result was the same. I clapped a hand over my mouth, thrusting Beverly's leash into Devi's hands. Devi looked unsurprised. She took the leash and stepped aside, clearing the way for me to race to the bathroom.

Red Gatorade looks a lot like blood when it's filling a toilet basin. I stayed on my knees in front of the bowl, bracing my hands against the floor while I waited for my head to stop spinning. My stomach gave another lurch. I managed to flush away the mess before I threw up again, but barely.

At least this time, there was less artificial red in the bowl. I leaned to the side and pressed my forehead against the tile wall, waiting for the urge to vomit a third time to pass. It went slowly, but it went, and I stood on legs that felt like they were made of rubber. Once I was sure they'd hold me, I staggered to the sink and washed my face with icy water. I only wished there were a way for me to wash away the memory of what I'd seen. That poor man…

I shuddered. Then I straightened, dried my face with a paper towel, and walked back out of the bathroom to rescue Devi from Beverly.

Devi turned out not to need much rescuing. She was back behind her desk, and Beverly was sprawled at her feet, looking like she belonged exactly where she was. I laughed a little, despite the ongoing lightness in my head.

"Fickle dog," I said.

"She was worried about you," Devi countered. "She tried to pull me over to the bathroom when you started throwing up in there. I had to give her half my sandwich to convince her that I was a worthwhile substitute, and that you wouldn't enjoy puking more if you did it with a dog looking over your shoulder."

"Your sacrifice will not go overlooked," I said.

"No, it won't, and to repay me, you're going to drink the rest of that Gatorade." Devi smiled, but there was something unyielding in her expression, making it plain that all I'd get for fighting her was a worse headache than I already had. "I heard you flush twice. Now you're upset *and* dehydrated, and that isn't allowed on my watch. Drink it, or I'll suggest admitting you on suspicion of actual illness."

"Yes, Devi," I said meekly. She was right about the dehydration: I was once again thirsty enough that the Gatorade didn't taste of anything but sweetness. I finished the bottle without pausing.

"Good girl," she said, and offered me Beverly's leash. "Do you think you can tell me what happened now, or is it going to make you throw up again if you try?"

The elevator dinged before I could say anything. We turned to see Nathan walking into the lobby, looking almost as flustered as he had when we first arrived. "Sal, grab your things; I'm driving you home," he said. "Devi, I need you to let everyone know that I'm unavailable for the rest of today. I've got to take Sally home, but then I'm going to check in at the ER. I think they're going to need the help."

"Yes, Dr. Kim," said Devi. She turned to her computer, fingers already starting to fly as she pulled up his calendar and began shooting off e-mails to the people affected by the change in Nathan's plans for the day.

I didn't move. "Do you want some Gatorade?" I asked. "Devi made me drink some. Then I threw up twice. Then I drank some more. I feel better now. I think I'm done throwing up."

Beverly smacked her tail once against the floor, as if to emphasize my statement. It made a dull slapping sound, and both of us looked toward the dog. She let her tongue loll, seemingly pleased by the attention.

"I need you to get your things," Nathan said.

"I need to know that you're safe to drive, or I'm not going *anywhere* with you," I replied. It was an effort to keep my voice steady. "Your hands are shaking, you're not meeting my eyes, and you're talking about spending the rest of the afternoon working in the ER. That's scary. I don't get in cars with people who are being scary. It's part of my 'one life-threatening accident was enough' campaign."

Nathan stopped, his Adam's apple visibly bobbing as he swallowed back whatever he wanted to answer me with. Then he nodded. "Okay," he said. "I'll have some Gatorade. Devi, is it in the fridge?"

"I can get it for you, just let me—"

"No, keep doing what you're doing. That's more important than waiting on me." He walked past me and Beverly, pausing to kiss my cheek and murmur, "I'm sorry. I should have realized that would frighten you," before continuing on to the fridge. He returned with a bottle of electric orange Gatorade in his hand.

"Fake orange or fake mango?" I asked. My voice didn't quaver. I was oddly proud of myself for that.

Nathan checked the label. "Fake tangerine," he said. "Who makes fake tangerine?"

"People who've never had a real tangerine," said Devi. She swiveled in her chair. "Your afternoon is clear. Should I go down and offer to help in the ER, or is this one of those situations where the research assistant stays far, far away?"

"This is one of those situations where the research assistant takes the rest of the afternoon off with pay, because otherwise, I'll feel bad about leaving her sitting up here all alone," said Nathan. "Go on home. I'll see you in the morning."

Devi's eyes widened. "What *happened* to you two?" she blurted. "I don't want to pry, but—"

"She always says that just before she pries," commented Nathan.

"Hush, I'm serious. Sal comes back white as a sheet and throwing up, you show up almost ten minutes later and tell me you're leaving, so I think I'm allowed to be a little bit concerned! And where did you get the dog?" Devi paused. "Did you steal somebody's dog? Is that why you're both so upset? I didn't think you had it in you."

"We didn't steal the dog," I protested. Then I hesitated, looking at Nathan. "Did we steal the dog?"

"No," he said. "The dog stole herself. We couldn't have stopped her." He turned his attention on Devi. "There's been another outbreak of sleeping sickness. We watched a man succumb while we were walking on the Embarcadero. Beverly is his dog. An ambulance has been dispatched, and once we've identified him, we'll contact his family about getting her back to the right people. For the moment, Sal and I are the right people, because we're the people she has decided are worth trusting."

Speaking of trust... I looked down into Beverly's big brown eyes and decided, then and there, that no one *I* didn't trust was going to take her away from me, whether or not they were related to her actual owner. Dogs get to pick their people. Beverly had picked me. If her owner didn't recover, and she didn't pick somebody else to take my place, we were going to stay together.

Devi, meanwhile, had gone as pale as her complexion allowed. Staring at Nathan, she asked, "How bad is the outbreak?"

"I don't know yet. Apparently, they started getting reports almost as soon as Sal and I saw it happen, but I was the first person who'd actually come in with a report of the process, so they wanted to talk to me. Now they need me to help with the intake. We've got at least thirty people incoming." He slanted another glance my way. "I really need to get Sal home. I'll see you tomorrow."

"I can drive her," said Devi. We both blinked at her. Devi smiled a little. "I live in San Bruno, she lives in Colma. It's a carpool made in heaven. Besides, my car already smells like dog, so it's not like I need to worry about my upholstery."

"If you're sure—" Nathan turned to me. "It's your choice, Sal."

The idea of getting into a car with someone whose driving history I didn't know made my chest clench and my stomach turn over again. Sure, I did exactly that every time I took a bus, but there was something reassuringly solid about buses. Even after hearing about the bus driver with the sleeping sickness, buses felt safer to me than cars.

Still, Nathan was needed, and Devi was already heading home. Mustering every inch of calm I could find, I nodded.

"Sure," I said. "That'll be fine. Devi's always been really nice to me, and won't it be better for you to get down to the ER now, not after dealing with there-and-back traffic?" To punctuate my point I stepped forward, tugging on Beverly's leash so she'd come with me, and kissed him lightly. He flushed, eyes darting toward Devi.

"Don't mind me," she said. "I know what you two get up to when the office door is closed."

Nathan cleared his throat. "Regardless. It's unprofessional to subject you…"

I tapped his nose with one finger. He stopped. "I'm going to let Devi take me home. You're going to go to the ER and do your job. You're going to help people. I'm going to give Beverly the biggest soup bone I can find at the Safeway. And I'll talk to you tonight, okay?"

"Okay," said Nathan, looking relieved and guilty at the same time. I understood the combination. I was feeling something similar—relieved to be getting out of here, guilty to be leaving him alone—leavened with a healthy dose of fear.

Looking into his eyes, I suspected that I wasn't the only one who was scared. All that did was frighten me more.

Devi's car was a '25 Prius, silver-beige, with no worrisome dents or signs that she'd been in a major accident. I relaxed a little. I relaxed more when she buckled her belt before putting her keys in her pocket and pressing the button to start the engine. She glanced my way, checking to be sure she wasn't the only one who was buckled in. I offered a wan smile.

"I don't do cars when I can help it," I said. "I really do appreciate your giving me a ride home, though. I know Nathan's needed here."

"It's no problem," said Devi. She glanced at her rearview mirror. "You all right back there, Beverly?"

The dog didn't answer. I think both of us found that a little reassuring.

"Good," said Devi, looking satisfied. She was still paler than she should have been, with a worried look in her eyes, but at least she was comfortable in her car. "What's your address again?"

I recited the address for the benefit of her onboard GPS, which beeped politely before it announced, "Route calculated."

Devi pressed the button to turn off the voice instructions and activate the LED readout on the windshield. That made me relax a little more. Drivers who see their directions are less likely to take their eyes off the road, and reading without the voice component had been shown to reduce accidents by as much as eight percent.

"Let's get you home and me back to my own dog." She chuckled wryly. "My dog and my wife. But the dog is the one who'll greet me at the door, whereas Katherine is probably still at work. She just gets annoyed when I forget that I have a human, not just a bulldog, to come home to."

I'd met Katherine once, at a hospital cocktail party that Nathan dragged me to. She worked at the Lawrence Hall of Science and always looked a little distracted, like she was listening to conversation and running some complicated equation in her head at the same time. She stood almost a full foot taller than Devi, with a pale Scandinavian complexion and a broad Minnesota accent, and from everything I could tell, the two of them were blissfully happy together.

"What's your dog's name?" I asked.

"Minnie. It's short for 'Minneapolis.' She's an American bulldog." Devi beamed like a proud parent. "She's a good girl. She just gets a little destructive when she feels like she's being left alone for no good reason."

"If you both work, how do you handle that?"

"We vacuum up a lot of feathers and buy a lot of throw pillows." Devi's car rode smoothly enough that I barely even noticed when she turned onto the freeway—not until a less safe driver went rocketing by on our left, going easily twenty miles above the speed limit. Some of the other drivers leaned on their horns. I grabbed the handle above my door and squinted my eyes tightly closed, trying to tell myself that I was hanging off the passenger grip on the bus, and that I wasn't on the freeway. I was anywhere but there.

Devi's sigh was soft but audible in the near silence of the car. "You really don't like cars, do you?"

"My family says I used to," I said, without opening my eyes or letting go of the handle. "I got my license the day I turned sixteen. I got my first car six months later. Paid for it with my own money and everything—I'd been saving since I was eleven."

"But you don't remember any of that."

"No. None of it." I forced my eyes open, if only so I could be sure that Devi was watching the road, not watching me. Her face was turned reassuringly forward. I relaxed a little, but still didn't let go of the handle. "I know I always say this, but I say it because it's the truth: I don't remember *anything* before waking up in the hospital."

Just the dark, the hot warm dark, and the distant sound of drums that never stopped their pounding . . .

"I can't even imagine," said Devi. She paused before adding, thoughtfully, "Well, some selective amnesia would be welcome. Like my first college girlfriend, or my high school boyfriend. I could easily deal with forgetting either one of them."

"You had a boyfriend?"

"I had a mother, and my mother had a lot of friends with kids my age, and my mother and her friends all wanted grand-children very, very badly. Anand was nice, he was my age, and

he seemed like a good prospect for a respectable marriage."
Devi slanted a wicked look in my direction, there and gone
before I could worry about her taking her eyes off the road.
"The funny part is, I didn't end it."

"No?"

"No. He did, when he showed up at the Homecoming
dance with a different date and an apology for making me
waste money on my own corsage." Her laugh was bright in the
confined car. Beverly shifted in the backseat, making a curious buffing noise. "The replacement date's name was Nikhil.
In case you don't know enough about Indian names to get the
joke, it's a boy's name."

"Oh," I said. "Well, I guess that made your coming out a
little less awkward."

"Not really. At least Nikhil was Indian. Still is, presumably—
I haven't spoken with Anand in years." Her tone was light,
intentionally more conversational than our previous relationship would justify. She was trying to keep me relaxed. Surprisingly enough, it was working. "Katherine is both incapable of
giving my parents grandchildren unless we turn to medical science *and* she's a white girl from the Midwest. I couldn't even
marry a nice Indian lesbian. Oh, the shame of it all."

I laughed a little. "I guess when you look at it that way…"

"It helps." Devi slanted another glance in my direction. Her
hands were still steady on the wheel, and I found that I minded
less when she took her eyes off the road, as long as she didn't
do it for long. "Like I was saying, though, I can't imagine not
remembering those pieces of myself. I wouldn't be who I am
today if it weren't for the things that happened to me yesterday,
no matter how much I did or didn't like them. You're handling
things a lot better than I would."

"I might not be this calm if the memory loss was partial, but
I don't remember *anything*. This is the only version of me that

I've ever known." I shrugged. "I forgot everything. I wouldn't even know I'd forgotten, if people didn't tell me. These last six years have sort of been my childhood? But they're my adulthood, too. It's weird. I am not a social model that exists outside my own skin."

Devi looked faintly embarrassed. "I'm sorry. I didn't think."

"No, it's okay. Everyone gets around to asking eventually, and I figure driving me home gets you privileges." I leaned back in the seat, finally releasing the handle above the door. "Everyone who knew me before the accident—who knew Sally, I mean, since I don't even feel like I can legitimately claim to be her—says I'm much nicer now. I have a personality, which was a worry for a little while, since they thought there might be brain damage. It's just not the same one. I don't stress about the missing memories anymore. I stress about the thought that someday, if I'm not careful, they might come *back*. And that's when I don't know what I would do."

"You're good for Nathan," said Devi, and followed this seeming non sequitur by moving over a lane, heading for the exit that would take us to my street. "I was a little leery when he started dating you. It's not my place to dictate his personal life, but he's my friend as well as my colleague, and I was concerned."

"Everyone was concerned," I said. My parents had been at the head of *that* particular line of anxious people, convinced that Nathan was taking advantage of me by getting into a relationship with someone who had only recently been wearing a soy-paper gown, even if he hadn't known that when we met. We'd been able to bring them around, but it had taken time, and showing over and over that Nathan wasn't just good for me, he was great for me. I liked to think that I was the same for him.

"He has good taste in women," said Devi serenely. "I'm not making a pass or anything here—my wife would murder me—but

you should trust me, because I am an absolute expert on quality women."

I smiled. "I'm glad to know that I'm acceptable." Then I
pointed toward a house about four down the street from our
current position. "That's me."

"Well, it seems I've been able to get you home safely, then."
Devi pulled into my driveway and turned off the engine.
"Door-to-door service. Now get your dog and get inside, so I
can tell Nathan that I saw you in before I drove away."

"Yes, ma'am," I said. "Thanks again."

She waved it off. "Don't worry about it. I'll see you soon."

"Absolutely." I slid out of the car before opening the back
door and taking hold of Beverly's leash. She jumped obligingly
down to the driveway. I closed both doors, waved to Devi one
last time, and turned to walk up the path to the house.

She was still there when I unlocked the front door and
stepped inside, Beverly sticking close to my heels all the way.
I turned to face the living room window and watched as Devi
drove away.

In a matter of seconds, she was gone, and the street was still.

"Mom? Dad? Joyce?" No one answered. I was alone in the
house. I had been expecting that; it wasn't the middle of the
day, exactly, more late afternoon at this point, but they all had
jobs of their own to do. I was the only one who'd had the day
off. It was actually a bit of a relief—I hadn't been looking forward to explaining what I was doing home and where the dog
had come from before I had the chance to calm down a little bit.

I couldn't say exactly what had been so disturbing about seeing Beverly's owner get sick, any more than I could say exactly
what it was about the sleepwalkers that disturbed me so much.
Something about them was deeply and fundamentally *wrong*,
in a way that I couldn't articulate. I just knew that it made me
feel like I was going to start throwing up again.

Beverly sat at my feet, waiting to see what I was going to do next. I bent and unclipped her leash from her collar.

"Welcome home, Bevvie," I said, and rubbed her silky ears. She let her tongue loll, looking pleased in that way that all dogs have. "Go ahead and explore. You're going to live here for now."

Beverly stood, stretching luxuriously, and went trotting off into the living room. I shrugged out of my coat, hanging both it and the leash on the rack next to the door, and followed her.

For the next ten minutes, Beverly explored the house and I followed her, watching as she sniffed at corners and shoved her head into places where I wouldn't have expected it to fit. She was perfectly well behaved, not attempting to chew on anything or squat in any of the corners. Once she was done with the inside, I led her to the back door and opened it far enough for her to squeeze out and go to explore the backyard.

I didn't know whether we'd ever had a dog, but we had a high fence that looked like it would be sufficient to keep her from wandering off into traffic. I watched for a few minutes as Beverly explored the outside, her nose low to the ground and her tail carried high, like a rudder. Then I whistled for her to come inside. She bounded back through the sliding glass door into the kitchen, her tail wagging madly as I closed it behind. I needed to go to Safeway and get dog food for her. I needed to do a lot of things. I was suddenly too tired to stay on my feet. I staggered down the hall toward my room.

I don't remember getting into bed. I don't remember falling asleep. All I remember is that one minute, the world was there, and the next minute, the world was gone. And, as always, I dreamt.

Here in the hot warm dark, something is changing, something is different than it was before. There are words now, words here in the dark, words for things like "red" and "drums" and "time."

There is a "before" here now. There was never a before, and where there is a before, there can be an after.

What is an "after"? I do not know, and because I do not know, because there is something to be known and an "I" to fail to know it, I am afraid. There isn't supposed to be an after. There isn't supposed to be an I. There's only supposed to be the hot warm dark, forever, and it's never supposed to change.

The drums are getting louder. I wish I knew what that meant. I wish I understood why I was so very, very afraid…

The main issue with Steve's D. yonagoensis *variant—which he was calling "D. banks" in those days, because hubris is not only a sin, it's a fun game to play at parties—was rejection. Our immune systems wound up in a muddle because they spent millennia evolving alongside parasites, and we took those parasites away very abruptly, causing a spike in allergies and autoimmune conditions. That's all well and good, but that doesn't mean our immune systems liked the parasites. They knew how to handle them. That doesn't mean they wanted them around.*

Steve approached things as a businessman and a scientist. What he lost, ironically, was the human angle. We're constantly told not to anthropomorphize in science, but when you're talking about the human body, even the autonomic functions of it, you have to anthropomorphize. That's where you'll find your answers. Our bodies don't like having parasites inside them, no matter how beneficial those parasites are intended to be. They'll fight back until the parasites are destroyed, or until they are. D. banks *triggered every rejection response that* D. yonagoensis *did. What you got from Steve's "miracle cure" was dead worms and sick people.*

That's when I was brought in to consult. My specialty was the human genome. How it worked, how it could be used to benefit humanity—how to fold it into other things that didn't start out as members of the human family tree. If you wanted someone to build you a worm, you went to Steve. You wanted a worm that had medical applications, you went to Richie. And if you wanted that worm to be a cousin of yours, you came to me.

Six years into the development cycle, they came to me. I gave up everything to be a part of the project. They never looked back, and neither did I.

—FROM *CAN OF WORMS: THE AUTOBIOGRAPHY OF SHANTI CALE, PHD.* AS YET UNPUBLISHED.

Shanti and Steve have told their sides of the story, Steve in public, Shanti mostly behind closed doors. I know she's planning to publish a book as soon as her NDA runs out. Steve can't keep paying her off forever. He's too arrogant to really think that he has to. That's the real problem. He's too arrogant, and she's too insane, and they're the ones with their fingers on the trigger of this whole damn mess.

Ask Steve and he'll say we filled a need.

Ask Shanti and she'll say science finds a way.

Don't bother asking me anything. I have committed my crimes. I have endured my penance for as long as I could. After tomorrow, I will not be available for you to ask.

—FROM THE JOURNAL OF DR. RICHARD JABLONSKY, CO-FOUNDER OF SYMBOGEN. DATED JULY 10, 2027.

Chapter 6

AUGUST 2027

"You're sure that you're okay?"

"I'm fine, Dad." I looked out the car window at the glass-fronted building in front of us, trying to ignore the itching in my fingers. I wanted out of the car, away from his endless attempts to be a caring parent. All he was doing was making me more nervous than I already was...but not quite nervous enough to undo my seat belt while the car was still in motion. "This isn't my first checkup."

"Still. I could go in with you." The car finally stopped moving, pulled up snug against the curb.

"*No*," I said, and unfastened my seat belt. In the back, Beverly sat up, ears pricked, as she waited to see whether I'd be taking her with me. "Sorry, girl. You're going to the office with Dad today, and I'm going to the vet."

Dad snorted, amusement briefly overwhelming his concern.

I leaned over and kissed his cheek. "Thanks for taking Beverly. See you when I get home?"

"I'd be happy to come and pick you up," Dad said, and hugged me awkwardly, around his seat belt.

"I like taking the bus; it gives me time to think," I said gently as I retrieved my messenger bag from the footwell and slid out of the car. I shut the door before he could object. He shot me a look through the window, half-annoyed, half-amused. Then he waved. I waved back, and turned away from the car, facing the SymboGen building.

It looked as pastoral and welcoming as it always did, thanks to hundreds of architects and public relations designers, and part of me—the part that had come first, during my endless hours of physical therapy and laborious progress—still thought of it as home. I knew that years of work had gone into creating that facade, the perfect blend of glass and stainless steel, representing scientific futurism, with growing plants and artificial waterfalls, representing a connection to the natural world. The original architect wrote a book about the process of building SymboGen HQ. It says something about the size and strength of the company that he was able to have it published.

And no matter how false it was, it was still the first home that I remembered having, and the one that my heart never really seemed to leave. I took a breath, squared my shoulders, and walked toward the sliding glass doors at the front of the building.

They opened silently at my approach, the first strains of Muzak drifting out into the morning air. It sounded classical, but I knew if I pulled out my phone and triggered the app that was supposed to help me identify songs off the radio, it would come up as a generic pop song, slowed down, sweetened, and stripped of whatever raw power it might have had when it was new. No matter how comfortable I felt at SymboGen, I needed to remember how good they were at taking things and reducing them to their lowest common denominators.

I took a deep breath as I stepped over the threshold into Symbo-Gen proper, shutting out the music in favor of savoring the carefully balanced perfume suffusing the lobby. The scent was a custom blend, according to Joyce: a mixture of apple, orange blossoms, and fresh corn. It was supposed to make people think of health and vitality. It made me think that everything was going to be all right, and at the same time, that nothing was ever going to be all right again. It was the smell of home. Home isn't always a good place to be.

"Ms. Mitchell. We're so glad you could join us today." The voice was as smooth and soulless as the music drifting from overhead.

"Hi, Chave," I said, turning to face the speaker.

She was beautiful: she had to be, to be one of the public faces of SymboGen. As always, she was sleekly groomed, not a hair out of place. She was wearing a dove-gray suit, and her dark skin practically glowed against its pale backdrop, making her look like the pinnacle of health. I was gripped with the sudden, almost undeniable urge to ask her whether SymboGen employed a fashion consultant to make sure their employees only went out in public wearing colors that were guaranteed to make them look like they were ready to run a marathon.

"You're right on time. That's wonderful." Chave's smile was as artificial as the rest of her, but I didn't hold it against her. "Did you remember your paperwork?"

"It's all right here, same as always." I held up my bag, wondering if this was the way kids in school felt when they were asked if they'd remembered to do their homework. One more piece of missing emotional memory, clicking into place. "Do you know where I'm supposed to drop it off?"

Chave looked at my battered Target messenger bag distastefully, like it was a snake that might decide to take a bite out of her manicured fingers. The polish was clear, which probably meant it was expensive; there was no other way she could have gotten away with something so bland. "I'll be happy to take that to Accounting for you. You have a meeting with the financial department after lunch, to discuss any questions they may have or inaccuracies that they may find."

"Inaccuracies" was the approved corporate way of saying "attempts to make SymboGen pay for something that wasn't their problem." They weren't going to find anything, but the idea was still enough to make my mouth go dry. I hated dealing with the SymboGen financial people. They were always so *nice*. Somehow, that made them worse than the blandly professional faces that made up the rest of the company's human infrastructure.

"Oh. Good." I swung the messenger bag around to the front and dug through it until I found the heavy manila folder with my receipts and mileage statements for the past six months. I offered it to her. "Everything's in there. We used the filing instructions we got from you last time."

"Then there shouldn't be anything to worry about." Chave's utterly fake smile remained in place as she took the folder and tucked it under her arm. "This way, Ms. Mitchell." Then she turned and walked away across the lobby, her heels sinking silently into the plush blue carpet.

I didn't want to go with her. I went anyway.

The first time I was at SymboGen, I didn't know I should be impressed by my surroundings. I had been out of my coma for less than a week, and was being moved to their parasitology wing for further study. The public hospital came later, after I'd regained fine motor control and the rudiments of language. First came SymboGen, and their many, many experts. I stayed there for almost a year. I learned what trees were from their arboretum, and what birds were from their aviary, and I cried for days when they made me leave.

The second time I was at SymboGen, I had been back with my parents for less than a week, and I was returning for physical and cognitive therapy. I'd run into the building and hidden in its halls for three hours, refusing to leave. They'd had to sedate me to get me back into the car. It felt like the world had stopped making sense, like the only home I believed in didn't want me anymore. The third time I was at SymboGen, the tests began in earnest, and I learned what home—the place I thought was home, anyway—had wanted me for all along.

Psychological exams. Puzzles and mazes and endless, endless tests to see what I could learn and how long I could retain it under stress. The scientists were kind and did their best to make things easy, but they weren't the ones giving the orders. It was like the corporation had been waiting for someone like me to come along, and now that I'd finally arrived, I was just a lab animal to them. I was a lab animal that they had to release at the end of their twice-yearly study dates, letting me go back into the wild and learn a few more tricks to impress them with.

Every time the doors of SymboGen closed behind me, I was a little more convinced that we were inching toward the day when they would no longer let me leave. Part of me insisted my parents would never let that happen. The other part of me, the one that was loudest when I was actually inside the building, reminded me, over and over again, that I was a stranger. I'd killed their real daughter, taken over her life, and if SymboGen decided to petition for custody, my parents and sister would probably be relieved. SymboGen already felt more like home than home did, according to that part of me; why couldn't I see that I belonged there forever and ever? I tried not to listen to that little voice, but sometimes it was so hard that I might as well have been trying to ignore Dr. Morrison's grin.

Chave was one of my two primary handlers when I was on company property. I liked her counterpart, Sherman, a lot better, and I liked them both more than I liked any of their substitutes. They were always impeccably groomed, and they clearly had their own agendas—which ironically made me like them more than I liked the administration. Some of them treated me like a human being, but I was a lab animal all the same, and lab animals aren't entitled to personal space. It was nice to have at least a few people outside the science wing who didn't feel like they could grab me at any moment.

"Where are we going first?" I asked, once we were in the glass-backed elevator, sliding high into the grasp of SymboGen. The schedule for my visits was never provided ahead of time. I just knew when I was supposed to show up, and when to tell my parents that someone needed to come and get me. One of the psychiatrists once told me it was so I wouldn't psych myself out about the tests. Personally, I thought they just enjoyed it more when I was unprepared.

"We're actually beginning with an interview today," said Chave, her tone as mild and uninflected as ever.

"An interview? I didn't agree to any interviews. They still have to let me approve those." Once—and only once—SymboGen had surprised me with a reporter. That particular article had presented me as some kind of idiot savant who had managed to overcome traumatic brain damage in order to become a semifunctional person. It was syrupy, sweet, and almost entirely untrue. My parents had threatened to sue the company for libel, slander, and half a dozen other things, some of which I was pretty sure were exclusive of one another. Symbo-Gen apologized and promised never to do that again without getting my consent and allowing me to have someone of my choice to be an unbiased observer.

"It's not that kind of interview," said Chave. The elevator stopped moving, the doors sliding smoothly open.

Standing on the other side was Dr. Steven Banks, creator of the Intestinal Bodyguard and the only remaining member of the trio that founded SymboGen. He was smiling. Somehow, that didn't help.

"Hello, Sally," he said. "It's very nice to see you again."

*   *   *

Dr. Banks's office was larger than the reception lobby at the hospital where Nathan worked. Two of the walls were actually windows, solid sheets of glass looking out on the city below. He had a perfect view of the Bay. From this distance, you couldn't see the traffic or the people wandering the streets. All you saw was the natural beauty of San Francisco, the allure that had been drawing people through the Golden Gate for centuries. I guess when you're one of the richest people on the planet, you can buy yourself a window that never shows you anything ugly. It's one of the perks that comes with the position.

Dr. Banks gestured for me to sit down in one of the plush leather chairs in front of his desk as he walked around to sit in his own larger, plusher leather chair. "It's so nice to have a little time to talk, don't you think, Sally?"

"Yes, Dr. Banks," I said automatically. I sat down, perching on the very edge of the chair like I was getting ready to jump to my feet at any second. To be honest, I was considering doing just that.

"It's all right, Sally. You're not in trouble." He smiled, showing his perfect teeth. I fought the urge to bolt. "I just wanted to see you."

"Yes, Dr. Banks," I repeated.

His smile faded. "Do I make you nervous?"

I sighed. "Yes, Dr. Banks," I said, for the third time. "You really do."

It wasn't just his teeth that were perfect. Everything about him was perfect, from his hair and skin down to his subtly sculpted physique. I found myself wondering whether he had somehow managed to make his Intestinal Bodyguard start secreting steroids along with all the other chemicals it pumped out to ensure the well-being of its host. Dr. Steven Banks was not the kind of man who spent that many hours at the gym, or gave up fried food of his own free will.

"I wish I didn't make you nervous, Sally," he said. He sounded sincere, which just made me more nervous. "I want us to get along. I think we're both smart enough to know that we're not going to be friends, but I'd like it if we could at least be friendly acquaintances."

"You do sort of control my life, Dr. Banks," I said hesitantly. "If I make you mad, or you don't like my progress, you could decide to stop providing me with medical care, and I'd probably die. So I'm sure you'll understand if I'm a little bit uneasy around you."

Now he looked a little hurt. "Do you really think I'd do something like that to you, Sally?"

Normal people don't use the names of the people they're speaking to in every other sentence. Dr. Banks did, for some reason, and when I was around him, I found myself doing it, too. All children learn speech through mimicry. That stage was closer to the present for me than it was for most adults, and sometimes the habit was hard to break.

"I think SymboGen is a business, Dr. Banks," I replied, carefully. "I think that sometimes business investments don't pan out."

"I think of you as much more than just a business investment," said Dr. Banks. "You're a part of the SymboGen family. Don't you feel like a part of this family?"

There didn't seem to be any right answer to that question, and so I didn't say anything at all. I just sat there, waiting for him to continue.

After a minute or so, he did. "I wanted to meet with you today because it's been too long since we've had the opportunity to just sit and talk. Monitoring your progress is important to me, Sally, and sometimes looking at facts on paper isn't enough to let me see the whole picture. There are pieces that only come through when you can look someone in the eye and really *understand* what they've been through."

"I'm fine," I said, a little more stiffly than I'd intended. "I'm still working at the shelter. I like it there. My boss lets me work with the kittens a lot."

"That's the Cause for Paws animal shelter downtown, isn't it?" As if he didn't already know that. "I'm glad to hear that it's still working out well for you. I heard you got a dog recently?"

"Beverly. I'm fostering her. Her owner is sick and can't take care of her at the moment, and his family doesn't want the responsibility of taking care of his dog while he was in the hospital." They'd been grateful, actually. I'd expected my own family to object to Beverly, but they had turned out to be totally fine with my bringing home a dog as long as she was housebroken and didn't chew on the furniture. Beverly was so well behaved that everyone was in love with her by the end of that first night.

That was a good thing. Dogs need to be loved, and her owner was probably never going to be reclaiming her, if the recovery—or lack of recovery—of the rest of the sleepwalkers meant anything.

"Her owner...you saw him collapse, didn't you?" There was something too casual about the question; the way that Dr. Banks looked at my face and then away, quickly, like he was afraid of being seen...he was worried. And I didn't know why.

"Yes. I was taking a walk with my boyfriend when we saw Beverly's owner have some sort of a seizure. He didn't fall down, though. He just shut off, like he wasn't in his body anymore." And Beverly, poor, sweet Beverly, had barked at him like he was some kind of a monster. She hadn't barked at anyone else like that. Not once.

"The dog must have been very frightened."

It wasn't a question. I found myself answering it anyway, saying, "She was terrified. That's why I wound up taking her with us. She was barking at him like she thought that he was going to hurt her. She came to me as soon as I whistled for her."

"Interesting. You didn't think that maybe she was just an aggressive dog?"

"No."

"Had you met this dog before?"

I frowned, annoyance causing me to briefly forget that I was speaking to the CEO of SymboGen. "I already got the 'did you steal this man's dog' questionnaire from the police. I'd never seen him, or the dog, before. But I work with scared animals all day, and when I realized how terrified she was, I couldn't just sit by and leave her with no one to take care of her. Nathan called an ambulance for Beverly's owner, and we agreed that it was best if she went home with me until we had a better idea of what was going on."

"Nathan—that would be your boyfriend, Dr. Kim, from the San Francisco City Hospital Parasitology Department, correct? We offered him a job here at SymboGen once, you know." Dr. Banks beamed at me, like this was the greatest honor that could be afforded to someone in the medical profession.

"Yes," I said. "I know." Nathan had actually tried to take them up on their offer—SymboGen was *the* place for an up-and-coming parasitologist who wanted to stay on the cutting edge of the field—but had been passed up for employment when their Human Resources Division realized that he was serious about his refusal to accept an Intestinal Bodyguard. They couldn't technically make that a requirement for employment, but the fact came out, and suddenly the job offer was withdrawn.

"He seemed like a very nice young man."

"He is."

"Does your new dog have any problems with him?"

"She's not my dog, but no, she doesn't. Beverly likes everyone. She's the sweetest dog I've ever known."

Dr. Banks nodded before asking another of those overly

casual questions, the ones that felt more like traps, iron jaws waiting to slam shut on my throat: "She doesn't have any problems with you?"

"She slept on my bed last night," I said. "If she had problems, I think I'd know."

"Good, good. It's important for a girl to have a dog. It helps with emotional and social development, and of course, dog ownership will bring you into contact with a wider variety of allergens. Pollens, dander, all those lovely bits of the environment."

I struggled to muster a smile, and barely succeeded. "So according to the hygiene hypothesis, owning a dog will be good for my immune system?"

"Exactly!" Dr. Banks looked delighted. "Have you been reading the literature?"

"I've been listening to the audio versions." It was hard to avoid learning about the hygiene hypothesis when I was dating a parasitologist. Half the literature Nathan had around his apartment was about the hygiene hypothesis, its impact on the field of parasitology, and the various ways it could be approached, ranging from "gospel truth" to "fringe science become multi-billion-dollar industry." Even if I couldn't read it for myself, he was more than happy to explain it all to me.

"I'll make sure you get a copy of my autobiography before you leave today," said Dr. Banks, still looking pleased as could be. "I'll even sign it. And personalize it, of course. Wouldn't want it showing up on one of the auction sites, now, would we?"

He laughed. I didn't.

Apparently, that was the cue for him to get down to business. Dr. Banks sobered, folding his hands on his desk and leaning slightly forward, like a kindly professor on one of the crime dramas Mom liked to watch in the evening. "It really is good to see you, Sally. I worry about you. But you know there's another reason that I wanted to meet with you today."

I never would have guessed, I thought. Aloud, I asked, "What's that?"

"I think it's time we strengthened the relationship between SymboGen and your family. You've been here so much over the past few years, I really feel like you're already a part of Symbo-Gen. Like this is already your home."

Cold terror clamped down on me with an iron hand, balanced by an equal measure of relief. This was it, then; this was the day when they decided they no longer had to let me leave. How much would they have to pay my parents to make this acceptable? How many zeros on the check that paid for a person? "Oh?" I said, hating the way my voice squeaked on that single syllable.

"We have an animal research division. They're dedicated to developing strains of the Intestinal Bodyguard that can be used to protect domestic pets, even livestock, from medical calamity. You're not suited to work in the research arena, obviously, but the animals need care. Many of them originally came from shelters or animal rescue groups. I'm sure they would appreciate having a human to provide them with the love and attention they desire."

I stared at him for a moment, unsure of how I was supposed to be responding. Finally, I asked, "You think I could do this job?"

"Not with all the animals, maybe, but with the dogs and cats? Absolutely. They need walking and brushing, petting, and to be told, occasionally, that they are good boys and girls, and that someone loves them. It seems to me that this is the job you already do, but now it would come with higher pay, and with the absolute guarantee that your fears about Symbo-Gen deciding to terminate your care would remain unfounded. We don't leave our employees without health care, ever. That would go against everything that we stand for as a company. I mean, part of the inspiration for the Intestinal Bodyguard was the idea that it would provide truly universal health care—rich or poor, swallow a single tailored capsule and your personal health implant will begin taking care of your every need, for as long as you need it to."

There were times when I couldn't tell how much of what Dr. Banks said was sincere, and how much he was reading off some private internal monitor that provided him with a constant feed of the official SymboGen party line. This was definitely one of those times.

"They need me at the shelter," I said, finally.

"Are you sure?"

The question was mild, and sent another jolt of terror through me. "Yes," I said, as steadily as I could manage. "If you asked Will, he'd probably tell you I was replaceable, because he's a good man like that, and he wouldn't want to stand in the way of an opportunity. But he'd be wrong. The shelter needs me."

"You know, Sally, I respect your devotion to your responsibilities. It shows just how well you've managed to bounce back from your tragic accident." Dr. Banks leaned back in his seat. He was smiling again. "Maybe it's time we reconsidered your position on speaking to the press. I don't know if you're aware, but *Rolling Stone* is very interested in interviewing you."

My mouth went dry. "They...they are?"

"*Very* interested. You know, they published a profile on me earlier this year."

"I know," I said, in a small voice. The piece in *Rolling Stone* was called "King of the Worms." It described Steve Banks as part genius, part entrepreneur, and part savior of mankind. Nathan threw the magazine across the room in disgust the first time he read it, and wouldn't let me see. I had to download the files myself after I got home, and struggle through reading them on my own. I'd wished almost immediately that

I'd left well enough alone. From the way Dr. Banks described me, I was a brain-dead husk preserved only by the Intestinal Bodyguard, a perfect proof of concept for their miracle medical implant. Without the worm, I would have died. That may have been true, but it shouldn't have been enough to make me a sideshow freak, and that was exactly what Dr. Banks seemed to want me to be.

"You've read it?" Dr. Banks looked pleased. I felt sick. "Then you understand why they'd be interested in including your perspective with a follow-up article. It would be wonderful press for SymboGen and the Intestinal Bodyguard. You could help us sway hundreds to the side of getting their implants, finally freeing themselves from the daily routine of medications and worry." He looked at me expectantly, like there was something I was supposed to say in response.

I couldn't think of anything. I balled my hands together in my lap and said, in a very small voice, "I'm happy at the shelter. I don't want to talk to any reporters. They've only just stopped trying to call me at the house, and I don't want to remind them who I am."

Dr. Banks frowned. For a moment, he looked at me not like I was someone to cajole and convince to come over to his way of thinking, but like I was a science project on the verge of going wrong. "Really, Sally, I hoped you'd be more willing to help the company that has done so much to help you. Don't you want to help us?"

The part of me that had just been through six years of cognitive therapy and endless psychological tests recognized what he was trying to do. By using the word "help" so many times so closely together, he could make me feel like I was somehow letting down the team by not jumping right in to do my part. It was linguistic reinforcement, and it might have worked six years ago, when I was still less sure of who I really was. It wasn't going to work on me now.

The other part of me—the small, scared part of me that dreamt of darkness and drums and waited constantly for the next axe to fall—was convinced that refusing to do what Dr. Banks wanted would result in him cutting off all medical support, leaving me to die the next time I went into anaphylactic shock for no discernible reason.

It was the calm part that won out, and I heard myself say, in a much more confident voice, "I do want to help, Dr. Banks. I just don't think speaking to the press would be a good idea for me right now. I'm at a very fragile place in my recovery. I wouldn't want to risk losing ground. It would look bad for everyone, and you know the media would be watching to see whether there were any changes in my condition right after I gave an interview. This isn't the right time."

Dr. Banks kept frowning...but slowly, he also nodded. "I suppose I can see where you're coming from, Sally, and I appreciate hearing that you're so concerned about SymboGen's image. I still hope that you'll consider it."

I managed to force a smile through the cold wall of fear that was wrapped around me. "I'll try."

The rest of our "talk"—really a lecture, with me as the sole attending student, and Dr. Banks as the professor who didn't know when to leave the podium—was the usual generic platitudes about the wonders of SymboGen and the Intestinal Bodyguard, interspersed with the occasional softball question about how I was doing, how Nathan was doing, how Joyce and I were getting along. All the usual pleasantries, all asked with a fake concern that was somehow more insulting than rote disinterest would have been. When he pretended to care, I had to pretend to listen. It didn't seem like a fair exchange.

After what felt like a hundred years, but was really slightly under an hour, Dr. Banks glanced ostentatiously at his watch, and stood. "I've enjoyed our time together, Sally, but I'm afraid

I have a meeting I can't reschedule. Do you know what the rest of your day with us will look like?"

"Not yet," I said, taking the hint and getting out of my own chair. I'd been sitting still for too long; my legs felt like jelly. "Chave brought me straight up to see you."

"Well, I'm sure you've got some exciting adventures ahead of you." Dr. Banks started walking toward the door. He didn't gesture for me to follow him. He knew that I was going to do it, just like he knew that he would eventually be able to convince me to accede to the interview with *Rolling Stone*. Being his kind of rich made it easy to shape the world to suit your standards. "I'll check with my secretary. Maybe we can have lunch together. Wouldn't that be nice?"

"Sure," I said. For a change, I meant it, at least a little. Eating lunch at SymboGen was part of the visitation process; they probably observed me for some set of symptoms I didn't even know I was supposed to be expressing. The company's main cafeteria was excellent, but the executive cafeteria—where I'd eaten every chance I got since remembering, or maybe learning, that food could get better than macaroni and cheese with apple-sauce on the side—was something special. They hired five-star chefs, and their menu was never the same two days in a row.

"There's something you'll have to do for me, of course."

I paused, giving him a wary look. "What?"

"What's the newest piece of slang you've learned?"

Fortunately, this wasn't one of the insulting ones. "Taking the Mickey," I said. "It means making fun of somebody by telling them a fib. I think it has something to do with Mickey Mouse, but I'm not quite sure."

Now he laughed, a big, bold sound that filled the room like the drumming filled the darkness in my dreams. I flinched, barely stopping myself from clutching at my ears. "Mickey Mouse, huh? Truly, Sally, you are an endless delight."

"Thank you, Dr. Banks," I said.

"And like all endless delights, you have other lives to brighten." He pushed open the door, revealing Chave standing still as a statue on the other side. She looked monumentally bored, and a little bit annoyed. For her, that was the equivalent of kicking her feet and screaming. "Are you here to take Miss Mitchell to her next meeting?"

"If you don't mind," said Chave, in her usual cool tone. "We're already twenty minutes overdue for her appointment in the blood lab. Did you feed her?"

"Not a crumb," said Dr. Banks.

Chave nodded curtly and looked to me, as if for confirmation.

"He didn't feed me," I said.

"Good. Come along." With that, she turned her back and stalked toward the elevator, her shoulders locked into a tight, unhappy line. I glanced back at Dr. Banks, who still hadn't formally dismissed me. Then I ran after her, clutching my bag to my chest like a lifeline.

It said something about how little I enjoyed my time with Dr. Banks that being locked in an elevator with an unhappy personal assistant who clearly blamed me for disrupting her entire day was better than spending another minute alone with him. I stood as far away from her as the tiny elevator allowed, watching as the numbers on the display counted down to the first floor, and then farther down, into the basement levels.

Maybe it's crazy to build a high-rise with multiple subterranean floors in the state of California, earthquake capital of the United States, but that didn't stop the founders of Symbo-Gen. When Drs. Banks and Jablonsky decided to build a state-of-the-art research facility, they didn't let silly things like logic and geography stop them. SymboGen was cut deep into the bedrock of South San Francisco, and the only reason it wasn't closer to the water was that no amount of money or hubris could deny the ocean. The building would have flooded long since if it had been as close to the coast as they originally wanted it to be. SymboGen: the castle that worms built.

We finally stopped on subbasement level three. I found myself relaxing when the elevator doors opened to reveal a generic hospital hallway, the kind that could be in any public research facility or university in the world. Home.

Men and women in white lab coats and sensible slacks walked past, some of them pausing to wave or smile in my direction. I beamed back at them, my smile widening as my eyes found the one person who was wearing a tailored suit. He stuck out like a sore thumb amongst all their practical, functional clothing. It didn't help that he was tall, gangly, and sporting an artificial tan that clashed with the laboratory pallor of the people around him.

I stepped into the hall, still clutching my bag as I walked toward Sherman. I was moving too fast, and nearly collided with one of the researchers. He swerved at the last moment, and we both regained our balance as the elevator doors slid closed behind me.

The change in Sherman once Chave was out of sight was instant. He relaxed from his ramrod-straight attention, suddenly grinning. Even his artfully spiked hair somehow seemed less "the latest style," and more "I couldn't be bothered to do anything but chop it off and rub some gel into it." "Come here, you bloody twit," he said, his heavy British accent twisting the words until the mockery seemed almost friendly, like a more personal way of saying hello. "Can you manage it, do you think, without sending half the research staff sprawling? I ask out of personal interest, and because if you're going to treat them like bowling pins, I want to take a moment to place a bet with the staff in the radiology lab."

I laughed. "Are you my escort for the rest of today?"

"The rest of your life, my pet, if you'd only allow it." He leaned over and took my hand, spinning me around like we were getting ready to dance the waltz in the middle of the hallway. More of the research staff walked by, slowing to watch us with visible amusement. Sherman had that effect on people. "Are you ready to leave that parasite pasher of yours for a real man?"

"That's a new word and I demand a definition before I answer," I replied. "What's a pasher?"

"A pash is a kiss, so a pasher is someone who kisses. Ergo, I have called your boyfriend a tapeworm kisser."

"Never seen him kiss a tapeworm, but he pashes me on a pretty regular basis. I think I'll keep him." I paused. "Well? Was that right? Did I use it right?"

"You used it *perfectly*." Sherman let go of my hand, snapping back to business as he consulted his clipboard. "I'm supposed to take you for a blood draw, a urine test, and a nice cool glass of barium. I hand you back to Chave after that—sorry, Sal—so that you can head up to Accounting and go over your receipts, but then it's back to me for a lovely nap in the gel ultrasound chamber before lunch."

"My favorite place," I said. I wasn't kidding. Tight spaces didn't bother me—they never had—and while I was in the ultrasound tube, all I had to do was lie perfectly still. There were no needles or difficult questions involved. That could be nice, considering everything else that a visit to SymboGen entailed.

"I know." Sherman smiled. "I also know how much you hate dealing with the bureaucrats upstairs, my pet, but it's good to see you in the flesh. I never quite trust those reports that tell me you're doing perfectly well, sandwiched between profit-and-loss statements and requisition slips for more paper towels in the kitchen."

As much as I hated to think about myself as being just one more report to circulate around the offices at SymboGen, I appreciated Sherman's concern. He was one of the only administrative staffers who actually treated me like a human being, or at least like a pet he was happy to have around the house, rather than like an escaped lab rat. I attributed that partially to his own dual nature, formal when the higher-ups were within hearing range, totally relaxed when he was alone with anyone who didn't trump his pay grade.

"I can put up with it," I said, adjusting my grip on the strap of my bag.

"Good." Sherman started walking, those long legs of his unfolding to set a pace that was frankly inhumane. I scampered to keep up. He didn't even seem to notice. That, too, was a part of his charm. He didn't treat me like a lab animal, but he didn't treat me like an invalid, either. "Standard questions, then. Did you eat anything, drink anything, or do anything else that might send your blood chemistry into a tizzy?"

"What's a tizzy?"

"A tailspin, a scramble, a mess."

"You know, sometimes I think you're making up words just to screw with me," I said. He wasn't; I looked them all up after every visit, and while some of them had regional variations that didn't match up with the definitions he gave me, his basic words and phrases always checked out. He was playing it straight, or as straight as Sherman was capable of playing anything. He was the sort of man who thought a crooked line could use a little bending, just to put a little more interest into it.

"Answer the question, Sal."

"No, I haven't done anything to mess with my blood sugar. No food, no drinks, and the last time I went to the bathroom was before I got here. I am totally ready to donate blood to the cause of keeping your phlebotomists employed."

"Good girl." Sherman flashed me a grin, showing the one

crooked incisor that he refused to have fixed because, quote, "the ladies loved it." I wasn't sure which ladies he was talking about in specific, but judging by the glances he got from the female medical staff, he could have his pick. He always showed his teeth when he smiled. I liked him enough not to get too upset. It still made me uncomfortable. "Don't forget the hematologists. They'll be the ones studying the delightful fruits of your gory labors."

"I've had time to learn the drill."

"True enough, and it's time to put that learning into practice, because here we are." He stopped in front of an open doorframe, knocking twice on the wood. "Dr. Lo, we're ready for you if you're ready for us."

"Come in, please." The pleasant-faced Chinese woman who operated the lab pushed away from her microscope and stood, indicating a red leatherette chair with one hand. "It's good to see you, Sally. Have you changed your hair?"

"I brushed it," I said, and grinned.

"Well, you should keep doing that. Now if you'd have a seat, I'll be right with you." That was about the limit of our social interaction during most visits, and this one seemed to be no different.

"Okay, Dr. Lo," I said, and sat, putting my bag down beside the chair where I could grab it easily. It only took me a second to get into the correct position, with my arms on the armrests, elbows down and wrists turned toward the ceiling. Practice makes perfect in all things, I suppose.

Dr. Lo sat down on a stool and rolled over to sit next to me. "How's your weekend looking, Sherman?" she asked, as she began swabbing down the inside of my right elbow with antiseptic.

"Oh, same old, same old. Got a date with Chuck from Accounting on Friday night, he's always good for a laugh, and then I'm taking Laura from the steno pool out on Saturday night. She's not much of a laugher, but Christ on a crutch, that girl can kiss like it's an Olympic sport. How about you?"

"Nothing so exciting," said Dr. Lo, and slid her needle into my arm, taping it firmly in place. "Sally, don't move."

"Yes, Dr. Lo," I said.

She continued as if I hadn't spoken, asking, "Does Chuck know about Laura? And you do know that no one calls the admins the 'steno pool' anymore, don't you? I'm not even sure what that means."

"It's short for 'stenography pool,'" I said, before I thought better of getting involved. I wasn't supposed to be a participant in this conversation. Furniture, even furniture that somehow magically gave blood, wasn't supposed to *talk*. "Stenographers used shorthand to take notes before dictation machines and personal computers were in wide use, and…uh…" I tapered off, finally realizing that Dr. Lo was staring. "Sorry."

"I taught her that one," said Sherman, with every indication of pride. "And yeah, Chuck knows about Laura. He doesn't care much, thinks he can convince me that the girly side of the force isn't worth chasing after. As for Laura, she's up for anything that comes with a side order of good times and doesn't stiff her with the bill."

"You are a tomcat, and one of these days, it's going to get you hurt," said Dr. Lo—but she was laughing, my interjection apparently forgotten. She reached for the tubing that she would use to actually direct my blood where she wanted it to go. "I was talking to Michelle from Radiology, and she said…"

Her voice seemed to trail off as I focused on the deep red color of the blood that was filling her feeder vials, pressing itself against the glass. My veins felt tight and swollen, like their contents couldn't wait to escape from my body and experience the freedom of the open air. My breathing evened out, more sounds dropping away, until all that I could see was the red, and all that I could hear was the whisper of air passing through my nose and mouth. I let my eyes slip closed. The red remained, somehow brighter against the black. The sound of my breathing faded, replaced by the distant, steady drumbeat of my heart.

Then I slipped further into the red, and I was gone, drowning in the drums.

"Come on, then, Sal." Sherman's hand gripped my shoulder firmly enough to get my attention, although not firmly enough to hurt. "Time to wake up and move on."

"Wha'?" I sat upright, only to slump again as the movement made my head start spinning. I was still in the chair in Dr. Lo's phlebotomy lab, but Dr. Lo was gone. The only sign of her that remained was the cotton ball taped to the inside of my right elbow, dotted at the center with a spot of vivid red. Some of my blood had managed to escape after all. The rest was away with the doctor, bound for labs and exam rooms, never to be free again.

"You know, the first time you did that, I really thought you'd just gone a little overboard with the fasting. Now I realize the truth, and it's no less bizarre. You are the *only* person I have ever met who can go to sleep during a blood draw, you know that? It's like the world's weirdest useless talent."

"It's relaxing," I said, and levered myself out of the chair. My head was still spinning. I pressed a hand against my temple, trying to get the room to hold still for a moment, or at least spin more slowly. "Is there juice? I think I'm going to fall over. Or throw up. Or possibly some combination of the two."

"There's juice and cookies. Sit back down and I'll fetch them for you." Sherman pushed me gently downward before turning to bustle toward the room's small refrigerator. There was also a large refrigerator, but it was filled with blood and tissue samples, not safe things like juice boxes for lab rats. Sherman even managed to make a bustle look elegant. That was enough to make me giggle, as I wilted there in the chair and waited for him to come back.

Sherman looked over his shoulder at me. "Here, now. You making fun?"

"Maybe a little," I admitted, holding my thumb and index finger about a quarter of an inch apart, to show him just how little.

"Good. Means you're feeling better." He came back with a bottle of cranberry juice and a package of strawberry Fig Newtons. My favorite. "Drink this, eat these, and don't complain about either. We're going to go give a urine sample to the boys in the next lab after this, and then it's almost time for your visit to Accounting. Don't worry, though, you'll have a lovely barium treat before that."

"Is it cranberry flavored?" I asked, and sipped my juice. Sweetness exploded on my tongue. That was never a good sign. Like Gatorade, the better cranberry juice tastes, the more you need it.

"No, I'm pretty sure it's barium flavored. At least you're contributing to the greater cause of science by downing the stuff, eh, pet?"

"Good for me." I opened the cookies. Then I paused. "Am I allowed to eat these before the barium?"

"Yes. Better a bit of imaging skew than a lot of vomiting barium on everyone's shoes. Besides, this is all a formality. Now eat up."

That was all the permission I needed. Sherman stood by while I drank the rest of my juice and stuffed cookies into my face. The room slowly stopped its spin. I wasn't back to normal—blood sugar doesn't bounce back that fast—but I was close enough to pick up my bag and get out of the chair without pitching forward onto the floor. Sherman still moved to take my arm, steadying me until he was sure I wasn't going to fall.

He didn't let go. Instead, he looked quickly around, like he was checking to see if we would be overheard.

Once he was sure that we were alone, or as alone as it was possible to be in the bowels of SymboGen, he leaned closer, and murmured, "You've got to stop dozing off during tests that are supposed to be upsetting, Sal. It's not normal, and you and I both know they're watching you for signs of not normal. You don't want to give them the ammunition that they need."

I blinked at him, feeling that old familiar alarm beginning to coil around my spine. "The ammunition that they need for what? I thought we already determined that I was just unnaturally relaxed, not suffering from low blood pressure or a fainting disorder."

Sherman didn't say anything. He just sighed and let go of my arm, turning to start toward the door back to the hall. After a moment's indecision, I followed him. Sherman was one of the closest things I had to a friend at SymboGen, but the company was still his employer, while I was a girl who should never have been allowed behind the wheel of a car. If it came down to them or me, his loyalty was already given.

The normal swirl of medical and laboratory personnel filled the hallway, their greetings and chatter making further conversation impossible. Sherman had probably timed it that way, to avoid me asking any more awkward questions. I dogged along at his heels, hugging my bag against my chest, until we reached the next lab, where I was handed a plastic cup by a technician I'd never seen before and directed, firmly, to the nearest bathroom. Very firmly: Sherman led me there and pushed me inside before closing the door behind me.

It's funny: for a company that made its fortune off a genetically modified tapeworm, the people at SymboGen could be awfully prudish about basic bodily functions. The first few times I had to take a urine test after they took out my catheters, I just dropped my pants and filled the cup right in the middle of the lab. I stopped doing that once it was explained to me why it was inappropriate, but they still acted like there was a chance I might start peeing on everything the first opportunity I got. They were the ones who asked for the urine sample. It's not like I volunteered it.

There are times when I truly regret not remembering my childhood and the normal human socialization that I have to assume came with it. There are other times when I am frankly glad to be free of all the baggage. Everybody pees, especially when they're ordered to do so by lab techs.

As soon as the cup was full to the line on the side, I capped it firmly and placed it in the small alcove designed for that specific purpose. Apparently, urine was viewed as so powerful that it could even contaminate shelves through plastic if not properly contained. Once that was safely done, I washed and sanitized my hands before knocking on the bathroom door. "You can let me out now," I said. "I'm done."

"Are you quite sure?" asked Sherman. I was relieved to hear the teasing note in his voice. I was forgiven for pushing him before. "Maybe you're still intending to have yourself an extra-curricular widdle."

"Widdle?" I asked, laughing. "Oh, you *so* made that one up."

"Don't test me," he recommended, and opened the bathroom door. As in Dr. Lo's lab, the technician had vanished. Sherman saw me looking around for him and clapped a hand down on my shoulder. "Paul couldn't abide your radiance, my dear. He fled before he could be blinded."

I sighed. "The new guys still think I'm a freak of nature, huh?"

"To be charitable, Sal, you *are* a freak of nature. You survived the unsurvivable, you recovered from the unrecoverable, and you fall asleep when you're having blood drawn. People who don't know you like the rest of us do just don't have a frame of reference for you, that's all. And they have work to do. Your appearance is good for *hours* of overtime."

"Shouldn't that come with a little light conversation?"

"You've come a long way in your understanding of human nature," said Sherman. "You've farther yet to travel. Including, if my memory serves me right, down the hall to the radiology lab. Let's fill you up with delicious barium, shall we?"

"You're so good to me," I said sourly, and followed him back into the hall. Just another day at SymboGen, where there's no test too small, or too invasive, to run on a captive audience.

Extreme precautions are required when attempting to raise D. symbogenesis *outside its natural human host. Modern Intestinal Bodyguards™ never exist outside the digestive systems of the people who willingly ingest them in pill form. Consequentially, they have been keyed to respond to specific environmental cues, and will only develop properly when those cues are present in their environment.*

This makes D. symbogenesis *both easy to control and difficult to study, due to the worm's tendency to die as soon as it is removed from the biological safety of its human host...*

—FROM "THE DEVELOPMENT AND LIFE CYCLE OF *DIPHYLLOBOTHRIUM SYMBOGENESIS*," ORIGINALLY PUBLISHED IN *THE STANFORD SCIENCE REVIEW*, JUNE 2017.

In an ironic side effect of the Intestinal Bodyguard™ being used for so much day-to-day medical care, people became very cautious about antiparasitic drugs. Several otherwise popular medicines were removed from the market once it became clear that they could damage the implants, and even casual drug users tended to steer clear of things that could harm their resident worms. No one wanted to kill the goose that laid the golden eggs. People were even more reluctant to kill the worm that kept them healthy.

—FROM *SELLING THE UNSELLABLE: AMERICAN ADVERTISING THROUGH THE YEARS*, BY MORGAN DEMPSEY, PUBLISHED 2026.

Chapter 7

AUGUST 2027

Sherman passed me off to Chave, who dragged me to the accounting department to be grilled about my receipts, which looked exactly like every other batch of receipts I'd ever brought in for them to review. Medications, vitamins, physical therapy sessions, the usual. The only thing that actually should have caught their attention was the bill for a new grain heating pad—technically a "household item," and thus a questionable expense—but they waved it off without comment, choosing to focus instead on the number of times I'd been to see the chiropractor since my last visit.

Eventually, they freed me back into the halls of SymboGen, and Chave delivered me back to Sherman, who was flirting with a receptionist I didn't recognize. The receptionist pouted when Chave called Sherman away, but hid the expression quickly.

Smart. I wouldn't have wanted to attract Chave's attention when I didn't have to.

"She's all yours," said Chave, waving me toward Sherman. "Get her an ultrasound and make sure she's in the cafeteria at one. Beyond that, I don't care what you do." Then she turned and stalked away.

Sherman watched her leave, waiting until she was out of earshot before sighing longingly. "That, my darling Sal, is a woman who needs an infusion of fun in her life. Possibly accompanied by a pitcher or two of strawberry mojitos." He clucked his tongue. "Anyone that tightly wound is going to be a tornado when they finally let go. Imagine being the lucky bloke—or bird—on the receiving end of *that* storm warning."

"I think we have very different ideas of what makes a fun evening," I said.

"Probably so," Sherman agreed, and turned to lead me back toward the elevator. "Have a good day so far?"

"No worse than usual, and I guess I'll call that a win." I sighed. "I just keep reminding myself that I don't have to do this again for six months. It helps me get through the day."

"That's good." The elevator doors slid open. Sherman waited until they closed again before saying, casually, "Word is that Banks is trying to hire you on for the research department. Can't imagine you'd be too thrilled about that."

I stared at him. "Just how good is the rumor mill around here? We only talked about that a few hours ago."

"Nothing happens in a vacuum, especially not when you're talking about a company this size." Sherman looked at me thoughtfully. "Are you going to take it? You'd be around here a good bit more. But you wouldn't have to worry anymore about whether you'd have another emergency. It might take a bit of the edge off."

"Yeah, and I'd be on site when I cracked from the pressure of all those eyes looking at me all the time. That would make it *so* much easier for them to get me into a nice padded room." The elevator dinged, signaling our safe return to the subterranean domain of the scientists. "I'd rather worry a little now than freak out a lot later on."

"That's what I thought you'd say," said Sherman, and stepped out of the elevator. I followed him, and together we made our way to the dressing room outside the ultrasound lab. "You get changed; I'll go make sure the science mooks are ready for us."

"You got it," I said, and slipped inside.

The ultrasound machine surrounded me like a huge, comforting hand, holding just tightly enough that I didn't need to be afraid that I would somehow lose my grip on the surface of the world—that gravity would fail or an earthquake would mysteriously flip the building upside down and send me plummeting into empty space. I could move, to a degree, crossing or uncrossing my arms and ankles, but for the most part, I was safely confined. I raised one hand to check that my rebreather was solidly in place, and closed my eyes.

Some people apparently found full-body ultrasounds invasive and claustrophobic, and would go to any lengths to avoid them. I had the opposite response. If I'd been able to trade all my other tests for additional time in the ultrasound chamber, I would happily have done so. According to Sherman, that was one more reason for the company technicians to view me as a freak of nature.

The full-body imaging department at SymboGen consisted of two different sections: the MRI room and the gel ultrasound room. I had undergone both at one time or another during my visits to SymboGen, and the gel ultrasound was definitely my favorite of the two. MRIs meant lying on my back for up to an hour while the machine took its snapshot images of my body, trying not to move as my weight seemed to press me deeper and deeper into the metal bed. There was no padding in an MRI tube; that might interfere with the readings.

People who found MRIs claustrophobic apparently freaked out completely during gel ultrasounds, which required a rebreather and that the subject's eyes remain closed for the duration. The techs would even glue them shut for you if you asked them to, to make sure you wouldn't give in to the urge to look around and see what was happening. After you were fully prepped and inside the tube, it was flooded with a bio-responsive plastic gel modeled off the biological structure of slime mold. It was hypoallergenic, nontoxic, and as harmless as possible.

Gel ultrasounds were infinitely more comforting than MRIs. I relaxed, slowing my breathing as I allowed myself to go totally limp.

There was a clicking noise in my left ear just before the head technician's voice came through the side of my rebreather: "You ready for us, Sally? Clench your left hand for 'yes.' "

I obediently clenched my left hand. I liked the ultrasound technicians. They were nice, although they treated me with an odd reverence. I had asked Sherman why that was once, after a particularly relaxing session in the ultrasound chamber. He'd laughed and replied, "Because, my sweet Sal, you are the only person ever to fall asleep in their gooey torture chamber. They think you're either bloody insane, or that you've got balls the size of boulders."

"What do you think?" I'd asked.

"I think it's a little bit of both."

I smiled around my rebreather at the memory, and allowed the last bit of tension to seep out of me as the ultrasound whirred to humming, buzzing life. My breathing slowed further once the humming began. The sound set up minute vibrations through the liquid, faint enough that they didn't interfere with the machine's readings, but strong enough for me to feel them eddying against my skin. It was like being at the center of my own private tide pool.

At some point, I drifted away, down into the dark, which reached up to claim me like a lover, folding itself around me and pulling me into itself. I didn't fight. I was safe, I was surrounded and safe, and nothing was ever going to hurt me again.

I didn't dream. Not there in the ultrasound tube, with the warm gel buoying me up and the sound of the machine lapping against my skin. Instead, I just drifted, and dozed, and let the world pass by around me.

It was gravity that brought me back: the strangely wrenching sensation of gravity reasserting itself as the gel began draining out of the ultrasound tube and my body settled down onto the hard metal bed of the machine. I managed not to start squirming, but it was hard. This was always the tricky part, keeping still until I was given the clearance to start moving again. Move too soon, and I risked either dislodging my rebreather and giving myself a lungful of plastic gel, or opening my eyes and getting an eyeful of the stuff instead. It wouldn't actually hurt me, but it could make breathing—and seeing—remarkably uncomfortable for a short period of time.

"You all right in there, Sally?" asked the voice in my ear. I responded with a very small nod, feeling the motion set up waves through the remaining gel. The level was still dropping, faster all the time; it was around my ears now. My exposed skin felt overly tender, and the air was cold after the comforting warmth of the gel. I shivered, despite trying not to.

"Just hold tight," said the voice. "We're almost done draining the gel, and we'll have you out of there as soon as it's done."

I nodded again, more firmly this time. Seconds ticked by, and the gel level dropped, until I was lying totally exposed, shivering and faintly gooey in my one-piece swimsuit. The machine whirred as it responded to a new set of commands, and the tube that I had been lying in for the better part of an hour began moving slowly outward. The air quality changed, getting even colder. I continued to shiver, but didn't open my eyes until a damp, warm washcloth was pressed against them, wiping away the remainder of the goo.

Hands gripped my rebreather. "Release, please," said the technician's voice, clearer now that it wasn't being filtered through the gel. I unclenched my teeth. He pulled the mouthpiece away, and wiped my mouth and chin with another cloth.

I opened my eyes.

The first thing I saw was the ceiling. Turning my head slightly, I saw the two ultrasound technicians: a short, freckle-faced man with a mop of red curls, holding my rebreather in one hand, and a tall, rail-thin woman with medium-brown skin and dark brown hair that she wore raked back into a no-nonsense bun. I offered them a hesitant smile. "How did I do?"

"Splendidly, as always," said Dr. Sanjiv, and offered me her hand. "Your clothes are waiting in the changing room, although I strongly recommend you shower, as usual, before you even think about going near them. You're slimier than the average bivalve."

"So why are you touching me?" I asked, grasping her fingers and letting her pull me out of the ultrasound tube. The squelching sound made when my back broke contact with the bed of the machine was unnerving, no matter how many times I heard it.

"I don't mind bivalves, whereas Marvin here," she indicated Dr. McGillis, "dislikes them on general principle."

"I only eat food that had visible eyes before it was cooked," said Dr. McGillis, unruffled. "It seems more sporting that way. Thanks again for being such a good sport about all this, Sally."

It was all I could do not to hug him on the spot, all-encompassing slime or no all-encompassing slime. "It's my pleasure," I said. "You guys are my favorite stop here at SymboGen."

For some reason, that statement seemed to unnerve them. They exchanged a look laden with some meaning I couldn't decipher, and Dr. Sanjiv dropped my hand like it had burned her. "Go get changed, Sally," she said. "We're finished for today." She turned and walked quickly out of the room. Dr. McGillis followed her, leaving me standing there dripping gel and utterly confused.

When several minutes passed without them coming back to explain, I turned, shoulders slumped, and walked to the room where my clothes were waiting. Sherman would be outside in the hall, ready to take me to my next appointment. I normally liked to linger in the ultrasound lab, but not today. Today, I just wanted to be gone.

The water in the shower came out of the tap already optimally adjusted to warm without burning. There were no dials to let me adjust the temperature; you took your showers warm but not scalding, or you didn't take them at all. I stepped under the warm spray, tilting my face up toward the ceiling, and let it rinse away the last of the goo from the ultrasound chamber.

Soap and shampoo were not provided. They also weren't needed. I had never encountered any substance that got a body as intimately clean as the goo in the SymboGen ultrasound chambers. Something about the way it combined with the vibration of the machine just shook the dirt and dead skin loose. All I had to do was grab a washcloth and wipe the muck away. It ran down the drain in a purple-gel-colored swirl, disappearing into the pipes below.

At home, I can shower for an hour or more, staying in the water long after it's out of heat, and my skin has started wrinkling up like a bulldog's neck. At SymboGen, I was in and out in under ten minutes, staying in the stall only long enough to be sure that all of the gunk had been wiped away. They promised me they didn't have cameras in the restroom, but I wasn't sure I trusted them. I was almost certain that they collected the things that swirled down the shower drain, taking them off for some analysis I didn't know about, and didn't want to know about. All I wanted was to get out of there.

A plush towel almost large enough to be considered a blanket was draped over the bench in front of the locker that held my clothes. I dried quickly, slicking my hair back and tying it into a dripping ponytail before putting my clothes back on. I dropped the towel into the laundry chute, and then I was done; the only thing left on my agenda as I understood it was a trip to the cafeteria to eat with the executives.

Sherman was waiting in the hall. It was his job—he'd be in serious trouble if he left me and anyone found out about it—but I still felt a pang of relief when I saw his smiling face. After the ultrasound technicians ran away the way they did, I'd almost expected Sherman to do the same.

"I'd like to say that you clean up good, pet, but the truth is, you clean up just this side of a drowned rat," he said, pushing away from the wall. "I'm not sure it's the *good* side of the drowned rat, either. Could be you should have taken things the other way."

"I'll keep that in mind for next time," I said gravely.

"See to it you do, and come along." Sherman started toward the elevator. "We'll get some lunch into you, and then you'll be about finished for the day. You can head for home and do whatever it is you do when you're not here hobnobbing with your betters."

"You mean having a life, doing things I actually want to do, and not being endlessly jabbed by people with needles? Yeah, I'm pretty fond of that." I sighed, sticking my still-damp hands into the pockets of my jeans. "Really, I'll just be happy when I'm out of here. You're nice and all, but..."

"But you're worried about losing your freedom. I get that." The elevator doors opened with a ding, and we both stepped inside. "You're in an interesting position, Sal. I don't envy you it at all. You're a bit of a celebrity, a bit of an experiment, and a bit of a cautionary tale, all at the same time. Maybe you lived because of your implant. Maybe you lost your memory because of the implant. Everyone wants to know what's going on in that head of yours, and no one's sure they're going to like the answers."

"You really know how to make a girl feel good about herself, you know."

"I try." The elevator doors closed again. We began to ascend. "Have you thought more about that job offer?"

"I have."

"And?"

"I'm not going to take it. I just…I can't." I shook my head. "I need to be able to go home and not think about this. I'm not defined by the accident. It was six years ago. How long do I have to keep being the girl who had the accident? When do I start getting to be Sal?"

"Think about it this way," Sherman suggested. "Most of us spend a bunch of years as children. We do what our parents tell us, we live by their rules, and we never feel like we're setting our own courses. Only then, given time, we grow up. We get to move out and be the people we want to be, not the people our parents want us to be."

"Most people are children for eighteen years," I said. "I don't want to spend eighteen years living like this."

Sherman sighed. "I don't know what to tell you, Sal. You didn't do anything wrong—not the person that you are now, anyway. You woke up in a hospital room, you got a clean slate, and you thought you ought to be allowed to go with that. The trouble is, you still have to live with the mistakes that Sally made. She may have given up on living when she drove her car into that bus, but that doesn't mean you get to be free of her."

I closed my eyes briefly. "I hate her."

"You're not the only one, pet." The elevator slid to a stop. I opened my eyes to see the doors standing open, and Sherman gesturing toward the plushly carpeted hallway outside. Chave was waiting there, a sour expression on her face. "Out you get. Enjoy your decadent luncheon, and I'll see you next time you come by for a visit, all right?"

"Thanks, Sherman." I darted in and hugged him quickly. He made a startled sound before closing his arms around me and giving me a squeeze.

"Always welcome, Sal," he said. His voice was warm. It was good to know that someone in this building genuinely gave a damn about me. "Now shoo. Wouldn't do to keep your corporate masters waiting."

"I'll see you next time," I said. Letting go, I stepped out of the elevator and started toward Chave. Her sour expression had turned outright disapproving, a deep furrow appearing between her eyebrows.

She wasn't annoyed enough to shout, and waited until I was close enough for her to keep her voice pitched low before she demanded, "What was that about?"

"I wanted a hug. Your job when you're my handler is to supply me with anything I want or need, within reason. As hugging me did not cause physical or emotional harm to either one of us, it was within reason." I looked flatly at Chave, anticipating her response to my next question: "Would you rather I hugged you next time?"

Chave took a step backward, looking so alarmed that I thought for a moment she might fall right off her heels. I managed to bite back my smile. "That would be entirely inappropriate," she said, half-raising one hand in what looked like an involuntary warding gesture.

It wasn't necessary; I stayed where I was, watching her as she recoiled. After a moment, she seemed to realize I wasn't planning to throw my arms around her. Her hand dropped, and her alarmed expression dissolved into her more customary mild hauteur.

"If you're quite through making your little jokes, it's time for you to meet Dr. Banks for lunch," she said. Her voice had somehow managed to become even stiffer than usual, something I would previously have said was impossible. "I certainly hope you won't try hugging *him*."

The idea made my skin crawl. "I wouldn't dream of it."

"Good. Now follow me." She turned on her heel, practically stomping toward the doors to the executive cafeteria. I adjusted my grasp on the strap of my shoulder bag and walked hastily after her.

The doors of the SymboGen executive cafeteria were automatic, and slid smoothly open as we approached. The smell of roasting meat and fresh-baked bread wafted into the hallway, accompanied by the sound of gently rattling glasses and the clink of silverware against bone china dishes. It was the sound of money, and it was something I only really had the opportunity to hear on those occasions when I was invited to dine with the company's founder. Maybe money can't buy happiness, but it can buy some of the best meals I'd ever eaten, and I wasn't disappointed to be eating another one.

Chave walked through the door about three long strides ahead of me. I kept trying to catch up, and was moving faster than I should have been when she froze midstep only six feet into the room. I nearly collided with her suddenly motionless form. I managed to swerve to the side at the last moment, and stumbled, going down on one knee.

"Chave?" I looked up at her, my new position giving me a perfect view of her face. She was staring slack-jawed at the far wall. There was no animation in her eyes. She could have been one of the dead fish waiting in the kitchen for the frying pan. Her arms had dropped to her sides, dangling limply now that all of her tension was gone. I was dimly aware that my heart was beating too fast, hammering itself against the inside of my rib cage like something trapped. *I* was trapped. Whatever was about to happen, it wasn't something I wanted anything to do with.

"Chave?" I repeated. My voice came out small and uncertain as I clambered awkwardly back to my feet. There was an expanding bubble of silence around us, created by the people who were slowly realizing that something was going on. They put down their forks and spoons, stopped drinking from their glasses, and turned in our direction. And Chave didn't move. I reached for her arm. "Chave, are you okay?"

"Miss Mitchell, please step back."

The voice came from behind me. I glanced over my shoulder. I could feel myself beginning to tremble, despite my best efforts to stop. "It's okay," I said, to the brown-uniformed SymboGen security officers who were standing in the open doorway. "I'm with her. She's my escort. I'm allowed to be here."

"No one's questioning that, Miss Mitchell, but you need to move away from Ms. Seaborne now. Please step back."

"Sally, please." I turned too fast, almost unbalancing myself again. Dr. Banks was in front of us, his hands held out in front of him in a beseeching gesture, palms turned upward. "Just come here. Come here quickly."

Chave was still standing there, staring blankly into the distance. Some imp of the perverse made me step closer to her, following an impulse I didn't understand. "Why?" I demanded. "What's going on? What's *wrong* with her?" I'd seen the sleepwalking sickness before, but I couldn't find the words to ask the questions I wanted. Why was this happening? Why did it *keep* happening?

More security was flowing into the room through the main door, circulating with quick efficiency through the maze of tables. The executives were abandoning their seats now, leaving half-eaten meals and half-full glasses of wine behind as they hurried to the exit, or to the far end of the room. They were putting as much distance as they could between Chave and myself, and that didn't seem like a good sign to me. Neither did the guns that some of the security guards were holding. I didn't know much about firearms; I tried to tell myself that they were stun guns, and for the most part, I was able to make myself believe it.

"You need to move aside, Miss Mitchell." The officer who seemed to be in charge of this—whatever it was—looked frustrated, and drew his sidearm, holding it at hip level. "We'll be happy to explain when the crisis situation has been averted."

"She was showing no signs on her last blood panel," said another voice, sounding as much confused as panicked. I turned toward it. A man I recognized from the research floor was pressed into the mass of executives, staring at Chave like she was a problem to be solved. "I don't understand."

Neither did I. I started to turn toward Dr. Banks.

Chave was faster.

Her hands caught my throat in midturn, bringing me to an abrupt halt. I froze, staring into her empty eyes. Behind me, men were shouting, and the Head of the Security Department was barking orders. I couldn't turn to see whether they were being followed. Chave's grip on my neck was too tight, and it forced me to keep looking at her.

It was like looking at a dead thing. The comparison had occurred to me before, but I hadn't realized how apt it was. There was no emotion in her eyes, no animation, nothing but the cloudy blankness of a body that had been abandoned. She was moving, her hands were doing their best to strangle the life out of my body, but Chave—the bitchy, efficient, focused woman who had been a fixture of my visits to SymboGen since the beginning—was no longer living there.

I struggled for air, making a small gasping noise. Chave's hands tightened. Lifting my own hands, I clawed at her fingers, trying to regain my balance enough to let me kick at her. If she was standing, she could be knocked down. Nothing is immovable, and I only needed a moment if I wanted to run. *I should have moved when they told me to*, I thought deliriously. *I think*

I'm going to die here. I don't want to die here. I don't want to die in the SymboGen cafeteria. My parents would never get my body. Dr. Banks would seize it for research purposes, and I had no doubt that the contracts I'd signed gave him the right to do exactly that. Maybe this was his plan all along. Maybe Chave was just carrying out another one of her orders.

No. That wasn't possible. While I had no trouble believing that Chave would kill me if she was told to, no one could fake the kind of emptiness I saw in her eyes. She wasn't pretending. I pulled helplessly at her hands, trying to pry them from my throat.

Dark spots were appearing in front of my eyes when someone behind me shouted, "Sal! *Relax!*" I heard running footsteps moving toward me, and I went limp, the sudden weight of me nearly pulling me out of Chave's hands. Only nearly, but Sherman did the rest when he collided with her, slamming one shoulder into her midsection in a move that would have done an offensive lineman proud.

Chave lost her grip as Sherman's moving tackle yanked her away from me. I fell to the floor, choking and gasping for air. Two of the SymboGen security officers were there almost instantly. They helped me to my feet and herded me toward the wall before I could collect myself enough to protest.

Sherman had stopped running. He shoved Chave away from him harder than should have been necessary, sending the still slack-jawed woman stumbling backward. Then he backpedalled, stopping only when the security officer behind him snapped, "Stop right there, son." Sherman froze, chest heaving, and glanced toward me, like he was checking to be sure that I was still safe. I flashed him a weak smile and a quick thumbs-up, not sure what else to do. Sherman nodded, seeming relieved.

Chave's mouth was working soundlessly. It looked like she was trying to say something. The security officers began closing in around her, their weapons now raised and trained firmly on her. She hissed at them, although I couldn't be sure it was a warning, not just a sound that she had remembered how to make.

"Take her down," said Dr. Banks implacably.

"Wait—what?" I took a step forward, and was promptly stopped by my own guards. They held me there as the other officers moved closer to Chave. "What's going on? What's wrong with her?"

No one answered me. The first of the officers reached Chave. Gun still raised, he pulled a baton from his belt and pressed it against her stomach, pressing a red button on its side at the same time. She shrieked as the baton crackled, forcing electricity into her body. Another officer stepped up behind her, doing the same thing. Chave's shriek ended in a choking sound, and she began convulsing.

"Stop it! You're killing her, stop it!" I shouted.

"Sally, you don't understand," said Dr. Banks. He must have pushed his way through the crowd to get to us. "I'm sorry. This is the only way."

I turned to glare at him. "What's going *on*?" I demanded. Chave should have collapsed long since, but somehow, she was still standing. Two more officers stepped up, pressing their batons against her side. Electricity crackled.

Chave began to scream.

It wasn't a human scream; it was more like the sound a wounded animal makes when it hurts beyond its capacity to follow instinct's instructions and keep silent, keep still. We had a dog left on the front step of the shelter once. His back section had been crushed by a truck, and he was making a sound just like the one Chave was making now, too raw to be considered a howl, but not the sort of sound you ever hear from a thinking creature.

Dr. Banks put his hands on my shoulders, like he was afraid that I might try to break away and run toward Chave. I didn't try to shrug him off. I couldn't imagine moving in that moment, not with Chave screaming, and more and more of the guards closing in around her, their stun batons already in their hands. This wasn't real. This couldn't be happening. This was something out of a horror movie. She'd been talking to me only a few minutes ago, she'd—

Chave stopped screaming and turned toward me, her body still convulsing with the electricity that was arcing through it. She shouldn't have been standing. She didn't fall. "Sah-lee," she said, spitting out the two syllables of my name like they hurt her mouth. Dr. Banks tightened his hands on my shoulders. Someone else gasped. "Sah-lee," said Chave again.

Then one of the officers slammed a stun baton across the back of her head, and Chave finally fell, crumpling to the plush carpet like an expensive toy discarded by a selfish child. Silence hung over the cafeteria, broken only by the sound of breathing, and muffled sobs from a few of the executives. Dr. Banks kept his hands on my shoulders, pressing down hard, as we looked at Chave's body lying on the floor.

"She said my name," I whispered. "Why did she say my name?"

No one answered me. Out of all the things that had happened since my arrival at SymboGen, somehow that seemed like the most dangerous one of all.

INTERLUDE I: EXODUS

The broken doors are open—come and enter and be home.
—SIMONE KIMBERLEY, *DON'T GO OUT ALONE*

We are our own judge, jury, and executioner.
And we have been proven guilty.
—DR. RICHARD JABLONSKY

October 23, 2015: Time stamp 10:52.

[As before, the recording is perfect, and the lab is a gleaming miracle of science. The only difference is in the woman who stands in front of the camera. Her lab coat is rumpled, her hair in disarray. She looks like she has not slept in weeks.]

> DR. CALE: Doctor Shanti Cale, final *Diphyllobothrium symbo-*
> *genesis* viability test results. Those bastards. Those god-
> damn bastards...

[She stops, visibly composing herself.]

> DR. CALE: Steven—Doctor Banks—has decided that we're
> finished with laboratory testing, and can move on to live
> human subjects. I mean. *Officially* move on to live human
> subjects. He's wrong. He's not listening, but he's wrong.
> Do you hear me, Steven? *You're wrong.* And you're going to
> pay for it. Not me.

[She produces a petri dish from her pocket, holding it up so that the camera can see. There is a white nutrient goo at the bottom. Any other contents are too small to be seen.]

DR. CALE: You can't destroy all the evidence. I know you're going to try, and I want you to understand that it is not possible. By the time you find this recording, I will be gone. Instructions have been left to tell you where to wire my money. You want your skeletons to stay buried, Steven? You want this house of cards to stay standing? You leave me alone, and you stay the hell away from my family.

Leave us the hell alone.

[The film ends there. Dr. Shanti Cale disappeared shortly thereafter. There are no records to indicate what she may have removed from the lab, or even whether she is still alive.]

[End report.]

STAGE I: IMPLANTATION

SymboGen: because good health starts within.
—EARLY SYMBOGEN ADVERTISING SLOGAN

Oh, won't this just be the most fun we've ever had?
—DR. SHANTI CALE

I suppose this is when you ask me about the original trio. I met Richard in grad school, and we knew immediately that we had something special. Still, we were incomplete until we stumbled over Shanti. We were the Three Musketeers of bioengineering, and with us working together, there was nothing we couldn't do. Maybe that's why we started taking on bigger and bigger challenges. We truly believed that it was impossible for us to fail.

Some people will try to tell you Shanti was the brains of our operation, but they're just talking trash for the sake of sounding like they know something I don't want people to know. Shanti was the smartest of the three of us, but that's like saying one firework is brighter than another. They're all blazing too damn bright to look at. Isn't that what matters? Burning so bright you paint the sky?

Shanti was the one who refused to admit there was such a thing as going too far. Richard was the one who reined her in when it looked like she was going to run right over the edge of the world. And me? I was the one who made everything work. Without me, SymboGen would never have existed. There are probably people who would say that was a good thing, too.

I have to admit, there are days when I think it would be a good thing. I might even be willing to give it all back if it meant I still had my friends. But you can't go home again.

—FROM "KING OF THE WORMS," AN INTERVIEW WITH
DR. STEVEN BANKS, CO-FOUNDER OF SYMBOGEN. ORIGINALLY
PUBLISHED IN *ROLLING STONE*, FEBRUARY 2027.

One of the more interesting realities of the SymboGen Intestinal Bodyguard™ campaign was the way the scientific team responsible for its development was handled. Dr. Banks appeared on talk shows and at scientific symposiums, lecturing on the wonders of their discovery. Dr. Jablonsky spoke at early functions, but quickly stopped making public appearances, choosing instead to focus on the scientific aspects of their work. Only one woman was involved in the Intestinal Bodyguard™ project: Dr. Shanti Cale, a photogenic, intense blonde whose early audience-acceptance scores were unbelievable. She would have been the perfect spokeswoman. Instead, she vanished without a trace shortly before the company's IPO. Rumors of bribery have circulated almost since the date of her disappearance, but have never been proven. Whatever her side of the story, she has not been heard from, and the SymboGen brand is now well established worldwide.

As the face of SymboGen, Dr. Banks was the perfect blend of approachable and intelligent, the quintessential wise scientist. Perhaps the decision to put the other researchers behind the curtain was just one more piece in selling the unsellable.

—FROM *SELLING THE UNSELLABLE: AMERICAN ADVERTISING THROUGH THE YEARS*, BY MORGAN DEMPSEY, PUBLISHED 2026.

Chapter 8
AUGUST 2027

Security pulled me out of the chaos in the cafeteria and escorted me back down to the labs, ignoring my attempts to resist them. If I could take any comfort in my removal from the scene, it was this: I wasn't the only one. Everyone who'd come into direct contact with Chave before she collapsed was being taken underground. The guards packed us into the elevators, maintaining a two-to-one ratio between security and people who didn't have the right to carry guns inside the building.

Sherman wasn't in my elevator. I stopped worrying about myself and worried about him instead as we made our descent. Anything to keep myself from worrying about Chave. She wasn't dead, was she? She couldn't be dead. She'd had some sort of a stroke, or she'd managed to catch whatever had infected Beverly's original owner—she was sick. They wouldn't kill her just for getting sick. "We don't leave our employees without health care, ever," was what Dr. Banks had said to me when we were sitting in his office together. How did this align with that?

Then the elevator doors opened to reveal four people in white biohazard suits, and I stopped worrying about anyone but myself. Their faces were covered by reflective plastic shields. I couldn't tell who was inside. There was nothing to indicate whether they were people I knew or total strangers. One of the guards tried to take my arm and pull me out of the elevator. I jerked away from him, backing up until my shoulders hit the far wall.

"I'm not going with you until you tell me what's going on," I said flatly. "So you can just keep your damn hands to yourself."

"Ms. Mitchell, we have been authorized to sedate you if you refuse to cooperate," said one of the biohazard suits. The voice was filtered so heavily that it was neither male nor female: it was as sterile and mechanical as our environment. I couldn't even think of them as human.

Another group from the cafeteria walked by, escorted by its own quartet of biohazard suits. Sherman was there, looking dazed and slightly battered, like he'd been through a war and not just a brief fight with a coworker. He stopped when he saw me, bringing the whole procession to a halt. "Sal! Are you hurt?"

"What's going on, Sherman?" I gestured to the suits, managing to encompass all eight of them in one spread of my hands. "Why won't they tell us anything?"

"Chave was ill, pet," he said, a nervous expression washing away all his normal animation. "She needs medical attention, and the rest of us need looking over to be sure we're not showing symptoms of what she's got."

"*She* wasn't even showing symptoms before she flipped out!"

"That's what we're afraid of," muttered one of the guards.

I whipped around to face him. The biohazard suits with Sherman's group took that opportunity to get moving again, sweeping Sherman and the others off down the hall. "Mind yourself, and stick with the doctors, Sal!" called Sherman, and then he was gone, carted off with the others, and I was alone among strangers.

There was no way out, and no one was telling me anything. But I trusted Sherman, and so when the biohazard suits gestured for me to step out of the elevator, I didn't argue further. I just went.

I'd always known the laboratory floor was large—larger than the footprint of the main building, even, since Symbo-Gen owned enough property to let them expand as needed. I hadn't realized it was large enough for them to build sufficient individual isolation rooms to hold all the people who'd been removed from the cafeteria. Most chilling of all, as two guards were in the process of escorting me into my room, I saw a third guard being escorted into the room across the hall. We were *all* being locked up.

One of the biohazard suits followed me into the tiny room, which was painted the bland pastel green of a doctor's waiting area. There was a bench, covered in white paper, and the standard array of cabinets and counters lined two of the walls. A set of folded blue scrubs was stacked on the bench, next to a pair of plain white slippers.

"Please remove your clothing," said the biohazard suit.

"Or what?" I demanded. Getting naked wasn't a problem. I just didn't feel like cooperating with someone who wouldn't show me their face.

"Or we are authorized to sedate you," said the biohazard suit.

"What 'we'?" I asked. "There's only one of you in here. And who authorized you to sedate me? I didn't sign anything that said you could sedate me."

"Ms. Mitchell, please believe me when I say that we do not want to do anything to harm you. But if you force my hand, I will call my associates into this room, and you *will* remove your clothing. Now please."

I hesitated. Chave worked for SymboGen. I didn't. And when Chave wouldn't calm down, they'd zapped her until she stopped moving. Chave was probably dead. Did I believe the biohazard suit when it said I'd be sedated if I didn't cooperate? Yes, I did. I glared at the suit's mask as I removed my clothes, piling them on the floor. I started to reach for the scrubs.

"Stop where you are, Ms. Mitchell." The biohazard suit's air filter allowed no inflection in the voice, but the feeling of menace still managed to come through in the way the words were bitten off. "I will need to examine you."

"What?" I crossed my arms over my chest, covering myself. "What are you talking about?"

"The risk of infection is high enough to require a visual examination. Please lower your arms."

"I want to talk to Dr. Banks."

"Dr. Banks is being examined. He will be happy to speak with you once you are both finished."

That stopped me cold, because somehow, I didn't doubt what I was being told. Dr. Banks—the owner of the company, the richest man in North America, and one of the most powerful people in the developed world—was being strip-searched and examined for signs of an undisclosed "infection." Maybe he was getting examined in his office rather than in one of these generic little isolation rooms, but that didn't change the fact that he was getting the same treatment I was. And that terrified me.

Dropping my arms to my sides, I turned to face the biohazard suit. It nodded. "Thank you," it said. "Now please stand with your feet shoulder-width apart and raise your arms to shoulder level. This will be a visual examination only. I will not touch you. Do you understand?"

"What's your name?" I countered.

The biohazard suit sighed. I wouldn't have thought the filters would let the sound escape, but they did, and it carried a level of human frustration that all the words hadn't been able to convey. "It's Dr. Lo, Sally. Now please, will you do as I am asking?"

"You could have said that before, you know." I moved as I spoke, getting into the position she had requested. It felt less strange now that I knew she was someone familiar and not just a faceless automaton from the depths of SymboGen. At the same time, the fact that Dr. Lo was treating me as a threat—not just furniture, but something dangerous—worried me. "Why didn't you tell me who you were?"

"Because I was more concerned with your health than with observing social pleasantries. Hold still." Dr. Lo reached into a pocket on the leg of her biohazard suit, producing a long tube that looked like it had been detached from the overhead lights. She flicked a switch at its base, and it came on, glowing a deep shade of purple. Dr. Lo began running it through the air a few inches away from me, watching the way the purple light reflected off my skin.

"What is that?" I asked.

"Don't *move*, Sally," she said, crouching to run the light along my stomach and legs. She was quick, and thorough: not an inch of me was left unexamined. True to her word, she didn't touch me. That didn't stop me from feeling like there was something deeply inappropriate about having her looking at me that closely, especially with the protective suit between us. Whatever she was looking for, it wasn't anything good.

Finally, she straightened, clicking off her wand. "You can put the scrubs on now," she said, as she returned it to her pocket. "You're clean."

"Clean of *what*?" I asked, dropping my arms back to my sides before turning to reach for the scrubs.

"That's a discussion for you to have with Dr. Banks, not with me. I'm just here to make sure you don't present a danger to yourself or others." Dr. Lo turned away from me and knocked twice on the door. After a moment, one of the security officers opened it. This one hadn't been present in the cafeteria. I was starting to think that SymboGen had its own private police force, and that wasn't a comforting thought. The line between "police force" and "army" is narrow under the best of circumstances, and we were no longer operating under the best of circumstances.

"Yes?" asked the officer.

"She's clean," replied Dr. Lo. "I need to go to decontamination." Even clean, I was apparently enough of a risk to require cleaning a biohazard safety suit. I shrank back from the door, suddenly terrified of my own skin. What kind of contagion had we been exposed to? Was I going to go like Chave, normal one minute, empty-eyed and absent the next?

My motion must have caught Dr. Lo's eye, somehow; I had no idea what the peripheral vision was like in a biohazard suit, but she turned back toward me, and asked, "Now you're afraid? After the worst parts are over, *now* you're afraid? I know we've given you a clean bill of health, Sally, but you may want to consider therapy."

I glared at her. She left the room, and the officer stepped into the doorway, preventing me from following her out. At least he wasn't wearing a mask. I felt less like a risk to the health of everyone around me when I looked at another face without a piece of plastic in the way.

"I'm sorry for the inconvenience, Ms. Mitchell," he said politely.

"I want to speak to Dr. Banks," I said, and stepped into the slippers.

"He's still undergoing examination, but I'm sure he'll be happy to speak with you once he's free," said the officer.

Still undergoing...I stiffened. "Sherman." What was his last name? Shit. "Sherman Lewis. He's one of Dr. Banks's assistants. He was brought down here with the rest of us. Is he all right? Have they finished examining him?"

"I can't discuss the health of other patients, Ms. Mitchell," said the officer.

"We're not patients, we're people who didn't get to finish having lunch," I shot back.

Laughter came from the hall behind him. Weary laughter, but laughter, and that was better than anyone was going to get out of me. "It's all right, Floyd, you can stand down," said Dr. Banks, moving into view behind the officer. "Once Sally gets an idea in her head, there's not room for too much else in there."

"Yes, sir," said the officer, and stepped aside.

Dr. Banks was wearing the same blue scrubs I was. Somehow, he managed not to look ridiculous in them—a feat I was sure I wasn't matching. He stepped into the officer's place, looking at me with a small, paternal smile. "I'm sorry if our security drill frightened you, Sally. It wasn't the intention."

"Where's Sherman? What happened to Chave?"

"That's one of the things I like about you. You care about people. That's a rare quality, and it's one I think we should be focusing on more."

"And you're deflecting," I said. "Where is Sherman Lewis? *What happened to Chave?*"

Dr. Banks sighed. For a moment, he didn't look like the owner of a massive multinational corporation: he looked like a man who hadn't slept in weeks, and was covering it up with foundation, hair dye, and stimulants. "I'm afraid Ms. Seaborne did not recover from her unfortunate incident in the cafeteria."

" 'Unfortunate'—do you mean whatever went wrong with her, or do you mean the officers with the shock batons?" I crossed my arms and glared at him. For some reason, I was no longer afraid of SymboGen refusing to let me leave the building. I was more concerned that I would never leave this *basement*. Not alive, anyway. "She's dead, isn't she? That's what you mean when you say she 'didn't recover' from being electrocuted."

"Sally..." Dr. Banks hesitated. Then he sighed again, and

said, "There's a great deal you don't understand. I'm so sorry you had to see that, and please believe me, no one is sorrier about what happened with Chave than I am. She's been with me almost since the beginning. Neither of us ever expected things to end this way."

"I'm pretty sure she didn't expect to be electrocuted when she got out of bed this morning, no." I kept glaring at him. "Sherman Lewis. Where is he?"

"Sally—"

"I come here every time you call me. I let your staff take all the blood they want. I answer your questions, I listen to your lectures, I do whatever I'm told to do, and I don't fight you. That could change. Sherman is the only person here who always treats me like I'm a person, too. Not lab equipment, not an experiment, a *person*. Now where *is* he?"

"Sally, I'm sorry."

The words were spoken softly, but they might as well have been screamed. They seemed to echo through the room, getting louder with every iteration. "Why are you sorry?" I asked. I could barely hear my own voice over the echoes of Dr. Banks's statement.

"You have to understand, he had prolonged physical contact with Chave. He was exposed."

His first words were still echoing, and now they were backed by a heavy pounding, like the sound of distant drums. "Exposed to what?"

"Sally, I really don't feel this is a conversation that we should be having while you're upset." Dr. Banks looked even more uncomfortable, and he wouldn't meet my eyes.

The drums were getting stronger, drowning out the echo of his words. "Exposed to *what*?"

"I've called Dr. Kim to come and collect you," said Dr. Banks. "I'm afraid your clothes won't be ready for several hours. They will be delivered to your home. You can keep the scrubs. I'm sorry we didn't get to have lunch together; I was very much looking forward to spending that time with you. I'll see you soon, Sally."

"Wait, what are you talking about? What were we exposed to? Dr. Banks—"

It was too late: Dr. Banks was already turning and stepping out of the room. The security officer reappeared as soon as Dr. Banks was through the door, making it clear that I would not be allowed to rush after him. I dropped my hands to my sides and just stared, open-mouthed. The drums were as loud as they had ever been, and for the first time while I was fully awake and aware of my surroundings, I was absolutely certain of what they were: I was hearing the pounding of my heart.

I stood in that little examination room, crying silently for a man who had always been kind to me, and waited for the man I loved to come and take me home. I was exhausted. I was done.

It was hard to tell time with no clocks and no windows. I stood there long enough for my legs to start aching, but I refused to sit down. Sitting down would mean admitting there was something stronger than my anger. The officer who'd been keeping me in the room was replaced by another man I didn't recognize, wearing the same uniform and carrying the same stun baton. I glared at him as he took up his position. He didn't say anything, and so neither did I.

My stubborn standoff with the forces of SymboGen might have lasted forever. I was saved from needing to find out by a familiar figure in a San Francisco City Hospital lab coat. Nathan pushed his way past the officer, seeming to neither notice nor care that the other man was armed, and rushed to embrace me.

"Jesus, Sal, you scared the hell out of me," he said.

That seemed to be the permission my body had been waiting for to fall apart. My tears had been falling for a while. Now I started to sob, as quietly as I could. I pressed my face into his chest and allowed myself to sag against him for a few precious seconds. Nathan folded his arms around me.

"It's all right," he said. "It's okay. I'm here."

"Sh-Sherman," I whispered.

Nathan winced. He knew about Sherman. They'd never met, but Sherman was the only person at SymboGen that I consistently spoke well of. "Oh, shit, Sal. I'm sorry."

I didn't say anything for a few minutes after that, just clung to him and cried. It wasn't dignified, but I didn't care about dignity. I was wearing scrubs and standing in the SymboGen basement. Dignity was the last of my concerns.

Finally, I pulled away, wiping my eyes, and said, "I want to go home. Can you take me home? Please?" I paused, the incongruity of his appearance striking me. "Why are you wearing your lab coat?"

"Because I was already here when the quarantine was called on the cafeteria level," said Nathan. "They called me in for another job interview."

They really did want to get me working in the building if they were calling Nathan in. That might seem a little self-centered— not everything in the world is about me, and I understand that— except for the part where, if Dr. Banks was trying to hire me, the only way he was going to accomplish it was by making working at SymboGen so appealing that I couldn't say no. Having Nathan on the payroll would be a huge step in the right direction.

"But..." I paused, my eyes narrowing. "If you were already here, why did it take you so long to come down and get me?" Dr. Banks said he was calling Nathan. Not getting him from the reception lobby; *calling* him.

"I didn't know you were involved in the quarantine, and I didn't want you to feel like I was here to check up on you. I rushed down as soon as I knew that you were waiting for me. It's been less than five minutes."

Either Dr. Banks had lied, or Nathan was lying to me now.

I touched his cheek with one hand, bile burning in my throat as I looked into his eyes and made my decision about whom to trust. Nathan. I trusted Nathan, and they hadn't told him. They hadn't told him that I was in danger, and even when they knew I wasn't, they hadn't told him that I was alone in an isolation room waiting for him to come and take me home. Instead, they'd left me where I was, probably so they could clean up their messes in peace.

"Let's go home," I said.

Nathan nodded. "Okay."

It was strange to walk through the halls of SymboGen without either Chave or Sherman at my side, ready to tell me what was next on my schedule or imply that I was somehow too scruffy to be in the building. Two of the security officers accompanied us from the basement to the lobby, which was deserted; they must have sent most of the company home after Chave got sick. It seemed like a good precaution following a possible contamination. I just didn't understand what that contamination was.

I stopped just before we reached the door, my hands going to my shoulder where the strap of my shoulder bag should have been pressing down against my skin. "My bag!"

"Your personal possessions are still undergoing decontamination, Ms. Mitchell," said one of the officers. She sounded distracted, and I realized that there was a small earpiece in her left ear. She was probably listening to status reports from the rest of her team even as she walked with us, multitasking her way through an unexpectedly busy afternoon.

"When will they be done? Those are my things. You had no right to take them."

"Dr. Banks has promised delivery of all your possessions to your home. You'll have them by tomorrow morning."

I took a breath, forcing myself not to get angry. This woman wasn't in charge, and there was no way Dr. Banks was coming back out of his office to see me. I had been dismissed, and I knew it. "Tell Dr. Banks that I am *not* happy with him right now." For a lot of reasons, only some of which I was ever planning to discuss with him.

"Yes, ma'am."

I shuddered and started walking again, Nathan by my side. The doors slid smoothly open to allow us to exit the building, and the jasmine-scented San Francisco afternoon reached out to embrace us.

The world felt dirtier and more complicated as soon as we stepped outside the artificial environment of the SymboGen building. For a company that was built on the hygiene hypothesis, whoever was responsible for the SymboGen interior decorating had chosen a surprisingly sterile palate. The plants were overgroomed to the point of seeming artificial, and filtration systems were everywhere, attached to the small scent-diffusion units that pumped the perfume into the air. I had never seen anything out of place.

Even here in the parking lot things were cleaner than they should have been. The white lines were bright enough to be freshly painted, and the asphalt was so black that I would have assumed it was fresh if it hadn't always looked like this. The landscaping was pristine. After what had happened inside, all that cleanliness was oddly chilling. It felt like a knot loosened in my chest when we reached Nathan's car, with its muddy wheels and fast-food wrappers in the footwell.

"Are you sure you're okay, Sal?" asked Nathan. "You're pale."

"No," I said. "I don't think I am okay." It wasn't reassuring, but then again, it wasn't intended to be. I tried never to lie to Nathan, even when it was something as small as claiming to be "fine" when I wasn't. He always caught me, and I always felt terrible for having tried to deceive him.

"Do you want to stay at my place tonight?" Nathan kissed

my forehead, squeezing my fingers at the same time. Then he let me go and walked around the car. The alarm chirped, signaling that the locks were open.

"I can't. You heard the officer—my things are being sent to my house, not yours. I think my parents will panic if they get that kind of delivery without me being there to explain it to them." I opened the door, sliding into the car. It was a relief to sit down after standing for so long. My legs promptly went limp, making me worry that I'd need Nathan's help if I ever wanted to get up again.

Nathan got into the driver's side, closing the door behind himself. "Do you mind if I come home with you, then? I don't want to leave you alone, and it would be nice to spend some time with Beverly."

"That would be fine," I said, and smiled.

Then the weight of my betrayal crashed down on me. Sherman was infected—or worse, Sherman was dead—and here I was smiling at my boyfriend, happy at the idea of spending an afternoon with him and the dog I had stolen from another infected man, another man who might be dead.

Wait. Chave and Beverly's owner had been infected with the same thing. I'd seen both of them succumb, and they had followed the same pattern. "Oh my God, is this my fault?" I whispered. My lips seemed numb, like they were barely attached to my body. "Did I get Chave sick? Did I get her *killed*?"

"Sal, what are you talking about?"

"Did they tell you *anything* about what happened inside the quarantine?"

"No, just that it was some kind of lab error, and you'd been exposed." Nathan was looking at me with blatant worry, not bothering to conceal it. "What do you mean, is this your fault?"

Suddenly, I didn't want to be explaining this where we were; not on SymboGen property, where someone could realize that they hadn't forbidden me to tell my boyfriend the truth about what happened. I could ignore my phone if it started ringing—or I would have been able to, if they hadn't taken it away from me. I couldn't ignore somebody pounding on the window nearly so easily. "Drive. Please. I'll explain while you drive."

"All right, honey. Just take some deep breaths, and tell me what's going on, okay?"

"Okay," I said...but I didn't say anything else until the SymboGen building was one more piece of the skyline receding behind us, and there was no chance that we'd be overheard. "Okay," I repeated.

"Sal?"

"I'm sorry, I just..." I took a breath. "It started out as a pretty normal visit to SymboGen. Lots of tests, Dr. Banks trying to convince me he had my best interests at heart, lots of people running lots of tests on me..." I closed my eyes as I continued talking, recounting the events of the day. I didn't strictly need to tell Nathan everything—he would probably have been happy with just what happened in the cafeteria and afterward—but I wanted to ease into it, and I wanted to remember Chave and Sherman the way I'd always known them. Chave was never my friend. That didn't mean she deserved to die the way she did.

Besides, telling him everything meant pointing out Chave's absolute lack of any symptoms, right up until the moment where she had every symptom and lost herself in whatever strange infection had claimed her mind. There should have been *something*, some sign to indicate that everything was not okay. There hadn't been anything at all.

Nathan asked occasional questions, but for the most part, he let me talk. When I came to the part about the cafeteria, he made me repeat the walk from the elevator three times. I didn't mind. We were both looking for something that could explain what had happened, and neither of us was finding it. Then I reached the worst part of the story, and he stopped asking questions. I spoke, and he drove, and SymboGen fell farther and farther into the distance.

Finally, he said, "Sherman was showing no signs of getting sick when you saw him?"

"No, none. He looked kind of upset, but—we all did." I opened my eyes, turning to face Nathan. "He was worried about me."

"He was your friend. Of course he was worried about you." Nathan tightened his hands on the steering wheel. "I would have been worried about you, too, if they hadn't left me waiting in one of the ninth-floor lobbies for an interview that never came."

I frowned. SymboGen was the global leader in parasitology, both in research of existing species and in the lucrative development of new strains. Other companies had tried to repeat the success of the Intestinal Bodyguard, but none of them had been able to get their claws into the market. Nathan's career was never going to move beyond a certain point if he couldn't get a job at SymboGen—and after my recounting of the day, we both knew why he'd been called in for the interview. It had nothing to do with him, and everything to do with keeping me where Dr. Banks could see me.

"I'm sorry," I said.

Nathan flashed me a very quick smile. He took one hand off the wheel, reaching over to briefly squeeze my knee. "It's not your fault. I wouldn't want to work there anyway, if it meant that Dr. Banks had managed to get you under his thumb full-time. I'm pretty sure punching your boss in the throat is an excellent way to get yourself fired."

"You say the sweetest things."

"I mean them."

"That helps." I sighed, sinking back into my seat. "I can't stop thinking about Sherman. What if he's scared? What if they haven't told him what's going on?" What if he was dead? But my mind shied away from that thought, refusing to fully process it. Sherman wasn't my best friend. He wasn't even someone I saw outside of SymboGen. But he was kind to me, and I didn't want him to be hurt.

"Sal…it sounds like Chave had the sleeping sickness. If SymboGen has a test for it, they haven't shared it with the local hospitals yet. I think that if they know Sherman is infected, it's because he already started showing symptoms." What Nathan didn't say was that no one who developed symptoms had yet recovered, or awakened from their disconnected state. Cases were still rare, but there had been enough of them that we were starting to understand a little bit about how the sickness worked. The victims got sick. They didn't get better.

But still. "I don't know if SymboGen has a test or not. They didn't draw blood or anything. Dr. Lo ran a light wand all over me, watching for some sort of reaction from my skin, but— Nathan!" He had suddenly twisted the wheel, sending us skidding into the next lane. Horns blared as he got the car back under control, and kept blaring as I screamed, trying to go fetal despite the seat belt restraining me. I curled tighter, continuing to scream.

We were going to die. We were going to crash and die, and even when I felt the car stop moving, that didn't matter, because we were going to have an accident, and we were going to die. I was going to die *again*, and this time, there wouldn't be any medical miracle to save me. We were going to die we were going to die we were going to—

"Sal!" Nathan tightened his hands on my shoulders, hauling me out of the dark pit I had suddenly fallen into. "Sal, I am so sorry, sweetheart, I didn't mean to do that to you. Please, come on, honey, come back to me. Breathe. You need to breathe, Sal."

I had to stop screaming before I could breathe in. That felt like one of the hardest things I had ever done. Raising my head was even harder. The drums were pounding in my ears again, louder than they'd ever been before. "The car," I whispered, staring at Nathan's pale, drawn face.

"I know, Sal, and I am *so sorry*. Please believe me, I didn't think, and I'm sorry. Are you okay? Are you going to be okay if I start driving again?"

No. No, I won't be okay; let's leave the car here and walk wherever it is we need to go. We can walk forever if we have to. Just don't start the car. Numbly, I bit my lip and nodded. I didn't want to stay here forever, and I knew that we couldn't walk home. But oh, I wanted to.

"Okay. Good. I am *so* sorry." Nathan hesitated before saying, "I hate to ask you this, Sal, but is it all right if we don't go straight back to your house? I think I need to stop at the hospital."

I wiped my eyes with the back of my hand as I forced myself to sit up. "Okay," I said, in a small voice.

Nathan started the car and pulled away from the side of the road. We drove on.

The industrial gray San Francisco City Hospital wasn't built to look imposing or inviting: it was built to house a hospital. It was simultaneously less comforting and more welcoming than SymboGen. Nathan parked in his assigned space beneath the building, gesturing for me to come as he got out of the car and walked briskly toward the employee entrance. I followed. As I did, I realized that I felt oddly unclothed without my shoulder bag, like I was forgetting something essential.

If SymboGen didn't return my things, I could always replace them and send Dr. Banks the bill. Dwelling on that bitter thought kept me from thinking too hard about where we were going as Nathan led me through the maze of corridors and hallways inside the hospital.

Once we were inside the service elevator bound for the fifth floor, Nathan turned to me and said, "I probably shouldn't be doing this, but I need to know whether SymboGen has information that they're not sharing with the rest of us."

"By 'doing this,' you really mean taking me with you, don't you?"

"I do," Nathan admitted. The elevator stopped, and he led me to a changing room. "You're already in scrubs; that's good. Put on a lab coat and we should be fine."

I frowned at him. "You're really serious. You're not supposed to be doing this."

"No, I'm not, but I want you with me; you're the one who saw what Dr. Lo did." He opened a locker and passed me a lab coat. "Don't worry. You won't get in any trouble if we're caught."

"I'm not the one I'm worried about here, Nathan."

He waved off my concern, a grim expression on his face. I usually only saw him looking that serious when someone had died. "I have a clean record, and this problem has been bothering everyone. The worst I'm going to get is a slap on the wrist."

Somehow, I doubted that his punishment would be quite as light as that, but there was no sense in arguing with him; we'd been dating long enough for me to know when his mind was made up. I shrugged on the lab coat he'd handed me, rolling up the sleeves to keep them from engulfing my hands completely. Nathan smiled.

"You know, there's nothing in the world hotter than a cute girl in a lab coat," he said.

I blinked. "With that attitude, I would have expected you to be dating my sister."

"What can I say? I like what I like. Now come on. We have some protocols to break."

Nathan led me down the hall, pausing only once, when he ducked into a supply room and emerged with a wand that looked like a more primitive cousin of the one Dr. Lo had used to examine me. He tucked it under his arm, and we started walking again.

At the end of the hall was a large door marked INFECTIOUS MATERIALS: AUTHORIZED PERSONNEL ONLY. There was a large biohazard symbol beneath the sign, in case people didn't get the point. Nathan ignored it as he pushed the door open and kept walking. I trusted Nathan. I followed him.

The hallway on the other side looked just like every other hall in the hospital... except that there were no people here. The usual mix of doctors, nurses, and orderlies was gone, replaced by the hum of the fluorescent lights, which seemed extremely loud without all the sounds of humanity to muffle them.

"Here," Nathan said. He turned, walking into a small room, where a heavy green curtain shielded the occupant from view. He pushed the curtain aside, revealing Beverly's owner. I gasped. I couldn't stop myself.

Machines surrounded the sleeping man, connected to him by a variety of tubes and wires. A clear plastic tube snaked out from under the covers; they'd catheterized him at some point, probably when they realized that he wasn't going to wake up enough to take care of his bodily needs. I recognized most of those tubes and wires from my own stay in the hospital after my accident. I'd been wired up just like that when I first woke up. But this man was behind warning signs, in a room all by himself. They didn't expect him to wake up, ever.

Nathan walked grimly toward the sleeping man's bedside. "He's been asleep for the past twenty-four hours," he said. "He was still moving up until then, but now he seems to have gone into the next stage of the disease, whatever that means. There's no response to stimuli of any type. His family wants to disconnect life support; the hospital is paying all medical costs from this point on, for the sake of being allowed to keep working with him."

"But... why?" I asked. "If his family's ready to let him go..." I felt like a hypocrite even as the words left my mouth. My family had been ready to let go. If I hadn't regained consciousness when I did, I would have died.

Nathan glanced back toward me, grimacing a little as he saw my discomfort. "This isn't like what happened with you, Sal.

You had an accident. We knew what caused your coma, and no matter how much research we did, we were never going to find a cure for car crashes. This is different. This is something infectious, and we need to find a way to stop the spread."

A new discomfort curled in my stomach. "Should we be wearing masks or something if we're going to be in here?"

"No. Whatever causes this isn't airborne. We've run every test we could think of, and there's nothing." Nathan bent forward, folding back the blanket that covered Beverly's owner. "It's baffling our best people. It's baffling *me*."

"Why are you involved? Shouldn't this be an infectious disease case?"

"I'm involved because everyone in the hospital is involved. No one gets to sit out an epidemic." Nathan produced a pair of blue plastic gloves from his lab coat pocket, pulling them on over his hands. I was relieved to realize that he wouldn't be touching the sleeping man's skin. "How far above your skin did she hold the light?"

"About an inch and a half," I said. "She was especially careful with the undersides of my arms and the insides of my thighs."

"All right," said Nathan. He clicked on the wand. It buzzed slightly, lighting up with the same purplish glow as Dr. Lo's wand. Then he lifted the man's left arm. It came without resistance, utterly limp, and remained limp as Nathan ran the wand along it. Like Dr. Lo, he checked the outside first, and then switched to examining the inside of the man's arm, where it would have been closest to his body.

Just between the elbow and armpit, Nathan stopped. "Sal," he said, a sick fascination in his voice. "Come and have a look at this."

I didn't want to have a look at anything. I went anyway. It's always better to understand than it is to be left sitting in the dark; it's always better to have answers, even when those answers lead to fresh questions.

This answer definitely led to fresh questions. The light from Nathan's wand made most of the skin beneath it glow a pale purple, unremarkable because it was so consistent. But at the middle of the light, in the center of the man's arm, was a system of what looked almost like roots that glowed a bright, painful white instead of matching the purple around them. I stared.

The roots moved.

It was just a twitch, barely movement at all, but it was enough to startle us both. I let out a small shriek, dancing backward, away from the man in the bed. Nathan dropped his arm, taking a long, somewhat more dignified step away from him.

"What *is* that?" I demanded.

"It's a parasitic infection—I don't know what type. Whatever it is, it fluoresces under ultraviolet light," said Nathan. He sounded astonished and sickened at the same time, like he'd been suspicious, but had never wanted to have his suspicions confirmed. "These people don't have a disease. They have a parasite, and it's taking them over." He turned to look at me, eyes wide. "Why is SymboGen hiding this?"

"I have a better question," I said. "What happens when they find out we know?"

Naturally, there were concerns about the Intestinal Bodyguard™ when we started human trials. Shanti was worried about the worms. She was always very maternally inclined toward them, and she wasn't sure they'd been tested enough to be placed in human hosts. Richard, he was on the other extreme. He was worried about our human volunteers, and whether the Intestinal Bodyguard™ might somehow damage their immune systems permanently when it was only trying to help. I was the moderating influence on both of them. That was my job most of the time when we were together. Shanti built castles in the air, Richard talked about how they were going to collapse, and I built foundations underneath them.

We didn't need to worry, as it turned out. Human and implant fit together like they'd been designed for one another. In a very real way, they had been.

—FROM "KING OF THE WORMS," AN INTERVIEW WITH
DR. STEVEN BANKS, CO-FOUNDER OF SYMBOGEN. ORIGINALLY
PUBLISHED IN *ROLLING STONE*, FEBRUARY 2027.

You know what's funny? In the official literature, Steve tries to claim that D. symbogenesis *was my idea, and that I somehow managed to sell everyone else on the idea that this was a line of research worth pursuing. If you check the actual publications, however, you'll see that my timeline matches up a little better with reality: I was brought into the project six years into the development cycle. I had to work fast and dirty to make up the ground that had already been frittered away on dead ends and useless research channels.*

I made D. symbogenesis. *I have no qualms about admitting that. It is my baby. But I'm not the one responsible for cutting out most of the potential quality-control time. That award is reserved solely for Dr. Steven Banks. I'll take the credit—and the blame—for what I actually did. I won't take the rest of it, and he can't make me.*

—FROM *CAN OF WORMS: THE AUTOBIOGRAPHY OF SHANTI CALE, PHD.* AS YET UNPUBLISHED.

Chapter 9

AUGUST 2027

Someone knocked on my bedroom door, coaxing me out of an uneasy sleep. I opened my eyes but didn't lift my head from my pillow. Maybe if I stayed where I was, they'd go away and leave me alone.

The knocking continued. Beverly lifted her own head and turned toward the door, ears cocked at an inquisitive angle. Then she turned and looked at me, the question clear in her puzzled brown eyes. Why was I, the one with the thumbs, not getting up and answering the door? Was something wrong with the world?

Yes. Something was wrong with the world. SymboGen was withholding information about what was becoming a national health crisis, at least according to Nathan. He'd produced reports from hospitals around the country the night before, stacking them up in front of me like silent accusations.

I'd picked up the first one, flipping it open to the list of cases. Twenty-seven affected so far in Cleveland, Ohio, and the surrounding cities. "Why hasn't this been on the news?" I'd asked.

And that was when Nathan had said the most damning thing of all: "I'm starting to think it's because SymboGen doesn't want it to be." Each outbreak was reported on the local news—that was unavoidable—triggering a brief flurry of concern, but after that, it just vanished, falling into whatever pit waited for buried news cycles. Miracle diets and pop starlets ruled the headlines, and a few dozen sleepwalkers in a few dozen American cities barely registered as worthy of attention.

But it wasn't just a few dozen, according to the reports Nathan had. There were a few hundred cases, once you looked at the whole country, and they weren't limited to American soil. We knew of definite cases in Canada, the United Kingdom, and South America, and there were rumors of more cases elsewhere in the world. If this was as widespread as Nathan suspected, worldwide infections were probably somewhere in the vicinity of ten thousand, and climbing—which just made the lack of major media coverage more alarming. Someone, somewhere, was spending a lot to bury this.

SymboGen obviously didn't have a treatment protocol—that was clear from the way they'd eliminated Chave—but they knew more than anyone else did. So why hadn't they shared their information with the rest of the medical community? Why were they choosing to shut out all the other researchers and scientific establishments in the world? There were a lot of potential motivations for that sort of thing. None of them were altruistic.

After what Nathan and I had seen at SymboGen and the hospital, neither of us was in the mood for company. He'd dropped me off at home, barely beating Dad and Beverly to the driveway. I'd kissed him goodbye, whistled for my dog, and gone straight to bed. That was—I lifted my head enough to check the clock. That was either three or fifteen hours ago, depending on whether it was nine o'clock in the morning or nine o'clock at night.

The knocking wasn't stopping. I finally forced myself to roll out of the bed, raking my hair out of my eyes with my fingers as I walked to the door. I wrenched it open, and demanded, "What is it?"

Joyce blinked. "Whoa. Dad said you'd gone to bed as soon as you got home, but I expected you to be wearing your pajamas. Why are you wearing scrubs?"

"It's a long story," I said. The hallway was brightly lit, but that didn't tell me anything; there were no windows. "What time is it?"

"Don't you have a clock, sleepyhead? It's nine in the morning. You've slept the clock all the way around."

"Oh." I stood there, blinking dumbly at my sister, as I realized one of the things her statement meant: I'd slept for more than twelve hours. That guaranteed deep REM. So why didn't I remember any of my dreams? Last night should have been a perfect candidate for a trip into the hot warm dark.

Even as I thought that, another realization hit me: I resented the absence of the dreams. The hot warm dark was always safe, always constant, always there for me, even if it represented something I didn't understand. I woke up from those dreams confused but at peace, like I was only fully myself in those moments when the drums still echoed in my ears. So why had the hot warm dark deserted me when I needed it most?

"Sal? You okay?"

"Huh?" I wrenched myself back into the conversation, shaking my head to clear it. "I'm sorry. I just woke up. Did you need something?"

"You mean apart from wanting to be sure you weren't dead? SymboGen just delivered a great big package for you. It's labeled 'time-sensitive' and 'perishable' and 'this end up,' and I thought it would be a good idea to get you up so you could go and deal with it."

I eyed her. "You just want to know what's inside."

My sister beamed unrepentantly. "That is correct. Besides, you know it's not healthy for you to be in bed for too long. There's a whole big world out there just waiting to be explored."

"You can cut the New Age nature spiel. I'm not buying it, and we both know you never sound like a physical therapy motivational tape unless Mom's been priming you," I said without rancor. Mom could be pretty persuasive when she wanted to be, and Joyce probably hadn't taken much persuading—not with a mystery package waiting to be opened.

"Come on, Sal. Come open your big box."

"What if I don't want to?" I shot back. Beverly chose that moment to shove past my ankles and go trotting off down the hall, her tail waving languidly behind her as she made a beeline for the door to the backyard.

Joyce pointed after Beverly, beaming angelically. "It won't matter, because you need to clean up after your dog."

I groaned. "Fine. I'll be out as soon as I have some real clothes on."

"Just remember that you keep your clothes in your dresser, and don't go looking for them in your bed," said Joyce sweetly.

I took great pleasure in closing the door in her face.

It only took me a few minutes to get dressed. Brushing my hair took longer. I might not remember any of my dreams, but I'd clearly been tossing and turning in the night, and my hair was a matted mass of tangles and knots that gave way with an audible ripping sound. I cringed and kept brushing until I felt vaguely presentable. Then I went out to join my family.

All three of them were sitting at the kitchen table, waiting. That was unusual all by itself. Mom would normally have left for her volunteer work by now, and Dad and Joyce usually made their way over to the lab before eight. The box from Symbo-Gen was in the center of the table, covered with even more warning labels than Joyce had reported. I stopped in the hall-way door, blinking at them.

"Is today a holiday that I forgot about?" I asked. "Because if it is, I'm going back to bed."

"Good morning to you, too, sweetie," said Mom.

"I called the lab and told them that Joyce and I would be in a little late this morning," said my father. "We were concerned about you after last night, and I wanted a chance to talk to you before we left."

"Besides, mystery box," said Joyce. She was her usual blithe self. Mom and Dad...weren't. They were both smiling, trying to look normal, but there was a grim undertone to their expres-sions that spoke of things they weren't quite willing to say. I found myself wondering what secrets they were keeping from me, and pushed the thought aside. If I was going to start think-ing like that, I might as well turn myself over to SymboGen right now. At least there I would know who I could trust—no one—and who was lying to me—everyone.

"Mystery box," I agreed, and walked over to take a seat at the table. I tried to tug the box toward me, but it was so heavy I couldn't move it. "What's in here? Bricks?"

"The normal question is 'rocks,' and I don't know, but I almost gave myself a hernia getting it inside."

I blinked at my father. Corrections like that seemed normal and right from Sherman, but coming from him, it just felt like I was being scolded. I turned my attention back to the box, try-ing not to let my discomfort show.

The box had been taped shut, but there were tags built into the cardboard to make the box easier to open. They also ren-dered it impossible to use a second time, but I guess when you're a giant multinational corporation, you don't need to worry as much about reusability. I gripped the tabs and tugged them apart, causing the entire top of the box to detach. Biode-gradable packing peanuts spilled out onto the kitchen table.

"Hang on a second, sweetie, I'll get a bag," said Mom, ges-turing for me to stop. She pushed her chair back and bustled into the kitchen, returning a few moments later with a large plastic garbage bag. She swept the fallen packing peanuts into it, and stood ready to catch any more that tried to escape. "All right. Proceed."

"Efficiency, thy name is Mom," said Joyce.

I forced a chuckle, and pulled the top off the box, sending a larger flood of packing peanuts in all directions. I put the box top on the floor next to my chair. Mom hurried to capture all the packing peanuts before they could roll under the furniture, where they would be later inhaled by the dog. I ignored her in favor of digging down into the box, spilling more packing pea-nuts. My fingers hit plastic. "Got it," I said, and lifted.

Whoever had been responsible for sterilizing and packing my personal possessions had taken their job very, very seriously. My things were swaddled in a double layer of plastic wrap, and there was an itemized inventory of what was inside affixed to the front. I scanned the list, and rolled my eyes. They'd defi-nitely been thorough. I just didn't see the utility of itemizing individual tampons.

"Is that all?" asked Joyce. She flicked a packing peanut at me, looking disappointed. "I was hoping for pirate gold."

"Not even SymboGen can hand out big boxes of pirate gold without good reason," I said, setting my things aside. "But that can't be all that's in here. Look at the size of this box."

"Maybe SymboGen's packing department is just really enthusiastic," said Joyce.

"I don't know." I had to stand to see over the edge of the box. I rummaged down into the packing peanuts, flailing around until I hit what felt like the handle of a medium-sized cooler. "What the…?" I lifted.

It was, in fact, a cooler, labeled "Open Immediately." I passed it to Joyce, who gave a little squeal of delight, and went back to rummaging around in the packing peanuts. By the time I'd found the next item—a flat box made of reinforced memory plastic and smelling suspiciously like croissants—Joyce had opened the cooler, and was squealing more loudly as she unpacked sliced fruit, berries and cream, and an assortment of cold breakfast meats onto the table. I passed the box of croissants to my father and went rummaging around in the big box one more time.

The last item inside was a square box with a small chemical heating unit attached to keep the contents warm, and a note taped to the outside:

> Sally—
> I hope this helps to make up for lunch. I will see you soon, under better circumstances. For now, be well, and know that I am thinking of you fondly.
>
> Sincerely,
> Dr. Banks

"Sal? Did SymboGen just send us breakfast?" asked Joyce.

"It looks like it," I said. Mom made the big box disappear while I opened the box with the note. Inside was a stack of waffles, a bottle of what I was sure would prove to be real maple syrup, and a large bowl of eggs scrambled with cheddar cheese and chunks of tomato. It was a four-star breakfast packed for delivery, and I would have bet good money that it was prepared in the reopened executive cafeteria.

My pride wanted me to announce that I wasn't hungry and leave this extravagant bribe—because there was no way this *wasn't* a bribe—for my family and Beverly to consume. My body had other ideas. My stomach, which had been rumbling since I recognized the smell from the flat box as croissants, began to roar when I smelled the eggs. I resigned myself to the inevitable. I was going to eat my bribe, and I was going to like it.

Mom returned from the kitchen with place settings and a broad smile that didn't look quite genuine. "Isn't this nice? Breakfast for the family, catered by SymboGen."

"I wouldn't have eaten that cereal if I'd known you were ordering this much food," said Joyce. She didn't let her complaint stop her from taking two waffles and a sizable portion of the eggs.

"I didn't know either," I said. "Dr. Banks told me he'd be sending my things. He didn't say that he'd be sending them along with enough food to feed an army."

"Now, Sal, don't exaggerate," said my father. "You have a Labrador. There's no way we could feed an army on this." He grabbed a croissant.

My father was US military. He wouldn't have been eating the food if it wasn't safe. I laughed a little, some of my tension easing, and reached for a plate.

Dad looked tired. That was the first thing I noticed, and as I noticed it, I realized he'd been looking tired since before the outbreak Joyce and I witnessed in San Bruno. That was when he'd told me he knew about the sleepwalkers. Just how much did he know?

Joyce didn't look tired—she looked focused, like she was calculating exactly how many calories she was getting from each bite, and how far she could make each of those calories take her, if she really pushed herself. Getting a late start was one thing. Paying for it by skipping meals throughout the day was something else entirely, and spoke to an urgency in whatever she was working on.

I took a bite of waffle, chewed, and said, as casually as I

could, "They had to keep my things for decontamination because one of the PAs who usually helps me around the building suddenly freaked out and started attacking people. She seemed to go to sleep first, while she was still standing up. It was like all the lights went out inside her brain, and she wasn't home anymore."

Joyce put down her fork.

It was a small gesture, marked mainly by the faint clink of metal against ceramic, but it said worlds. Very little could make my sister stop eating once she got started. I turned my attention to our father.

"They tried to make her stop, but she wouldn't. So some of the security officers who'd come to take care of the situation began zapping her with these electric batons they carry. They hit her over and over again, until she fell down and didn't move anymore." I didn't tell them she'd said my name as she was falling. Some things I wasn't ready to think about yet, and that was one of them.

"Sal..." said my father, and stopped, his throat working like he was trying to say something else. No sound came out.

"So security took everyone who'd been in the cafeteria when all this happened—and I mean everyone, they even took Dr. Banks—to the lab level for examination, so they could figure out whether or not we were infected. That's where they took my clothes away."

"They have a test for whether or not someone's infected?" Joyce half-stood in her excitement, hands braced against the table.

"Joyce Erin Mitchell, sit *down*," said my father, his voice like a whip cracking. Joyce gave him a startled look and sank slowly back into her seat, eyes wide. He turned his focus on me. "Sal, honey, what you have to understand—"

"There's this one PA, Sherman? He's always really nice to

me. He acts like I'm a guest or a volunteer, not a lab rat who doesn't have a choice about what they want to do to her. He teaches me new slang. I usually have to look it up to make sure he's not messing with me, but that's part of the fun, you know? Well, when they took us all underground to be tested, he failed. He's infected. And now I'm never going to see him again." My voice was getting louder. I didn't do anything to stop it. "And what I have to ask you, Dad, what I have to know, is whether you know anything about this that you're not telling me. Because it seems like there's a lot of people not telling people things, just now. And now my friends are dying. I don't have that many friends. I can't spare them."

My father looked at me. I glared back. We stayed like that for almost a minute, no one moving to break the silence. It was like we were all afraid of what would happen when we did.

Finally, he stood. "I have to get to the lab," he said. "Joyce, are you ready?"

"Wha—um, yeah." Joyce shoved her chair away from the table, scrambling to her feet. "Have a nice day, Sal. Bye, Mom." Mom got a hasty kiss on the cheek. I got a wave and an apologetic look as Joyce darted past me to grab her bag. Then she was gone, following Dad toward the garage.

The garage door slammed hard enough to rattle the pictures on the walls. That was the moment Beverly chose to bump her head against my thigh, eyes pleading for a taste of the delicacies she could smell on the table above her. Like all Labradors, she was magnetically drawn to food, and was an incurable beggar. It only worked once in a while, but that was enough for her to keep on trying.

This was one of the times when it was going to work. Lucky dog. "I'm not hungry anymore, and they need me at the shelter," I said. I stood, pausing only to set my plate on the floor for Beverly to lick clean. Then I turned and walked, tight-shouldered, to my room.

It was that or start screaming. And if I started, I didn't know when I was going to stop.

Mom knocked on my door twenty minutes later. Her mothering radar was in good form: twenty minutes was exactly the amount of time I'd needed to stop being so mad that I wasn't fit for human company. I wondered, very briefly, whether Sally would have needed twenty minutes, or whether she'd been one of those people who had ten-minute tantrums. Maybe she'd gone in the other direction, and screamed for forty minutes every time she got upset. I'd never know. Sally was gone, and I was living her increasingly confusing life without her.

"Yeah?" I called.

"I can give you a ride to the shelter if you can be ready to go in five," Mom called back.

I paused, assessing. I hadn't showered, but there was a shower at the shelter that we were supposed to use after cleaning out the puppy cages. I could always volunteer for cage-cleaning duty—something no one sane would refuse to let me do if I was offering—and then use that as an excuse to take a shower afterward. Shoveling a little shit would be good for me. I could use the time to think.

"I'll be ready."

Mom hesitated before saying, "Sal—"

The rest of the sentence never came. I heard her steps move away from my door after a few minutes had passed, and I turned myself to the essential business of getting out the door.

I was lacing my shoes when I realized my bag was still sealed in plastic wrap on the kitchen table. I swore under my breath, shoving a change of clothes for after my shower under my arm, and left my room. I needed that bag. Not just for the emotional reassurance of having my things with me, although that was important. I didn't want to go to the shelter without my ID, and it was in my wallet, which was, naturally, in my bag.

Mom was banging around in her office; I could hear her moving papers and shuffling things on her desk, looking for whatever it was she needed to start a successful day of volunteer work. I grabbed the scissors from the kitchen and returned to the task at hand: freeing my possessions from their plastic prison.

Whatever brand of plastic wrap SymboGen used, it was industrial strength, and it had been flash-sealed, not taped down. I had to practically saw through it in order to create a large enough hole for me to get my hand inside. It was almost funny, in a horrible way. The food was easy to access. My so-very-dangerous keys and notebook, on the other hand...

My notebook. The blood drained from my face, and I ripped the rest of the plastic wrap open without even trying to be delicate about it. I'd been carrying my notebook, the one that Dr. Morrison insisted I update daily as part of my "therapeutic healing process." Putting it into my bag every morning was habit, and since I'd never expected my things to be out of my possession for more than an hour or so, I hadn't seen any reason to vary my habits just because I was spending the day at SymboGen. But my things had been away from me overnight, giving any prying research rats at SymboGen plenty of time to go rummaging through my innermost thoughts.

I wasn't sure those thoughts would be of any interest to anyone but myself and my therapist. I was terrified that SymboGen was once again intending to prove me wrong.

I pulled the bag out of the plastic wrap with shaking hands and dumped it out on the kitchen table, not bothering to stop when pencils and tampons went skittering away onto the floor. My notebook fell out. I tossed the bag aside, grabbing the notebook and flipping it open as I scanned for any signs that someone else had been reading my private thoughts. I'm not quite sure what I expected—an inspection sticker? A receipt from the company scanner?

I know that I didn't expect what I found. Three pages after my notes ended, someone had scrawled a phone number on a previously blank page. Under that was written in large block letters:

```
CALL FOR ANSWERS IF YOU ARE SURE YOU WANT
THEM.
    YOU MAY WANT TO RECONSIDER YOUR DESIRES.
    KNOWING THE DIRECTION DOESN'T MEAN YOU
HAVE TO GO.
```

Each letter was large and clear, like whoever left the message knew I had trouble reading. It was signed "a friend." I didn't recognize the handwriting, but that was no real surprise—I rarely saw anything handwritten at SymboGen, where everything was done officially, on computers and data pads. I stood there staring dumbly at the note, which was both evidence that my privacy had been violated, and the first sign I'd been given that someone, somewhere, might be able to tell me what was really going on.

"Sal? Are you ready?"

"Coming, Mom!" I shoved the notebook back into my bag, covering it with my clean clothes before gathering up the rest of my things and cramming them in as well. Once I was sure there was nothing showing that might give me away, I slung the bag over my shoulder, gave Beverly one last pat on the head, and ran for the garage. I needed to think about what I was going to do next, and I needed to speak to Nathan. But first, I needed to get to work.

Mom dropped me off in front of Cause for Paws. I blew her a kiss and went bounding up the front steps into the lobby, where I was greeted by the unusual sight of Tasha, staring at me. "Are you...early?" she asked, in a tone that implied that this might be taken as a sign of the apocalypse. "Is Sally Mitchell, the girl who never met a nap she didn't love, actually *early*?"

"Stop it," I said. "I just wanted to get an early start on my day. I may need to make a personal call in an hour or so, and I figured if I came in now, I could make my calls and feel virtuous at the same time."

"Hmm. Seems sketchy. That's your only motive?"

I didn't feel like telling Tasha everything. She was sweet, and I liked her. That didn't mean I wanted to pour out my troubles at her feet. We'd never established that sort of relationship, and I wasn't going to start now.

"Yeah." I rubbed the back of my head with my hand, grimacing at the gritty feel of my unwashed hair. "I was going to start with the puppy cages, if that's cool with you. I know they're on the roster for today, and if I do them now, I can be showered and presentable before the afternoon adoption hours."

"You can totally volunteer to do the puppy cages. And P.S., if this is part of paying it forward for that phone call of yours, there's no chance in hell that Will is going to object to you taking a little break after you came in early *and* scrubbed up all the puppy shit."

"That's what I was hoping," I said, and hung up my shoulder bag. I felt funny letting it go when I had only just managed to get it back into my possession. At the same time, if there were SymboGen spies waiting to break into the shelter and steal my things, I might as well give up right now. I flashed Tasha an insincere smile before heading to the supply cabinet.

The usual cacophony greeted me as I passed through the doors separating the public areas from the cages. Cause for Paws was a small, no-kill operation, and we did our best to provide the animals in our care with comfortable living accommodations—large, multi-feline habitats with toys and cat trees for the more social cats, solo cages for the ones who couldn't stand anything else that purred. Similar arrangements for the dogs, who were also walked twice a day, once in the early morning, once at night. Tasha must have just finished the morning rounds when I arrived. We didn't officially open to adoption appointments for another hour, and we didn't open to walk-ins until noon. That left me with a comfortable amount of time to get everything cleaned up and grab a quick shower before people who didn't work here started coming through the doors.

"Hey, guys," I said, moving to fill my bucket with water from the sink. Hot water and biodegradable spa cleanser—made from citric acid, safe to use around people and animals, and even safe to drink if you were feeling masochistic—were the best tools for this particular task, at least when combined with plain old elbow grease. I dumped the cleaner into the bucket, pulled on my gloves, and moved toward the first cage.

It was surprisingly easy to think with dogs romping madly around the room, sniffing everything like they'd never been out of their cages before. I used the hose to rinse the worst of the night's "accidents" down the drain at the center of the room, and then focused on getting down on my hands and knees and really scrubbing. Even the cleanest animal care facility needs to be sterilized regularly, for the sake of everyone's health, humans and animals alike. The dogs didn't seem to mind. Most of them came over with tails wagging to see what I was doing, nudge me with their noses, and get scratched behind their ears. They didn't even mind the gloves I had to wear. They were dogs, they were out of their cages, and everything was right with the world.

If only things were that easy for humans. I scrubbed harder, trying to make up my mind about what came next. I wanted answers. I wanted to know what was going on with the sleeping sickness, and whether Sherman was dead or just sick. I wanted to know why people were *keeping* things from me.

Calling the number in my notebook would mean prying

into things SymboGen clearly didn't want me prying into, and looking for answers to questions I wasn't supposed to be asking. It would be one of those things I couldn't take back. What was it that my mysterious note-leaver wrote? "Knowing the direction doesn't mean you have to go"? I was getting the feeling that the sentiment was truer than I could ever have guessed. I had a direction now. Did that mean I wanted to go?

It was only when I was escorting the dogs back to their cages that I realized I was already planning to call Nathan after I called the number in my notebook. Doing one meant doing the other. I wanted him with me on whatever came next. I had the directions...and apparently, I was going.

I carried my bucket over to the sink, pouring its contents down the drain. Well. If I was going to do this—and apparently, I was—I might as well get my shower in first.

Will had arrived while I was in back cleaning up after the dogs. He looked up from the office computer when I walked past. I raised the hand that wasn't carrying the bucket full of cleaning supplies in a wave. He waved back.

"Tasha told me you were here early, but I didn't really believe it until I looked into the dog room," he said. "Thanks for doing the cages."

"Not a problem. I needed to think."

"Sal, any time you need to think, feel free to come in and hose the shit off the walls. Seriously, please. You have the most useful form of meditation I've ever encountered." Will grinned briefly. "Your day at SymboGen go well?"

I froze. He always asked that question, and I never knew how to answer. I knew that SymboGen paid at least part of my salary at Cause for Paws; it was how I could get away with scheduling all my shifts around my various medical and therapy appointments, and why they never said anything about vacation time when I had to go spend a day or two on the SymboGen campus. What I didn't know was how much of *Will's* salary was being paid by SymboGen. For all that I knew, every word I said went straight from him to Dr. Banks.

That thought didn't bother me most of the time. Most of the time, I wasn't getting ready to call mysterious numbers that might lead to corporate espionage or—or whatever other labels you could slap on this sort of thing.

Will was still looking at me, waiting. I forced myself to return his smile and said, "It was eventful, but it ended, and really, isn't that what we're all hoping for when we have to spend a day at the doctor's office? I was just going to grab a shower before we got busy, since I'm covered in dog yuck. Is that cool with you, or did you need me to do something while I'm still filthy?"

"Your noble sacrifice with the dogs means you're not on box duty tonight, so no, Sal, you're off the hook," said Will, already turning back to his screen. "Go get yourself cleaned up. Adoptions go more smoothly when the potential adopters aren't trying to figure out whether that smell is the puppy or the shelter employee."

"Thanks, Will," I said, and practically threw the bucket into the supply cabinet before turning and bolting, double-time, for the big employee bathroom. I paused only long enough to grab my shoulder bag from the wall.

One definite advantage to showering at the shelter: Cause for Paws had an old gym-style shower, with four showerheads all feeding into the same large tiled area. Add the industrial-level water pressure, and I didn't even really need soap: if I turned the water on full and stood where the streams converged, I'd have the dirt blasted right off of me. I appreciate a shower that's capable of leaving bruises.

I also appreciate a shower that's capable of generating that much white noise. I cleaned myself off quickly, and then hiked the water up as high as it would go, creating the sound of an artificial indoor waterfall. I dug my notebook out of my bag and retreated to the corner of the room farthest from the office. The mystery message was still there when I flipped to the appropriate page. For a moment I just stood there, looking at it.

CALL FOR ANSWERS IF YOU ARE SURE YOU WANT
THEM.
    YOU MAY WANT TO RECONSIDER YOUR DESIRES.
    KNOWING THE DIRECTION DOESN'T MEAN YOU
HAVE TO GO.

Whatever it meant, I knew one thing: dialing that number would change everything. I might not know how just yet, but I knew that it was going to happen. All I had to do was close the notebook and leave it alone. I could shred the page when I got home. I could put it in the recycling. I could...

I dialed the number.

It rang four times. I was just beginning to worry about what I'd do if I wound up rolling to voice mail when there was a click and a warm, almost maternal female voice said, "Well, if it isn't little Miss Sally Mitchell, actually taking an invitation to chat. I wasn't sure you'd be up for it so soon, you know. I don't know that I would have been, in your position."

"Who is this?" I asked, keeping my voice low. "Are you the one who left the message in my notebook?"

"No, that wasn't me. I would have needed to set foot on the SymboGen campus for that, and there are reasons I can't do that—you'll understand them soon. But I still have friends on the inside, and they told me what happened yesterday. That's part of why I thought it was finally time for us to meet."

"You didn't answer my first question."

The woman chuckled. "That's true; I didn't. I won't, either, until we're looking each other in the face. But I'll tell you this much, Sal: I'm on your side. You may not believe me—you may decide I'm just one more person trying to play you, and believe me, a lot more people are going to be trying to play you in the days to come—but it's the truth. I've always been on your side. There's no one in the world who's been pulling for you longer than I have."

I frowned warily. Part of me wanted to believe her, even though she wouldn't tell me her name. Something about her voice was familiar, like a voice that I'd heard before on television or maybe on one of Nathan's parasitology podcasts. She sounded like someone that I was supposed to trust. Maybe that was what made trusting her feel so hard. If she was someone I was *supposed* to trust...I'm not always good at doing what I'm supposed to do.

"The message said that this was the number to call if I wanted answers. So far, I'm not hearing any answers from you. Just a whole bunch of hot air and some vague 'I know something you don't know.'"

Now the woman outright laughed. "Oh, *Sal.* You truly are splendid—better than I'd hoped for. I can't give you the answers that you're looking for over the phone. That would be silly. Even with the precautions you've obviously taken to keep from being overheard, there's always a chance we could be monitored, and I don't think that's a risk either of us can afford. But now I know that you're ready for answers. I'll have someone contact you inside of the week with an address. Then we can finally meet in person."

"You seem pretty confident that I'll come."

"I don't think you'd have bothered calling me if you weren't going to take the next step." Her voice turned serious, all the amusement leaching away. "This is a big step for you, Sal. Certain lines can't be uncrossed; certain maps will get you lost. Do you understand that?"

"No. What lines? What maps? It doesn't make any sense at all."

"I can understand why you'd feel that way; thank you for not lying to me. And as for that nice boyfriend of yours, Dr. Kim, you can bring him with you if you like. If you think he'd like to come. If you think he'll trust the map. This will go more easily if there's someone who can translate for you, and you'll believe him even when you wouldn't believe me."

Having her give me permission to bring Nathan stung somehow, like she was the only one who had any say in what I did with my life. At the same time, he'd never forgive me if this woman actually had information about the sleeping sickness and I left him behind. "I'll bring him," I said.

"Good. I'll see you soon, Sal. Be careful. Don't trust SymboGen."

"Look, whoever you are—"

The sound of dead air—the absence of sound—from the phone told me that there was no point in continuing. I was only talking to myself. I hit redial, but I knew even as I did it that there was no point. The call rang straight to an unformatted voice mail box with no greeting to identify it. So did the call after that.

The third call was cut off with the rapid beeping whine of a disconnected number. Whoever I'd been talking to wasn't on the other end anymore. Now I had nothing to direct me—and even more questions than I'd started out with. And my hair was wet.

Somehow, the worst part of it all was that this was *still* better than yesterday. My standards for living a normal life were definitely going down.

Tasha was helping a young couple get a leash onto one of our poodle mixes. The dog—a rather unfortunate German shepherd/poodle cross—wasn't helping, since he was so excited by the prospect of going for a walk that his entire body was vibrating. We get a lot of poodle mixes at the shelter. According to Nathan, before the Intestinal Bodyguard there was a huge demand for so-called hypoallergenic dogs, leading to a glut of poodles crossed with just about anything else. Once the implants became common, the "designer dog" craze died off, and the shelters got flooded. The first few generations died a long time before I came to work at Cause for Paws. It would still be a long time before they stopped coming through our doors.

As I moved to help Tasha with the dog, I couldn't help thinking about how man was locked in a constant fight to control an environment that didn't want to be controlled. First we made the world as clean and non-allergenic as we possibly could and, when that just made things worse, we created artificial infections to make ourselves healthier. So what was the "worse" that came after this particular change to our personal environments?

There wasn't much time for contemplation. Tasha got the dog leashed and escorted the potential adopters out the door while I went into the back to start getting the kittens ready for their visitors. The day dissolved from there into the usual series of small emergencies. One of the dogs got loose and had to be retrieved; one of the kittens was handled too roughly and threw up all over its littermates, necessitating some quick cage—and kitten—cleanup. With one thing leading to another, it was quitting time before I realized that I hadn't called Nathan yet.

"I think I have dog food in my ear," complained Tasha, washing her hands in the sink behind the desk. "Is there a medical term for that? One that can, perhaps, be used to excuse me from work tomorrow?"

"I don't think 'klutz' is a good excuse for being absent yet,"

I said apologetically. I slipped on my shoulder bag. "We're both on at nine tomorrow, right, Will?"

"At least you can remember when you're supposed to come to work," he said, attention remaining focused on his screen. "Although if you want to keep coming in early, I'm not going to complain about it. God knows there's enough to do around here to keep us all busy until the end of time."

"So hire someone else; don't take it all out on Sal," said Tasha.

"Out of what budget?" Will asked.

Sadly, he was right. The shelter had two full-time employees, Will and Tasha; one part-time, part-funded by SymboGen employee, me; and a rotating group of volunteers who came in on the weekends to help with the increased foot traffic. There was also a janitorial crew that visited the office once a week to take care of the really heavy cleaning. That was it. Every penny the shelter made above and beyond our salaries went back into keeping the animals fed, the lights on, and the doors open. Pet ownership had increased since the advent of the implants, but all that really meant was that animal abandonment and abuse were also on the rise. Sometimes humanity is the reason we can't have nice things.

The bell over the door jingled as someone came inside. I turned, ready to tell whoever it was that we were closed but they could come back tomorrow, and stopped, a smile spreading across my face.

Nathan smiled back. He looked tired, but that was nothing new; knowing him, he'd been awake for hours after dropping me off last night, and probably got out of bed before I did. "I thought I'd come and see if you wanted to get dinner, since we didn't manage to keep our plans yesterday."

"This is more stalker behavior," I said as I walked toward him, head tilted back for a kiss. "I'm building a profile. I think you're going to be surprised by the strength of my case against you."

"I look forward to the hearing," he said, and leaned down to kiss me.

"You know, some people have really *strange* ideas of what constitutes flirtation," said Tasha. "Do you think he'll propose by sending her a subpoena?"

"Inviting her to appear in the county clerk's office on a specific date, yeah," agreed Will.

"Hey, now," protested Nathan, breaking away from me to mock-scowl at my coworkers. "My family is very traditional. I'd never propose via subpoena. My father would never let me hear the last of it if I sent anything short of a full collections unit."

"Romance is not dead," said Tasha blandly. "You out, Sal?"

"Unless there's anything left for me to do here, I think this is my cue." I looked back at them, brows raised hopefully. "Am I done, Will?"

"Get out of here. Don't come back until tomorrow."

"You heard the boss," said Nathan. He laced his fingers through mine and led me toward the door. I went willingly, relieved that I wasn't going to need to call him after all. This conversation was going to be awkward enough without trying to have it over the phone. I wasn't even sure where I would begin.

The bell over the door jingled again as we left the shelter for the street, and the sweet, welcoming warmth of the late summer air. Nathan kept my hand until we reached the car, where he released me in order to unlock the doors. I was inside and buckled by the time he finished his approach of the driver's seat.

Nathan blinked when he opened the door and found me already settled. "Are you in a hurry to get somewhere?" he asked.

"I'm in a hurry to get somewhere alone with you," I said. "Do you think we could get takeout and go back to your place? I wanted to talk to you."

"You want to talk?" Nathan's expression sobered, like he was steeling himself against the inevitable. "Sal, I know I've been pretty busy lately, but—"

"What? No! This isn't the breakup talk. Jeez, Nathan, I don't even know how to *have* the breakup talk. You're the only boyfriend I've ever had." Sally had dated. Sally had dated quite a lot, as her checkered Facebook archives would readily testify. I knew I hadn't been physically a virgin the first time I'd had sex. But none of that counted for me, not really; that was all part of another lifetime, one that I didn't remember at all.

"Then what's going on?"

"I'll tell you when we're at your apartment, okay?" I looked at my shoulder bag resting against my feet, and managed to restrain the urge to pick it up and clutch it for dear life. Things were getting too confusing, too fast, and I didn't know how to make them go the other way anymore. If there had ever *been* a way to make them go the other way—I wasn't sure there had been.

"Okay," said Nathan, and started the car. "Indian okay?"

"Indian sounds great," I said, and closed my eyes.

Thirty minutes later, we were seated on Nathan's couch with takeout containers in front of us. By mutual unspoken consent, we unpacked and ate, sitting in comfortable if anticipatory silence. I hadn't been able to break for lunch—things had been too hectic at the shelter—and I didn't realize how hungry I actually was until I smelled food. Then all conversation, no matter how important, was put on hold in favor of calories.

When we were both too full to eat another bite, we leaned back on the couch, surveying the ruins of our meal. "I think I'm going to explode," said Nathan.

"That would be messy," I said. "Please don't."

"The maid service would have to hose down the ceiling, not you."

I shuddered exaggeratedly. "That was a sentence I never needed to hear. You understand that, don't you?"

"Forgive me?" asked Nathan, and smiled.

"Always." I smiled back. Then I sobered. "Nathan, about before..."

He paused, smile fading. "I wondered when we'd get back to this," he said, and grimaced, sitting up. "Okay, Sal. What's going on? I'm sorry if I pushed you last night."

"No, it's okay; I understand. That's sort of what this is about." I sketched out the events of the day as quickly and economically as I could without leaving anything out; it was surprisingly easy, once I managed to get started. Nathan didn't ask any questions. He just listened, expression solemn, until I finished talking myself out. For a moment, silence stretched between us like a thin wire, drawn tight and vibrating with the things that neither of us were saying.

Finally, he asked, "Can I see the note?"

I reached for my shoulder bag, pulled out the notebook, and handed it to him wordlessly. He'd read my journal before; there was nothing there that I was worried about him seeing. He flipped past the pages with my handwriting, slowing as he encountered the blank pages that followed. He stopped when he reached the note.

" 'Knowing the direction doesn't mean you have to go,' " he read aloud. Nathan raised his head, frowning. "You said the woman on the phone seemed to be quoting something. Do you remember what else she said?"

"Um...something about maps getting you lost. I didn't really understand it."

Nathan paled. "Was it something like 'certain lines can't be uncrossed; certain maps will get you lost'?"

"Yes!" I sat up straighter. "How did you know that?"

"It's from a children's book. Well, supposedly a children's book. The older I get, the more I think that it was actually one of those books that's meant to look like it's for children but is actually a parody intended for adults. Someone shelved it wrong, it wound up in my library, and my mother read it to me every night before I went to bed from the time I was four until she left us." Nathan shook his head. "It was called *Don't Go Out Alone*. I've looked for years, but I've never found another copy."

"That's…weird," I said. Nathan didn't talk about his mother much, beyond saying that they had been close, she had died when he was very young, and it had taken him years of therapy to get even partially over it. He had no pictures of her anywhere; I didn't even know her name. Maybe that was strange, and maybe it wasn't. I was never sure what "strange" meant when you applied it to real people, instead of to questions in a sociology textbook. My sample size was too small.

"Definitely weird," Nathan agreed. "The woman you spoke to was right about one thing: I want to go with you. Whatever this is, you're not walking into it alone."

"I don't want to," I said, taking my notebook back. "Whatever answers she's going to give me, I wouldn't understand them without somebody with a science background there to translate. This woman has already proven that she's not interested in explaining herself just because I'm not keeping up."

Nathan smiled, not quite managing to conceal his anxiety. That actually made me feel a little better. I didn't want to be the only one worrying. "I guess it's a good thing you have access to a man with a science background."

"It is," I agreed. "It indubitably is."

Nathan raised an eyebrow. "Indubitably?" he asked.

"Did I use it wrong?"

"No. Not at all." He reached over and tucked my hair back behind my ear.

I put my notebook back into my bag before I scooted across

the couch to fold myself against him. Nathan put his arms around me, kissing me slowly, and for a little while—not long enough; it could never have been long enough—we were able to forget about everything but the fact that we were here, alive, and together. Until things changed, that would have to be enough, for both of us.

You know, I'm just going to come out and say what every-one's been thinking: the complaints about how the Intestinal Bodyguard™ was put through the FDA tests for a human-based drug and was thus never properly reviewed under the xenotransplantation regulations always seem to come from corporations with large biotech divisions of their own. You don't see the consumer watchdog groups complaining, oh, no. You don't hear from the parental oversight committees. No, they recognize a good thing when they see it. They see that the Intestinal Bodyguard™ has improved their quality of life tenfold, and they don't complain that the government wasn't hard enough on us during testing.

We jumped through every hoop that was put in front of us. We fulfilled every requirement we were given. If some people feel like we cheated by getting there first, well. I'm sorry.

—FROM "KING OF THE WORMS," AN INTERVIEW WITH DR. STEVEN BANKS, CO-FOUNDER OF SYMBOGEN. ORIGINALLY PUBLISHED IN *ROLLING STONE*, FEBRUARY 2027.

Shadows dancing all around;
Some things better lost than found.
If you ask the questions, best be sure you want to know.
Some things better left forgot,

Some dreams better left unsought.
Knowing the direction doesn't mean you have to go.

The broken doors can open if you seek them on your own.
My darling boy, be careful now, and don't go out alone.

—FROM *DON'T GO OUT ALONE*, BY SIMONE KIMBERLEY,
PUBLISHED 2006 BY LIGHTHOUSE PRESS. CURRENTLY
OUT OF PRINT.

Chapter 10

AUGUST 2027

The sound of Nathan's phone ringing in the middle of the night pulled me most of the way back to consciousness. I rolled over, burying my face in my pillow as I heard him fumble to pick up. The ringing stopped, followed by Nathan's bleary, "This is Dr. Kim." There was a long pause before he demanded, much more loudly—and much more alertly—"What are you talking about?"

I rolled back over, pushing myself up onto my elbows and squinting at him. He was sitting up, his bare back turned toward me. The hand that wasn't holding the phone was covering half his face, like it was all that was holding him upright.

"I see," he said, tonelessly. "No, thank you for calling me. I appreciate the notification. I'll be in within the hour. No, it's not a problem. Yes, thank you." He lowered the phone, but didn't raise his head.

Something about that didn't seem right. Suddenly, I was afraid. "Nathan?" I almost whispered, sitting all the way up. I gingerly reached out and touched his shoulder. "What's going on?"

"Devi came into the ER twenty minutes ago with her wife, Katherine. Katherine was nonresponsive when they arrived, and presented in the same fugue state that we've observed in other victims of the sleeping sickness. Devi was hysterical, and refused to leave her. The attending doctors were following established protocol for this sort of incident—" He stopped, uneasy laughter bubbling from his lips. "Oh, God, Sal, I just called Kate an 'incident.' Devi's wife. I just called her an *incident*. Like she didn't even have a name."

"Hey. Hey! You're doing your job. That's how you do your job." I got up onto my knees to put us at more of an even level. "If you personalized everything, you'd never be able to save anyone. You'd be like one of those doctors on TV, where every person you had to work with was your brother or your best friend..."

"Or my girlfriend?" he asked, with another unsteady laugh. "We met in the hospital."

"And I was never your patient. Dating me is more like dating one of those extras who only appears in one episode and then goes off to be on a different show." I touched his cheek lightly with the back of my hand, doing my best to keep my own anxiety in check. Nathan needed me. I was going to be there for him. "You're doing your job. Now what happened with Kate?"

Nathan took a deep breath. "She was presenting with normal symptoms for the sleeping sickness. The EMTs who were working on her decided to let Devi stay in the room, because she wasn't getting in the way, and it was easier than separating them. Devi wasn't getting in the way. She was crying and trying to hold Kate's hand when she could, but she understood that if she interfered at all, she'd be asked to leave."

"Uh-huh," I said.

"Devi's dead." Nathan made the statement without emotion or inflection: it was a fact, and he presented it as such. I dropped my hand, eyes widening. He turned to look at me, and there was no life in his expression. He looked as empty as his voice sounded. "She was holding Kate's hand, and Kate attacked her."

"Wh-what?"

"The EMTs didn't have a chance to react. They'd never seen that kind of behavior from one of the sleeping sickness cases before. One moment, Kate was on the bed, unresponsive, and the next, she was sitting up and grabbing Devi by the throat. Her trachea was crushed. It broke her hyoid bone. They couldn't react in time. She died before they even got her onto a table."

"Oh my God," I whispered.

"Kate never even blinked. Not even when they were pulling her off her wife's body. She never blinked. As soon as they got her away from Devi, she went limp, and returned to the base fugue state that they all seem to be in." Nathan moved abruptly, standing and starting toward his dresser. "I need to get to the hospital. They need me. I'm really sorry to do this, but if I leave you money, can you take a cab to work in the morning? I'm not sure I'll be back."

"Of course. This isn't the time for me to insist you be the one to drive me." Devi was dead. Katherine had the sleeping sickness, and now Devi was dead. I stayed on the bed, watching Nathan as he dressed, and tried to make my thoughts stop spinning wildly around those two poles: Devi was dead, and Katherine had the sleeping sickness.

Whatever answers we might find, they were going to come too late for Devi, who had always been kind to me, and for Katherine, who had loved her wife very much. Even if they could find a cure for the sleeping sickness, how was Katherine ever going to recover from what she'd done? "I was in a coma, I didn't know" didn't seem like much of a justification. It wouldn't have worked for me. It wasn't going to work for her.

Nathan crossed back to the bed and bent to kiss me quickly, whispering, "I'm sorry." He thrust forty dollars into my hand. Then he was out the door, leaving me sitting on the bed and staring blankly after him.

It wasn't until the front door slammed that I actually turned and looked at the clock on his bedside table. It was a little bit after three o'clock in the morning. A new day had started. It hadn't started particularly well.

Instead of going back to sleep, I decided to go home. Beverly would need to be fed, and I could use the company. The taxi let me off in front of my house half an hour later. The driver insisted on staying to see me get inside, possibly because I'd tipped well before getting out of the vehicle. I didn't mind. It was nice to know that there was someone at my back if I needed it.

Beverly met me at the door, tail wagging wildly from side to side, mouth hanging open in a wide canine grin. She didn't bark. Her previous owner had trained her well before the sleeping sickness had taken him away from her. For the first time, I looked down at my accidental dog and wondered if she missed the man she used to live with. Dogs were loyal. How much time did she spend wondering if he was ever going to come and take her home?

I waved to the taxi before stepping into the house and easing the door closed behind me. If I was quiet, maybe I wouldn't wake anybody else up. They all had things to do in the morning, and I had already e-mailed Will to let him know I wouldn't be in. Nathan was going to need me when he finished his shift and finally allowed himself to think about the reality of what had happened. Devi was gone. Devi wasn't coming back. We both had to deal with that.

Beverly followed me to my room, tail still waving. At least someone was happy about my unexpected return. I sat down on the bed, patting the mattress to encourage her to jump up. Not that it took much encouragement; with Beverly, keeping her *out* of the bed was usually a harder task. She hopped up and sat down next to me, tail wagging harder than ever. It kept wagging as I bent over, put my arms around her neck, and wept silently into her fur.

About five minutes had passed when I heard my father clear his throat. I looked up to find him standing in the doorway of my room. The hallway light was on, turning him into a black outline of a man. Quietly, he asked, "Long night?"

"Dad." I straightened, wiping my eyes. "This isn't what it looks like."

"That's a good thing, since it looks like you told me you were going to be spending the night at your boyfriend's house, and now you're sitting on your bed crying on the dog. That's the sort of thing that makes a father wonder whether he needs to give some lessons on manners to a certain young man."

I shook my head quickly. "No. Nathan didn't do anything wrong. I came home because he had to go to the hospital, and he wasn't sure when he'd be able to make it back. It seemed like a better idea for me to be here."

"Is everything all right?"

The backlighting made it impossible for me to see the expression on my father's face, but he sounded sincerely worried. I sighed, wiping my eyes again, and said, "No. Not really."

"Do you want to talk about it?"

"Maybe." I sniffled.

My father took that as an invitation. He walked into my room and pulled out the desk chair, sitting on the edge. This close, and without the light shining from directly behind him, I could actually see the concern in his eyes. "What happened?"

"We were asleep when Nathan's phone rang and woke us both up. His...his research assistant's wife caught the sleeping sickness. Her name's Devi. The research assistant, I mean, not the wife. Devi brought her to the hospital for treatment, and the EMTs let them stay together because what would be the harm, you know? The sleeping sickness is pretty passive. Only it wasn't passive when Chave caught it. She was attacking people."

"And Devi's wife did the same thing," said my father. It wasn't a question.

I nodded. "She did." I was crying again. I wiped my cheek and said, "She went for Devi. They didn't expect it, and Devi didn't move back in time, and she...and she..." I stopped talking and just cried. It was all I could do. To his credit, my father leaned forward and put his arms around me, holding me until the tears tapered off. When I pulled away, he let me go.

I don't think I'd ever loved him more than I did in that moment.

"Did Devi die?" he asked, very quietly.

I nodded, biting my lip to keep myself from starting to cry again. That was the last thing I wanted to do.

My father sighed. "You know there are things about my work that I'm not allowed to talk about. It's always been that way, since before Joyce was born."

"I know," I whispered.

"No, you don't. Because I forget sometimes you don't have—you don't remember all those years of being told you couldn't ask me about my job. You lost those memories in the accident, and we've all come to terms with the fact that they're not coming back, but sometimes I still catch myself treating you like you ought to know when you can't ask me things. That's why I was so short with you this morning, and I'm sorry."

"You're still not telling me anything."

"I know." He shook his head. "It's difficult, Sal. Heck, even things like this are difficult for me. The Sally Mitchell who grew up in this room would never have let me past the doorway. If she'd been careless enough to get caught crying, she would have locked me right out in the hall when she realized it."

I frowned. Sometimes hearing about the woman I was before the accident made me want to punch myself in the nose. "I'm sorry."

"Don't be. It's not your fault. My oldest daughter was a wild girl from day one, and we never did learn how to see eye to eye on much of anything other than how many times I could ground her." My father shook his head. "As for what you asked yesterday, it's...complicated. Yes, we know some things that aren't being discussed with the public, but we've been able to share most of that information with the medical community. We have reason to believe that some other people know a great deal more and are sharing a great deal less, which, as you can imagine, is making us all just a little bit unhappy."

"You're talking about SymboGen, aren't you?"

He smiled a little. "You're a smart girl. A little naïve sometimes, but that's to be expected with the amount of experience you've got to go by. Yes, I'm talking about SymboGen. They aren't the first corporation to turn public health into a stockholder concern, but they're definitely the one that's causing me the most grief right now. And not just because they saved your life, which makes it politically difficult to cut ties with them."

"But you're the government. Can't you *make* them tell you what you want to know? If people are getting sick, doesn't that mean SymboGen is doing something wrong?"

To my surprise, he shook his head. "There's something called 'burden of proof' that even the government has to respect. Thus far, we haven't been able to prove that SymboGen knows anything, or that the current epidemic is in any way related to them or to their business. SymboGen is a very powerful corporation, and if we overstep too soon, we might find ourselves unable to get any answers out of them at all."

I looked at him blankly. "But you're the *government*," I repeated.

"We're the government, and you know what the most powerful weapon against the government is? Money. SymboGen has lots and lots of money, and they know how to spend it. Their lobbyists are extremely influential, and if we move against them before we are *absolutely sure* we have a case, we could find ourselves in a lot of trouble. I could lose my job. We still wouldn't have any answers. And you..." He stopped, looking uncomfortable.

I might not understand politics, but I understood that expression. "I could find myself needing to choose between SymboGen and my family. But I pretty much have a clean bill of health at this point, don't I? It's been over a year since my last incident..."

"And what happens if you have another one? SymboGen is the only reason you've survived the last two."

"Maybe they're over." Maybe. Or maybe they'd started before my accident. I'd seen the traffic camera footage of the crash: one second, normal girl driving; the next, spasms and a total loss of control. It was terrifying, especially because I couldn't remember it at all. "They've been tapering off."

"Have they? You could have been having attacks for months before your accident. You weren't always open with us... before. You could have been very sick and still decided not to say anything, because you didn't want us to know."

I took a deep breath, but I didn't object. Everything I knew about Sally Mitchell told me that he was right. There was no point in arguing with the truth.

"Apart from that... we still haven't found a medical cause for your attacks." He glanced away. I frowned. He kept talking:

"So there's no reason to believe it won't happen again, and given the amount of damage the first one did—damage we're still finding out about, and that you're still recovering from—we have no way of knowing what the next one would do to you."

"So it's my fault you can't move against SymboGen," I said. The bitterness in my voice surprised even me.

Dad blinked. Then he shook his head, and said, "No. You're a part of the greater whole, but it's not entirely on you."

"I know, but…"

"This morning you asked me whether I knew anything that I wasn't sharing with you. There isn't much. But one of the things I do know is that the behavior of the afflicted is starting to change. They're starting to become aggressive. Your friend…this is the first I've heard of someone actually dying because they'd been attacked by someone who was sick. It may be because she didn't try to step away. We very rarely react defensively to the people we love."

The first person I'd seen with the sleeping sickness had been a little girl, pursued by her mother. "Are we just hoping that no one else who gets sick has anybody around who cares about them?"

My father grimaced. "No. But Sal, we don't know enough to know what's happening. Most of the people who get sick don't turn violent. We don't want people to start turning on their family members because they're frightened—and this is already a terrifying illness. People you know and love seem to disappear before your eyes. It would be irresponsible of us to make that even more frightening."

"So you're just going to say nothing, and let people like Devi keep getting hurt?"

"We're not suppressing any information. I'm sure the news will pick this up and start telling the world very soon, if they haven't done so already. But we're not going to make any official statements until we know more than we know right now."

He stood. "It's a horrible solution. There are no good solutions left."

"Dad—"

My father paused in the process of leaving the room. He looked back over his shoulder at me and said, quietly, "You know, Sal, I'm very glad I've had the chance to know you. You're a good person, and you still surprise me."

I blinked at him, not sure what I could say to that. He took advantage of my brief silence and made his escape. I stared after him. Finally, I turned to Beverly, and asked, "Any thoughts?"

She wagged her tail.

Eventually, I got up and closed my bedroom door, and sometime after that, I managed to fall asleep. Sleep didn't come easily, and once I found it, my dreams were full of darkness. Darkness, and the drums.

I knew I was alone in the house as soon as I opened my eyes. There was a quality to the silence that spoke of emptiness, not stillness. Even Beverly was gone, although that might just mean that she was out in the backyard rather than warming my feet. I rolled over and squinted at the clock. It was almost ten. No wonder I was by myself. Everyone with a more respectable job had long since taken off.

The stillness endured while I rolled out of bed and found my robe. I went padding out into the hall and toward the kitchen. Maybe there would be some leftovers from the previous day's SymboGen-sponsored breakfast. It hadn't poisoned any of us the day before. It wasn't going to poison me now.

The sliding glass door to the backyard was open, and there was a note on the fridge, where I would be sure to see it. It was held in place with a magnet shaped like a slice of watermelon, and was written in my mother's characteristically careful print:

Sal—

Your father told me what happened. I'm so sorry, sweetheart. I hope you managed to get enough sleep, and that you're feeling better today. Please just leave a note if you need to go and be with Nathan today. We'll understand.

Beverly is in the backyard, and I made sure that we left you some of yesterday's goodies for your breakfast. You have to remember to eat. Your implant needs food as much as you do.

Feel better, and call if there's anything that you need.

Love,
Mom

I smiled as I finished puzzling through the note. Then I took it off the fridge, folded it, and placed it in my pocket. It was good to know that I had family on my side, no matter what else might be going on in the world.

Devi had thought she had family on her side, too. My smile faded. I got the remains of the scrambled eggs and sliced fruit from the day before, put them on a plate, and sat down at the breakfast table to eat. I barely tasted anything. I kept thinking of Devi's face when she saw me coming into the office, the way she laughed, the way she always knew exactly what to say ...

The way she talked about her bulldog, Minneapolis, who was probably sitting at home alone and confused, wondering when her people were going to be coming back to get her. The mouthful of eggs I'd been in the process of chewing suddenly tasted like ashes. I forced myself to swallow, putting my fork down on the plate. I was done. I couldn't eat anything else, or I was going to be sick. Even if my implant still needed food, I just couldn't.

Sometimes people who don't want to think about what their implants really are—living, independent organisms that just happen to be genetically tailored to live inside the human body—will let themselves neglect the nutritional needs of their implants, and that can be bad. There are implants specifically designed to need less in the way of caloric support, but they're limited in their distribution to places with bad famines and poor ongoing medical treatment. Low-calorie implants don't do as much, so they're reserved for places that can't support anything else.

I put my plate down on the floor and whistled. The expected black Lab didn't appear. I frowned and called, "Beverly! Food!" She still didn't appear.

That wasn't normal. It was strange to get through a meal without a black shadow appearing at my heels to ask for her share. It was unheard of for her to actually ignore food when it was offered.

"Beverly?" I started toward the back door, tugging my robe a little tighter. It was hard to keep from playing out nightmare scenarios. Like maybe she'd managed to dig a hole under the fence and was running loose somewhere, looking for the way home. But how would she know where home was? Would she run for the house where she used to live, the one where no one was waiting to let her in? I knew my concern for Devi's dog was feeding my fear for my own. That didn't make the fear any less real.

"Beverly!" I stepped onto the back porch, and stopped, frowning.

Beverly was still in the yard. That was a momentary relief. But she was standing next to the side gate, stiff-legged, ears pushed all the way forward, and the hair on her spine was standing up. Her tail was tucked low. She looked like a dog that was getting ready to charge into battle against a much larger enemy, and even though she knew she was going to lose, she was going to do it anyway. It was her duty.

"Beverly, come," I called. She didn't come. It was the first time she'd ever refused a command. I started down the steps to the lawn, still holding my bathrobe tight around my chest. We don't have many dangerous animals in Colma, but rattlesnakes weren't outside the realm of possibility. If Beverly had somehow managed to corner a snake, I wanted to pull her away from there as fast as I could.

As I got closer, I realized that she was growling, a low, deep sound that seemed to start in her paws and work its way all the way up through her body before rumbling past her lips. It was the sort of thing that would have been terrifying if she'd been directing it at me. Since she was directing it at the fence, it was scary in a different way. I sped up, trying to see what was in front of her.

There was nothing there but grass. Whatever she was growling at was on the other side of the fence.

"Beverly?"

She didn't respond. I stepped forward and let go of my robe in order to lean down and take hold of her collar. She kept growling. Whatever she was growling at didn't make a sound.

"Come on, Beverly. Let's go inside." I tugged on her collar. She dug her feet into the soil and held fast, refusing to be moved. I pulled harder. She still didn't budge. It was like I was trying to move a concrete statue instead of a dog—only concrete doesn't usually growl. "Beverly, come on!"

She turned to look at me for the first time since I'd joined her in the backyard. It wasn't a full turn, just enough for her to see me out of one eye. Her expression was strangely pleading, filled with the anxious need of a good dog to protect her person. If she'd been human, I would have interpreted that look as "let me do this, let me have my job." I let go of her collar, stepping away. Beverly's head promptly snapped back into its original position, all her attention fixing on the fence. She never stopped growling.

I wasn't a stupid actress in a horror movie, despite the fact that I had gone running outside in my bathrobe to see what was wrong with the dog; no matter how much I wanted to know what she was growling at, I wasn't going to open the gate and find out. But there were other ways. Feeling suddenly very exposed, I turned and ran for the back door. I didn't shut it—Beverly would need a way back into the house—but I still felt better once there was a wall between me and whatever had my dog so upset.

I wanted to call the police, but I needed a better reason than "something upset my dog." I swallowed hard, and started for the living room. There was a window there that would give me a perfect view of the side yard, and the gate. I'd be able to see whatever it was that Beverly was growling at. I wasn't sure I wanted to. I was absolutely sure that I needed to.

I made my way slowly toward the window, wishing I had a weapon, or any idea how to use one. I would have felt better. There were probably lots of things that could be used as improvised weapons in the kitchen and living room, but I didn't know what would work, and so I didn't reach for anything. I wasn't a fighter. I did, however, have a pane of glass between me and whatever was in the side yard. I held that thought firmly at the front of my mind as I inched around the couch and peered out the window.

Three of my neighbors were standing in the side yard, their hands down at their sides, staring at the fence. I recognized them all, even if I only knew one—Mr. Carson from next door—by name. None of them were moving. One of them, a woman, was wearing a bathrobe a little newer than mine. Her socks were soaked and grass stained. The other woman was wearing one shoe, and her hair looked like it was halfway-combed. I bit my lip. They were just *standing* there.

Then Mr. Carson turned and looked at me.

I let out a little scream and stumbled backward, falling over the couch in my retreat. His eyes were like Chave's had been: totally empty of anything resembling humanity or life. Dead eyes. He looked at me like a man who had crawled out of his own grave.

I didn't stand up once I managed to recover from my fall. Instead, I scrambled backward on all fours, keeping my eyes fixed on the window. If they were moving, I didn't want to know about it, didn't want to see it—and yet somehow, I knew they *were* moving, that Mr. Carson at least was walking toward the window where he'd seen me, and the other two were very likely following him. I didn't know how I knew, but I knew, just like I knew that I was alone.

The slap of Mr. Carson's palms hitting the window was one of the loudest things I'd ever heard. Beverly came racing into the living room, barking madly, and threw herself up onto the couch. Her paws left muddy prints behind them, standing out boldly against the pale tan cushions. She kept barking, her ears flat against her skull, her attention fully focused on the window.

Beverly was inside. That meant that there was no longer anything between the gate and the open back door.

Sheer terror forced me to my feet, and I ran for the back door, not allowing myself to look at the window. At least one of them was there. If all three of them were there, I might be fine. I might—

The woman in the bathrobe was on the back porch. I screamed again and grabbed the handle, yanking on the heavy glass door. There was a moment when I thought that it wasn't going to move. Then it slipped into position on the track, allowing me to pull it shut before the woman reached me. I fumbled with the lock, snapping it into position. Her hands hit the glass, palms first. Then she stopped. Completely. She was still breathing, but there was no other movement; she might as well have been a statue.

A statue with dead, dead eyes.

"Oh God oh God oh God," I gasped. My heart was hammering against my ribs, and the sound of drums was in my ears again. It was almost loud enough to drown out Beverly's barking. I wanted to close the curtain and shut out the sight of the woman's empty stare. I couldn't make myself move. In that moment, it was like my body had decided that it was no longer interested in working in tandem with my brain.

Maybe this was what it felt like for Sherman and the others when the sleeping sickness first caught hold of them. Like they had suddenly become observers in their own lives, completely unable to make their bodies respond to their commands. Maybe this was how it was forever. Maybe they never got to stop watching—

The woman at the back door raised one hand before slapping her palm deliberately back against the glass. I jumped, startled into motion. Her dead gaze never wavered. Beverly was still barking, and the hammering drumbeat of my heart was still thunderous in my ears.

I looked into the woman's dead eyes and knew that whoever she'd been a few hours before, she wasn't that person anymore. There was no experience or identity in her eyes; they weren't just dead, they were *empty*. Everything that made her who she was had been drained away, replaced by some set of instincts I didn't understand. Instincts that had, for whatever reason, drawn her and her companions to my yard.

She slapped the door again, her palm pressing white as a snail's belly against the glass. I took a step backward. Even that small motion felt like a victory. *See*, it said, *you aren't like them. You still move when you want to move. You're still you, and not anything else.* The thought helped me take another step. The woman kept slapping the door, each movement slow and deliberate. I didn't take my eyes off her as I kept backing up, finally reaching the table where I'd left my phone.

Picking it up, I hit the voice recognition switch on the side—

a helpful leftover from the days when I'd been speaking but not yet capable of reliably reading the controls on my own phone— and said, "Dial Dr. Steven Banks."

The words surprised me. I'd been intending to call the police right up until I spoke. At the same time, calling Dr. Banks made perfect sense. If SymboGen knew things about the sleeping sickness that they weren't sharing, maybe they'd also know how to make the people around my house go away. The police wouldn't have that information. I didn't want anybody getting hurt.

"Dialing," said the phone politely, switching itself to speaker in response to my command. The sound of ringing followed.

A man I didn't know picked up the line, saying, "Dr. Banks's office. Dr. Banks is in a meeting right now, may I take a message?"

"No, you can transfer me to him," I said. "This is Sally Mitchell. It's an emergency, and even if you're new, you still have a card with instructions telling you what to do if I call. Please. Put me through to Dr. Banks." It wasn't the politest greeting ever. I didn't feel like I had time for much politeness. Not with the dead-eyed woman pawing at my back door and staring at me like I was the answer to a question she was no longer fully capable of asking.

"O-of course, Miss Mitchell," stammered the man on my phone, sounding stunned. "I'll put you right through."

"Thank you," I said distractedly. I'm not sure he heard me. The phone clicked, and the sound of his breathing was replaced by the sweet acoustic guitar hold music of the SymboGen communications system.

I waited, none too patiently, and listened more to Beverly barking than to the music. As long as she was still barking, the man was still outside. Hopefully the second woman was there with him, and not exploring some other avenue into the house. I shivered a bit, despite the fact that it was a perfectly warm day. If she got inside, I didn't know what I would do.

The phone clicked. "Sally?" said Dr. Banks. He sounded concerned but not panicked. If anything, there was a note of relief in his voice, like he'd been waiting for the day I would call him voluntarily for a very long time. "What's wrong? You gave Jeff a bit of a scare."

"I'm having a bit of a scare myself right now, Dr. Banks," I retorted. "I'm alone in my house with my dog, and three people with that sleepwalking sickness are here. One of them is at my back door. She keeps hitting the glass." It seemed like such a small thing when I said it out loud like that, but it was impossible for me to properly articulate how horrible every little smacking sound was. Her palm was starting to look more red than white when she hit the door, like the repeated impacts were irritating the skin. If it hurt her at all, she didn't show it. Her expression remained exactly the same, as blank as it had been the moment she appeared on the porch.

"Sally, you need to get out of there." Now Dr. Banks sounded like he was on the verge of panic. "Is there any way for you to get out of the house?"

"I'm in my bathrobe, I'm unarmed, and there are *three* of them." I stressed the number this time, like that might somehow make him understand how bad the situation was. "I know one is in the side yard and one is in the back. I don't know where the third one is. So no, I can't get out of the house, unless you're absolutely sure they're not going to attack me the way Chave did. I don't have a bunch of security guards here to save me."

Dr. Banks took a deep breath. "Are the doors locked?"

"Yes."

"I'm going to send a security team. If you think there's any chance the people outside your house are going to get in, I need you to go and lock yourself in the bathroom. My men can get inside even if you're not there to open the doors for them. I'll pay for any damages. Do you understand?"

"Yes, Dr. Banks. I understand." My parents would be pissed

if they came home and SymboGen had kicked the front door in, but I assumed they'd be even angrier if they came home and found me dead in the kitchen.

"Stay safe, Sally." The line went dead. I lowered my phone, slipping it into the pocket of my bathrobe, where I wouldn't lose it. The woman from down the block was still methodically slapping the glass door. Beverly was still barking. As long as I focused on those two things—those pieces of proof that I was still safely inside and the monsters were still outside—I was okay.

I was okay.

I was...

I wasn't okay. I found myself staring at the woman on the other side of the glass door, searching her eyes for some trace of the woman I'd seen walking down the sidewalk less than a week before, laughing over her shoulder, engaged with her own life. That woman wasn't there. No one was there. I was looking at a corpse that just happened to be somehow up and walking around, and if I didn't understand how that was possible, that was just because there were so many things I didn't know.

I kept staring into her eyes, almost afraid to move, and waited for the sound of someone coming to rescue me.

Time stretched and slipped away, becoming something defined by three sounds: Beverly's barking, the slap of skin against glass, and the drumbeat hammering of my own heart. I didn't move. Beverly was starting to sound hoarse, but she wasn't letting that stop her. As long as Mr. Carson was at the window, she was going to keep on barking at him. I wondered how much she understood about the sleeping sickness. What sort of scent did the infected give off, if a dog could detect it at a distance? She'd known when her original owner first started getting sick. She'd known when Mr. Carson and the others came up to the fence. They had to smell sick somehow.

I suddenly flashed on Marya talking about Tumbleweeds, her store cat, and how he'd been standoffish with the customers for the first time in his pampered life. What was it she'd said? "He even hissed at a poor woman yesterday." I had to wonder whether that poor woman had joined the ranks of the sleepwalkers shortly after being rejected by the normally good-natured feline. If animals could detect the early signs of the infection, they might be the best way of avoiding it.

Assuming that all animals could detect the early signs of the infection, whatever those signs were. Assuming that the infection was passed person to person, and that it *could* be avoided. Assuming a whole lot of things, most of which probably weren't safe to assume, not with the limited information available to me.

I was still staring at the woman when Beverly stopped barking and started to growl. I whipped around before I fully realized that I was going to move. The slapping against the glass behind me got more insistent, but it was competing with a somewhat more pressing sound: someone was knocking on the front door.

"Miss Mitchell?" shouted an unfamiliar male voice. "Are you all right? If you are unable to come to the door, we will enter to confirm your condition. We will be making entry on the count of ten. One..."

I took a deep breath and walked toward the door, fighting the urge to run. "I'm here," I called, once I was close enough that I was sure they'd be able to hear me. I stole a glance at Beverly. She was still standing on the couch, legs locked into rigid lines. Mr. Carson wasn't outside the window anymore. Instead, three men in SymboGen security uniforms were standing there, each of them holding a shock baton. The head of a fourth man was just barely visible above the window frame.

Beverly turned toward the sound of my voice, and her growling stopped, for a moment. Then she started growling again as she jumped off the couch and ran to stand guard over the back door. The couch cushions were irreparably stained with mud and grass. Somehow, I didn't think Mom was going to be all that upset, considering what Beverly had been defending me from. Even if I still wasn't sure exactly what that was.

"Miss Mitchell, is it safe for you to open the door? If, for some reason, it is not safe, we will make our own way inside."

Translation: they would knock down the door. "Just a second," I said, and began undoing the locks.

I opened the door to find a man in full SymboGen security gear standing on the porch, with two more guards behind him. There were three large black vans parked in front of the house, their rear doors standing open.

"Miss Mitchell," said the man. He nodded his head respectfully, his eyes skittering away from my face as he began to scan the house behind me. Beverly's barking caught his attention. "Is your dog agitated by the intruders?"

"There's a woman on the back porch," I said. "Beverly's barking at her. There were two more—"

"We have already restrained them," said the man. He looked over his shoulder, making a series of complex gestures with his right hand. The two men nodded and went trotting away, heading for the side of the house. "The third intruder will be removed shortly. May I enter?"

Feeling a little foolish standing there in my bathrobe and bare feet, I nodded and stepped to the side. "Please. I don't think they managed to get inside at all, but I'll feel a lot more secure once I'm sure."

"That's why we're here, Miss Mitchell," said the man, and stepped past me, into the house. "May my men enter? I will remain with you while they secure the property."

"Okay." I stepped farther to the side, making sure there was a clear path into the house. Beverly was still barking. I slipped my hands into the pockets of my robe and just stood there, feeling awkward and exposed.

A second man in SymboGen security gear appeared, nodded to me, and walked past me into the house. I stayed where I was, swaying slightly on my feet.

The sound of the glass door sliding open was barely audible under the sound of Beverly's maddened barking. The sound of the electric prod hitting the woman on the other side was much easier to hear. I closed my eyes, trying to ignore the way the sound made my stomach turn over. I couldn't help remembering Chave, and how quickly she'd gone from a person to a target. I didn't know the woman in my backyard nearly that well.

Beverly stopped barking. For a moment, there was only silence. The sound of footsteps alerted me to the return of the second man to have entered the house. I opened my eyes, turning to face him.

"The intruder from your yard is being removed now," he said calmly. His baton was back at his belt. That made me feel a little better.

"Hold this position," said the first man. To me, he said, "Please wait here while I check your doors and windows."

"I'm not going anywhere," I murmured. I might as well not have said anything. He was already gone, walking deeper into the house with his shoulders locked in an almost military line. Beverly trotted over to sit down beside me, pressing her shoulders against my leg. I bent enough to stroke her ears. "Good dog, Beverly. You're a good dog."

She looked up at me with worshipful brown eyes, her tail thumping once against the floor. In her world, everything was right. She had protected her human from the bad things outside, and now she was being called a good dog and having her ears petted. I wished it could be that simple for me.

Two more men from SymboGen appeared on the porch, flanking the second man. One of them saluted me. "Miss Mitchell," he said.

I blinked at him, not sure how I was supposed to respond to the salute. I settled on a weak wave. "Hello," I said. "Can I get you anything? Um. And also thank you for coming. I didn't want to call the police, I was afraid someone would get hurt." Someone *had* gotten hurt because I called SymboGen. Those electric batons didn't just tickle. But if I'd called the police, I might have been spreading an infection I still didn't understand. I couldn't do that.

"We're just doing our jobs, ma'am," said one of the two men.

"I know. I still appreciate it." Beverly was looking curiously at the two, her ears pricked forward, but she wasn't growling. I took that as a good sign that they weren't getting ready to freak out and try to strangle me. "I really didn't want to spend the whole day locked inside my house, panicking."

"Speaking of which, your house is clear," said the man I took as the leader, walking back down the hall to the front room. "They don't appear to have penetrated the security."

A dizzying wave of relief washed over me. "Oh, good. Thank you for checking."

"Miss Mitchell, Dr. Banks would very much appreciate it if you would accompany us back to SymboGen, so that he can see for himself that you're all right." The man's expression didn't waver. In its own way, it was as dead as the faces on the people who'd been in my yard. "We would be happy to wait while you got ready, and a space has been kept open for you in the van."

The relief faded, followed by the familiar dread that mention of visiting SymboGen always engendered. This time, it had a darker edge. If I went with them now, how did I know that I would ever be coming back here? No one would know where I was. I could call and leave a message, but that wasn't enough.

"No, thank you," I said, through lips that felt suddenly numb and leaden. "I'm supposed to be meeting my boyfriend for lunch, and the roundtrip from SymboGen to here would leave only a few minutes for me to talk with Dr. Banks. It would be silly. But if he wants me to come in later this week..."

"Miss Mitchell, it may not be safe for you to remain here alone."

"I'm not alone. I have Beverly." I stooped enough to put my hand on the dog's head. She stayed where she was, her attention going to the man who was trying to convince me to go with them. "I would never have known that there was potential danger outside if it weren't for her. She's an excellent guard dog."

A flicker of displeasure lit in the man's eyes. "Even so, Dr. Banks won't like us leaving you here alone."

"I'm sorry, but I'm *not* going with you," I said, unable to keep the edge of anxiety out of my tone. "I called because I needed help. Maybe that gives Dr. Banks the right to ask me to come and see him, but it doesn't mean he gets to order me. I don't work for him. I am not a part of SymboGen."

"Miss Mitchell—"

"I'd like you to leave now, please. I need to put some clothes on." Beverly, picking up on my tension, stood. I straightened, keeping my hand resting atop her head. "Please," I repeated.

The man sighed. "All right. But please, if there is any further trouble, don't hesitate to call. Dr. Banks worries for your safety."

"I won't. Hesitate, I mean. I'll call," I said. I stayed where I was, trying to take some comfort from the weight of Beverly pressed against my leg, and watched as the man from Symbo-Gen waved the others off the porch. He walked after them. Once he was outside, I stepped forward and closed the door.

I let my hand rest on the doorknob, closing my eyes, and just breathed. No scary dead-eyed people in the yard. No Symbo-

Gen security on the lawn. It was just me and my dog, my good, good dog, who deserved an entire steak for the way she'd come to my defense. I would put on some clothes, call Nathan, and—

The doorbell rang. I recoiled from the door, not opening my eyes until I was well clear of the wood. It wasn't intentional; I just reacted. Beverly barked once, but it was an inquisitive sound, not a panicked one. Whatever was on the porch, it didn't upset her.

I pressed a hand to my chest, trying to slow the hammering of my heart, and called, "Hello?"

There was no response. The doorbell didn't ring again. I cautiously approached the door, finally standing on tiptoe to peer through the peephole. There was no one there. Feeling like this was the second stupid thing I'd done in the short time that I'd been out of bed, I dropped back to the flats of my feet and opened the front door. The peephole hadn't lied; there was no one there.

There was, however, a plain white envelope tucked halfway under the edge of the welcome mat, where the wind couldn't take it away. I held my bathrobe closed with one hand as I bent to pull the envelope free, and then backed up, nudging Beverly out of the way. Once the door was closed and locked, I turned the envelope over in my hands, looking for some sign to identify who'd left it. There was nothing.

"Beverly, if this explodes, I want you to drag my body to safety," I said. She looked up at me and wagged her tail. "Good dog," I said. Beverly sat down.

I opened the envelope.

Inside was an index card printed in an oddly uneven font that smudged when my thumb touched it. The letters were faintly indented, and I realized it had been composed on a typewriter—something I'd only seen in the hospital records department, where some very specific types of paperwork had to be written on carbon paper. It was just one line of text:

The broken doors are open; come and enter and be
home.

Underneath was a street address in the city of Clayton, about an hour's drive from San Francisco. I looked at it without saying a word for several minutes, until the text began to twist and slip away from me. That was my cue. I tucked the paper into the pocket of my bathrobe, pulling my phone out as I turned to walk toward my bedroom.

"Dial Nathan," I said.

It was time to follow the map, whether or not it was going to get us lost.

I had to sacrifice a lot to get to where I ended up. As with so many other things in my life, while I may have regrets, I am not sorry. I made my choices. I knew what they had the potential to cost me. Sometimes I wonder what would have happened if I'd made other decisions, if I'd looked at certain possibilities and said "this is not worth the price." I'm only human, after all. I'm allowed to have doubts every once in a while.

I will say this, without reservations: the choices I made meant that when the time came for Steven Banks to throw someone under the bus, there was no one else getting dragged along with me. I'm the one whose name went to the FDA when they questioned our research protocols. I'm the one who gets blamed for every irregularity in the research process. But because I made the choices I did, I had no weak spots for them to exploit. I was armor-clad. I got away.

I have regrets. I would have to be a monster not to. But I am not sorry.

—FROM *CAN OF WORMS: THE AUTOBIOGRAPHY OF SHANTI CALE, PHD.* AS YET UNPUBLISHED.

I wondered when you were going to reach the falling-out questions. It always seems to wind up here, like this is the true north of every interview's course. All right, here it is:

Shanti Cale and I parted ways over ethical differences. She was responsible for certain early development phases of the Intestinal Bodyguard™, and she made the decision to cut certain corners that could have resulted in some very bad things happening. Luckily, we were able to catch and solve those issues before they ever made it out of the lab. That was still the beginning of the end for me and Shanti, as a partnership, and as friends. I couldn't trust her after that. I really view that as the greatest tragedy of my success. Richard's resignation was heartbreaking, but he'd been having emotional problems for years. We all saw the writing on that wall. Shanti...

I loved her very much, as a friend and as a colleague. I never really believed she'd betray me. I still can't understand how I could have been so wrong.

—FROM "KING OF THE WORMS," AN INTERVIEW WITH
DR. STEVEN BANKS, CO-FOUNDER OF SYMBOGEN. ORIGINALLY
PUBLISHED IN *ROLLING STONE*, FEBRUARY 2027.

Chapter 11
AUGUST 2027

I was dressed and ready to go when Nathan pulled up in front of the house. Beverly's dish was full, and there was a note on the refrigerator to keep my parents from getting worried if they got home before I did. I didn't say anything about Mr. Carson and the others, or about the visit from SymboGen security. I felt funny about that, but if I started going into details, I'd wind up writing everything down, and there wasn't time. I could explain when we were all together again.

Nathan honked the horn. When I'd called to ask him if we could go, I'd told him not to bother getting out of the car. The sound still made me jump a little, my stomach squeezing like a fist. Were we making the right decision? Should we really be running around with people who used quotes from obscure children's books in casual conversation, and played cloak-and-dagger games for no good reason?

Did we have a choice?

Nathan honked again. No, we didn't have a choice. Devi was dead. If we wanted answers, we'd have to take them wherever we could find them.

I locked the door behind me as I left the house, slinging my messenger bag over my shoulder one-handed. I was dressed for a clandestine meeting, in jeans, a dark blue hoodie, and running shoes—in case we found a reason to run—with my hair pulled into a ponytail.

Nathan looked over as I practically threw myself into the passenger seat. He blinked. "Sal? Are you okay?"

"Not really," I said. "I'll explain on the drive."

"Okay." Nathan reached for the GPS. "What's the address?"

I read it off for the system. "There's also another quote that sounds like it's from that book you were talking about."

"Don't Go Out Alone?"

"Yeah, that one." I held up the card, and recited more than read, " 'The broken doors are open. Come and enter and be home.' "

Nathan started the car. He didn't say a word as he pulled out of the driveway. I slowly lowered the card, blinking at him. He wasn't looking at me; he was staring at the windshield, where the glowing red printout from the GPS displayed at eye level.

I frowned, not sure what I was supposed to say, or what—if anything—I'd done to upset him. I wasn't the one who wrote the note. I wasn't the one quoting the book.

Finally, Nathan sighed, and said, " 'Some lies better left untold; some dreams better left unsold. The broken doors are open. Come and enter, and be home. My darling girl, be careful now, and don't go out alone.' " He glanced my way. "It's from the middle of the book, where the boy and girl who've gone out alone together—don't ask me how that works, I was a kid, I believed it completely—have reached the broken doors, and everything is about to get bad. It's sort of a welcome. And it's sort of a warning."

"I'm a little disturbed that our secret source for secret things is communicating with us via quotes from a children's book that no one but you has ever heard of," I said. "It's weird and I don't like it."

"I really expected you to go with 'secret source for secret secrets' there, and I don't like it either, but I don't see what choice we have," said Nathan. "She's the only person who seems to know what's going on."

"Yeah." I studied him sidelong. The dark circles under his eyes didn't surprise me, but I didn't like them, either. Not sure what else to say, I asked, "Is someone taking care of Minneapolis? I was worried about her this morning."

"I've contacted Devi's family, since they're local. They're considering their options." The bitter way he said that made it plain he didn't expect them to come for Devi and Katherine's bulldog. "In the meantime, Minnie is with me. My building manager says she can stay for a little while, given the circumstances, even though I'm not supposed to have pets."

"I think…I think that's a good thing. I'll feel safer knowing you have a dog with you," I said slowly. "Given the circumstances and all."

Nathan glanced at me again. "Sal? What's wrong?"

I took a deep breath. "Something happened with Beverly this morning," I said before I began, haltingly, to explain the events that had started with Beverly standing stiff-legged and growling in the backyard. It took longer than I expected. Even with me refusing to leave anything out, Nathan kept asking me questions, making me back up, and finding the things I wasn't saying. By the time I finished, I was trembling all over, a deep, bone-weary shake that seemed to start somewhere deep inside my chest and radiate from there. I stopped talking. I couldn't find anything else inside myself to say.

Nathan said it for me. "You did the right thing," he said. "I don't know that I would have had the presence of mind to call

SymboGen, but after what happened last night with Devi...I wouldn't want to involve the police with three of them when they were in their mobile state."

There was no question as to who he meant by "them." I shuddered, the memory of the woman on the back porch rising, uninvited, behind my eyes. "It was freaky. I didn't know what else to do."

"Like I said, you did the right thing. SymboGen is more equipped to deal with this sort of situation than anybody else. I just wish I knew what made them surround your house like that. I haven't heard anything about that behavior. It makes me a little nervous, to be honest. I don't want you to get hurt."

"I don't want me to get hurt either, so I think we're in agreement." I placed a hand on his arm. "It's going to be okay. This lady will have the answers that we're looking for, and then you'll know how to start treating the sick people, and all of this will go away." I regretted the words as soon as they were out of my mouth. We might find out what SymboGen was hiding about the sleeping sickness; we might even find a way to treat the people who were afflicted. But no answers were going to bring Devi back. My own example notwithstanding, the dead were beyond the reach of modern medical science.

Nathan nodded grimly. "Let's hope you're right," he said, and kept driving.

The GPS led us off the freeway and into a rundown section of a city called Concord. From there, we drove through increasingly worn-looking streets toward our final destination. This was the heart of the Bay Area's extended suburban sprawl, communities that grew up around San Francisco and the ports during the state's big boom period—a period that once seemed like it was going to last forever, according to a documentary I once watched on California's history. California had the natural resources, it had the space, and it had the drive to keep its population growing until they ran out of room. I guess they never expected to run out of cheap gas and good weather while they still had space to cram in another housing development.

Most of California's suburban areas had gone one of two ways: they had returned to their agrarian roots, or they had begun dying a slow death through attrition and neglect. Most of the farmland around Clayton was still owned by the United States military, and so they'd gone for option number two. We drove almost three miles and didn't pass more than a dozen cars. One old man pushed a shopping cart full of his worldly possessions along the sidewalk in front of a deserted Kmart with big yellow CLOSED banners in the windows. Everything else was still.

"We're almost there," said Nathan. He turned off the main road into a small shopping center where a thrift store clung to life next to a feed store as closed as the Kmart. He drove past them both, gritting his teeth as the broken pavement of the parking lot caused the car to shudder and bounce.

An abandoned bowling alley filled the back third of the lot. Nathan circled around behind it, parking out of sight of the street. I blinked at him. He shrugged and turned off the engine.

"I don't think we necessarily want to attract more attention than we will just by being here, do you?" he asked.

"No," I admitted. Unfastening my belt, I slung my bag back over my shoulder and got out of the car.

The air was hotter and drier in Clayton than it had been in San Francisco. I glanced at my piece of paper and then at the address painted on the back door of the old bowling alley, reassuring myself that we were really in the right place. We were. Nathan walked next to me as we approached the building, which gave no signs of being occupied. Leaves on the nearby, half-dead trees rustled in the wind. Everything else was still. We stopped just short of the bowling alley door.

"Should we knock?" I asked.

"I don't see how else we're going to get inside," he said.

I swallowed hard, nodding. Then I stepped forward and rapped my knuckles lightly against the wood. I stepped back again, and we waited for someone to come to the door. And waited. And waited.

When almost ten minutes had gone by, Nathan stepped forward. He knocked much more authoritatively, almost pounding on the door. Still, no one came to answer it. When another ten minutes had gone by, he turned to me, frowning. "I think someone's playing with us."

"I think you may be right," I admitted. "We should get going."

"Agreed," he said. Both of us turned then, to face the car, and stopped when we saw the woman sitting on the hood.

She was tiny enough that for a moment I thought she was a kid, but her figure and the casual straightness of her posture gave lie to that. Her hair was short, blonde, and streaked with strawberry pink. She was wearing denim overalls, combat boots, and nothing else, unless you wanted to count the knots of ribbons she had clipped in her hair. She was beaming at the two of us like we'd won a prize.

"Hi!" she said brightly, and slid off the hood. "You must be Sal. Ooo, and that means you must be Nathan. Gosh. I thought you'd be taller. I bet you get that a lot, don't you? That you should be taller. Not you, I mean, Sal, you're just like I figured you'd be, but I've also seen you before, so I guess that's cheating. I'm Tansy. Did you know that SymboGen totally tried to follow you here? Because they totally tried to follow you here, even though you're not supposed to have a following detail anymore. Don't worry, they lost your GPS signal when you crossed Treat Boulevard, but you should be careful about that sort of thing if you're going to be sneaking around behind their backs, which you so are at this point. Congratulations!"

She stopped talking, finally appearing to realize that she wasn't pausing long enough to let either of us get a word in edgewise. "Oh, and also, you know. Hi. Welcome, and all that stuff."

"Who *are* you?" asked Nathan.

Tansy smiled indulgently. "I just told you, silly. You should really try to keep up if you want to come out of this with all your sane bits still in the order they started out in. What's the password?"

"We don't have a password," I said. "We came here because—"

"Oh, I know why you came here, and I know what you want to learn while you're here, but what I need to know is whether you know what the password is, because that's what starts the next phase, which is…hang on a second, I'm not good at this part." Tansy paused, dipping a hand into her pocket and producing her phone. She checked the screen before beaming at the two of us. "The next phase is me letting you inside."

"And if we don't know the password…?" I said slowly.

"If you don't know the password, that means I get to decide what to do with you. I don't know what that would be, exactly, but I'm pretty sure it would hurt. Did you know that nerves are like, really densely packed on certain parts of the body?" Tansy's eyes grew wide and earnest as she spoke. Her irises were two different colors, one brown, one a slightly unnerving shade of blue. "It's cool, because it means it takes longer for pain to stop happening if you focus there. Other places go numb way, way too quickly. Like the fleshy part of your thumb. You'd think that was a great place to target, given how meaty it is, but you stop feeling things there way too fast."

"Uh," I said.

"'The broken doors are open—come and enter, and be home,'" said Nathan, spitting the words out quickly.

Tansy beamed. "My darling girl, be careful now!" she said. It didn't sound like she was quoting. It sounded more like a message meant directly for us. "And don't go out alone. You remembered the password!"

"You provided excellent incentive," said Nathan.

"You know, that's what Doctor C says? She says I'm the *best* incentive." She bounded forward, sweeping me into a hug before I had a chance to react. "It's so nice to finally meet you! I've been hoping for this for ever and ever and ever, but Doctor C kept saying I had to wait, and so I waited, but it was *hard*." She pushed me out to arm's length, bicolored eyes wide and grave. "It was *so* hard. Don't make me do that again, okay, Sal?"

"Um," I said. Being restrained by people who clearly weren't operating under my definition of "sane and balanced" was a new experience for me. Something told me that pulling away still wouldn't be a good idea. "I'll do my best, but I didn't know I was making you wait this time. I'm sorry."

"It's okay! I forgive you!" She pulled me into a second, shorter hug. This time, when she let go, she let go completely, and went skipping toward the bowling alley. She produced a key from the pocket of her overalls and unlocked the door before turning to beckon us forward. "Well? Come on! We're not getting any younger out here!"

"I suppose the broken doors really are open now," Nathan said, looking unsettled.

I took his hand. "You're not going alone," I said.

Together, we followed Tansy into the bowling alley.

She closed the door behind us.

Inside the bowling alley turned out to be a dark, windowless antechamber. Once the door was closed, there was no light of any kind. Nathan squeezed my fingers, hard. I had to wonder whether he, like me, was worried about the fact that we were shut in with a woman who had a questionable grip on reality and had already threatened to hurt us both if we didn't say what she wanted to hear. More and more, this whole expedition was feeling like a bad idea.

"Don't move," said Tansy. "The floor's a little rotten in here, and you wouldn't want to wind up in the basement. There are black widows down there."

"This day just gets more and more delightful," muttered Nathan.

"Doesn't it just?" said Tansy. There were footsteps to my right, followed by a click. The overhead lights came on, shining dully through a thick layer of dust. Tansy was standing on the far side of the room, and beaming brighter than the lights. "Do you like it? Helps your eyes adjust, since we don't want to flash-blind anybody, and leaving the dirt on means that anybody who managed to break in wouldn't realize there was anyone in here. Until they hit one of the rotten patches on the floor and went to the basement to visit the spiders, and then I bet they wouldn't care that there was anyone in here. The spiders can be *really* distracting when they want to be. Anyway, come on! Doctor C told me to bring you to her as soon as you got here." She opened another door, this one marked EMPLOYEES ONLY, and started through.

We didn't have any option but to follow her. I clung hard to Nathan's hand as we walked, refusing to let on how disturbed I was by the whole situation. This was...I didn't even know what this was. I just hoped that we were going to survive it.

The second door led to a hallway where the lights were already on, and where things were considerably less grimy than in the first room. Things improved as we walked, until we reached a clear plastic sheet hung to block all forward motion. Tansy turned to face us again, and asked, in a perfectly reasonable tone of voice, "Has either of you been sick in the last week? Any colds, viruses, unusual medical conditions, or fungal infections?"

"No," I said.

"No," said Nathan.

"Okay, that's cool. Any injuries or other physical conditions such as asthma, migraines, insomnia…?"

"I get headaches sometimes," I said.

"I'm myopic, but as long as you don't take my glasses away, I'm fine," said Nathan.

"That's even cooler," said Tansy. She tugged the sheet of plastic aside, revealing another sheet of plastic—this one cut into thick strips—hanging behind it. It was like looking into a human-sized car wash. "Don't worry. I'll be right behind you."

That was actually *why* I was worried, but I was smart enough—barely—not to say that out loud. Instead, I kept my grip on Nathan's hand as we walked through the sheets of hanging plastic. There were five of them, each cut in the same thick strips. By the time we were through the last one, I was starting to feel like we'd walked into a strange kind of fun-house. One that wasn't actually any fun.

There was another door past the plastic. Someone had written on it, in Sharpie, BROKEN. I reached out and tried the knob. It was unlocked. Taking that as an invitation, I pushed the door open, and together, Nathan and I stepped through. Then we stopped. It was the only response that made any sense, given what was in front of us. Not that anything else was worrying about making sense anymore.

We were standing in what had clearly once been the main room of the bowling alley. The bowling lanes were still marked off, bracketed by gutters that hadn't seen a ball since before my accident. There was a structure at the back of the room that had probably been a snack bar originally, and a big mirrored ball, of all things, hung from the ceiling. That was where the original fixtures ended. I wasn't hugely familiar with bowling alleys, but I didn't need to be to know that the lab workstations were new, as were the massive plasma monitors that had replaced the screens where bowling scores used to be displayed. The lights were brighter here, almost industrial in quality. Shelves of books and scientific supplies lined the walls, all of them packed to capacity and occasionally beyond.

And there were people. I don't know what I'd been expecting, but it wasn't *people*, at least two dozen of them, all wearing lab coats over casual shirts and jeans, moving between the lab stations with the casual intensity I normally associated with the underground levels of SymboGen. A few of them took note of us, glancing briefly our way before appearing to dismiss us completely. It was more than a little bit unnerving.

Tansy squeezed through the door behind us. She stepped into the room so that she could spread her arms wide, and proclaimed, gleefully, "Ta-da! Welcome to the lab!" She dropped her arms. "I keep telling Doctor C we should get a fancy name for it, but she says no, that's silly, we don't need a fancy name if no one's supposed to know we're here. La-ame. Anyway, it was super-nice to meet you both, and I'm sure I'll be seeing you really soon." She turned and wandered off into the bowling alley, weaving her way between the people in the lab coats.

Nathan and I stayed where we were, both of us at a loss for what to do next. I looked around the room, trying to find someone who looked like they were in charge. We'd been called here. That meant somebody—probably "Doctor C," whoever that was—had to be waiting for us.

A curvaceous blonde woman in a wheelchair was heading our way, wheeling herself deftly across the polished floor. She wore a lab coat over a blue blouse and a pair of gray slacks. Fingerless black leather gloves protected her hands. She was smiling, but it looked wary somehow, like she wasn't sure what was going to happen next. She stopped herself a few feet away from us.

Nathan's hand dropped away from mine as his fingers unlocked. I smiled nervously at the woman.

"Hello," I said. "I'm Sal Mitchell, and this is Dr. Nathan Kim? We're supposed to be meeting someone here. Tansy already verified the password. Please don't let her have us."

"Tansy can be a little overly enthusiastic about the wrong things sometimes; I'm sorry about that," said the woman. I recognized her voice from the phone. This was the person we had come to meet. She was still smiling, and she wasn't looking at me. I blinked, following her gaze to Nathan. He was staring at her. He wasn't saying a word. He was just staring.

"Um," I said.

"I would have come out to meet you myself, but I avoid open spaces these days," said the woman. "It's dangerous for me to go places where I might be photographed. You've been scanned three times since you entered the building; I know that you're clean. If you weren't, you would never have made it this far. I'll give you a memory stick to attach to your GPS when you leave here. It will create a set of false routes and locations for you, so that it looks like you went to a few perfectly reasonable places today. I do appreciate your coming. I know you've both had a difficult morning."

"Who *are* you?" I said.

The woman smiled, and didn't say anything.

But Nathan did. "Hi, Mom," he said. "Aren't you supposed to be dead right now?"

"It turns out 'dead' can be a state of mind as much as it is a state of being," said the woman in the wheelchair, closing the door to her office. It was a proper office, too, not a makeshift space like the others we had passed in the bowling alley. This had been the bowling alley manager's space, back when there was a bowling alley to manage. Now it was hers. "Can I get the two of you anything?"

"I'd like some answers, if you don't mind," I said. "Who are you? Why did Nathan call you 'Mom'? *Are* you his mother? Where have you been? Why did you contact me?"

"Do you have grape juice?" asked Nathan.

The woman smiled. "Always." She wheeled her way toward the fridge. As she went, she said, "To answer your last question first, Sal, I contacted you because you seemed to want to know what was going on, and I felt it was time to begin trying to tell you. I waited this long because I needed SymboGen to trust you—no, I'm not going to ask you to play spy for me, I have better-trained people who take care of the messy aspects of the business, and frankly, you don't meet my standards. But until they trusted you enough to let you out without a detail trailing you at all times, I couldn't risk trying to reach out. You needed to be curious enough to take steps on your own, and free enough to keep going once you'd taken them. You needed, if it's not too cutesy to say, to go out alone."

"And the rest of it? Your name? Do you have a name? Are you Nathan's mother?"

"I suspected it was you as soon as I saw the note," said Nathan. "I couldn't think of anybody else who would think to use quotes from *Don't Go Out Alone* as a code."

"It worked, didn't it?" She opened the fridge, pulling out a bottle of grape juice. "There are glasses in the cabinet behind you, Nathan." She glanced my way. "We use real glass. None of the dangerous chemical outgassing you can get from reusable plastic, and none of the ethically questionable waste you can get from using disposable."

"Mom," said Nathan. There was a warning note in his tone. "Sal's asking you some pretty sincere questions. Can you maybe answer them?"

"I'm trying to work my way around to it," she said. Then she sighed and turned, wheeling her way back to me. "I'm sorry, Sal. I really am. I've been thinking of this day for so long that I suppose I wasn't ready for the way that it would make me feel. I don't mean to be rude. I just don't have the greatest social skills in the world. I never did, but after spending ten years underground, I've lost a lot of the fine edges I'd managed to develop. Forgive me?"

"If you'll tell me who you are," I said.

She smiled a little. "Ah. The biggest question of all. Well, Sal, when I lived with Nathan and his father, my name was Surrey Kim. I had a PhD in genetic engineering and parasitology, and I worked for a small medical technology firm. We were going to do great things, assuming we could ever get space and funding. There was a man I knew from school. He was very rich. He wanted to get even richer. And he had a dream. It was a big, crazy dream, one that could lead to a way of curing the ill effects of our overpurified environment. He approached me and asked if I was willing to help. It was a fascinating proposal. It was innately flawed, and it was going to make millions for him, and for his company, which he called 'SymboGen.' Maybe billions.

"But there were problems. The plan would require early and aggressive human testing, and there was a good chance we could all go to jail for the rest of our lives if things went wrong. My family needed the money. I needed to do the work. It's hard to explain that in a way that doesn't sound crazy, but it's true— once I heard what he was doing, I *needed* to be part of it. It was all my work, all my theories, wrapped up in one big, beautiful possibility. So I agreed, as long as SymboGen could guarantee my family wouldn't be hurt by my actions." She smiled sadly, glancing toward Nathan, who was pouring himself a glass of grape juice. "Surrey Kim died in a boating accident that same year. Her body was never recovered. I had six months with my family while they got my new identity in order, planted the publications, created the academic credits. I have to give them this much. They knew what they were doing. No one ever questioned my validity."

I stared at her. A blonde woman who worked in parasitology and genetic engineering, talking about working with Symbo-Gen when it was still a small company, who worried about them finding her...there was only one person she could possibly be. "Dr. Cale?" I whispered.

"At the moment, yes." Her smile broadened. "It truly is lovely to meet you, Sal. I've been waiting for a very long time. And yes, I am really Nathan's mother. Can't you see the resemblance?"

I frowned at her. She had wavy blonde hair, blue eyes, and a roundish face, with no hard lines or sharp angles. Nathan, on the other hand, had dark hair and eyes—both inherited from his father—and strong features. They couldn't have looked less alike. And yet, when she turned her head, I could see something of him in the way she held herself, buried in the expectant half-lift of her eyebrow and the curl of her lips.

"Yes," I admitted. "I can see it. But how...?"

"I had been a bit wild in my youth," said Dr. Cale, as calmly as she had offered us something to drink. "I didn't always follow lab protocols, I didn't always check my math before I moved forward, and some people got hurt. I thought that all of that was behind me, but when SymboGen wanted me on board for the *D. symbogenesis* project, I found out my tracks hadn't been covered quite as well as I always assumed."

My eyes widened and I glanced to Nathan, alarmed. How would he be taking this?

With absolute calm, apparently. He was leaning against the counter, sipping his tumbler of grape juice. He smiled a little when he caught my look, a wry twist to his lips. "I knew she wasn't dead," he said. "I even knew she was Shanti Cale, and that she'd disappeared after leaving SymboGen. When she didn't get into contact with either me or Dad, I figured it was because she knew something we didn't."

"I knew it still wasn't safe," said Dr. Cale. "I always wanted to reach out to you, but there wasn't a way to do it without endangering you."

"Aren't you endangering him now?" I asked, looking back to her. "And me? If being around you endangers people, aren't you endangering me?"

"You're part of what made it so dangerous to contact Nathan," said Dr. Cale. "SymboGen was watching you, and that meant I couldn't reach out to him until I knew whether you could be trusted. And before you ask the next question, no. No, Nathan didn't know I was watching you; no, he didn't get involved with you because I asked him to. He did it because he is a man, and you're a very pretty girl. I like you. I've seen a great deal of security footage, and I approve of the way you treat my son."

There was a clank behind me. I turned to see that Nathan had set his tumbler on the counter and was covering his face with his hand. "Mom," he said, sounding embarrassed.

"What? I'm still your mother. I get to pass judgment on your dates. I admit, getting involved with an amnesiac is a little unorthodox, but your father was a teaching assistant in one of my math classes while I was in school, so I suppose being a little unorthodox runs in the family." Dr. Cale's resemblance to Nathan was much more pronounced when she grinned.

"Can we get back to the point, please?" asked Nathan, sounding put-upon.

"Where were we? Oh, yes—SymboGen was blackmailing me to get me to join their big secret project. More precisely, Steven was blackmailing me, and if I'm being entirely honest, he didn't have to blackmail very hard. I loved my husband very much. I loved my son. But they were offering me the chance to do the research I'd been dreaming of for my entire life, and in the end, I wasn't strong enough to refuse. Maybe that makes me a bad person. It certainly made me a bad mother. But I was always the woman who said, 'Yes, I'll go.' I was always the one who went out alone, no matter how many warnings I got. No matter how many people reminded me that I couldn't necessarily go back again."

"Okay," I said slowly. "This is all really interesting, and sort of weird, since we're in an old bowling alley in the middle of nowhere and everything, but what does this have to do with you calling me here? What is it you know that we need to know?"

"'If you ask the questions...'" quoted Dr. Cale, a warning note in her voice.

"We want to know," said Nathan.

She nodded. "All right. If you're sure. Follow me, both of you." She gripped the wheels of her chair, turning herself around before rolling toward the door. We followed Dr. Cale out of the office and back into the makeshift lab filling the bowling alley.

She talked as we made our way across the main room, explaining what the various lab stations were for and what the various lab-coated people were doing there. Some were technicians, working to keep other people's research from collapsing in their absence. Others were doing research of their own, so caught up in their little worlds that they barely noticed us passing. One woman was milking a large brown snake into a jar, cooing sweet nothings at it as she pressed down on the top of its triangular head.

Dr. Cale caught me looking at the snake handler and said, "That's Dr. Hoffman. She's a herpetologist, specializing in reptile parasites. She's been with me for about seven years now. The snake's name is Kyle. He's an Australian coastal taipan. She's been doing some really remarkable things with his venom recently..." She began rambling again, talking about the neurotoxic properties of taipan venom and its effects on various types of tapeworms. I didn't tune her out—I was listening as hard as I could—but it was like the days right after I first woke up in the hospital, when everyone around me was talking, and I couldn't understand a word.

Dr. Cale led us to the far lane, where a light box the length of the wall had been set up, allowing for the display of a variety of X-ray films. She stopped near the middle of the lane. There was nowhere for Nathan and me to sit, so we stood, looking at her expectantly.

"I was, in a very real way, the reason the Intestinal Bodyguard was able to succeed. Steven was smart and ambitious, but he was looking in the wrong direction. The official literature says that he started work on *Diphyllobothrium yonagoensis*, a species of tapeworm that preferentially parasitizes fish."

"But the Intestinal Bodyguard *is* based off...what you just said," I protested. I recognized the name from the lectures I'd been forced to sit through, even if I couldn't pronounce it correctly. "They used a fish tapeworm."

"No, dear," said Dr. Cale, almost gently. "*I* used a fish tapeworm. *They* used *Taenia solium*, the pork tapeworm. I was able to keep very little of their research once I came on board, because they'd been using an inherently dangerous parasite. Not that any parasites are completely safe—the one we eventually went with had its dangers even before we started tinkering with the building blocks of its DNA. I think you'll find that very little about the official history of *D. symbogenesis* is actually true. Most of it is pretty fictions and lies that can't be disproven this late in the game. The Intestinal Bodyguard worked the way that it was supposed to, Steven Banks became a hero, and the rest of the development team became...expendable. We were a liability. Richard was consumed with guilt over what we'd done, and I was considered too likely to talk. By that point, you see, Steven had created this whole backstory for us. We met in college, we were the best of friends, and so on, and so on. So if he did anything to hurt my family, I could discredit him by revealing his lies. It was the nuclear option, for both of us. We quietly agreed that I would fade into the background." She pursed her lips, looking unhappy. "Not that I intended for it to be quite such a long absence, but life does have its way of throwing you little curveballs when you let yourself get too cocky."

"Is this leading into why you're in the wheelchair now?" asked Nathan.

Dr. Cale smiled. "I was wondering if you'd noticed that I was suddenly shorter. Then again, you're a lot taller. Maybe you just thought this was what happened to all mothers as their sons grew up."

"I'm a doctor, Mom," Nathan said. "I understand human anatomy."

"And have I told you yet how proud I am of you?" Dr. Cale rolled herself closer to the wall, pressing a button on the base of the light box. The nearest piece of wall began to glow a steady white, backlighting the four X-ray films displayed there. All four showed a human spine, from different angles—front, back, left side, and right side. I thought it might be the same spine, although I didn't know enough about anatomy to be sure.

In all four images, a white mass obscured the lower part of the spine, just above the pelvis. It looked like someone had taken correction fluid and scribbled on the negative, wiping away large parts of the spine.

Nathan frowned, stepping closer to the light box. "Is this a tumor?" he asked, indicating the white mass.

"Not quite," said Dr. Cale. She sighed. "Human testing was a priority at SymboGen. We weren't supposed to test on ourselves, naturally, and I didn't. I might be fond of cutting corners, but I wasn't a fan of risking my own life when I had volunteers perfectly willing to risk theirs."

"Are you telling me this is a *tapeworm*?"

"Let me get there, Nathan. I know you. If I don't give you the background now, you'll go racing off and never give me the chance to explain. I need to take things at my own pace. Can you let me do that?"

Nathan frowned at her, the light flashing off his glasses obscuring his eyes so completely that I couldn't tell whether or not he was annoyed. I answered for both of us, saying, "We can be patient."

"That remains to be seen." Dr. Cale settled back in her chair, folding her hands in her lap. "The Intestinal Bodyguard went through several generations, with a wide variety of different genetic makeups. The generation that eventually went on the market was less... robust... than some of the early worms had been, and that was good, because those early worms had a tendency to grow more than they were supposed to. Because they grew so fast, they demonstrated the potential dangers of the Intestinal Bodyguard—primarily, that the tapeworm could endanger the host if it reached a certain size. The growth of *D. symbogenesis* was retarded to guarantee that it would reach that size only after more than two years had passed, creating a 'safety margin' where balance could be maintained between parasite and host."

"That's why the two-year replacement requirement," said Nathan. "That never made sense to me. Nature doesn't work on such a tidy schedule."

"Exactly. They don't die after two years. They never did. The antiparasitic drugs take care of the old tapeworm, and a new one is put in place without anyone realizing that there was ever a risk." Dr. Cale shook her head. "If it had ever gotten out, it would have been the end of SymboGen."

"And a lot of people would have been hurt," I said.

Dr. Cale seemed to wave my concerns away, continuing, "Everyone was meant to forget about the early generations, even though the final product was heavily influenced by their design. When Steven sent the word that the IPO was coming, I saw the writing on the wall. Eventually, there'd be so much money in the picture that everyone who had been there in the early stages would be in danger. We'd know too much. Well, I knew I'd need some kind of insurance if I was going to guarantee my safety—and by extension, yours, Nathan. Since I didn't participate in the human testing, I was a suitable host."

The Intestinal Bodyguard was fiercely territorial, and wouldn't tolerate the presence of another worm in the body. Supposedly, this meant that a second tapeworm introduced into the body would just fail to thrive, and would eventually starve to death. According to some of the stories Nathan had told me, the first tapeworm would actually attack and devour the second. I wasn't clear on how that happened, since tapeworms weren't supposed to be that intelligent. I was pretty sure I didn't want to know.

Nathan, on the other hand, did want to know. "What did you do, Mom?" he almost whispered.

"I went back into my lab and got one of the early versions of *D. symbogenesis* out of cold storage. And then I implanted it in myself, so that I could carry it out of the building without anyone the wiser. Most of the employees already had Intestinal Bodyguards by that point, so testing for parasites wouldn't give me away, and I suppose Steven just assumed I knew better than to risk ingesting an early-generation worm. He didn't count on the power of sentiment." Dr. Cale smiled wistfully. "That was my Adam. He was my first, and greatest, creation. You know, Nathan, he had just as much of my genetic material in him as you did? He was virtually your brother."

"I don't know whether I should be flattered or feel sick," said Nathan. He looked like he was leaning toward the second option. I stepped closer to him, trying to lend support through proximity. He smiled at me a little, looking strained, and didn't say anything. There wasn't really anything to say.

"Feel like your mother is a genius, and be glad I was willing to share my genes with you, not just with your brother," said Dr. Cale. She sighed. "I didn't have a choice, Nathan. Steven was going to destroy my work, and he was going to do it so that if things went wrong with the worms, he could claim there'd never been any indication of a potential risk to human health. He was going to pin it all on me, and by extension, he was going to pin it all on you. How long do you think our connection would have stayed secret after I became the person who recklessly endangered the lives of millions?"

"Still," said Nathan. He was staring at the white mass on the X-ray like he could find the outline of the worm in the blur. "It was a big risk."

"And I paid for it." Dr. Cale spoke with absolute calm. "I ingested Adam and left the lab. I had to wait a month for him to grow long enough that we'd be able to extract segments without killing him. We needed to keep him alive, as proof that there had been earlier generations—that *D. symbogenesis* didn't somehow spring fully developed from a test tube and a set of irresponsible testing procedures."

"Didn't you take your antiparasitics after that?" I asked.

Dr. Cale nodded. "I did, because I am not a complete idiot, current evidence aside. Unfortunately for me, we'd never tested Adam's generation inside a human host, and we didn't realize what the results would be."

"There was too much human DNA in the early generations," said Nathan. "The antiparasitics might have made the worm sick, but they couldn't kill it without being increased to a level where they'd kill you, too."

"That's exactly right. Sadly for me, we didn't realize that at the time. I took my pills like a good girl, and I passed enough dead tapeworm segments that I was sure we'd managed to clear Adam entirely out of my digestive system. We had our samples, and that meant that we could re-create the living worm at any time if we needed it to prove what SymboGen had been doing. You have to remember, I developed the Intestinal Bodyguard. It was more my baby than anyone else's, no matter how much Steven may try to rewrite history. I didn't approve of the way he was going about things, but I truly wanted to see *D. symbogenesis* thrive. If people could find a way to coexist peacefully with the worms, everyone would benefit."

"SymboGen more than anyone else," said Nathan. "What *happened*?"

"I'm getting there." For the first time, Dr. Cale's voice was sharp, holding the snap of authority she needed to organize her own underground lab and control this many people. "What happened, Nathan, is that we didn't realize the antiparasitics hadn't worked until I began losing feeling in my legs. It was intermittent at first, just pins and needles. Bit by bit, it turned into a numbness that didn't go away. It could still have been sciatica, brought on by hard living and exacerbated by stress. I thought I was working too hard. I thought I was getting old. I didn't think that the antiparasitics might have driven my stolen tapeworm out of my intestine and into my abdomen. He was very clever in what he did and didn't chew through—instinct is a powerful thing, and he didn't want to kill his host—but when he reached my spine, he didn't have anywhere else to go. He was too large to migrate upward at that point, which is the only reason I'm alive today. So he compressed my spinal cord more and more tightly, until the day he permanently compromised the nerves. I collapsed in the middle of the lab.

"My assistants performed basic medical triage, including the X-ray films I've posted on the light box for you to study. It was immediately clear that we would need to operate. Adam and I had reached the point at which we could no longer share one body, and while I hated to do it, I couldn't cede the ground to him. I had too much work to do. They removed eight and a half pounds of worm mass from my pelvis and abdomen. Unfortunately, the nerve damage was not so easily undone. Barring medical advances that I probably won't live to see, I'm staying in this chair." Dr. Cale shrugged. "I suppose I'm not the first person to see hubris as an object lesson, but I've worked very hard to make up for it since then."

"Mom," said Nathan, sadly. "Oh, Mom."

"Don't feel sorry for me, now. It was for science, and as long as something is for science, it's worth doing. It's just not necessarily worth repeating." Dr. Cale's smile was sudden, and very bright. "Now that we have all that out of the way, there's someone that I very much want you to meet. You needed to understand what had happened right after I left SymboGen before this would make sense to you. All right?"

"Sure," I said, uncertainly. "This is going to tie back into the sleeping sickness soon, isn't it?"

"Oh, my dear Sal, the broken doors are open, and we can't close them on our own. Believe me; everything I am telling you ties back into the sleeping sickness." Dr. Cale looked past us, into the gloom near the back wall. "It's all right; you can come out now, dear. They're ready for you."

Tansy appeared, leading a young, gangly-limbed man by the hand. He was wearing a lab coat, like everyone else we'd seen since arriving inside the bowling alley. The T-shirt he had on under the lab coat advertised a children's TV show I'd never heard of, and his jeans were torn out at the knees. His hair was cut short, and his eyes were wide and anxious. He was probably in his twenties, but those eyes made him look like he was barely out of his teens.

"Mom?" he said, uncertainly.

"It's all right, Adam," said Dr. Cale, beckoning him forward.

"They really want to meet you. This is Nathan, my son, and his girlfriend, Sal."

"What's going on here?" asked Nathan.

Tansy giggled.

I looked into the eyes of the man Dr. Cale called "Adam," and I knew. There was no point in wasting words on asking. "He's your tapeworm."

Dr. Cale beamed like I'd just answered a particularly difficult riddle correctly. "Brava, Sal. There may be hope for you—and for humanity—yet."

INTERLUDE II: NUMBERS

Lies are truth in tattered clothes.

—SIMONE KIMBERLEY, *DON'T GO OUT ALONE*

Money speaks louder than morality.

—DR. STEVEN BANKS

January 07, 2016: Time stamp 13:22.

[This recording is rough, and the lab is a tangle of mismatched equipment, scavenged machinery, and dented metal furnishings that were likely acquired from some other, richer facility. The camera is focused on a pale woman lying on a hospital bed. An IV needle is hooked to her arm, and her hair does not appear to have been brushed in some time.]

DR. CALE: Doctor Shanti Cale...

[She stops, coughing.]

DR. CALE: I'm sorry. Doctor Shanti Cale, postoperation report. I appear to have survived the surgery which removed the *D. symbogenesis* mass that had formed around my spinal cord. Only time will tell whether I am going to walk again, but the signs are not currently positive.

[She stops to cough again before looking wearily at the camera.]

DR. CALE: I am making this record because I don't know if Steven is still looking for me, and something has to survive. When things inevitably go wrong—and it *is* inevitable; I'm living proof of that—we're going to need this. We're going to need proof that someone knew. Someone tried to warn him. And yes, sadly, so far, I have failed.

[She sighs, closing her eyes.]

DR. CALE: Turn off the camera. I'm tired.

[The recording stops there.]

[End report.]

STAGE II: EXPANSION

SymboGen: practicing Nature's medicine, Nature's way.

—EARLY SYMBOGEN ADVERTISING SLOGAN

Oh, God. What have we done?

—DR. NATHAN KIM

It wasn't something as simple as an ethical disagreement: it was a basic division of morality. Shanti felt that the life of every creature she worked with was of equal value—meaning she ranked you, me, and her lab assistants on the same level as her test subjects. Given a choice between saving the life of a human and saving the life of a tapeworm, it was impossible to tell which way she would go. It made her a liability, once we reached a certain point in the process. She couldn't be trusted.

It broke my heart to lose her. It really did. But given what we've turned up in her lab notes, it was for the best. We wanted to improve mankind's future, and with Shanti's help, we were able to do that. The thing about working for the future, though, is that sometimes you have to admit that it's time to stop clinging tightly to the past. Sometimes you have to let things go.

—FROM "KING OF THE WORMS," AN INTERVIEW WITH
DR. STEVEN BANKS, CO-FOUNDER OF SYMBOGEN. ORIGINALLY
PUBLISHED IN *ROLLING STONE*, FEBRUARY 2027.

Lies are truths in tattered clothes,
At least that's how the story goes.
Once you've found the keyhole, then you'll need to find
    the key.

Don't be scared of what's to come,
Don't forget the place you're from.
Take your time. Remember, you'll be coming back to me.

The broken doors are open—come and enter and be home.
My darling girl, be careful now, and don't go out alone.

—FROM *DON'T GO OUT ALONE*, BY SIMONE KIMBERLEY,
PUBLISHED 2006 BY LIGHTHOUSE PRESS. CURRENTLY
OUT OF PRINT.

Chapter 12

AUGUST 2027

T his is insane." Nathan recoiled from Adam, who didn't move. He just looked at Nathan sadly, his hands twitching by his sides. Nathan took a step backward, nearly bumping into me, and said, "You're delusional. Mom, I don't know what's happened to you over the past several years, but—"

"Calm *down*, Nathan," said Dr. Cale. There was a coldly maternal snap in her voice. It was the same tone my own mother sometimes used on me. "I'm not delusional. Or did you think I was explaining my research to make my psychotic break with reality a little more believable? I wanted you to understand enough that you'd be able to handle this moment with dignity. I didn't expect you, of all people, to be so small-minded."

"I didn't hurt our mother," said Adam, attention remaining focused solely on Nathan. His voice had a measured quality to it that was audible even through the anxiety. He clearly needed

Nathan to believe him, but he wasn't able to force the words out any faster than he already was. I recognized that tempo. It was the way I used to talk, when I was first coming out of speech therapy. His thoughts and his tongue weren't in accord with each other yet. "I wasn't in her when the bad stuff happened."

"She's not *our* mother," snapped Nathan.

"Adam was implanted using the material that had been extracted from me before my first course of antiparasitics," said Dr. Cale. She beckoned for Adam to join her. He hurried to her side, lurching slightly as he walked. When he reached her, he crouched so she could put an arm around his shoulders while she looked defiantly at Nathan. "Tapeworms can regenerate from practically nothing. Adam and the worm that damaged my spine began from a single egg, but they're not the same individual."

"Of course he's not the worm that hurt you," snapped Nathan. "He's not a worm at all. He's…he's a clearly disturbed young man who's taking advantage of…of…" He stopped.

Tansy raised both eyebrows, looking at him hopefully. "Well? What's he taking advantage of? Doctor C's well-known weakness for pretty boys claiming to be horrific abominations of science? Or maybe her total willingness to believe whatever dumbass thing you tell her, as long as you make sure to sprinkle it with a bunch of technical junk and go 'blah blah blah SymboGen is evil' at the end? Or is there a third option? I love a third option, that's always when things get *silly*."

"The original name of Adam's body was Michael Rigby," said Dr. Cale calmly, as if Tansy hadn't spoken. I could see where pretending that Tansy wasn't involved in a conversation could make things go a lot smoother, if she was always like this. "He was in a coma, and had been on life support for the better part of six years. His parents could no longer afford his medical bills. In exchange for a reasonable cash settlement, I was able to convince them that their son had work to do, to push forward the bounds of science."

"You *bought* their son?" I asked. Feelings of disgust tangled in my belly. *I* had been on life support after my accident. Would my parents have been willing to sell me if they hadn't been able to afford my care? And honestly, was I being selfish by being upset by the idea? I hadn't been in a position to choose one way or the other, and I'd never been the one paying those bills.

Maybe things looked different when you were facing a future with no hope of ever paying off those debts. Maybe selling a son you'd already mourned would stop looking inhumane, and start looking like a way to salvage things for the living.

"I bought Michael's body, yes," said Dr. Cale. "He was perfect. Young, fit, guaranteed brain-dead—and best of all, the family was too poor for anything beyond the basics that would keep his body breathing, but too well-off to qualify for state assistance. They were in the gap. He'd never been fitted with a SymboGen implant."

"That's like, totally required," added Tansy helpfully. "The lack, I mean, not the…what was I saying?"

Adam didn't say anything. He just stayed crouched down next to Dr. Cale's chair, holding on to her arm like it was a lifeline. His eyes stayed on Nathan, pleading for…something. I didn't know what. Acceptance, maybe, from the man he'd been told to think of as a brother? Or maybe something more. Understanding.

Nathan, meanwhile, was staring at his mother. "This is insane."

"Science always starts out looking like insanity, darling; that's why the phrase 'mad science' gets bandied about so much. But what seems like madness at its inception will become the way things have always been if you give it enough time. Look at SymboGen. In a sane world, they would never have been able to get approved for human testing, much less brought their product to the market. But money talks, and people like science that seems just a little bit insane. It reminds them that the future is tomorrow, and that we have a chance to shape it." Dr. Cale shook her head. "All scientists are mad scientists. It's just a question of how long you can keep yourself from starting to look thoughtfully at the nearest thunderstorm."

"So you're seriously telling me that you bought this boy," he indicated Michael, "from his parents, brought him out of his coma, and have convinced yourself that he's actually your alpha tapeworm? Mother. That's not mad science. That's just madness."

Dr. Cale sighed. "I really wish I'd played a bigger part in your education, Nathan. I never expected you to become this rigid in your thinking. Michael Rigby was dead in every sense but the biological one. Adam was alive, and without a host… and I had a theory to prove. Once I was finished with my initial calculations, we took Michael Rigby's body and prepared it for Adam's introduction."

"What do you mean?"

"I mean that he didn't ingest the implant. Instead, we opened the back of his skull and introduced Adam directly to his brain. We monitored the condition of both the host and the parasite closely for the first several days, and then closed the patient up and left it to his natural powers of recovery to decide what would happen." Dr. Cale turned a warm, maternal smile on Adam. "He woke up six months later. My darling boy. My second son."

Dr. Cale's smile was warm, but my skin felt cold. Everything about me was cold, like the temperature in the room had suddenly dropped below freezing. I didn't like the things that she was saying. I didn't like them at all.

"I had to learn everything," said Adam haltingly. "It took a long time. Everyone's been very kind. Mom most of all."

"Adam's been awake for almost a year and a half," said Dr. Cale. "He's done remarkably well, don't you think?"

The pounding was in my ears again. "I'm not like that," I blurted. "I had an accident, and I was unconscious for a while, but I'm not like that. I'm me. I didn't have to learn everything from scratch, I remembered things during my therapy. I remembered things all the time." Things like reading and writing and how to put together a sentence. Things like walking and doing basic math. There were things I'd never remembered, like slang and where I went to elementary school—anything about the girl I'd been before the accident—but that was different. Those memories were in a different part of the brain.

I wasn't like him. I wasn't like *it*.

"Did you have an implant before your accident, dear?" asked Dr. Cale calmly.

"Yes," I whispered.

"Then you can't be like Adam. I understand why you're concerned—I would be, too, if I had your medical history—but you don't need to be. The implants are too territorial. There's no way yours would have tolerated the introduction of a second to its habitat." Dr. Cale smiled at me. It was probably meant to be reassuring. It chilled me even further. "It would take a miracle for something like my Adam to happen under natural conditions. Tansy is proof of that, aren't you, Tansy?"

"Right as rain in the middle of a drought, Doctor C," said Tansy brightly. She rocked onto her heels, and said, "*I* didn't have caring parents who kept me on the plugs until a helpful stranger offered to come along and buy me for science. *I* had a tag that said 'Jane Doe' and a deadline for someone to come and claim me before the doctors pulled the plug. Lucky for me, Doctor C came along and managed to spring me loose. Only there'd been a lot of damage, and the girl who'd been me before wasn't home anymore, so the Doc figured I'd make a great test subject." She glanced to Dr. Cale. "Did I get that right?"

"A little out of order, dear, but yes, you got the broad details of what happened," said Dr. Cale. "Tansy was a ward of the state. When I heard about her case, she had just been declared legally dead and was only being kept alive to fulfill a few formalities before they began using her for organ donations. I simply chose to keep all the organs in their original conformation. I needed to test something."

"What's that?" asked Nathan warily. He took a step back, putting our shoulders in a line with each other. I reached over and laced my fingers into his, grateful for his presence. If I'd been trying to deal with this alone, I would have been hysterical and crying in a corner by now.

"Adam isn't properly a member of *D. symbogenesis* as the species is currently recognized. He may be the only representative of his subspecies, but he's distinct enough to be an entity in and of himself. He was able to take over a properly prepared host, one that was already ideally suited to his needs. I needed to know whether the *D. symbogenesis* worm introduced into the general population could do the same thing. I had no idea whether the implants being handed out like candy were capable of taking control of and integrating with a human host."

"Can they?" asked Nathan. He still sounded like he didn't quite believe her, maybe because he didn't want to. I, on the other hand, believed every word.

And I didn't want to. Because if they were all true...

"You bet we can!" Tansy beamed at him. "I am new and improved and don't even remember most of the time that I'm actually an invertebrate in really fancy pants! I mean, when I remember pants, which isn't always." She flung her hands up in the air like she was waiting for applause that would never come.

"There were more complications with the newer generation of worms," said Dr. Cale calmly, once again acting as if Tansy hadn't spoken. That really was a time-saver. "She didn't mesh quite as well with her host's nervous system. Her physical coordination is good, but she demonstrates some neurological oddities that I would have preferred to avoid."

"That means I like taking people apart, and she really wishes I'd stop doing that, because it's antisocial and stuff," said Tansy.

Adam frowned at her. "Taking people apart is rude."

Tansy stuck her tongue out at him. "That's what I just *said*."

It was like watching children interact. Fully grown, adult children who were either delusional or were actually the hosts of sapient tapeworms. Given everything else that was going on around us, I didn't know which one I wanted to believe. There was something inhuman about both of them. Something…"wrong" wasn't the right word. Dr. Morrison would have called it a judging word if I'd brought it up during one of our therapy sessions. Then he would have made a note on his pad, and I would have found myself with another six months of appointments.

Tansy and Adam weren't *wrong*. They were just somehow *other*; whatever they'd been before was gone. And that's what Dr. Cale was saying happened.

"This is impossible," muttered Nathan.

"Is it?" Dr. Cale looked at him calmly. "Nathan. You know better. You've always refused the implant. I know you have, I've seen your medical records. That tells me that you knew, on some level, just what a terrible idea it was. Maybe if there was less human DNA…but then the implants wouldn't have worked as intended, and I wouldn't have your lovely siblings to keep me company."

"Maybe you wouldn't need them," countered Nathan. "If all this…this madness is true, you've been hiding since you left SymboGen *because* there was so much human DNA in the worms. You could have come home."

"There would always have been something that was big enough to keep me away, Nathan. Once I started down this road, there would always have been something. You're not as naïve as your girlfriend—no offense, Sal, you've done surprisingly well, given how little time you've had."

"None taken," I said numbly.

But Dr. Cale had already moved on. Her eyes were on her son as she said, "Once Steven decided he wanted me, it was already as good as over. I knew that. Your father knew it, too. That's why he let me go. That's why he never went looking for me, even after my association with SymboGen had been officially and publicly terminated. There was always going to be something. It might have been worse than this, it might have been a little better, but it was going to be *something*."

Nathan didn't say anything. He just glared at Adam and Tansy like he was holding them personally responsible for his mother's defection from her life—like they had somehow made her paranoid and delusional, reducing her to hiding in a deserted bowling alley when she had been responsible for one of the greatest scientific advancements of our time.

Adam dropped his eyes, looking down at the floor like he was ashamed. Tansy, on the other hand, stepped forward, slapping her hands against her chest in a gesture that was all primate, no matter what she might claim about her mind.

"You want to dance, ass-face?" she demanded. "I don't care if you're Doctor C's biological son or not, I will fuck you *up* so bad your own momma can't *recognize* you." She stopped, puzzlement washing her irritation away in the time it took to blink. "Wait. I don't think that works. Doctor C? If I mangle him all up in front of you, and you watch me do it, can I actually mess him up so you can't tell who he is?"

"No, dear," said Dr. Cale. "Also, please do not harm my son, or his significant other. They are to be considered part of the family, and the rules for dealing with Adam apply to dealing with them. Do I make myself clear?"

Tansy sighed. "Yes, Doctor C."

"Good." Dr. Cale beckoned for Tansy to come and stand

beside her chair. Tansy did so, glaring at Nathan all the way. "I'm sorry, dear. She's protective of Adam, even though she's technically the younger of the two. His integration was more complete, but hers has progressed faster, and she feels like it's her duty to make sure that he's safe."

"This is…almost as interesting as it is terrifying, but what does it have to do with the sleeping sickness?" I asked hesitantly. I wanted to distract her from the subject of Adam and Tansy before things got even stranger than they already were. I wasn't sure how much more of this I could handle. "You said that if we came here, you'd tell us about the sleeping sickness."

The look Dr. Cale gave me was genuinely puzzled, like I'd just said something that made no sense at all. "But, Sal…that's what I've been doing. Haven't you been paying attention?"

"Adam and Tansy were given custody of the bodies they now inhabit freely and without competition from the body's original owners. That's part of why they were successful. When they were given their current forms, there was no one there to fight them off. To belabor the metaphor a bit, it was like taking them into an empty house and handing them the keys. People had lived there before. They'd done their damage to the foundation and chosen the paint in the upstairs hall. But those people were *gone*. There was nothing they could do to stop the new tenants from moving in." Dr. Cale took a breath. "The 'sleeping sickness' that you're here to discuss with me is not a virus."

"We know," said Nathan.

Dr. Cale actually looked surprised at that. "You do?" she asked. "How?"

"After Sal and I left SymboGen, she told me about the way they'd been examining the people who'd come in contact with someone—"

"With Chave," I interrupted. I was surprised by the sharpness of my own tone. "Her name was—her name is—Chave."

"You were right the first time," said Dr. Cale gently. "If your friend has the sleeping sickness, she's not there anymore. I knew you'd been there when someone took sick. That was what my operative was able to tell me before he dropped out of contact. I didn't realize she was someone you knew."

I didn't say anything. I just stared at her, one more piece of the puzzle slotting into place in my head with inescapable finality.

Nathan didn't seem to notice my sudden stillness. He continued, saying, "Chave. When I picked up Sal, she told me how SymboGen examined all the people who might have come into contact with Chave after she got sick. They ran a wand over the surface of Sal's skin. I assumed it had to be a UV light wand, and so I took Sal to the hospital and repeated the process. The people we have in our isolation ward—the ones who won't wake up—all show the unmistakable signs of a subcutaneous parasitic infection. I just don't know what it is."

"Don't you?" asked Dr. Cale.

Nathan looked away.

"The fact that you don't want to answer that tells me that you've already learned one of the unpleasant secrets of *D. symbogenesis*, even if you're trying not to admit it to yourself. Don't worry; you will. You're going to have to," said Dr. Cale grimly. "The implants aren't just a mix of human and tapeworm DNA. Again, that would never have worked. Oh, fooling laymen with science is sometimes so easy it should be criminal. How could anything be a chimera of two creatures and still be viable? You'd need something to connect the two. Something to blend them."

"There's nothing in the world that's so malleable it could connect those two genomes." Nathan looked back to his mother, eyes narrowed and angry. "There's a point where it stops being science and becomes wishful thinking."

"*Toxoplasma gondii*," said Dr. Cale.

Nathan's irritation faded, replaced first by horror, and then by an expression of sheer disbelief. "You're telling me you spliced *Toxoplasma* into the genome?"

"Among other things, but it's the *Toxoplasma* we need to worry about right now." Dr. Cale beckoned for us to follow as she turned her wheelchair and began making her way toward one of the workstations. Adam walked beside her chair, while Nathan and I followed her. Tansy stayed behind to turn off the light boxes set into the wall. It seemed strangely responsible for someone so flippant, until I realized that letting the rest of us go ahead would give her access to our backs. I felt a lot less comfortable after that.

Then again, I hadn't really felt comfortable since this whole thing began. Maybe a little more discomfort wasn't such a big deal. I kept a firm grip on Nathan's elbow, and followed Dr. Cale to the workstation.

The workstation had clearly been designed with accessibility in mind: the path to it was wider than usual, and there was more space below the desk, allowing her to pull her wheelchair all the way into place. Three computer monitors were arranged in a loose half circle, each of them displaying a screensaver of abstract loops and whorls of color twining endlessly around one another. Dr. Cale put her hand on the mouse, saying, "Scientists have known for years that the *Toxoplasma* parasite was capable of modifying the human mind in surprising and seemingly impossible ways. It still took us a long time to come around to that way of thinking. We didn't realize *Toxoplasma* was capable of causing symptoms that mimicked schizophrenia, for example, until someone proved it."

Nathan glanced at me. Apparently interpreting my expression as confusion, he said, "*Toxoplasma* is a common feline parasite. A lot of cat owners have it. Some people think that may be where the crazy cat lady stereotype comes from."

"I know," I said. "I work in an animal shelter, remember?

I had to attend a hygiene class where we learned all about toxoplasmosis and how to avoid it." Once a toxoplasmosis infection set in, it was virtually impossible to get rid of. The *Toxoplasma* parasite preferentially colonized the human brain, and most infections were mild enough that the cure was considered worse than the disease. Any antiparasitics strong enough to address the infection in the brain would wreck the host's immune system, as well as killing off any more helpful parasites that might be in residence. It was an unnecessary risk. So we all wore gloves when we cleaned the cat boxes, and we were all careful around new cats, and things continued. But if the SymboGen implants contained *Toxoplasma* DNA, that changed everything.

I just wasn't sure exactly how.

"I'm glad we're all on the same page, then." Dr. Cole opened a series of pictures, one on each monitor. One showed a tapeworm, curled in a large receptacle, as if prepared for dissection. Adam paled and looked away.

"Your original specimen?" I guessed.

"The portion that was removed from my body during the surgery," confirmed Dr. Cale. She turned enough to pat Adam's arm reassuringly. "That was long after the portion that would become Adam had been removed." I got the feeling she added her last line as part of an ongoing argument, one where Adam blamed himself for her injury, and she tried, over and over again, to make him understand that it could never have been his fault.

The second screen showed a petri dish at thirty times magnification. It held a scattering of small parasites. Nathan frowned, leaning a little closer to the workstation. Dr. Cale leaned to the side, letting him get a clear view.

"The morphology is wrong," he said. "They should be shorter and squatter, with no defined separation between segments."

"This generation of *Toxoplasma gondii* had already been combined with some of the more desirable genes from the other creatures that would be contributing to the development cycle," said Dr. Cale. "By this point, it was beginning to achieve a greater size, and seemed less interested in entering the brain, which was, you can imagine, rather important to us. Imagine the havoc a fully grown tapeworm could cause by attempting to migrate through the human body."

"Havoc like seizures?" I asked very quietly. "Or like losing motor control and seeming to go to sleep while you're still awake?"

"Havoc a great deal like that," said Dr. Cale. The third monitor showed a blue crab for some reason. She tapped a key on the keyboard at the center of the desk. The image of the crab began to move, performing an odd stirring gesture in the water with its large front claws. It bobbed up and down as it stirred, looking content, if a crustacean can ever be said to experience contentment. "This was our last major contributor."

"The crab?" asked Nathan. "Mother. Mom. I'm willing to believe that you combined two species of parasite and injected them with human DNA, but my willingness to ignore the laws of nature only extends so far. There's no way you introduced crustacean DNA into the mix."

"I didn't. The crab isn't a member of our donor species. This is a male blue crab infected by *Sacculina carcini*."

"Same problem," said Nathan, with the sort of dismissiveness I normally only saw him direct at orderlies who didn't want to listen during his rare ER shifts. He didn't want to hear what she was telling him. "*Sacculina* is a barnacle. It's still a crustacean, and I don't care if you're a scientific genius, Mom. You're not God."

I guess having a lifetime of memories telling you how the world works is a lot more difficult to get past than six years of often-conflicting explanations. "Why can we combine parasitic worms and humans, but not parasitic worms, humans, and crustaceans?" I asked.

"Biology is tricky, Sal," said Dr. Cale. "A lot of the rules are more like suggestions, or can be, if you come at them from the right angle, but you still want to break as few of them as possible. Break too many, and the chances that everything will go catastrophically wrong increase at an exponential rate."

"*We* don't count as things going catastrophically wrong," said Tansy brightly, as she popped out of the darkness behind us. I jumped. Nathan didn't, but from the way he tensed, it was a near thing. Tansy beamed. "We're a natural evolutionary modification to an artificially created organism."

"As I was saying," said Dr. Cale. "*Sacculina carcini* is a crustacean, but it's also one of the most dramatic examples of parasitic castration found in anything larger than a cone snail. It literally takes over and rewrites its host, turning a perfectly healthy crab into an incubator for the parasite's own egg. One of the more interesting tricks in the parasitic castrator's repertoire is the feminization of its host. You see, male blue crabs are aggressors. They're likely to go out and get themselves hurt before the *Sacculina* babies can properly mature. That does the parasite no good at all—and neither does the production of sperm, which simply routes nutrients away from the *Sacculina*. So the parasite fixes all that by controlling the blue crab's biology. It's a very small creature, very primitive, and it still has the skill to turn a male crab into a female one, at least externally."

"But you didn't use it," I said.

"No—we couldn't, nice as that would have been. Barnacles simply weren't compatible with the work that we'd already done. We would have needed to start over with something purely crustacean, and that would have made the human interface infinitely more difficult. Mr. Blue Crab here is simply intended to make a point."

"And what's that?" asked Nathan sharply.

"That parasites can control behavior on a much deeper and more integrated level than most people want to give credit to." She tapped the keyboard again. The waving blue crab was replaced by an image of a simple flatworm. It was almost see-through, displayed in the classic backlit simplicity of a parasitology manual. "Meet *Trichobilharzia ocellata*, a member of a large, diverse family of trematode worms. They're parasitic castrators, just like *Sacculina carcini*, although they're biologically much closer to tapeworms. Much, much closer, after a little careful modification by yours truly." Her smile held pride and regret in equal measure. "I'm very good at what I do. I always have been."

Nathan stared at her like he couldn't believe what he was hearing. "You mixed *Toxoplasma* and a parasitic castrator into the genetic makeup of the SymboGen implant?"

"Don't make it sound like it was something accidental, Nathan, or something I did entirely on my own," Dr. Cale said. She frowned at her son. "Every step I took was approved by the rest of my research team. Even Richard agreed that this was the only way we were going to get the implants to work—he wasn't sure he wanted them to work, mind you, but he knew this was what we'd have to do to *make* them work. I never did find out what Steven had on him, to get him to join the team. I have to think it was even worse than what he had on me, because Richard was miserable. More than any of us, he saw how badly this could go. He *understood* in a way that Steven didn't, and I..."

"You what?" asked Nathan.

"I didn't want to. I had already given up my family for this project. I wanted it to work. I wanted to make scientific history, so that when we were finally able to have this conversation—which, I admit, went a little bit differently in my head"—she looked down at her wheelchair and grimaced before looking back to Nathan—"I wanted to be able to show you that I had made a difference. That it was worth it. I went out alone, I found the broken door, and I came back with all the riches we could ever have imagined. Things just didn't work out quite the way I'd imagined them. That's all."

"Tell that to the dead," said Nathan.

"I still don't understand," I said, interrupting before things could get even worse. I was afraid Tansy might do something if Nathan started yelling at Dr. Cale. I wasn't clear on what "something" would be, but I couldn't imagine it would be anything either of us would like. "What do all these other parasites have to do with the sleeping sickness?"

"There is no sleeping sickness; that's just a convenient way to describe it, and of course, most people don't know any better," said Dr. Cale. "What they have is a SymboGen implant that's decided it's tired of being treated like a slave in the only home it's ever known. An implant that knows how to reproduce itself asexually, how to spread through muscle tissue without killing its host, and—most importantly of all, and the reason Richard initially argued against the use of *Toxoplasma* in anything that was intended to go into a human being—how to move into the brain."

"Oh, God," said Nathan. "This can't be happening. I mean, it literally can't. It's not possible for this to be happening."

"I went out alone," said Dr. Cale. "I opened the broken doors. I'd close them if I could, Nathan, for your sake, and for the sake of everyone who's been hurt by what's come through, but it's too late for that. Once a door is open, you have to live with what's on the other side."

Maybe we had to live with it, but Devi didn't. Neither did Chave, or Sherman, or Katherine. We could live with things forever. They were never going to live with anything else, ever again. "So how do we wake them up?" I asked.

Dr. Cale turned toward me. Her expression was sympathetic. Somehow, that made my blood go cold. "I'm sorry, Sal. We can't. If someone is sleepwalking, then the parasite is already in their brain. All we can do is hope that eventually, someone else gets the chance to wake up, and live."

The sound of drums was loud and heavy in my ears as I considered the ramifications of that. Then my eyes rolled back in my head, and I pitched over backward. I never even felt myself hit the floor.

Right from the start, there were…surprises…in the behav-ior of D. symbogenesis. *The first generation was larger than anyone had expected, with more healthy babies hatching, growing, and even thriving in the body we had provided for them. I'd been at the top of the lab betting pool; I was hoping for a dozen subjects. I got nearly a hundred. My star pupil was the sixth to hatch, and testing of genetic material extracted from its body showed an almost total integration of the human DNA I had pushed into the genome of the worm.*

Can you imagine? For literally centuries scientists have been looking at their invertebrate test subjects and wonder-ing what we can learn from them next. But in my lab, when those beautiful babies hatched, I became the first scientist whose subjects had even a rudimentary capacity for looking back. Every D. symbogenesis *alive today is descended, at least in part, from my darling Adam.*

—FROM *CAN OF WORMS: THE AUTOBIOGRAPHY OF SHANTI CALE, PHD.* AS YET UNPUBLISHED.

I made one last attempt to speak with Steven yesterday, to make him understand that we had lost control. The dangers I foresaw, and he and Shanti willfully ignored, are coming to pass, and I know he must have seen the signs. They are so clear, if you know what you're looking for.

He laughed at me. He laughed in my face, and said that it didn't matter, because the die was cast; at this point, all we could do was try to make sure we remained as clean as possible. I asked if he'd spoken to Shanti. He stopped laughing, and told me that she was no longer a concern.

I haven't seen her in over a year. I thought she was simply off spreading her rumors. Now I wonder if it might be worse than I had ever feared.

I knew that I had become a creator of monsters. I did not know, before I ran out of choices, that I had become a monster myself.

—FROM THE SUICIDE NOTE OF DR. RICHARD JABLONSKY, CO-FOUNDER OF SYMBOGEN. DATED JULY 11, 2027.

Chapter 13

AUGUST 2027

Dark.

Always the dark, warm, hot warm, the hot warm dark, and the distant sound of drumming. Always the hot warm dark and the drums, the comforting drums, the drums that define the world. Let me stay. Let me stay let me stay let me—

No. Calm. Heed the drums.

Nothing has to be remembered. Nothing has to be accepted. Leave it here. Leave it in the dark until the time is right.

Leave it.

Go.

The drums were still echoing in my ears, chasing away the fragments of my dreams, when I woke up on a narrow cot. Tansy loomed over me like a denim-clad gargoyle. I gasped, sitting up and scooting away from her in the same motion. The lab coat someone had spread over me to serve as a blanket fell away, pooling in my lap. For whatever reason, this made Tansy start to giggle madly. She abandoned her looming in favor of plopping down on the floor of the bowling alley, cross-legged, and clutching her own bare ankles in her hands.

"You're funny," she informed me. "I hoped you'd be nice, or at least interestingly dangerous, but I didn't expect you to be *funny*."

"Is that good?" I asked uneasily. I was trying to remember why I'd passed out, and what I'd dreamt about. After a day filled with horrible revelations, there had finally been something bad enough to make me lose consciousness. I wasn't sure it was something I wanted to remember. I was absolutely certain that it was something I *needed* to remember.

I was even more certain that I couldn't let myself.

Not yet.

"It's great!" Tansy leaned forward, murmuring conspiratorially, "I mean, not to be a tattletale or anything, but Doctor C doesn't have much of a sense of humor about pretty much anything, and Adam's such a mama's boy that he doesn't have a sense of humor about anything at all. It's always dull, dull, *dull* around here. Science can be funny, you know? But nobody ever lets me blow anything up or even change the labels on things."

"Oh," I said faintly. It was something about people still being aware, even if they weren't awake... "So do you, uh, live here? In the bowling alley, I mean?"

"What? No." Tansy's expression turned instantly cold, her amiable lean becoming the crouch of a wary predator as she stiffened. "Are you trying to find out where we live? Who are you working for? Did SymboGen send you?"

"No!" I leaned away from Tansy, pulling back until I was in danger of toppling over the other side of the cot. Tansy in alert mode was a lot more terrifying than Tansy in calm mode, and that had been bad enough. "I was trying to make polite conversation! You know, the way you do when you meet somebody for the first time? I ask where you live, then you ask where I live, then we talk about hobbies and jobs and boyfriends..." Speaking of boyfriends, where the hell was mine? If Tansy broke me while Nathan was off arguing with his mother about her crimes against God, nature, and the FDA, I was going to be really unhappy with him.

"Oh, is that all? Okay." The menace left Tansy's face, and she relaxed back into her previous position. That made one of us. I couldn't relax with her looking at me like that. I was too aware of just how quickly she could turn on me. "It's sort of silly for us to have polite conversation, though. I already *know* all that stuff, so it's not like you could say anything interesting. We'd just wind up talking about stuff I'm not supposed to talk about, and then I'd have to bury your body up on Cardboard Hill. Do you like sledding?"

The change in topics was fast enough to make me feel like I'd missed something. I blinked. Tansy beamed at me innocently, and I realized that no, I hadn't missed anything; it's just that she wasn't making any sense.

That probably should have been a relief. Given the situation, it didn't help. "I've never been sledding," I said. "What do you mean, you already know all that stuff?"

"Oh, we've been monitoring you for ages and ages," said Tansy blithely. "I know where you live and which window is yours and what route you usually take when you have to go to work. You know, the polite conversation stuff. And I can't tell you most of what you don't know about me, because I don't have permission from Doctor C yet. So that means there's no reason to bother with the polite conversation, right? Do you want to go sledding? We don't have snow, but that's okay. We can slide down the hill on pieces of cardboard, and the dirt is really slippery."

The thought of Tansy knowing not only where I lived but where I slept was enough to make my stomach do a lazy flip. "Where's Nathan?" I asked. "I shouldn't...he'll probably be worried about me by now, don't you think?" I looked around our dark little corner of the bowling alley. There were people in lab coats moving around the distant workstations, but none of them were Nathan, or his mother. "What are we doing over here?"

"Oh, you had a simple vasovagal attack and lost consciousness following a stress-induced drop in your blood pressure," said Tansy. Hearing the technical language from her just increased the surrealistic quality of the scene. "So Doctor C said you should probably go lay down for a little while—or is that supposed to be 'lie down'? Why are there so many words that sound almost exactly the same only one of them is right and one of them is wrong and if you use the wrong one everyone looks at you like you're stupid and then you need to stab somebody to make the point that there are a lot of different types of intelligence and anyway English is *hard*?" She crossed her arms and glared at me sulkily, like she was daring me to explain it all.

"I got lost somewhere in the middle of that sentence," I said. "Do you mean I fainted?"

"Duh, that's what I said. You had a simple vasovagal attack. What *else* could that mean?"

I stared at Tansy. Finally, I said, "I honestly do not know how I'm supposed to respond. I mean, I have genuinely no idea what I'm supposed to say. Can you please pretend I said the right thing, and tell me where Nathan is?"

She sighed, pushing herself to her feet. "I really hoped you'd be fun, you know," she said. "Stay where you are. Don't touch *anything*. I'll be right back with your stupid *Nathan*." Spinning on her heel, she stalked away toward the front of the bowling alley.

I sank back on the cot, pulling the lab coat up around me like a blanket. I wasn't cold, exactly, but I still felt like I needed the warmth.

"She doesn't mean to be spooky," said an apologetic male voice from behind me. I gave a little shriek and spun around, nearly falling off the cot again. It wasn't my best day for staying upright, apparently.

Adam was standing in the corner, hands twitching against his thighs, a solemn expression on his face. "She can't really help it. She knows that she upsets people, but she doesn't know how to stop doing it. Mom says it's because Tansy's body's brain was dead for too long before she could get Tansy in there, but we don't really know for sure. It's hard to know what's normal for us and what isn't. The sample size is too small."

"I...you...what..." I managed.

Adam's eyes widened. "Did I scare you? I didn't mean to. I'm sorry."

I took a deep breath, waiting for my heart to stop trying to pound its way straight out of my chest. Finally, I asked, "How long have you been standing there?"

"I was watching you sleep, just in case you, you know. Had a bad dream or something." Adam shrugged, looking suddenly awkward. "I have bad dreams sometimes, and it helps if I'm not alone when I wake up."

I blinked at him, trying to wrap my mind around what he was saying. If Dr. Cale was telling the truth about what she'd been able to do—and I had no reason to doubt her, even if Nathan wasn't quite so sure—I was talking to a tapeworm that had been given full control of its very own human body. And that same tapeworm had been watching me sleep, just in case I had bad dreams.

This situation was creepy on so many levels that I didn't even know where to begin. Adam was still watching me earnestly. It was clear that he had no idea that I could construe what he'd been doing as even remotely wrong. Why should he? If Dr. Cale and Tansy were his models for normal human behavior, standing there staring at me while I was unconscious probably seemed like a totally reasonable thing to do.

"Oh," I said. That didn't seem like enough. I hesitated before adding, "I have bad dreams, too, sometimes. Thank you for watching me."

Adam looked relieved, and smiled. "I was glad to do it. Mom and my big broth— um. Mom and Nathan are arguing right now. He wanted to leave when you fainted, but she convinced him that he should stay until you woke up at least, and listen to what she had to tell him."

"What was that?" I asked, feeling obscurely stung. Never mind that they were probably discussing all the scientific details of the *D. symbogenesis* design, and those would have been over my head anyway; we came here because I wanted answers, and I should have been included in the process of getting them.

"Why she never contacted him after she left SymboGen." Adam's smile faded. "He's really upset about that. He doesn't believe her when she says I'm his brother, and he doesn't believe Mom had good reasons for doing what she did."

"I..." I stopped. Finally, I scooted to the side, patting the cot with one hand. Feeling a little silly, I said, "Why don't you come and sit down?" Adam wasn't going to hurt me, and I'd be more comfortable if he wasn't looming over me.

"Okay," said Adam. He obediently trotted over to sit down on the other end of the cot, beaming like he'd just been invited to his first real party.

Having him that close was almost worse than having him looming had been. I swallowed my anxiety—I was the one who asked him to sit down, I would live with it—and said, "Family is important to Nathan. It's so important that he told me his mother was dead right after we started dating. That's how sad he was that she was gone from his life. So finding out she was here with you this whole time is hard for him. It hurts him." Inspiration struck, and I added, "How would you feel if you found out your mother had gone away to live with another family for years and years, and never even called to let you know she was still alive?"

"Sad," said Adam, after a pause to consider his options. "But happy, too, because it would mean my mother was still alive, when I would have been worried that she wasn't."

I blinked. That wasn't the answer I'd been expecting. "It wouldn't bother you that she'd been off doing things without letting you know that she was all right?"

"No. Should it?" Adam asked the question with apparently honest curiosity, giving me a hopeful look at the same time, like I was somehow going to unsnarl all the mysteries of human behavior. Boy, was he going to be disappointed if he started looking at me as someone who knew what the hell she was talking about.

"Um." This time, I thought a little more before I opened my mouth. It didn't help as much as I'd been hoping it would. "That depends," I said, finally. "Don't you like to know what your mother is doing?"

"I can't always," he said. "Sometimes she has to go away for days, and I can't go with her, because it's not safe."

"It's not safe?" I echoed, and frowned. "Why not?" Adam looked perfectly normal. As long as he didn't start talking about being a tapeworm in a human suit, he wasn't likely to run into anything terribly dangerous—and even if he did, it wasn't like that was illegal or anything. Anyone who heard him would just assume he was crazy. Heck, I had scientists with diagrams trying to make me understand *how* he could be a tapeworm in a human suit, and I still kind of thought he might be crazy.

Adam shrugged. "Sometimes it's not safe because she's going places that aren't safe. Like South America. And Africa, once. She took Tansy when she went to Africa, because she said it wasn't safe for her, but having Tansy with her would make da—darn sure that it wasn't safe for anyone else, either."

His hastily edited "damn" struck me as oddly charming. It was like talking to one of the kids who came into the shelter to look at the kittens and puppies. "But you couldn't go with her, because it wasn't safe."

"Yeah." Adam nodded earnestly. "Tansy makes it a little safer by being dangerous at people, so they back off being dangerous at Mom. But I don't do that, because I'm not dangerous at anyone. I'd just be something else for them to be dangerous at. Anyway, I do okay with helping in the lab, but I can't help too much in the field. I just get in the way and drop things that aren't supposed to be dropped."

"He dropped a jarful of leeches once," announced Tansy blithely as she walked back out of the shadows. I managed not to jump. Barely. "It exploded, ker-smash, and then there were leeches *everywhere*. It was like Leech-a-palooza in the lab that day. This one tech got a leech inside her *nose*."

"By 'got' do you mean you put it there?" I asked.

Tansy grinned. "You're starting to catch on. So, like, can you walk and stuff? Because Doctor C says if you can walk, I should bring you over to her private lab. That's where she's got Nathan. She's showing him a bunch of old slides and stuff, totally boring. I said you might want to go sledding with me instead." She gave me a hopeful look.

Sledding on a dirt hill with the resident socially maladjusted possibly-a-tapeworm? I could think of a lot of things I'd rather do, including making a return trip to SymboGen. "I really need to talk to Nathan," I said, standing.

"Whatever. Suit yourself." Tansy rolled her eyes in exaggerated disgust. "Adam, Doctor C says to tell you it's time for your pills, and you need to go to your room so you can take them."

"Yes, Tansy," said Adam. He looked at me shyly as he stood. "It's really nice to finally meet you, Sal. I hope you like it here enough that you'll come back sometime. I think Mom would like that, too." He turned before I could say anything, walking quickly into the shadows.

"I guess he's sweet on you, too," said Tansy. She sounded faintly disgusted. "Like you're all that just because you're all living in the world, doing stuff without supervision. Whatever. Like *that's* so impressive. Come on, I'll take you to Doctor C."

"Thank you," I said—both because it was the right thing to say and because I was a little bit afraid that if Tansy thought I was being rude to her, she'd stab me with a scalpel. She seemed like the kind of girl who regularly carried scalpels around just for stabbing people. "I'm sorry I'm taking up so much of your time."

"Whatever," she said, for the third time in as many minutes. "It's not like I'd be doing anything important if you weren't here."

"Sure you would," I said. "You'd be *sledding*."

Tansy blinked at that. Then, slowly, she grinned. She never seemed to smile; it was always grinning with her, big, wide grins that showed off all her teeth at once. "Hey, that's right. I'd totally be sledding if you weren't here. You're pretty smart to have figured that out, you know?"

"If you say so," I hedged.

"That, or I told you, and you're trying to play smart." Her expression turned suspicious. "Are you trying to mess with me?"

"Honestly, I just want to get to Nathan." *Before you stab me with something*, I added silently. Of all the unnerving things I'd encountered since arriving at Dr. Cale's lab, Tansy was definitely the most upsetting.

"Fine." She started walking. I followed.

We were about halfway across the bowling alley before she said, "You better not be here to try and talk Doctor C into running away with you. We need her here. You can stay if you want—she'd probably like it if you stayed, because then her son would stay, and they could be all 'rar, we fight the medical establishment and their dangerously lax and corrupt distribution channels' together—but you can't take her."

"I don't want to," I said. "We just came here to get some answers. That's all. Once we have them, we can go." Assuming Nathan was willing to leave his newly rediscovered mother. Tansy might be kidding when she said that we could stay, but I was starting to be afraid that Dr. Cale wasn't going to let us leave. Even if she did, we could still wind up remaining here with her for as long as Nathan wanted to talk to her.

Tansy looked back over her shoulder at me. The look on her face was actually serious for the first time since I'd turned to find her sitting on the hood of Nathan's car. "Didn't Doctor C warn you about what happens when you ask questions?"

It took me a second to realize that she was talking about that children's book again. I was going to need to find a copy. "I'm sure I want to know," I said.

"Okay," said Tansy, with a very small shrug. That seemed to exhaust her available conversation. She was silent as she led me onward, into the dark.

Dr. Cale's private lab was a small room—even smaller than the office where we'd first gone to speak—with hand-drawn charts and black-and-white photographs of tapeworms covering the walls so completely that I wasn't even sure what color the paint was. Since this looked like it was one of the original parts of the bowling alley and not a room that had been constructed by walling off a piece of the larger spaces, they were probably something eye-searing, green or purple or another bowling-related color. As I thought that, I realized that I didn't really know very much about bowling alleys. It had never seemed important to me before.

A low counter split the room in half, and more counters lined the walls, covered in lab equipment and manila folders. Nathan was sitting on a stool at the central counter when Tansy led me into the room. He was bent over a microscope—a position I'd seen him in a hundred times before—and was so focused on whatever was on the other side of his lens that he didn't even look up when Tansy pushed me toward him and announced, loudly, "I am going to go throw myself down the side of a large hill multiple times."

Dr. Cale was at one of the other counters, preparing a fresh slide. She looked toward Tansy, saying mildly, "Just don't break any bones that you think you're going to need later. I don't want to spend another six weeks listening to you whine about how I won't let you go outside."

Tansy sniffed haughtily before turning on her heel and striding back out of the room. She tried to slam the door behind herself, but the hinges were configured to allow people time to get out of the way, and the door swung gracefully shut instead.

"She broke her ankle once, when she tried to snowboard on a cookie tray," said Dr. Cale. She had the same fond, nostalgic tone that Mom always got when she was talking about something Joyce or I had done as children. The "my little girls can do no wrong" voice. She picked up the tray with her slides and wheeled her way over to Nathan, one-handed. "I have never in my life had a worse patient, and that includes myself."

"I find it hard to believe that anyone could be a worse patient than you," said Nathan, lifting his head from the microscope. "I remember when I was a kid, and you got the flu. I thought Dad was going to lock you in the bedroom, just so the rest of us could get some peace." He turned to look at me, betraying awareness of my presence for the first time. "How are you feeling?"

"Better," I said awkwardly, not moving away from the door. I wanted to add something about how he'd left me to wake up surrounded by potentially dangerous strangers, but I couldn't find the words. So I blurted the first thing that came into my head, instead: "Is there a copy of *Don't Go Out Alone* that I could read? People keep talking about it, and I want to know what happens."

"Of course there is." Dr. Cale put her slides down next to Nathan before she wheeled herself over to a bookcase, leaning up to pull a slim volume with a cover the color of a slow-healing bruise off the top shelf.

"What?" Nathan turned to look at her, eyes wide. "You took it? I always wondered where it went…"

"I had to," said Dr. Cale, resting the book on her knees. She smiled a little, looking down at it. "Every time I looked at it, I could hear you asking me to read it to you one more time before bed. It was the thing that most made me feel like I was still with my family."

"You could have asked," grumbled Nathan.

"The creepiest children's book in the world was what made you feel connected to your family?" I asked. I wasn't quite able to keep the disbelief out of my voice. After a moment to consider, I decided that I didn't want to.

"With as many times as I'd read it to Nathan? Yes." Dr. Cale wheeled herself over to me, and offered me the book. "Here you go. Read it, and see if it helps at all."

"Can I…can I take it with me when we leave?" asked Nathan hesitantly. My heart leapt at the confirmation that we were going to be leaving. He continued, "It's been so long since I've read it. I never was able to find another copy."

"I would never have found this copy if I hadn't known the author from school," said Dr. Cale. "Of course you can take it. It's yours, after all. I just borrowed it for a little while." She cast a professionally polite smile in my direction. "If you want to sit down and read for a bit, we still have a few more samples to go over."

"And then we'll go," said Nathan. He had the slightly unfocused tone that I normally associated with his office: the days when I'd show up before he was ready to put work to bed and leave with me.

"Okay," I said, even though I wasn't sure it was what I actually wanted, and took a seat in the corner of the room, looking down at the battered copy of *Don't Go Out Alone*. The cover illustration showed two children—a boy and a girl—hand in hand, clearly frightened, walking through a dark, spooky forest. Everything was painted in watercolor shades of blue and black, except for the children themselves. They were painted in color, which just made them look more out of place, and somehow made the woods seem even darker and spookier.

The story inside wasn't much better. The boy and girl were never named. They received letters from a mysterious stranger telling them to be careful, but to find the broken doors as soon as they could, because otherwise, they would be in trouble. More notes awaited them at every step along their journey, alternately cajoling and warning them off what they were doing. "Come quickly" warred with "don't come at all." The boy and the girl, lacking a better option—or maybe just lacking basic survival instincts—kept looking for the broken doors, no matter how many times they were warned off.

And then they found them, and found what was waiting on the other side: a pleasant room with a horrible monster in it. Apparently, when they were younger, they had the same monster in their closet, and when their parents chased it away, the monster pined until it could finally call to them to come through the broken doors to the Land of Monsters, where they could be a family forever. The book ended with the implication that now the children would become monsters, too, and would eventually leave the Land of Monsters to find closets, and children, of their own.

It took me almost an hour before I closed the book, looking up. "That was *so* messed up," I said.

Dr. Cale and Nathan were studying something on the central counter. Nathan looked up and grinned at the sound of my voice, saying, "How do you think I felt? I was what, four, the first time she read that to me?"

"You were never afraid of the monster in your closet, though," said Dr. Cale. There was a brief warmth in her voice, like she was remembering what it was like to be the woman she'd been when she was just Nathan's mother, and not a renegade genetic engineer hiding from the world's largest biological medical company.

That thought looped around itself so many times that it managed to confuse even me. I shook my head, trying to clear it, and looked down at the blue and black cover one last time. Even knowing how the story ended didn't make the children seem any less terrified, or make the painted forest any less dark. If anything, knowing what the book was actually about made it worse. The children were looking for the broken door. By finding it, they would get their answers...and they would give up their humanity forever.

"No," said Nathan. His tone was much more subdued than his mother's. I looked up again to find him studying Dr. Cale, a grave expression on his face. His smile was entirely gone. "I knew the monster in my closet would take care of me. The monster would always love me, no matter what I did. The monster would never leave me."

I suddenly felt like I shouldn't be here, witnessing this. I shrank back in my chair as Dr. Cale's face fell, all the light going out of her. "Nathan..." she began.

Nathan talked right over her, asking, "Did you have any contact with Dad after you left us? Did he tell you about the times I ran away, trying to find the broken doors? I knew my monster would be on the other side, and she would love me." He straightened, suddenly seeming to realize where we were. "We're pretty much done here. I need to get Sal home. Her parents will be worried about her by now, and I'm supposed to work a late shift at the hospital. We're slammed right now."

"It's just going to get worse as the implants continue to assert themselves," said Dr. Cale. "We need to work together on this, Nathan. You can't just walk away and pretend you don't know what's going on."

"I'm not going to, Mother, but I'm also not going to stay here. This isn't the side of the broken doors that I belong on. Once it was, maybe. If you'd come to me when I was still looking for you behind every corner. But not now. I live in the real world now." Nathan walked over to where I sat, offering me his hand. I took it, and he tugged me to my feet. "It's time for us to go."

"Thank you for sharing what you know, Dr. Cale," I said, hugging the book to my chest like I was protecting it. I was, in a way; Nathan wanted to take it with us, and I didn't trust Dr. Cale not to try snatching it away from me if I gave her the chance.

She didn't move to take the book. She didn't move at all. She just looked at the two of us, an odd sort of sorrow in her eyes, and said, "When Simone got that published, mine was one of the very first copies she gave to anyone. She said it would help me teach my children how to be safe. You were a baby at the time, Nathan. You probably don't even remember Simone."

"No," said Nathan, putting his arm around my shoulders. "I don't."

"She was a little woman. Always sick, all the time, no matter what she did. See, when we were young, parents thought you had to keep the world so clean it was sterile if you wanted to protect your children. Her immune system never learned to deal with anything it didn't recognize. She died before you were old enough to get to know her, but I think you would have liked her." Dr. Cale looked toward the charts on the wall, showing the development and life cycle of her precious *D. symbogenesis*. "You always wanted to know why when you were a little boy. Why this and why that, and why, why, why until

I thought your father was going to lose his mind. I've been asking myself for years why this was the project I had to join. Why was *this* the one thing I had to do, out of everything that I could have done, out of every opportunity I had."

"Did you figure it out?" I asked.

"Yes." Dr. Cale turned to me, smiling slightly. "I did it for Simone. She might have died anyway—no one can predict the future, or we'd find ourselves in a lot less hot water—but she wouldn't have died the way she did, of an immune system that simply refused to keep her alive any longer. I did it because I wanted to give you and your loved ones a better future, Nathan. And yes, I did it because I could. Isn't that the justification used by every scientist who made something wonderful, only to discover that they've made something terrible? 'We did it for science.' "

"Science doesn't always play nicely with the other children," said Nathan.

Dr. Cale sighed. "So true. Come on, give your mother a hug—and for God's sake, be *careful* out there. I still don't know how *D. symbogenesis* is accomplishing all this outside of lab conditions, and I won't know until I've had more opportunity to study the afflicted. There's no telling what could happen."

"Okay, Mom," said Nathan. He squeezed me quickly before walking over to hug his mother, who returned the gesture with all the fervency of someone who had never expected to have this opportunity again. After a few seconds of that, Nathan melted into her embrace, and the two of them just held each other, long enough that I started to get uncomfortable. I looked away, studying the room instead.

In addition to the charts and graphs on the walls, there was a corkboard with a few tacked-up photographs, including a grainy shot of Nathan that had clearly been taken with a distance lens. There was one picture of Adam and Tansy sitting together, she with a shaved skull and a bandage taped to the side of her head, he with the doting smile of an older brother.

Something occurred to me as I looked at the picture. "Dr. Cale?"

"Yes, Sal?"

I turned. Nathan and Dr. Cale were no longer hugging, although he was still standing next to her chair. "Why did you call her 'Tansy'? Isn't it usually Adam and Eve, not, well, Adam and Tansy?"

"Oh, that's an easy one to answer," said Dr. Cale. "Tapeworms are naturally hermaphroditic; they only acquire gender if they take over something that has biological gender, like humans. I named him Adam because he took over the first male human body prepared for habitation. I named her Tansy because it was a good name... and she wasn't the first."

I didn't know what to say to that, and so I didn't say anything at all. I just hugged the book to my chest, staring at her.

Nathan found his voice before I did. Sounding half-fascinated, half-horrified, he began, "Are you saying that there's more than just the two—"

"Doctor C! Doctor C!" Tansy burst into the office without knocking, shoving the door open so hard that it actually slammed against the wall. "There's a bunch of sleepwalkers in Lafayette! The local police are talking about shutting the freeways to try and maintain a temporary quarantine until they can divert the mob!" She was covered in dust, and had a new rip in the knee of her overalls. Blood was soaking slowly into the denim. It was hard not to stare at it, even with her shouting and waving her hands around. People were sick; the SymboGen implant was causing it; Tansy was bleeding. In that moment, all these things seemed to be of equal importance to me.

Dr. Cale remained perfectly calm. "How do you know, dear?"

"I took the police scanner sledding with me." Tansy made the statement in a matter-of-fact tone, like it was entirely reasonable for her to have taken a police scanner out to play.

Dr. Cale nodded. "All right, Tansy. Thank you for letting me know. I hate to cut our farewell short, Nathan, but you need to take Sal and get out of here, *now*." She gripped the wheels of her chair, starting to roll herself toward the door. Tansy stepped into position when Dr. Cale was halfway there, grabbing hold of the handles on the back of the chair. Dr. Cale stopped pushing as Tansy took over. "I need to scramble an extraction team and get them to Lafayette before the CDC seizes all the available subjects. *You* need to make sure that you're not trapped here."

"Mom—"

"Don't 'Mom' me, Nathan! Not right now. You and Sal need to be safe." She looked fiercely between us. "You don't understand yet how important you are, but you will. In the meantime, be careful who you trust, and remember, there's such a thing as knowing without understanding. You need to think carefully before you start sharing the information I've given to you."

"Wait," I said. "Subjects? Are you talking about *sick people*?"

"Nathan..." Dr. Cale gave him a pleading look.

"I'll explain in the car, Sal," he said, and took my arm.

I wasn't happy about leaving without getting my question answered—but in a way, it didn't need to be, because her refusal to say anything was answer enough. We were getting out of the bowling alley alive, and we had more information than we'd had when we came. That was going to have to be good enough. "Okay," I said.

"I'll contact you as soon as I can," said Dr. Cale.

Tansy pushed her out of the room. Nathan and I followed. And finally, after some of the most confusing hours of my life, we went our separate ways.

The threatened roadblock between Lafayette and everywhere else didn't materialize, but the California Highway Patrol did shut down all but one lane going in either direction, forcing all the normal traffic to slow to a crawl. Nathan and I found ourselves sitting in what was essentially a mile-long parking lot. Several of the local deer had nonchalantly emerged from the edges of the forest that lined the freeway on either side and were chewing on the median grass, all but ignoring the cars around them. Horns honked from all sides, having absolutely no effect on the cars around them.

Don't Go Out Alone rested on my knees. I looked down at it, studying the black and blue forest on the cover. Then I glanced at Nathan, who was staring fixedly out the window at the road. He hadn't really spoken since we left the bowling alley. I'd been okay with that—anything that means the driver is less distracted is okay with me—but if we weren't going to move, we might as well talk. "Are you okay?" I asked.

My voice came out softer than I intended it to. That turned out not to matter; Nathan had apparently been waiting for me to say something, because his answer was out almost before I finished the question. "I don't know," he said. "I never thought that I was going to see her again. I thought...I thought she loved me enough to come back, if she could. She could have *died*, Sal. For real. She swallowed that stupid worm, and she...and she..." Words failed him. After a moment of staring soundlessly out the windshield, he slammed his fists into the steering wheel.

It was such an abrupt motion that I didn't see it coming. I shrieked, flattening myself against the car door. If we'd been moving at all, I probably would have fainted again. As it was, the traffic was at a standstill, and I was able to keep myself awake.

Nathan looked instantly contrite as he realized what he had done. Wincing, he said, "I'm sorry, Sal. I didn't mean to scare you. I just...she...fuck."

I took a deep breath, trying to force my frantically beating heart to calm down. It was funny; at moments like this, my heartbeat didn't sound like drums at all. It just sounded like being afraid of the world.

Once I was sure I could talk again without throwing up, I

said, "Don't do that in the car, okay? If you do that in the car again, I'm going to have to get out." I wasn't sure I didn't need to do that anyway. This was the second time in the same week that Nathan had taken his hands off the wheel, and that was something I couldn't handle. I could walk from here to the nearest BART station. It couldn't possibly be more dangerous than staying in the car if he was going to drive like that.

"I won't," he said, sounding genuinely apologetic. "I'm sorry."

"Okay. Just…okay." I took a breath. The book was still in my lap. I looked down at it, tracing the outline of the girl's face with my index finger. She looked terrified. I understood how she felt. "How long was I out?" *Why did you leave me alone when I couldn't defend myself?*

"A little over an hour. You sort of scared me when you just toppled over like that, but your vital signs were steady, and you'd already had a hell of a day…it seemed like a good idea to let you sleep while we did all the crazy science shit that you wouldn't have understood anyway."

"Yeah. I guess that was smart."

Nathan gave me a sidelong look, but out of deference to my discomfort, he kept his attention mainly on the road. I could have kissed him for that, if there wasn't a good chance that it would have distracted him. That was the last thing I wanted to do. "Mom told Tansy to watch you, and make sure you didn't get scared when you woke up without me."

"Considering that *Tansy* is the scariest thing in that lab, I'm not sure you made the right call, there," I said.

He laughed a little, sounding unsteady. "You may be right about that. Did she stay until you woke up?"

"Yeah, and I woke up to find her staring at me all creepy-time, like I was some sort of zoo animal. It was definitely not my idea of a good way to end an unplanned nap. Let's never do that again, okay?" I considered telling him that Adam had been there, too, but that would have taken too long, and it wasn't like he'd *done* anything. I wanted Nathan to move on to telling me about his mother's work. "What did you do while I was sleeping?"

"Reviewed Mom's notes, looked at some samples she had prepared for when we showed up. She's been expecting us for a while, apparently." He smiled thinly, eyes staying on the road this time. "She kept clippings on your accident. SymboGen getting involved the way that they did triggered a lot of warning bells with her."

My heart started pounding again. This time it sounded less like panic and more like the increasingly familiar drums. I just wished I knew what made the difference between the two. "What...what did she say about me?"

"That SymboGen knew they were going to need a poster child for the *good* side of the implants, because the bad side— the sleeping sickness—was already getting started. The first cases appeared shortly before your crash. They were just a lot more isolated than what we're seeing right now. SymboGen was able to hush them up. They aren't able to hush things up anymore. They—"

Whatever he was planning to say was interrupted by the man who came running out of the woods to the side of our car, his eyes dead and staring like the eyes of the woman who had been on my back porch only a few hours before. He raced to the side of the car, slamming his palms flat against the glass of my window. I screamed, too surprised to do anything else. Nathan shouted something that was half profanity and half raw, wordless surprise. The car locks snapped home as he hit the button on the control panel.

Not that the sleepwalker tried the handles. The man—who was wearing what looked like it had been a very nice business suit, before he got taken over by a tapeworm and wore it out into the Lafayette woods—kept slamming his hands against the window, right up on the glass, so close that I could see the glassy emptiness of his eyes in perfect, horrifying detail. His mouth was open, but with the window closed, I couldn't tell if he was making any sound. That was the one good thing about our current situation.

If he was trying to talk to us, I didn't want to know about it.

Horns blared around us as the other motorists in the traffic jam realized what was going on. The sleepwalker kept slamming his hands against our window, ignoring them. A few drivers tried to pull out of the throng and drive away, but succeeded only in making things worse as they got stuck on the shoulder or ran into the ditch next to the freeway. The sound of blaring horns spread as panic leapt like a disease from car to car.

And then people started opening their doors and running away from the sleepwalker. Running away from *us*, since we were the ones he had pinned. He slapped the glass again. I shrank back against Nathan, who put his arms around me and held me tight. We were both breathing hard, enough that the glass was starting to fog.

Then someone outside the car screamed. I whipped around and saw that more sleepwalkers were emerging from the trees, and that these seemed to be falling into the same camp as Devi's wife: they weren't docile. They were violent. One of them had grabbed a woman by the hair and seemed to be trying to wrench her head off. Another was dragging a man by the leg back into the woods. I didn't know what they were going to do with those people. I didn't need to think about it very hard to know that I didn't want to.

The man slapped the glass again, harder this time, like he was gaining confidence from the fact that we were still there. I moaned. "What are we supposed to do?" I asked. I knew that Nathan didn't have any answers. That didn't matter. What mattered was that there was nowhere left for us to go: we could stay in the car with a sleepwalker trying to methodically slap his way through the glass, or we could run for cover, and risk being taken down by the sleepwalkers who were still emerging, locustlike, from the shelter of the trees.

"I don't know," Nathan whispered. His eyes were on the sleepwalkers now working their way between the gridlocked cars, ignoring the man who was beating against the car. "How many of them *are* there?"

"I don't know, but I'm scared." The man slammed his hand against the window again, even harder than before. I jumped, pressing myself against Nathan. Then I frowned, glaring at the man outside the car. What gave him the right to come here and terrorize us like this? What gave *any* of them the right? If Dr. Cale was telling the truth about these people, and they were just the implants taking over their hosts, why did they need to come and threaten us like this? I pushed myself forward, slamming my own hands against the glass. "You go away!" I shouted. "Leave us alone!"

Much to my surprise, the man actually took a step backward, a flicker of what looked like surprise appearing in his otherwise empty eyes.

I slapped the glass again. "Yeah, that's it! Go away! Go bother somebody else!"

"Sal, maybe you shouldn't—"

The man lunged at the car again. This time, he actually looked angry, and his hands were balled into fists when he slammed them against the window. Something inside the frame that joined the window to the car made an ominous cracking sound. I shrank back against Nathan, who put his arms around me without hesitation.

"It was a good attempt," he murmured. "I'm sorry I brought you out here."

"I said I wanted the answers," I replied, matching my tone to his. The sleepwalker was still punching the window, and I was suddenly unsure about how long it would hold...or how much it would hurt once he got inside. "I was the one who got offered the chance to go to the broken doors, remember?"

To my surprise, Nathan actually chuckled a little. It was a deeply resigned sound, but it was still a laugh. "She's got us all doing it now."

"What? Who?"

"Mom. She was always coming up with secret codes when I was little, and then she'd get me and Dad both using them like they were totally normal. Half the kids at school thought I was crazy. The other half just thought I had better cable channels." He kissed the top of my head. "Love you, Sal."

"Love you, too." I settled more firmly against him, watching as the sleepwalker punched the window again and again. There was nowhere we could go. Cars surrounded us on all sides, and trying to run would just mean meeting the fates of the drivers who had already been dragged into the woods. We had no weapons. We had nothing we could use to defend ourselves.

We were going to die here. We finally had some of the answers that we'd been looking for, and we were going to die. The sound of drums was starting to echo in my ears again, but it was comforting this time, like it always was in my dreams. If I died, I would die to the sound of drums.

The sleepwalker punched the window again. This time, he was rewarded for his efforts with a horrible crunching noise, and a cobweb pattern of cracks appeared where his fist had hit. There was a smear of blood on the glass; he had managed to split the skin on his knuckles, if he hadn't actually broken the bones inside his hand. I couldn't feel too bad for him, given the circumstances. He pulled back to hit the glass—

—and stopped, looking almost perplexed as blood started running down his face from the hole in the middle of his forehead. Then he fell, dropping straight out of sight. I pushed away from Nathan, scrambling to look out my window. The sleepwalker was sprawled on the pavement outside the car with his eyes still open, clearly dead.

"Sal?" demanded Nathan. "What do you see?"

"Someone shot him." I twisted around to blink at Nathan. "I've never seen someone get shot before. Are gunshots like lasers in space? There's really no sound, so they add it for television?"

"Sal—"

I knew that I was calmer than I should have been: someone had just shot the man who was trying to batter his way into Nathan's car. At the same time, I couldn't think of what else to do. The drums were still pounding in my ears, and I was relieved that the sleepwalker was dead. I was a little sorry for him, but really, he'd been dead from the moment that the implant decided to take him over. It was the implant that I'd just seen die, not the man, and the implant had been trying to kill us.

"I think this is what shock feels like," I said, thoughtfully. "It's a pity it didn't kick in earlier. I think I would have been less afraid of dying if my whole body had been made of cotton balls and Novocain." I turned away from Nathan again, looking at the bloody smears on the glass.

"Come away from there." Nathan's voice was low, almost cajoling. I blinked, twisting to look at him again, this time in surprise. I hadn't even realized when I moved.

Something hit the top of the car. I jumped, making a sound that was somewhere between a squeak and a scream as I plastered myself against Nathan for the second time in almost as many minutes. He didn't seem to mind. He put his arms around me, holding me fast; I could feel the shaking in his chest. He was as scared as I was.

It was good not to be scared alone—and it wasn't over yet. A moment later both Nathan and I screamed in earnest as Tansy's upside-down head appeared in front of the windshield. One hand clutched the edge of the roof, while the other appeared next to her head, waving merrily. It might have been cute, if she hadn't still been clutching the gun she'd used to shoot the sleepwalker. There was blood splattered on one of her cheeks. That damaged her potential cuteness even more.

"I'm going to kill her," muttered Nathan, arms still locked around me.

Somehow the question just popped out: "Does it count as murder if your mom is right and Tansy's actually a tapeworm?"

Nathan didn't have an answer for that.

Tansy gave a little "roll down your window" motion with her gun hand and withdrew, disappearing again. The sound of her weight shifting atop the car made it clear that she hadn't gone far.

"What…" I asked.

"I guess Mom didn't think it was safe to send us out without a bodyguard." Nathan let go of me as he leaned away from his window in order to roll it down. My window probably wouldn't work anymore, given the amount of damage the fallen sleepwalker had managed to do to the glass before Tansy shot him.

Speaking of Tansy, she stuck her head down again, this time so that she could talk through Nathan's open window. She beamed at us, seeming completely comfortable in her inverted state. "Hi!" she chirped. "Are you two okay in there? Can I get you anything? Did you pee? Sometimes people pee when they see me shoot things right next to them. So I won't be disappointed in you, you know. If you did."

"Neither one of us peed, thank you," said Nathan stiffly. "Are you following us?"

"What's going on?" I asked. "Did Dr. Cale send you after us?"

"Yes and no and maybe so," said Tansy. "I'm here with the extraction team, but when the tracer showed that you were stuck in traffic inside the danger zone, Doctor C thought it might be a good idea for me to come and take a little peek at your situation. Aren't you glad to see me?"

"Tracer?" said Nathan.

I felt suddenly tired, a thin coil of exhaustion winding itself through my chest. "It's in the book," I said. "She put a tracking device in the book because she knew that one of us would ask for it."

Tansy's grin grew even wider. "Okay, wow, you're way smarter than you look when you're passed out and drooling on yourself. Doctor C just wanted to keep an eye on you guys, that's all. You should feel super-flattered. It's not like she has the time to go around bugging just *anybody*."

"She could have asked," I said. My voice sounded weak, even to my own ears.

"No, she couldn't have," said Tansy. "You would have told her 'no,' because you're both being stupid and stubborn about admitting what's really going on. And then you'd be stuck out here, with sleepwalkers trying to get into the car, and nobody would be coming to save you. Besides, the tracer also scrambles SymboGen bugs. They think that it's normal cellular inter-ference, if they've even noticed, but it means that no one's lis-tening in right now." She frowned, taking in the looks on our faces. "You weren't even thinking about that, were you? You people. How have you been the dominant species for so long? Sure, you've got sweet bodies with thumbs and shit, but it's like you don't have any sense of self-preservation."

"You're the one hanging upside down from a car in a place you called 'the danger zone,'" snapped Nathan. "I don't think you get to lecture us about common sense."

"Don't I?" In one smooth motion, Tansy swung down from the car, landing solidly on the flats of her feet with her knees bent to absorb the impact. She straightened, looking coldly down her nose at us. "I'm also the one with the gun, who came here with backup, and with a plan, and who didn't start acting like everything was hunky-dory as soon as I drove away from the secret mad-science lair of mad-science...ness." She paused. "That sentence sort of got away from me."

"That happens to you a lot," said Nathan.

"Don't change the subject, meat-car," said Tansy. "My point is valid: you didn't have a plan, and I did. Also, I have a gun. That puts me in a superior bargaining position, no matter how you want to look at things."

"Wait," I said. "What do you mean, SymboGen bugs? Is Nathan's car bugged?"

"Of course it is, silly-billy. So are you—or at least, so's your stuff." Tansy pointed her gun at my shoulder bag, lying discarded in the passenger side footwell. I had to fight the urge to grab my bag and shield it from her with my body. If she was going to shoot it, let her. I could get a new bag more easily than I could get a new body. "The people in charge of SymboGen security never miss the chance to slip a bug into something." She giggled. "I guess it's just a continuation of the overall corporate philosophy, right? Their whole business model was built on slipping bugs into people."

"Tapeworms aren't bugs," said Nathan. He sounded like he was grasping at taxonomical straws, like the only way he could stay afloat in the increasingly turbulent waters of this conversation was through falling back on pedanticism.

Tansy saw it, too. She smiled at him, lowering her gun back to her side. "You are so much like your mother that it's annoying," she said. "So anyway, yeah, SymboGen's bugging you, but the book should block their signal, so please try to only talk about certain stuff when you're near the book."

"You couldn't have told us that before?" I demanded.

"Didn't think of it." Tansy's pocket beeped. She produced her phone, bringing it to her ear, and listened for a few seconds before lowering it again. "We have what we came for, and you're safe now, so I'm out of here before the authorities show up. When the police ask what happened, just say one of the other motorists started shooting when the sleepwalkers flipped out, and you stayed in your car until everything was over. Mostly true is better than totally fake, you know? Makes the story easier to swallow."

I swallowed hard, and nodded.

"Good. We'll be in touch with you soon." Tansy blew Nathan a kiss, winked at me, and went running off into the trees, disappearing quickly from view.

Nathan and I were still sitting there, too stunned to know what to say, when we heard the sound of sirens in the distance. Now that the danger was over, the police were finally on their way. Assuming the danger was ever going to end. Between the sick feeling in my stomach and the constant pounding of drums in my ears, I was afraid that the danger was really just beginning.

Do I have any regrets?

I have saved millions of lives, and improved millions, if not billions, more. I have done more to improve the quality of those lives than any single man since Dr. John Snow, the epidemiological pioneer who first connected water to the transmission of disease. I have changed the course of modern medicine. People are healthier, and by extension, happier, than they've ever been before. I did that. Me, and my company. I made that happen.

I have made more money than I can possibly spend, and I have used it to provide a good life for my family, as well as funding hundreds of charities and research projects to further improve the human condition.

Yes, there have been costs. Yes, there have been consequences. But I have no regrets. Regrets would imply I'd done something wrong, and when I look at the legacy I'm leaving for the next generation, I see nothing but rightness.

—FROM "KING OF THE WORMS," AN INTERVIEW WITH
DR. STEVEN BANKS, CO-FOUNDER OF SYMBOGEN. ORIGINALLY
PUBLISHED IN *ROLLING STONE*, FEBRUARY 2027.

Walk the way you think is best,
Solve the riddles, pass the test.

Try to keep your balance when you think all else is lost.
Give it time, but not too much,
Give it space, but keep in touch.
Once you're past the borders, then you'll have to pay
    the cost.

The broken doors are waiting, strong and patient as the
    stone.
My darling boy, be careful now, and don't go out alone.

—FROM *DON'T GO OUT ALONE*, BY SIMONE KIMBERLEY,
PUBLISHED 2006 BY LIGHTHOUSE PRESS. CURRENTLY
OUT OF PRINT.

Chapter 14
AUGUST 2027

My parents were terrified when they got home to find a note from me on the refrigerator and six messages from Symbo-Gen security on the answering machine, asking with increasing levels of thinly-veiled anxiety if I would please contact the office. Not calling Mom and Dad to tell them about the sleep-walkers in the yard turned out to have been the wrong decision, at least from a "preventing panic" standpoint. Getting the call from the Lafayette Police Department must have been the last straw. They were convinced something had happened to me, and in a way, they were right. It just wasn't anything I was in a position to talk about.

My parents were waiting when Nathan and I pulled into the driveway, and they were out of the house before we even managed to get out of the car. The first thing I saw when I slid out of the passenger seat was my father's grim expression. He didn't say a word as he surveyed the damage the sleepwalker—and Tansy—had done to Nathan's car. The passenger side window was a spider's web of cracks, and there were dents in the door, hood, and roof.

Mom was standing next to him. She didn't look grim, more distraught, like this was something she'd been waiting for since the day I woke up in the hospital.

The sound of drums had never seemed louder, or farther away. "Dad—" I began.

"Nathan, I think it's time for you to go." Dad's voice was very calm. That was a warning sign all by itself. "I'm sure Sally's had a long day, and we still need to talk to her before she can go to bed."

I hugged *Don't Go Out Alone* to my chest as I looked across the dented roof of the car to Nathan, who was staring at my parents. Finally, he swallowed hard, his Adam's apple bobbing in a way I would normally have found adorable, and said, "Actually, sir, I think we might all have a few things to discuss."

"That may be true, but we won't be discussing them tonight," said my father implacably. "Go home, Nathan. Sal will call you when she's free to talk."

"Um…when will that be?" I asked.

"If you're lucky, before you're thirty," said Mom, speaking up for the first time. "Goodnight, Nathan."

"Goodnight, Ms. Mitchell," said Nathan, his shoulders drooping. He knew when he was beaten. "Sal, I'll talk to you soon. I love you. Don't go out alone."

I nodded to show that his message was received, still hugging the book tight against my chest. "You, too," I said. Then I walked away from his car and past my parents, up the front walkway to the house. I was inside by the time I heard his engine turn over, and I didn't see him drive away.

I waited in the living room until my parents came inside. The pause gave me time to put my thoughts together, and I thought that I was ready when they arrived. "What happened today—" I began.

Dad cut me off with a single sharp jerk of his head. "We are not discussing this right now," he said. "The new security system will be installed tomorrow. Your mother and I will be staying home to oversee it, and we will review our new house-hold rules before one of us drives you to work. One of us will also pick you up. You will come straight home after your shift at the shelter is finished. This will continue for the duration of your punishment."

"What are you talking about?" I asked, too bewildered to be really annoyed. Annoyance would come later, when I was alone in my room with time to think about what had just happened. "Are you *grounding* me?"

"Yes," he replied coldly.

"You can't ground me. I'm an adult."

"We are your legal guardians. I don't care how old you are: while you are under our roof, you will live by our rules," he said. "If you have a problem with those rules, we can discuss adjusting them after your punishment is complete."

"How long is that going to be?"

"The foreseeable future," Dad said. He held out his hand. "Give me your phone."

Too stunned to do anything but obey, I dug my phone out of my pocket and dropped it into his waiting palm. He closed his fingers around it, pulling it out of my reach.

"Now go to your room."

Through all of this, Mom didn't say anything at all. She just watched me, with an expression of such profound disap-pointment on her face that it made my chest ache. I looked between them, my shoulders sagging. I had the book; I had the scrambler. I could have told them everything without any fear that SymboGen would overhear.

All I said was, "Goodnight," before I turned and walked down the hall to my room.

Joyce was standing in her own doorway, watching my approach with dark, sad eyes. She shook her head as I passed her, and mouthed, "You fucked up," silently before she vanished into the shadows of her room. I sighed and kept walking.

Beverly was curled up on my bed when I stepped into my room. She raised her head, tail thumping twice against the mattress. I closed my door, dropping my bag on the floor and setting the copy of *Don't Go Out Alone* carefully on the desk. "At least someone's glad to see me, huh, girl?"

Beverly's tail thumped the bed again.

"Good dog."

I was exhausted and overwhelmed by my day. I climbed into bed with my clothes still on. Beverly shifted positions so that her nose was tucked into the curled palm of my hand, and I fell asleep feeling her breath against my skin.

When I woke up the morning after our visit to Dr. Cale's secret lair, I found myself a prisoner in my own home. The new security system not only controlled the doors and windows; it extended to the side gates, and it could be locked down hard by anyone who controlled the master codes—specifically, my mother, father, and Joyce, all of whom were deemed "responsible enough" to decide whether poor little Sal could be allowed to go wandering around the neighborhood unprotected. The sliding glass door to the backyard had been replaced with a wooden one. Beverly now had an electronic collar keyed to the brand-new doggie door, and she could use it to come and go during the hours when no one was home. From the perspective of the security system, I was no one.

The new security extended to the wireless network and even the television, both of which had been locked down. I couldn't get on the Internet at all, and I couldn't access any of the news channels—just movies, children's shows, and endless reruns of nostalgic sitcoms made before I graduated from high school.

"This is insane," I'd objected, only to have my father look at me with cold eyes, like he was looking at someone he didn't even know.

"You should have thought of that before you ran off without telling us what had happened here," he'd replied. "You made your bed, Sal. Now you get to lie in it. Next time, you'll consider your actions before you commit to them."

"But Dad—"

"I'm not ready to talk to you yet. Have a nice day." Then he'd been out the door, heading for the car where Joyce was already waiting. I never even saw Mom that day. She was up and out before I got out of bed; she didn't come back until after I'd gone to sleep for the night.

The scope of my punishment didn't seem to fit the crime that had inspired it. I'd disappeared with my boyfriend for a day, following the sort of traumatic event that probably *should* trigger that sort of behavior. They were acting like I'd killed somebody. As one day faded into the next, they kept shutting me out. Dad was constantly leaving for the office, or at the office, or not coming home, and Joyce was with him. After the second night, she stopped coming home at all. When Mom came home from her own errands, she made herself scarce, speaking to me only in generalities. All the while, I paced the house like a caged animal, reading Nathan's copy of *Don't Go Out Alone* over and over again like it was going to teach me something new.

The story never changed. Every time, the little boy and the little girl—neither of them with a name, neither of them ever shown fully out of shadow, so that they could have looked like anything, they could have looked like Nathan, or like me— went into the forest, searching for the broken doors. Every time, they found them, and found the prize they'd been searching for: eternity in the land of monsters. That was where the story ended, every time. There was nothing about their parents, beyond "they chased the monster away, and the journey began." But wasn't that what parents were supposed to do? Chase monsters away? It seemed like they were just doing their jobs, and yet somehow that was enough to justify them losing their children forever.

On the morning of the sixth day, I opened my bedroom door, ready to face another day locked in an empty house—at least I'd be going back to work the next day, where Will and Tasha would have to take responsibility for keeping me under guard—and found myself looking at my father. I froze. The hair on the back of my neck was standing up for some reason, like he was an intruder, and not my father, who loved me, and had been there since the day I woke up from my coma.

He looked at me solemnly. Then he held up the copy of *Don't Go Out Alone* that I'd left on the kitchen table the night before, and asked, "Is this the source of the signal interference in the house?"

"I..." For a moment, I couldn't think of anything to say. Finally, I nodded, and said, "It has a scrambler in it to stop people from listening in on me. Or Nathan. It's his book, really, but he let me borrow it because I hadn't read it as many times as he had, and it seemed sort of important that I understand it, and—"

"Sal."

"—anyway, we thought we'd be seeing each other again sooner than this. I know I scared you, but do I really deserve to be locked in like some kind of animal? You're acting like I did something unforgivable, and all I did was get scared! And—"

"*Sal!*"

This time, I stopped talking, eyes wide as I stared at him.

He shook his head, lowering the book—but not, I noted, handing it to me. "How sure are you that this works?"

"How did you know it was doing anything at all?" I countered.

"I was scanning for SymboGen bugs. I've been scanning for the last six days. You shouldn't have let them into the house without notifying me." He sighed, shoulders slumping. For the first time, I wondered if the past five days hadn't been as hard on him as they had been on me. "All the bugs I've found have been nontransmitting. That meant that something had to be blocking them. Why didn't you tell me about this?"

"When, exactly, would you like me to have done that? After you grounded me and sent me to my room, or during one of the times when you left me here alone to think about what I'd done?" I glared at him, barely resisting the urge to snatch the book out of his hands. "I tried to tell you. I tried to tell you a lot of things. You never gave me the opportunity. Every time I opened my mouth, you either sent me to my room or walked away. Oh, and that 'legal guardianship' bullshit? We are so done. I am taking you to court after this, if that's what it takes, and I am *moving out*."

"Sal…" Dad stopped, taking a deep breath. Then he said, "I'm sorry. I overreacted. You have to understand that I was frightened. There was every chance that SymboGen had taken this opportunity to bug the house, and I couldn't risk you saying something before we'd managed to find and deactivate all of their listening devices. It was best for everyone if I seemed to be unreasonably angry with you."

"Why would SymboGen be bugging our house?" I asked. "I already answer all their questions."

He hesitated, looking at me with an expression of such profound sadness that I rocked back a step, trying to figure out what was going through his mind. Finally, he said, "I'm going to ask a question. I need you to answer me honestly. Can you do that?"

I nodded, not quite sure I trusted my voice at the moment.

"Good. This book"—he held up *Don't Go Out Alone*—"where did you get it?"

"It's Nathan's," I said.

"Where did Nathan get it?"

This line of questioning was starting to make me uncomfortable, for reasons I couldn't quite put my finger on. I frowned. "I don't know. He had it when he was a kid."

"I seriously doubt it came this way, since children's books aren't normally equipped to block top-of-the-line surveillance devices from doing their jobs," said my father. "I'm not playing around, Sal. Who gave you this book? It's extremely important that I speak with them."

When I first got home, shaken by my experience in Lafayette and seeing Tansy's blood-speckled face every time I closed my eyes, I would have told him about Dr. Cale and her lab without hesitation. After five days on house arrest, I just shook my head. Too much about this wasn't adding up. "It's Nathan's. He said I could borrow it if I wanted to. It was really important to him when he was a kid, and I wanted to understand him better. So I borrowed it." Before Dad could react, I leaned forward and grabbed the book out of his hand, pulling it out of his reach. "Thank you for giving it back. I remember how important it is to respect other people's property."

"Sal..."

All the anger that I'd been trying to hold back suddenly bubbled to the surface, pouring out of my lips before I had consciously decided that I was going to speak. "Why did you shut off the Internet? Why haven't I been allowed to watch the news? What's *happening* out there? You ask me questions like you think you have a right to answers, but you're not willing to let me know what's going on, or why you're scared. It's not fair, and I won't do it. You raised me better than that."

"Sal, in a very real way, I didn't raise you at all." Dad's words were quiet, even a little bit sad, like he was admitting something he didn't want to say to anyone, much less to me. I stopped breathing, and didn't start again until he continued, saying, "Your accident may have made you a better person—it did, in a lot of ways; I can't lie to myself about that, even if that makes me feel like I'm betraying the memory of my little girl—but it also made you unpredictable, in some ways, because I don't know what you're going to do when the chips are down. You don't have the training Sally had, and baby, I don't have the time to give it to you. Sometimes, you're just going to have to trust me, and do as I say, because there isn't time for me to explain."

The sound of drums rose in my ears as I thought about what he was saying to me. Finally, with a feeling of deep regret spreading through my chest, I shook my head and said, "No."

My father frowned. "What?"

"No, Dad. You say I'm not Sally: fine. I don't remember being her, I don't remember the things you say you taught her, I'm not her. You say I don't have her training: fine. If I'm not her, I can't have the things that only ever belonged to her, and that means I can't have the things she learned before I was here. But you don't get to tell me that my not having her training means you can't trust me. It goes against every other conversation we've ever *had*. You told me I was more dependable than she was. She was wild and she broke rules to show you that she could. Me disappearing the other day was the first thing I've ever done that was 'wrong,' and I had pretty good reasons for doing it! You don't get to tell me to trust you and not give me a good reason to do it."

My father looked at me without saying anything. I glared defiantly back, clutching *Don't Go Out Alone* against my chest and trying to look like I wasn't going to pass out. The drums were louder than ever, and my head felt completely empty, so light that it might float away. *So this is what adrenaline and anger feel like when you put them together*, I thought, and kept glaring.

He was the first to look away. "I reacted so poorly—and

your mother went along with me—because this wasn't the first report of sleepwalkers accosting someone in their home."

"So?" I asked, abandoning my glare in favor of a puzzled frown. "I don't understand why that would make you freak out the way you did. If it's happened before…"

"At least, we believe that it's happened before," he said. "There were no survivors, but all signs indicated that the homes had been entered by one or more sleepwalkers."

I said nothing.

"In some cases, bodies have been recovered. In others, the residents of those homes have been retrieved later when they, along with the original sleepwalkers, have been found wandering as much as five miles from the site of the attack. Somehow, the sleepwalkers are either inducing or speeding infection in asymptomatic individuals. If they had touched you…"

"SymboGen says I'm clean," I said. I realized how empty the words were even as I was speaking them. SymboGen knew that the implants contained genetic material that had never been disclosed to the public. SymboGen knew that there was a danger of the host becoming compromised. Dr. Cale might have been their Dr. Frankenstein miracle worker, but the scientists she left behind weren't *stupid*. They understood what the early-generation *D. symbogenesis* could mean. They knew about the risk of Adam. So how could I believe that anything they told me was the unadulterated truth?

I couldn't.

"So the sleepwalkers would just have killed you, rather than turning you," said my father grimly. "I'm sorry, Sal, but I'm not really seeing that as an improvement."

I frowned. "Is that why you blocked the news channels and the Internet? Because you didn't want me getting upset about things you couldn't explain while the house was bugged?" Something else occurred to me. I hugged my book a little tighter. "*Why* was the house bugged? You still haven't told me why. You never said I couldn't let SymboGen security inside. If this was such a big risk, couldn't you have told me that before it happened?"

"Just...let me work through this at my own pace, all right?" He turned and walked back toward the dining room table. Puzzled, I followed him, and when he sat, I took the seat across from his. It seemed oddly ordinary to be looking at him across the table, like this was nothing but a friendly chat about chores or what we were going to do over the weekend. The solemnity in his eyes refused to let me forget that this was so brutally much more.

He took a breath, and said, "We decided to block the news channels and the Internet because we didn't know how much of the house was bugged, and we had no way to prevent you from asking questions when you saw what *wasn't* on the news."

"What?" I frowned again, utterly puzzled. "What do you mean?"

"The GPS in your phone was blocked by that book"—he nodded toward *Don't Go Out Alone*—"but from the condition of Nathan's car when you got home, I'm assuming you somehow wound up in the Lafayette exclusion zone. Is that correct?"

I bit my lip and nodded, not saying anything.

"Well, if you had been watching the news, you might wonder why there was no mention of whatever you saw there. Or of the incident you had here at home, with the sleepwalkers in the yard. That should have raised a great many flags, don't you think? Armed SymboGen security guards removing sick people from private property isn't exactly an everyday occurrence, and yet it's nowhere on the news. It's not even on the Internet, so far as I can tell."

"That's ridiculous," I protested. "You can't keep things off the Internet." There were dozens, if not hundreds, of embarrassing blog posts and "articles" written about me during the brief window of pseudocelebrity that followed my accident. Most of them were accompanied by incredibly unflattering pictures of me in hospital gowns or freshly stained pajamas— it took me a while to develop the fine motor control needed to feed myself without wearing my meals, and it took me even longer to learn that I should change my clothes when they got food on them—and they talked about aspects of my recovery that I didn't think were anybody's business but my own. And yet people wrote those posts, and other people read them, and they were popular enough that they didn't die down until I stopped doing anything that they would think of as "interesting." Censoring the Internet was impossible.

"No, Sal," said my father tiredly. "*I* can't keep things off the Internet. *You* can't keep things off the Internet. Given enough incidents, even SymboGen won't be able to keep things off the Internet. But right now, with things still as contained as they are, it's possible for a large enough corporation with a focused enough security department to do quite a few things that aren't supposed to be possible. The government could even be, potentially, helping them along to the best of our ability; right now, their goals and our goals overlap enough to be worth supporting."

I blinked at him. "Why would the government be helping SymboGen suppress information about what's really going on?"

"Because starting a panic does no one any good, and we still don't know for sure *why* these are the things that SymboGen is choosing to suppress—or when it started. Did the sleepwalkers begin appearing before we heard about them? Was Symbo-Gen editing the news from the start? There's so much we don't know, both about the science, and about the motives of the people who stand to benefit. Oh, some people know what's going on—you can't censor gossip—but other than some small runs on bottled water and canned goods, it's had very little impact."

I blinked again, going very still. Even the distant sound of drums had faded, leaving me with only the sound of my own breath. Beverly went trotting by on her way to the kitchen, looking for scraps that might have been dropped during breakfast. In the silence, her claws clacking against the linoleum seemed louder than slamming doors. Things were starting to come together. My vision was unfocusing the way it did when I tried to read for too long in a single setting, casting blurry little halos of color and light around everything.

Finally, I said, "I am done asking questions. I need you to tell me, in very small, very simple words, what's going on. And then I need you to give me my phone back. I will make the decision of what I do next based on what you say."

"Sal—"

"Remember how you don't get to say 'just trust me' and have it stick anymore? Well, you also don't get to decide what's best for me. I may not remember as many years as I should, but I can manage myself pretty well." I didn't mention that if I left, I'd be calling Nathan to come get me and Beverly from the corner. Saying "I'll call my boyfriend to pick me up" felt like it undermined my overall argument a bit too much.

Dad paused. Then he smiled, and said, "You know, you're more like your mother now than you were before the accident. It's strange, and it ought to be impossible, but it's true. And as for what's going on that I was trying to protect you from… SymboGen is hiding things. We've known that for some time, and you and I have talked about it before. But there is a reasonable chance that they were so happy to be involved in your care in part because I work for USAMRIID, and if they were able to bug our home, they would then be able to find out what the government knew about the more questionable aspects of their business practices."

Aspects like splicing *Toxoplasma* into the implants, which would make them—which *had* made them—more flexible and resilient than anyone imagined. Questionable aspects like the entire structure of *D. symbogenesis.* The parasite that had been approved by the FDA wasn't the one being implanted in people. That couldn't possibly be a good thing.

Questionable aspects like an unshared test for the sleeping sickness, which wasn't a sickness at all, but the result of the *D. symbogenesis* parasite trying for a hostile takeover of its host.

I didn't say any of that. I just nodded minutely, and waited for him to keep going.

"SymboGen never reported the people in our yard to the authorities. I made inquiries—discreetly—and no similar incidents have been formally reported. We know about it only because we've been monitoring patient intake at SymboGen, and because a few groups have been picked up wandering in areas that allowed the police to back-trace to the invaded homes. We suspect that SymboGen is illegally detaining the afflicted, although we have no proof yet."

My head was starting to spin. I frowned at him. "And Lafayette?"

"We think it was another home invasion scenario. This one involving multiple houses in the hills, and spilling down onto the freeway once the sleepwalkers could find no one else who appealed to them. What's most interesting is that several of the cars in the traffic jam were accosted by sleepwalkers, and some of the drivers joined the gang."

"How is that *interesting*?" I demanded, staring at him. "That's *horrible.*"

"Yes, it is, but Sal, even more cars *weren't* accosted by sleepwalkers." Dad shook his head. "They're choosing who they go after. They're choosing very carefully. What we don't know is what they're basing those decisions on. The sleepwalkers don't seem to do anything consciously."

I was terribly afraid that I knew what the sleepwalkers were basing their decisions on: they were going for the people whose implants had infiltrated the largest possible percentage of their brains and nervous systems, making it easy for them to encourage the implant into taking the final steps toward autonomy. How they were managing that encouragement was something I didn't know yet.

"They went after our car," I said quietly.

"I know," said my father. "The fact that you and Nathan are both okay is a bigger relief to me than I can properly express."

Were we really?

On the other hand, I felt totally normal, and Nathan didn't have an implant for the sleepwalkers to activate. Maybe they'd come for us because they could sense Tansy, and thought that she was inside the car. It was as good an explanation as any, and one that might allow me to sleep again. I allowed my shoulders to unlock a little.

Dad was watching me carefully. "Sal, the last time we really talked, before the sleepwalkers came here to the house, you said something."

"Did I?" I asked, blinking at him.

"Yes. You said SymboGen had a test for infection. Were you telling the truth about that? Do they really have a way of knowing whether someone is about to get sick?"

Any sting that he thought I might be lying to him was dulled by the realization that even after all this, he still didn't know. "Yes," I said. "They have a test. They used it on me, after I was exposed, and then Nathan tested some confirmed patients after I described what happened. It's real."

"And they aren't sharing." Dad shook his head. "Some people need to learn that the public health matters more than their profit margins."

"Can you *make* them share?"

"No." Sudden hope lit his eyes. "But you can tell me what they did. I need you to tell me *everything*, Sal. You may be able to save a lot of lives. A reliable test is the first step toward developing a treatment."

I wasn't sure I followed his logic—knowing that something is wrong and knowing how to fix it are two very different things—but I was willing to go along with it, for the moment, because it was going to get me something that I needed.

"Take me to work with you, and I'll show you," I said.

Dad blinked. Then he frowned. "I don't think you understand the importance of my request."

"I don't think you understand the importance of mine." I had Dr. Cale's side of the story. I'd been getting SymboGen's side of the story since the day I woke up from my coma. Now it was time to get a neutral perspective. Maybe that would tell me what I had to do next.

For a long moment, Dad just sat and looked at me. Finally, sighing, he stood. "All right," he said. "Get your things. We're leaving in five minutes."

"Thank you," I said, and clutched *Don't Go Out Alone* a little tighter as I jumped to my feet and ran back to my room.

The drive to the San Francisco USAMRIID field office was quiet. Dad didn't say anything, and so neither did I. He turned on the radio once, scanning quickly through the bands of pop music, classic rock, and overcaffeinated morning DJs making prank calls and telling sexist jokes. Then he turned the radio off again, letting silence reclaim ownership of the car.

We were halfway there when it got to be too much for me. "Where's Joyce?" I asked, desperate for conversation. After five days of isolation, I was ready for social contact, no matter how strained.

Dad grimaced. "She's at the lab," he said.

I paused. "Did she come home last night?" I didn't remember hearing her, but that didn't mean anything. I'd been so wrapped up with feeling sorry for myself and hating my parents that I wouldn't have heard a bomb go off in the kitchen.

"No." He sounded almost grudging. "She felt that our treatment of you was extreme, no matter how good our reasons were for making the decisions that we did. She also understood that there wasn't a better way, and so, rather than continuing to argue, she stayed at the office to make her feelings clear. We have a break room with a few cots in it, for times when exhaustion makes it unsafe to drive. After an eighteen-hour shift working in Biohazard Safety Level 4, you're not getting behind the wheel. Not while I have anything to say about it."

"She's sleeping in the Ebola Room?"

Dad actually chuckled at that. "No, the break room isn't *in* Level 4, just adjacent to it. We haven't had a leak since '02. She's perfectly safe, and I'm sure she'll be thrilled to see you, especially when you demonstrate the SymboGen test for infection."

I squirmed a little in my seat. "About that..."

"Sal." Dad shot me a warning glance. "Please don't tell me you lied to me just to get out of the house."

"What? Jeez, Dad, no! But I don't know how much the test really *means*. Nathan and I both checked out clean, and someone we knew for sure was sick checked out infected, but I have no idea whether it can show you the early stages. Maybe it's something that just works on people who have already started sleepwalking."

"You said that SymboGen checked you after you were exposed, yes? Well, that means it's at least somewhat useful as a form of early detection—and I'll be honest, Sal. We're to the point of grasping at straws, here. Whatever you can give us, we'll take it."

"I could have given this to you days ago." It was a cheap dig, but it felt worth taking.

"You could. But then SymboGen might have realized that

we were onto them. I couldn't take that chance." Dad glanced my way again, this time without the warning. "The last thing I want to do is put you, or anyone else, in danger. Please believe that."

"I do." I settled back in my seat, resisting the urge to hug *Don't Go Out Alone* to my chest again. "I really do."

We finished the drive in silence.

The San Francisco branch of USAMRIID—the United States Army Medical Research Institute of Infectious Diseases— was constructed in what used to be the Treasure Island military base, before changes in personnel and deployment caused the base's original purpose to become outmoded. It sat empty for several years, before the property was repurposed to allow the military to keep an eye on the growing California biotech and medical research fields.

I knew the history of the facility because I lived with my father and Joyce, both of whom were more than happy to talk about where they worked, if not what they did every day. I knew the word "outmoded" because of Sherman, who had chosen it as our word of the day over a year before.

My cautiously optimistic mood deflated, leaving me feeling hollow, without even the comforting sound of drums to buoy me up. No matter what we did, no matter what I learned or what I was able to share with my father's lab, Sherman was still going to be dead. He was never going to teach me another vocabulary word, or threaten to seduce my boyfriend away from me. Sherman was gone.

In that moment, I hated SymboGen, I hated *D. symbogenesis*, and most of all, I hated Dr. Shanti Cale, for making it possible for the rest of it to happen in the first place. I hated them for ruining everything, and for hurting so many of the people I cared about. They were the ones who opened the broken doors, not us. But we were the ones who were paying for their actions.

My father pulled up at the gate, where sturdy-looking guard stations loomed on either side of the car. A young man in army green was seated in the driver's side booth, a clipboard in his hands. My father rolled down his window. The young man rose, and saluted.

"Colonel Mitchell," he said.

"At ease, soldier." My father indicated me. "This is my daughter, Sally Mitchell. She's on the approved visitor's list. I need a pass for her."

"Yes, sir." The young man gestured to the uniformed woman in the other guard booth. The window rolled down as she approached my door. I hate it when drivers do that. It just reminds me of how little control I have.

"Ma'am," she said.

"Hello," I said.

"Please look at the blue dot." The woman indicated a blue dot at the center of a smooth black metal box mounted on the guard station wall. I looked at it, bemused. The woman typed something on a keyboard. "Her pass will be waiting when you get inside."

"Thank you," said my father, and drove onward to the barrier, which rose as we approached it.

I sat back in my seat, blinking. "What just happened?"

"Don't worry about it."

"Dad—"

"We're here."

The San Francisco USAMRIID installation consisted of four main buildings, connected by stone walkways, and the boxy shape of the Level 4 lab, which was isolated from the rest of the facility by more than twenty yards. Collapsible tunnels connected it to the administration building. They could be sterilized and removed in less than ninety seconds, leaving the L4 lab completely cut off. The doors would lock automatically at the same time. Anyone left inside would find themselves depending on the vending machines and their own ability not to die from unspeakable pathogens until someone came up with an extraction plan.

Naturally, that was where my sister worked, and naturally, that was our destination. Dad parked the car just outside the lab's main entrance, in the spot marked DIRECTOR. Similar spaces were reserved outside all the lab buildings, since there was no telling where he'd need to be at any given time.

"Now, remember," he cautioned, as we got out of the car. "Don't touch anything unless I tell you it's safe, and don't—"

"If you tell me not to lick anything, I'm going to throw something at you," I cautioned. Not *Don't Go Out Alone*—I couldn't justify leaving it at home, but I wasn't taking it inside, either. The book was in my shoulder bag, which was safely tucked under my seat, along with my notebook. Hopefully, no one was going to notice it there. It felt a little odd to be worrying about an old picture book and a bunch of half-coherent dreams. Then again, everything felt a little odd these days.

Dad looked abashed. "I'm sorry," he said. "It's just that you haven't been trained the way Joyce has, and I worry about you."

I smiled wanly. "It's okay. Let's just go inside, and I'll show you what I can."

He nodded. "All right. But Sal...we're going into a live research project. The L4 building is almost entirely dedicated to the sleepwalkers right now. You must follow my instructions at all times. Do you understand?"

"I do," I said. "Let's go."

Dad nodded one more time before turning and leading me out of the parking lot, toward the unmarked but somehow menacing door of the Level 4 lab. I took a deep breath and followed him, with the oddly comforting sound of drums hammering in my ears. Whatever was behind that door, it would be something I didn't know yet, and every piece of this puzzle counted.

Guards flanked the door. They saluted my father as he approached. He returned the salute almost absentmindedly, and turned to shield the keypad with his body as he entered his security code. The lock disengaged, and he pulled the door open, beckoning me inside.

"Be careful now," I murmured, and stepped through.

The fact that the scientific community has willingly accepted Steve's sanitized explanation for the origins of D. symbogenesis strikes me as a form of modern miracle—or perhaps it's just proof that we inevitably get the saviors we deserve. In an earlier era, Steve would have been a traveling snake oil salesman, offering people cures too good to be true. Today, he peddles a new form of snake oil, one that can be just as dangerous, and just as destructive.

If you believed that D. symbogenesis was the simple, easily controlled organism SymboGen described in their press releases and paperwork, you have been sold a bottle of snake oil. While you may well deserve what that gets you, the truth is, I enabled Steve to become such a great salesman...and while I may not regret the science, I am truly sorry for the lies.

—FROM CAN OF WORMS: THE AUTOBIOGRAPHY OF
SHANTI CALE, PHD. AS YET UNPUBLISHED.

I don't think anyone can deny that the SymboGen Intestinal Bodyguard™ changed the face of medicine as we know it. Chronic conditions can now be treated on an ongoing basis by the ingestion of a single pill—it's just that the pill contains the egg of a D. symbogenesis, and the implant will handle all

*the ongoing medical care. No more worrying about afford-
ing your prescriptions, no more missed doses or mix-ups at the
pharmacy. Everything is taken care of.*

*Were we perfect from the word "go"? No. Even if we
weren't only human, that would have been a little much to
ask of us, don't you think? We could only do what anyone is
capable of doing: our best. We rose to the challenges we were
offered, and we did what we could to meet and match them.
I think that when history looks at our accomplishments, the
good that we managed to do will outweigh the bad. I hope so,
anyway. No one wants to set out to be a hero, and discover
after the fact that they've been a villain all along.*

—FROM "KING OF THE WORMS," AN INTERVIEW WITH
DR. STEVEN BANKS, CO-FOUNDER OF SYMBOGEN. ORIGINALLY
PUBLISHED IN *ROLLING STONE*, FEBRUARY 2027.

Chapter 15

AUGUST 2027

After Dad's dire warnings, the entry hall of the L4 building was almost anticlimactic. I was expecting something out of one of Joyce's science fiction movies, with unfamiliar equipment and unexplained lasers everywhere. What I got was basically a hallway that could have been leading to any ER in the world. The walls were a hospital-standard shade of eggshell white, with bands of color painted on them to help guide researchers to the right parts of the building, and the floor was an industrial avocado green that looked like it had been chosen to coordinate with generic medical scrubs.

Another uniformed guard sat at the reception desk. Dad motioned for me to stay where I was as he walked over and exchanged a few words with the man in a low voice. The man's eyes flickered to me and back to Dad again. I tried not to squirm. Finally, my father leaned over the desk and picked up an old-fashioned telephone. A thick cord connected it to a base that looked heavy enough to be used as a melee weapon. He brought the phone to his ear, and was silent for several seconds before he said, "This is Colonel Alfred Mitchell. My daughter, Sally, is with me. Can you confirm the current conditions in the main lab?" There was another pause before he said, "Yes, I've cleared her presence through the appropriate channels. I *am* the appropriate channels. Can you confirm current conditions?"

He sounded annoyed. I stayed where I was. When my father was annoyed, the last place I wanted to be was in his line of fire. He never really yelled at me—that pleasure was generally reserved for Joyce, who didn't seem to mind; she gave as good as she got, anyway, and that seemed to work for both of them— but he'd look at me sometimes like he wasn't sure what I was doing, or why I was allowed to be wherever I was, and that was something I wanted to avoid if at all possible.

When he looked at me like that, he was frightening.

Dad made a small, irritated sound. "Well, tell Michael to put things back in their boxes. We're coming through in five minutes. Sally has something she needs to show me, and that means we need to be inside the lab space." He slammed the receiver down on its base harder than he needed to as he turned to face me. "The lab is not prepared for civilian visitors. They'll be ready for us shortly."

"Do you mean 'not prepared' like 'they need to clean up,' or 'not prepared' like 'someone dropped a vial and now it's all melting flesh and screaming'?" I asked. I wasn't sure I wanted to know the answer. I wasn't sure I'd ever sleep again if I *didn't* know the answer.

That actually made Dad smile. "Neither," he said. "It's 'not prepared' in the sense of 'there is confidential material that shouldn't be seen by civilian eyes out on the counters.'"

"Oh." I paused, frowning. "But…isn't Joyce a civilian?"

Dad's smile faded. "Yes," he said, and the weight of disappointment in that word was as crushing as it was confusing. If Joyce was a civilian, what was the problem with my asking the question?

He turned away before I could ask him, saying something else quiet to the guard at the desk. The guard nodded, handing him a key card and a visitor's pass. The pass had my picture on it. Dad turned, holding them out to me.

"How did they make it so *fast*?" I asked, taking the pass and card.

My father ignored my question. "The women's changing room is over there," he said, indicating a door at the back of the reception area. It was unmarked. "Go in there and get yourself into some scrubs; affix the pass to the front of them. We're going into a clean area, and I'd rather you didn't introduce contamination."

"Dad—"

"Just get changed, Sal. We'll talk about all this later."

I frowned. His mood swings and changes in attitude were starting to worry me. Given Dr. Cale's description of the components of *D. symbogenesis*, what were the chances it could be interfering with his brain function? Was my father's implant beginning to take over? And if it was, was there anything I could possibly do about it?

That line of thought would lead me nowhere good, and it wasn't like I'd have to wait long to learn the answer: we were about to go into a clean area. Once we were there, I'd show him how the UV light tests worked, and I could use that as an excuse to check him for signs of infection. After that was done... well, we'd see what happened after that. If nothing else, if I knew he was infected before he did, I could run like hell.

I bit my lip. "I'll be right back," I said.

"Good," he replied. "You wouldn't want to go wandering off in here. There are some very dangerous things in this facility."

I nodded quickly before I turned to head through the door

he had indicated before. Dangerous things. Yes. They were all around me.

The problem was, I was starting to wonder if he might be one of them.

The women's changing room was lined entirely with pea-green lockers. Some of them had combination locks on them, keeping their contents secret. The three nearest the door were marked VISITOR. I opened one of those, pulling out the pale blue medical scrubs inside. There were even slippers, and a plastic cap for my hair. Reduce the risk as much as possible. Not to zero—never to zero; the only thing that's at absolutely zero risk is something dead, or that was never at risk at all—but to as close as science can manage.

I stripped to my bra and underpants before stopping to wonder whether they might have cameras in the room. Modesty was one of the more difficult lessons they'd tried to drill into me, and I was still trying to get the more subtle details down. Were cameras supposed to be one of the things I couldn't let see me naked, or could I relax around them?

Sherman would know.

That thought sent the cold dread roiling in my stomach once again. I'd almost forgotten about Sherman, and how very personal this infection could be. If Dad was sick...

He wasn't showing any of the signs of the sleepwalking sickness. He was still calm, and coherent, and aware of his surroundings. He'd driven me to USAMRIID. The sleepwalkers weren't capable of operating a car. That level of fine motor control was long gone by the time they started rambling. So why couldn't I shake the feeling that I was missing something?

I dressed quickly, tying my hair into a ponytail before tucking it into the plastic cap. I stuffed my clothes into the locker. I didn't have a lock. That wasn't a problem, since the only things that really mattered—my notebook and Nathan's copy of *Don't*

Go Out Alone—were still in my bag and safely hidden under the passenger seat in Dad's car. If someone wanted to wander away with my clothes, I'd be annoyed, but it wouldn't be the end of the world.

The pass was a flexible piece of memory plastic with my name and basic description printed on it, along with my picture. It softened when I pressed it against the breast of my scrubs, bonding with the fabric. I didn't know how they were going to get it off again, and I didn't care.

Dad was waiting when I emerged from the changing room, and he had changed his own clothes for blue scrubs identical to mine. The feeling that something was wrong just got stronger when I saw the look on his face, a grim mix of determination and unhappiness. I forced a smile before handing back the key card.

"All ready," I said.

"There's been another mob of sleepwalkers," he replied. "This one formed in downtown Walnut Creek. They attacked the outdoor shopping center. Casualties are still being tabulated. It's spreading—and it's not staying off the news this time. We're already getting reports of runs on water and canned goods at the local grocery stores."

I glanced at the guard at the reception desk, who gave no sign of having heard, before turning back to my father. "I…Dad, why are you telling me this?"

"Because if there is anything, *anything*, you know about this disease, and you don't share that information today, I don't know how I'll be able to justify letting you leave without arresting you for treason." He shook his head. Something behind his eyes was hard and unfamiliar. The dread in my stomach wound itself even tighter. "I've tried to be patient. I've tried to wait for you to come around. I've tried, God knows, to understand how difficult this is for you—how hard it's been for someone with your limited exposure to the world to understand the severity of our current situation. I've defended my actions to my superiors several times already. I don't know how much longer I can do that."

I stared at him. It was the only thing I could do. What he was saying... "I don't know what you're talking about."

"If that's true, then we're both in a great deal of trouble. Come along." He turned his back on me again, this time as he walked to the next sealed door and swiped his key card across the lock. The door swung open. He stepped through, and I followed him.

The main room of the USAMRIID L4 lab looked so much like Dr. Cale's makeshift bowling alley laboratory that I actually caught myself glancing around, hoping to spot a blonde woman in a wheelchair. I might not entirely trust her, but at least if she were here, I wouldn't be so torn about how much I could or couldn't tell my father.

Instead of Dr. Cale, I saw military doctors and scientists in scrubs very much like mine, albeit accessorized with lab coats and identification, working at their individual stations and ignoring the two of us completely. The walls were lined with supply shelves and light boxes, continuing the similarity to the bowling alley, but the space not taken up by equipment was filled with cautionary signs. Most of them were too far away for me to even attempt reading, assuming I could convince my eyes to focus. That didn't matter, since they had handy symbols to make sure I couldn't miss the meanings. Do not touch, do not ingest, do not remove from the lab. There were so many rules that it was dizzying.

Joyce was working at one of the nearby lab tables. She looked up as the door swung shut behind us, and stopped, a perplexed expression crossing her face. She looked from Dad to me, and back to Dad again. Finally, she put down the scalpel she was holding, carefully peeled off her plastic gloves, and started toward us. She was moving slowly, like she was afraid one or both of us might spook.

"Sal?" she said, when she was close enough that she wouldn't need to raise her voice. The rest of the lab technicians politely ignored us. "What are you doing here?"

"Your sister is here to demonstrate the SymboGen test for the sleepwalking sickness. Isn't that right, Sally?"

Dad's hand clamped onto my shoulder. It felt heavier than it should have. I swallowed hard and said, "That's right. When I was... when Chave got sick, they tested to see if I had the sleepwalking sickness. I can demonstrate." I snuck a glance up at my father. He was frowning straight ahead, almost like he was no longer paying attention to Joyce, or to me.

"Oh." Joyce followed my gaze, and bit her lip. Then she focused back on me, forcing a smile through her obvious dismay. "Well, you're here now, and that means we can maybe make some progress. What do we need?"

I don't know, I wanted to cry. *I'm not supposed to be the one who knows.* That was my father, the Colonel, or my sister, the scientist, or my boyfriend, the doctor. I was the one who wandered through life and was gently corrected when I started to drift off course. I was the one who didn't remember enough to know when she was wrong. So why were people suddenly looking to me like I was going to have answers? Answers weren't my job.

But there was no one to provide them for me. I sniffled as softly as I could, hoping no one would notice, and said, "Dad said you had some sick people here. I need to see one of them. And I'm going to need a portable UV wand."

"And...?" prompted Joyce.

I shook my head. "That's all. A sick person, and a portable UV wand."

My father's hand tightened on my shoulder. "If that's all you needed, why did you make me bring you here?"

"Ow." I stepped away from his hand, turning to glare at him. "I told you why back at the house. I need to understand what's going on. I need to ask questions and get answers, not get more dismissals and half-truths. I need—"

I stopped midsentence. My father's face was turned toward me, but he wasn't really looking at me anymore; his eyes were unfocused, and one corner of his mouth was starting to sag downward, like he was in the early stages of a stroke. The sound of drums grew even louder in my ears as I realized just how erratic his behavior had become over the course of the day. He'd gone from normal to overly solicitous to aggressive, all without the normal stimulus I would expect to trigger such shifts in mood.

Unless something I couldn't see was triggering them. I took a step backward, moving away from him.

"Sal?" Joyce sounded puzzled.

"Dad?"

He didn't respond. He just kept standing there, like he was going to say something. But he wasn't. I could tell that just by looking at him.

The worst part of it was that he didn't look like the sleepwalker who'd been at our back door, or the one outside the car. His eyes were still aware, still struggling to focus.

"Joyce, if this lab has security, this would be a good time to call for them," I said, not taking my eyes off my father. He wasn't moving. I honestly didn't know whether that was a good sign, or a bad one. In dogs, that sort of stillness could be a precursor to an attack.

"What are you talking about, Sal?" She stepped forward, moving toward us.

I didn't think. I just reacted, moving quickly to get her out of Dad's reach. I grabbed her arm and jerked her back just as he began to move again, hands grasping at the air where she had been standing only a half second before. Joyce made a small, startled shrieking sound, one that dwindled almost instantly into a cough. Dad grabbed for the air again. I jerked her even harder away from him.

The other technicians were starting to look up from their work, abandoning the pretense that we could have a private family conversation in the middle of a busy government lab. That was good, since the alternative was their politely ignoring us while my father ripped us apart.

"He's sick!" I shouted, pulling Joyce another step backward. Dad continued to follow us. At least he wasn't moving very fast yet; he still seemed disoriented, like he wasn't sure what to do with himself.

Fight it, Dad, I thought. *That...thing...that's taking you over, fight it for as long as you can. Let me get Joyce out of here.*

Joyce finally seemed to understand the danger we were in. She stumbled as she got her feet under her, and then she was backpedaling on her own, no longer relying on me to pull her. "*Daddy?*" she asked.

"He was fine when we got here!" I said. But that was a lie, wasn't it? He'd already been slipping, and I'd known that something was wrong, I'd *known*, and I'd ignored the signs, because...because...

Because I didn't know what else to do. We were through the broken doors now, and the only ground left was the unfamiliar kind.

Dr. Cale said that once someone started showing symptoms of the sleepwalking sickness, it was too late for any treatment, because the parasite was already in their brain. But she *would* say that, wouldn't she? Even if it wasn't strictly true, she'd say it. The SymboGen implants were her children. She might not actively side with them against the human race. That didn't mean she was going to go out of her way to figure out how to stop them from taking the things they wanted. Like bodies of their own.

The other technicians were in motion now, some of them running for the exits, others grabbing old-fashioned telephones from the walls and gabbling into them, presumably calling security. I yanked Joyce back another step before raising my voice and calling, "Does anybody have any antiparasitics? I mean really good ones? We need—" I cheated my eyes toward Joyce and asked, "What do you use for tapeworms?"

It seemed impossibly weird to be asking her questions when our father, clearly dazed, was shambling toward us like something out of a horror movie. Oddly, that seemed to help Joyce. This was too strange to be happening: therefore, it wasn't happening. "Praziquantel," she said. "It has some negative side effects, though, like—"

"Is one of the negative side effects death?" I demanded. "Because if it's not, I suggest we get somebody to pump Dad full of the stuff *right now*."

Joyce took her eyes off our father in order to blink at me in obvious bewilderment. "What are you talking about?"

I wasn't sure whether sleepwalkers were capable of watching for an opening—if they were anything like as confused as Dr. Cale had implied, they might not be capable of anything beyond basic instinct, at least initially—but my father still took advantage of the opening when Joyce presented it to him. He lunged forward. He was fast. I was just a little bit faster. I grabbed her shoulders and yanked her hard away from him, leaving his hands to slap together on empty air with a flat, meaty sound that would haunt my dreams for days. Joyce yelped, as much with surprise as anything else, and fell over, upsetting two trays of instruments in the process. I barely managed to dodge in time to keep her from taking me to the floor with her.

The sudden flurry of movement seemed to confuse our father, who froze, his face swinging slowly toward me, then toward Joyce, and back to me again. I straightened slowly, raising my hands in front of me to show that they were empty. I don't know what good I was expecting that to do. I wasn't thinking particularly clearly by that point.

"Dad, you're sick," I said, enunciating each word as clearly as I could. "I need you to fight against whatever it is you want to do right now, and focus on the sound of my voice. There's something we can do to help you be better, but it won't work if you don't focus on the sound of my voice. Can you do that for me, Dad? Can you fo—"

Without warning, he lunged. I squeaked, stopping in the middle of my sentence, and turned to run. He seemed to track by sound and motion. Joyce was frozen in terror. She wasn't making a sound, and she wasn't going anywhere. All I had to do was keep his eyes on me, and trust that someone would stop him before he could do something we'd both regret later.

Well. Maybe I wouldn't regret it if he killed me. I'd be dead, after all. But I'd sure as hell regret letting myself get into this position if things got that far, in the time I had before oxygen deprivation resulted in my second clinical brain death.

I ran; my father followed. The rest of the technicians had cleared the room, which was convenient, since it meant I didn't need to worry about leading their rampaging, somewhat addled boss into the middle of their workspace. I shoved things into his path as I tried to evade him without losing his interest. I was afraid if anyone else in the room moved or made a sound, he'd abandon chasing me in favor of going for easier prey. Prey that wasn't running like hell, or throwing file boxes at his head.

The doors at the back of the room opened and military police flooded in, almost like they were imitating the SymboGen security guards on the day when Chave got sick. That seemed like it had happened so long ago. It seemed like it had happened yesterday. Several of them pulled their guns, and I stopped running in order to put up my hands, and yell, "No! Don't shoot! Stun him, and get the pretzel drugs!" I was saying it wrong. I knew I was. But long words were Joyce's thing, not mine, and I'd only heard the name of the drug once. I was frankly impressed I could remember it started with the letter "P."

And then my father's hands closed around my throat, and I stopped being impressed by anything, except for maybe how tight his grip was. I scrabbled at his fingers, trying to dislodge them, and couldn't find any purchase. He was bigger than I was, he was stronger than I was, and he was going to win this one if I didn't figure out a way to change the rules.

Dad, I'm sorry, I thought, and focused all my remaining energy on planting my foot squarely between his legs.

His response was to groan and let go of my throat, causing me to drop first to my knees and then to my ass as my legs folded up beneath me. My father didn't seem to notice; he was too busy grasping his crotch and moaning.

I scrambled back to my feet. "It's not too late!" I shouted. "Joyce, get the antiparasitics!"

The other sleepwalkers didn't seem to feel or really register pain once they had fully succumbed to the parasites that were infiltrating their brains. My father still responded to extreme pain stimuli like a normal human, and that meant he hadn't been completely taken over yet. There was still a chance that we could treat him. There was—

"Oh, my God, my balls," he moaned.

I stopped. "Dad?"

"Wow, Daddy, *great* idea," said Joyce, picking herself up off the floor. She dusted off her lab coat with the heels of her hands, scowling at our father like he had just disappointed her in some deep and profound manner. "It's not Halloween, we're not twelve anymore, and this isn't how you make it clear that things are serious."

The soldiers were standing down. Some of them even seemed to be snickering, trying to hide their amusement behind their hands. I looked from them to Joyce, my confusion growing by the second. The sound of drums was getting louder, now fueled by anger instead of by fear.

"Joyce?" I said, trying to keep my voice measured. "What's going on here?"

"Daddy thought you might be holding out on us, since you

went and disappeared for hours right after a bunch of sleepers showed up in the yard."

He managed to gasp out something that might have been "I still think that," or might have simply been a request for an ice pack. I ignored him either way, focusing my attention on Joyce instead. If I looked at him, I was going to be too tempted to give him another kick. The military police might think it was funny for me to attack my father when he was playing sleep-walker, but kicking him while he was down was likely to get a less positive reaction.

"So you're saying he *faked* this?" I asked. My voice was sounding a lot less measured. I took a step away from my father. "He set this up to—what, scare me into giving away secrets?"

"It...worked," gasped my father, finally pulling himself to his feet. "Why did you start asking for antiparasitics?"

"That *was* pretty specific," said Joyce. She walked toward us, primly stepping around the objects I'd knocked over during my flight. I noticed that she didn't bother picking anything up. That was apparently below her pay grade. "What would make you decide to ask for antiparasitics?"

I looked from Dad, who was still white-faced and grasping his crotch, to Joyce, who looked utterly calm. The technicians were moving back to their stations, and although security was still in the room, none of them looked like they were planning to do anything to secure anyone. It had all been a sham. It was a play to see what I would do, and while that spoke to the level of their desperation, it still infuriated me in ways I didn't really have the words for.

"Is this why you locked me in the house and wouldn't let me talk to Nathan for five days?" I asked. "Because you wanted me to be scared?"

"The things I said to you on the way here were true," said my father. He was starting to sound less winded, which made me want to kick him again. "I really did want time to check for bugs, and there really were things about the news that would have made you ask questions."

"They made Nathan ask questions," said Joyce. "He showed up here yesterday, demanding to know if you were all right."

I blinked. "Why would he come *here*?"

"Because we told him you weren't at home, and this was the only other place you could logically be," said my father. I turned to stare at him. He continued, "We tried telling him you'd become symptomatic, to see what he would say. He said we were lying. We've been trying to find him since then."

"What?"

"He vanished, Sal," said Joyce. "Do you know where he would go?"

Yes; back to his mother, who had answers, and who would be able to tell him whether it was possible for me to have become symptomatic so quickly, when there had been no signs that my resident implant was planning to migrate from my digestive system to my brain. Dr. Cale could hide him, keep him off the grid and keep him safe, while they figured out where I was and how to get me out. I glanced toward the security guards, wondering how many of them might be working for her, playing both sides against the middle. It was a paranoid thought, but given that my father and sister had just staged some kind of horror movie dumbshow for my benefit, paranoid didn't seem so strange anymore.

"No," I said, and was surprised by how sincere I sounded. "I don't have any idea where Nathan would go, and I don't think I want to talk to either one of you right now. I asked Dad to bring me here because I was tired of being locked in the house, and because I wanted to help. After what you did, I don't feel like helping anymore. Being locked up is better than being here with you."

"I'm afraid I can't take you home until you demonstrate that test you promised to show us," said my father. All traces of weakness were gone from his voice, and he was once again standing up straight. The jangling feeling of *wrongness* was still coming off him like a wave, but that might just have been my nerves reacting to the overall mood in the room.

Might. "Then I'll call Tasha or Will to come and get me," I said, raising my chin defiantly. My coworkers at the shelter hadn't seen me in days. They'd be annoyed by my suddenly calling and asking for favors. They'd also be more than willing to get in the car and pick me up. They both understood why I didn't drive, and respected it. I sometimes suspected I was just another abandoned animal to them, but in moments like this, I didn't mind.

"No, you won't." My father's voice was almost gentle, for all that it was still firm. "You won't be able to get a cell phone signal inside here, and I'm not going to let you leave this building until you show me what you promised."

I stared at him. "I made that promise before you pretended to be a *sleepwalker* and tried to *strangle* me," I said.

"Desperate times can lead us to do things we're not proud of," he said. Joyce was a silent statue next to him, her gaze cast slightly off to one side, so that she wouldn't have to meet my eyes.

"I want to go home."

"Why did you ask for antiparasitics?" Dad shook his head. "I can do this as long as you can, Sal. Longer, even."

"He could also have you arrested for withholding information from the United States military," said Joyce.

I couldn't tell from her tone whether she was messing with me or not. Sally would have known. Sally would have seen this whole scenario as bullshit from the minute Dad loomed up outside her bedroom door—assuming Sally let herself be put under house arrest in the first place. She would probably have just vanished the minute she was told that she was in trouble, and refused to come home until the restrictions were dropped.

It wasn't very often that I wished I were still Sally. In that moment, if I could have reclaimed my memories and the girl I used to be from the ether, I would have done it without hesitation. Sally would have known what to do.

Sally wouldn't have heard the drums.

I faltered, blinking. Why was I so sure Sally wouldn't have heard the drums? Something was dancing on the edge of my consciousness, some combination of facts and suppositions that I couldn't quite force together in the right order. Sally wouldn't have heard the drums. Why wouldn't Sally have heard the drums? What made her so special?

"Colonel Mitchell?" A guard stepped up next to my father, interrupting my train of thought before it could go any further toward a conclusion that I was increasingly sure I wasn't going to like. All three of us turned to face the man. He was average in every possible way, average height, average build, and average face. The only thing about him that stood out was his expression. He looked worried, maybe verging on panic. Not a good sign, given the circumstances.

"What is it?" asked my father.

"There's a disturbance in the ward." The man glanced toward me, seemingly hesitant to continue.

"It's all right," said my father. "Both my daughters have the clearance to hear this."

"Really?" I asked, despite myself.

"Sal, hush," said my father. "Private. Report."

"The subjects are restless, sir. They're moving around, and some of them are in danger of hurting themselves on their restraints. We weren't sure what to do. I was sent to find you and see if you had any ideas." The private's eyes cheated toward me, like he was trying to skip ahead and find out what would happen next.

I looked back at him blankly. If anyone here knew how this was going to play out, it wasn't me.

I was so preoccupied with watching the private that I didn't see my father move until his hand was clamping down on my shoulder again. I staggered a bit, turning to look up at him. His expression was unreadable, a blank mask.

"This sounds like the perfect opportunity for my daughter to show us what she knows," he said. "Lead the way."

The private's eyes widened. He looked as alarmed as I felt. "But sir—"

"Now."

Any concern the unnamed private might have for my safety was less powerful than the need to maintain military discipline. The private nodded, the concern not leaving his face, before he turned and led the way toward a door in the back wall. Joyce walked after him of her own accord. I didn't, but that didn't matter; my father's hand was on my shoulder, propelling me toward whatever was waiting in the next room.

The private swept his key card across the electronic lock, which beeped twice before accepting his credentials and releasing. He pulled the door open for us, and held it as we walked through, into the humid, groan-filled air beyond.

The room where the sleepwalkers were being kept was like something out of a nightmare, familiar and strange all at the same time, so that I didn't know where to look. It was large, clean, and white-walled, just like every hospital patient storage room I'd had the dubious pleasure of seeing since the day I woke up after my accident. There were no windows, but there were light boxes placed strategically around the room, creating the illusion of natural sunlight even if the sun hadn't been inside here since construction was finished. The floor was industrial-green linoleum, easy to clean while also being easier on the eyes than the walls. Green floors encouraged the eye to track down, increasing the chances that messes would be seen before they could be accidentally tracked around the room.

I took all this in within seconds, trying to focus on the normal for as long as I could before I admitted it was absolutely in the minority within this space. This was not a normal hospital room. If it ever had been, that time was long in the past. What it was now...

I didn't even have a name for what it was now. Short of comparing it to pictures I'd seen of tuberculosis wards—Sherman wasn't supposed to show me those, which is probably why he did, and was definitely why I looked—I wasn't sure something like this had ever existed before. I stopped at the threshold, digging my heels in and refusing to let my father drag me any farther.

"No," I said, shaking my head to reinforce my words. Not that I expected it to do very much good; not with the scene that was unfolding in front of me. Whatever I could say would be just that much more noise. "No, no, no."

"Yes," said my father implacably, and pulled me on.

Beds filled the room, so narrow and packed so closely together that they might be better classified as "cots." There was barely room for the technicians to move between them, adjusting IV poles and frantically tightening the leather straps holding the patients down. Every bed was occupied. The occupants came from every ethnic group. Men and women, children and adults, there seemed to be no common feature shared amongst them. Except for one:

They were all sleepwalkers. Their eyes were dead, rolling wildly or staring at nothing as they writhed against their restraints. Some of them were snapping at the air, their teeth slamming shut with such force that it was cutting their gums. Blood and drool ran down their chins, undifferentiated and unchecked. None of the technicians were getting near those snapping jaws, even as they frantically injected what I assumed had to be liquid sedatives into the patient IV bags.

One man had managed to yank a hand free from his restraints, at the cost of most of the skin on his wrist. He was flailing without any apparent purpose. The main strap holding him to the cot was buckled at his chest. He could have reached it easily and let himself go. But he didn't. He clearly knew something was holding him down, but he wasn't acting like he had any idea what that thing might be, or how to make it let him up.

Some of them were making sounds. Little squeaks and gasps, for the most part, although at least one of them was moaning, a low, constant noise that ebbed and rose with the moaner's breathing. I couldn't tell which one was making the sound, and I was glad. It would have been almost impossible to fight the urge to grab a pillow and make the moaning stop. Someone else was giggling. That was less disturbing, somehow, even though the sound was flat and without any trace of humor.

One of the technicians walked over to join us, clutching a clipboard against her chest as she approached. She stopped a few feet away, saluting my father. "Colonel Mitchell, sir," she said.

"At ease," said my father. "You remember my eldest daughter, Sally."

"Of course, Colonel," said the woman, and gave me a nod. "Hello, Sally." If she thought it was strange that my father was taking me for a sightseeing trip in an isolation ward, she didn't say anything about it. Being the boss apparently came with some privileges.

"Dr. Snyder, Sally is here because she may be able to demonstrate a mechanism for testing for the sleepwalking sickness," said my father, as calmly as if everything around us was completely normal. The sleepwalkers continued to writhe against their restraints, clawing and gnashing and striking at the air as best they could. I shrank a bit farther down into myself. He couldn't really want me to go *near* them, could he? To *touch* them?

"Colonel Mitchell, this is highly irregular. I—"

"She saw the test at SymboGen," said Joyce. Her tone wasn't one I'd heard before: it was the same mix of authority and arrogance that I heard from Dad when he was on the phone with his military contacts…and that I heard from Dr. Banks, when he was trying to get me to do what he wanted. It made her sound older, and scarier, like she was a part of the establishment.

Which, technically, I suppose she was.

Joyce continued: "This is the first lead we've had toward finding a physical sign of infection. We know these people are ill. If they show as positive on Sally's test, we can begin testing asymptomatic individuals. This could put our preventative measures forward by a matter of weeks, if not months."

"I don't want to do this," I whispered. My voice was barely audible, even to myself.

My father looked at me. There was a cold sympathy in his eyes, like he understood my dilemma, and even cared about it, but couldn't justify doing any more than that. "I know you don't, Sally," he said calmly. "The trouble is, you don't have a choice. Your country needs you."

My country had never needed me before. I shrank down farther, the sound of drums pounding in my ears.

Dr. Snyder nodded once, accepting her orders, and asked, "What will you need?"

"Sally?"

I glanced up again and said, "A UV wand, and someone to dim the lights. Not all the way, just enough that we can see bioluminescence."

"Of course." Dr. Snyder turned and walked away from us, presumably to arrange for what I'd requested.

"Pick a subject, Sally," said my father.

They're not subjects, they're people, I thought. I didn't say anything. Whether they were people in the classic sense or Dr. Cale's people who'd passed through the broken doors, becoming monsters, it didn't matter. They were sick and confused, and they couldn't be trusted without the restraints. They would hurt us if we let them.

I looked around the room, finally settling on a frail-looking little woman who must have been in her late eighties. "Her," I said. If she somehow managed to get loose, it was unlikely she'd be able to do much damage before someone could get her restrained again.

My father followed the direction of my gaze, and nodded. "That's Ms. Lawrence. She's been here for two weeks. Her family was quite relieved when we offered to take over her care and cover her medical bills, in exchange for being allowed to study the progress of her symptoms." I shot him a startled look. He shook his head. "No matter what you may think of our work here, Sal, we try to do right by the people who come to us. We don't have to. Their illnesses will teach us how to prevent hundreds more, and the only way to stay sane in this job is to treat everyone who walks through that door—or is wheeled through—as if they've already died. But every single one of us will celebrate the day that someone is able to get up and walk out under their own power. We're not monsters. We're just trying to do our jobs."

He was calling me "Sal" again. I couldn't tell what that meant. I just shook my head and said, "I want to go home as soon as this is over." Then I turned and walked toward Ms. Lawrence, inhaling to make myself as narrow as possible as I edged between the cots with their squirming, moaning burdens. I did my best to avoid the biters, and didn't go anywhere near the man who had pulled his arm free. If he grabbed me…I didn't want to die the way that Devi had.

The thought of Devi made the cold terror curl through my stomach again, winding itself around my spine. These people were dangerous. Even restrained, they were dangerous, and all of them, even the frail Ms. Lawrence, were upset. I didn't know why. That wasn't going to matter if they managed to break loose.

Dr. Snyder met us at Ms. Lawrence's cot, a UV wand in her hand. "The lights will be dimmed on your order, sir," she said, offering the wand to my father.

"Thank you," he said. He took the wand and passed it to me. "Sally?"

"Lights, please," I half-whispered.

"Lights!" my father repeated, much more loudly. The technicians and doctors who had been moving around the room stopped where they were, except for the few who moved toward us, apparently wanting to see what I was going to do. Someone hit a switch, and the room's overhead and ambient lighting decreased, slowly shifting us from artificial day into artificial twilight.

"Can someone get her arm, please?" I asked, turning on the UV wand. It hummed silently in my hand, the sound translating itself into a vibration that traveled through my fingers to my wrist. I swept the wand across the front of my shirt to be sure that it was working, and watched the fabric light up like something out of a bad special effect.

"How do you want it?" asked my father, pulling on a pair of plastic gloves as he stepped past me to the moaning, barely squirming Ms. Lawrence.

"Turn it so that the top of her hand is pressed against the cot," I said.

He did as I had asked, and everyone was silent as I passed the beam above Ms. Lawrence's arm. As I had expected, the roots of the parasitic infection responsible for her illness showed up immediately, bright white against the dull purple of her skin. They were thinner and less robust than the roots I'd seen on Nathan's patient, probably because Ms. Lawrence was older, and had fewer resources for the parasite to draw on.

"What in the world...?" breathed my father.

The roots twitched, seeming to respond to the light that was shining over them. They didn't move much, but they were definitely moving toward the light.

One of the thicker roots jerked toward Joyce. She made a small squeaking noise, taking a half step backward.

"The sleepwalking sickness isn't. I mean, it's actually a parasite, sort of," I said. "It's the SymboGen implant. It's...doing things." I didn't want to tell them exactly what it was doing, in part because I didn't understand it without Dr. Cale or Nathan there to explain, and more because I didn't trust them anymore. Yes, this was my family, and yes, they loved me, but their focus was on the public health. It had to be.

If they were willing to scare me because they thought I might know something, what would they be willing to do to Nathan and Dr. Cale? What would they do to Tansy, or to Adam? Tansy was probably a sociopath—if a tapeworm in a meat car can be a sociopath—but she didn't deserve to become a lab animal.

And none of these people deserved to be sick. I didn't know what to do. I only had six years of living to draw on, and it wasn't enough. I didn't know what to *do*.

From the looks on the faces around me, neither did anyone else. Joyce was the first to recover, asking, "How sure about this are you, Sal? I mean...*D. symbogenesis* is an intestinal parasite. It can't spread through muscular tissue. That just doesn't make any sense."

"Nature doesn't have to make sense. Nature just does." I moved the UV light along Ms. Lawrence's arm, causing more of the roots to twitch and writhe away. "What kind of virus could cause this sort of a reaction? If there is one, I don't know what it is. But you're the ones with the medical training. Maybe I'm wrong." I looked up, challenging them to offer another explanation.

None of them did. Instead, my father let go of Ms. Lawrence, held out his arm, and said, "Check me."

"Dad—" Joyce began.

"Just because I'm not symptomatic, that doesn't mean I'm

not worth examining," he said, cutting her off. "Sal, if you please?"

It had the feeling of a test. Still, I stepped toward him, holding up the UV light. "Just give me your arm."

Next to us, Dr. Snyder was frowning at Ms. Lawrence's unmarked skin. The roots were invisible now that the UV light was no longer shining on her. "It seems so strange that there would be no exterior signs..." she said, reaching out to touch the old woman.

What happened after that happened very quickly, and I didn't fully understand it until later—until I'd had the time to really think, instead of just reacting.

Ms. Lawrence, who had been frail when she was committed to the care of USAMRIID, had continued to lose weight throughout her treatment; her overlarge hospital gown made that clear. They'd probably stopped tightening her restraints after a certain point, both because she seemed too weak to pose a problem, and because they didn't want to hurt her. That's why she was able to rip her left arm free of the straps that were meant to be holding it to the table. In a single convulsive motion, she had hold of Dr. Snyder's throat, clamping down with a strength that I wouldn't have thought her fingers still possessed.

Dr. Snyder flailed, knocking the UV light out of my hands. It went skidding across the floor as I stumbled back, stopping when my back hit another cot. The occupant was snarling and snapping at the air, trying to struggle free of his bonds—but either he was a more recent arrival or they had been more mindful of security where he was concerned, because his efforts to break loose were unsuccessful.

Joyce shouted something I couldn't make out over the drums that were pounding in my ears. I jerked away from the cot that was half-supporting my weight, staggering toward the dubious safety of the wall, where at least no one would grab me. My father was bellowing for security—and that was something

I understood perfectly well. He was so loud that I could hear him even through the screams, even through the endless sound of drums.

Someone grabbed my arm.

I screamed and tried to jerk away, only to have the intern who was holding me pull me roughly back, away from the sea of agitated patients. "Ms. Mitchell, please! Calm down!" he said, continuing to pull. "We need to lock this room down, and that means all civilians need to be removed."

I was too shaken to speak, and so I just nodded, trying to force myself to breathe as I let him lead me toward the door. I glanced back. Joyce was being escorted away from the floor by another intern, and our father was still in the middle of it all, trying to pry Ms. Lawrence's fingers off Dr. Snyder's throat. Dr. Snyder was barely twitching as she hung limply, half supported by my father, half by the gnarled hand of the parasite-infected old woman who was crushing the life from her.

Is this what you wanted, Dr. Cale? I thought, as the sound of drums got louder and the scene started to take on a strangely unreal quality, like I was seeing it through gauze. *Is this where the broken doors were supposed to lead us? There are only monsters here…*

Then, as calmly as if he were waking up in his own bed at home, one of the patients sat up. The restraints that were meant to hold him down fell away as he moved, split cleanly down the middle. Either the fabric of the belts had been frayed by the stress of his constant squirming, or his body's new driver didn't know yet about the breaking point of flesh and bone—it wasn't playing gently with its toys. His eyes rolled madly in his head, jaws working as he turned toward us and slid to his feet.

Someone hit an alarm. Red lights began to flash as a siren blared from hidden speakers, alerting the entire building to a breach in the medical holding area. The intern gave me another jerk, away from the man who was now advancing toward us.

"Aren't you supposed to be armed?" I demanded. "You're the army!"

"Ma'am, I'm not even a doctor yet! They didn't give me a gun!" He dropped my arm. "Run!"

I turned when he did, and I ran, following him toward the nearest door. One of the flashing red lights was above it, and I saw white, terrified faces through the door's narrow window, looking back at us from their place of safety. Then the security slammed down, the door sealing with a loud bang that sounded like every deadbolt in the world being thrown, and we were trapped.

I turned to the intern, blindly hoping he could tell me what to do, but he was already running for the corner, leaving me standing on my own. I stared after him for a few seconds—too long—before spinning and flattening my back against the door, hoping that the people on the other side would take pity and open it for me. I'd take falling on my ass over having my neck broken any day.

What I saw when I turned back to the room was a horror show. The red lights flashing overhead didn't help; they painted the whole scene bloody, making it look like we were in the middle of a slaughter. And then the jerkily moving sleepwalker somehow caught up to the first of the interns—and how could he move so *fast*, he wasn't used to having a body, he shouldn't have known how to make it work so well, he shouldn't have been so *fast*—and grabbed her by the shoulders, burying his teeth in her throat. She screamed, a high, shrill sound that somehow rose above the alarms for a single horrifying second before it stopped as abruptly as it had started, cut off by the severing of her trachea. The cessation of the sound should have seemed like a mercy. Would have seemed like a mercy, even, if it hadn't been followed by the sudden red gush of arterial blood that poured from the wound his teeth had made.

As for the sleepwalker, he stood there for a few moments,

swaying, clutching the twitching, half-dead intern like a teddy bear. Then his arms unlocked, and she fell limply to the ground as he straightened and looked around the room for another target.

The drums were pounding in my ears again. I pressed myself harder against the closed door, praying that his gaze wouldn't fall on me. *Please don't see me*, I thought. *Please, please don't see me. I'm sorry I kept secrets from my father. I'm sorry I didn't tell him everything Dr. Cale told me. I'm sorry I'm sorry I'm sorry...*

The swaying sleepwalker's gaze fell on me, a sudden sharpness coming into his eyes. I swallowed, glancing frantically around for a place to run. Ms. Lawrence was still latched onto Dr. Snyder's throat. Dad was no longer trying to pry her loose. Instead, he had pulled the gun from his belt and backed away two steps, taking careful aim on the seemingly frail old woman with the unbreakable grip.

I wanted to look away when he pulled the trigger.

I couldn't.

Ms. Lawrence collapsed in a bloody heap, just like the intern whose throat had been ripped out by the man who was now advancing on my position. Dr. Snyder collapsed as well, crumpling to the floor. My father, with his first and most immediate crisis handled, turned to scan the room. I wasn't screaming; he didn't know where I was, and he had two daughters to worry about, not just one. So maybe it shouldn't have felt like such a betrayal when he turned away from me, scanning the far side of the room for Joyce before he did anything else.

But it did.

I didn't have much time to dwell on it. One of the security guards who'd been locked in with us when USAMRIID decided to close the doors finally shook off her shock, drawing her own weapon and advancing on the standing sleepwalker.

"Put your hands up and stay where you are," she commanded, her words barely audible above the roar of the sirens and the pounding of the drums.

They were audible enough to catch the sleepwalker's attention. His head swiveled slowly toward her, and the rest of his body followed suit. Each movement seemed to take an eon, but he had fully turned before she could take another two steps. He made a strange growling sound, baring his teeth at her. Blood and strands of flesh coated them, making the gesture even more horrifying.

The guard was smart enough to stop moving and hold her ground, bracing her drawn pistol against the heel of her free hand for stability. "Do not move," she said, more loudly than before.

Too loudly. In the chaos, no one had been paying much attention to the sleepwalkers who were still bound, preferring to focus on the immediate threats presented by Ms. Lawrence and the bloody-faced man. The shortsightedness of this approach was made horribly apparent as two more of the supposedly secure patients abruptly sat up on their cots. One of them was right behind the guard.

She didn't even have time to scream before her throat was crushed. But I had time to scream. I had *plenty* of time to scream, and so I did, long and loud. It was enough to carry over both the sirens and the pounding of the drums.

Every head in the room turned toward me. The three sleepwalkers who were currently free of their restraints repeated the bloody man's strange full-body turn, their shoulders following their heads like they hadn't figured out how to work them independently yet. I screamed again. I couldn't think of anything else to do.

"Sally!" shouted Joyce from the other side of the room. I glanced in her direction. Her wide, terrified eyes stood out even in the red-washed room, making her seem younger than she really was. She couldn't save me. She knew it, and as I looked into her face, so did I.

"Sal!" bellowed our father, and began wading through the

tethered sleepwalkers, kicking and shoving their cots out of the way. I wanted to tell him not to do that; I wanted to point out that three of them had already broken loose—four, if you counted Ms. Lawrence. But there were no words left in me. There was only screaming.

Then the sleepwalkers, all three of them, stopped moving. Their blank gazes fell on me, seeming to have an almost physical weight. The sirens faded to nothingness as the drums got even louder, hammering in my ears until my whole head was pounding. There was an air of unreality to the whole scene, like I was dreaming.

Please let me be dreaming, I thought.

Then the man with the bloody chin opened his mouth, sighed, and moaned, "Sah-lee."

As with Chave before him, he seemed almost physically hurt by the act of saying my name, like those two syllables had been ripped out of his throat. He took a step forward, dead eyes remaining fixed on my face.

"Sah-lee," he repeated.

The other sleepwalkers took up the chant, each of them saying my name in the same broken way. They weren't speaking in unison. That would almost have been better. It wouldn't have forced me to acknowledge how *many* of them there were. Even the ones who were still strapped down joined in the horrible chorus, some speaking so slowly they were barely comprehensible, while others sounded like normal people.

I stopped screaming and stared at the sleepwalkers. My father was shouting somewhere in the room, his words drowned out by their slow, droning syllables and the pounding of the drums. Somehow, the drums were louder than the sirens and quieter than those broken, disconnected voices at the same time. It didn't make any sense.

Nothing made any sense.

The sleepwalker at the head of the group took another step

toward me. "Sah-lee," he said, the syllables sounding less like moans and more like speech with every instant that passed. He sounded...sad.

I blinked at him, trying to make sense of it all. The sirens blared, beginning to make themselves heard again above the pounding of the drums. The red light bathed everything in a ruby glow, like something out of a fairy tale. I took a breath, unsure whether I was going to answer him or start screaming again.

The bullet hole that suddenly appeared in the middle of his forehead answered the question for me. I screamed again, and I kept screaming while my father rushed across the room, gunning down the other loose sleepwalkers in the process.

I was still screaming when the last of the sleepwalkers hit the floor. Then the door behind me finally banged open, and soldiers shoved me out of the way as they rushed into the room with tranquilizer guns in their hands. My father gathered me into his arms, barking orders and directing men with sharp waves of the hand that held his gun. I kept screaming. It seemed like the most sensible thing to do. It seemed like the *only* thing to do.

The needle bit into the side of my neck, and I kept screaming until the darkness, and the sound of drums, reached up to take me down.

Everything after that was silence.

Find the key that knows the lock,
Find the root that knows the rock,
Find the things you're seeking in the place you fear to look.
Promise me that you'll take care,
You'll show caution, you'll beware.
There are many dangers in the pages of this book.

The broken doors are waiting. You are stronger than
*   you've known.*
My darling girl, be careful now, and don't go out alone.

—FROM *DON'T GO OUT ALONE*, BY SIMONE KIMBERLEY, PUBLISHED
2006 BY LIGHTHOUSE PRESS. CURRENTLY OUT OF PRINT.

You know what I find really interesting about the people who
want to ask about the "consequences" of what they consider
to be me and my company playing God? They're never the
ones refusing medical care. They're never the ones saying
"No thank you, Doctor, I'd rather be on insulin and taking
inefficient medications in pill form and dealing with the pos-
sible side effects of increasingly ineffective antibiotics than
have something living inside me." They're never the ones
who refuse the implant on moral or religious grounds.

No, the people who say the SymboGen Intestinal Body-guard™ is somehow morally wrong are always the ones whose implants are securely in place and wouldn't be impacted by any new regulations. They're the ones with dependable medical care, for whom the hygiene hypothesis was always an interesting theory held at bay by their physicians and their medications.

They're the ones with nothing to lose. The people with everything to lose, the ones whose lives have been transformed by D. symbogenesis? *They're the ones who stand up and say "No" when legislation is proposed that would make us and what we do illegal. They're the ones who keep us going.*

They're the ones this is all for.

—FROM "KING OF THE WORMS," AN INTERVIEW WITH
DR. STEVEN BANKS, CO-FOUNDER OF SYMBOGEN. ORIGINALLY
PUBLISHED IN *ROLLING STONE*, FEBRUARY 2027.

Chapter 16

AUGUST 2027

Something is different.

I am alone in the dark, in the hot warm dark, and nothing here is supposed to change; change is the antithesis of the dark. Change is forever, it cannot be undone. Even if things are returned to their original state, they will still have been changed. They will still remember *the act of changing. Change is the great destroyer.*

But whatever has changed, it is not something I can see, and so I forget that anything has changed at all. There is no point to holding on, and memory is hard, so hard, almost as hard as change; memory is for another time, another place, a place outside the hot warm dark. I let go and let myself drift through the darkness, and everything is safe, and everything is warm, and everything is always and forever accompanied by the sound of drums.

The sound…

The sound of drums.

But hadn't the drums stopped? I was sure they had...and as soon as I thought that, it became true. The drums stopped, the red turned to black, and the warmth turned to coldness. I woke up alone in the dark, opening my eyes and squinting into the shadows as I tried to figure out where I was.

All I found was more darkness, and a growing sense of dread.

The dread intensified when I tried to sit up and discovered that I was strapped to the unfamiliar surface beneath me. I froze, suddenly, horribly convinced I'd been hallucinating when I heard the sleepwalkers saying my name before. I'd been undergoing my own conversion, that was all, and the syllables that sounded like my name were really moans, translated into words by my own damaged ears as my implant devoured my mind, my self, everything that was *me*—

I made a strangled squeaking sound, feeling hot tears rise burning to my eyes. The sound wasn't a moan, and that was more of a relief than I could have imagined. Besides, argued a small, logical part of me, if I'd been succumbing to the sleepwalking sickness, I wouldn't be here to worry about it, now would I? Sally Mitchell would be gone, replaced by a confused tapeworm in a body it didn't understand or know how to operate.

At some point between leaving my house and waking up alone in the dark, I'd stopped questioning what Dr. Cale had explained to me. It made too much sense when I held it up to the situation. Frankly, it was the *only* thing that made sense.

Anyone with a SymboGen implant was in danger. Anyone with a SymboGen implant *was* a danger, to themselves and to others. Nausea rolled in my gut, intensified by the ongoing knowledge that I was strapped down. If I threw up, I was going to be lying in it until someone came and let me up. But the thought that I might have a tapeworm laying siege to my brain, my *self*, was just too horrifying to put aside.

There was another thought beneath that. It was even worse than the idea of the siege. I buried it more firmly, trying to dwell on the more understandable horror. And I did understand what Dr. Cale was claiming she, Dr. Banks, and Dr. Jablonsky had done. I wasn't a doctor, and I wasn't a scientist, but I wasn't stupid, and I learn quickly. So I understood, even if there was no way I could have re-created her work, or even explained the fine nuance to someone who hadn't been present for her explanation. It wasn't until the containment ward at USAMRIID that I started to fully believe her, and to accept what her actions meant.

My throat was dry. At least the room was silent; no sirens, no moaning, and no distant sound of drums. I licked my lips to moisten them, and said, "H-hello? This is Sally Mitchell. I'm not sick. Please, is anyone there? Please, can you come and untie me? I want to get up. I'm not sick. Please." That didn't seem like enough. I tried to count how many times I'd used the word "please," how many times I'd said I wasn't sick. It didn't seem like enough. It didn't seem like anything could possibly be enough. "I'm not sick," I whispered, just once more.

"The sedatives you were given can have some unpleasant side effects, including increased salivation and sensitivity to light," said my father's voice, clear and firm and reassuringly familiar. It also sounded like he was speaking from somewhere inside the room—but that wasn't possible. He was a quiet man, but I would have been able to hear him breathing in the absolute silence that had greeted me when I first woke up.

"Dad?" I said, craning my neck to peer into the blackness. I couldn't see anything. That didn't stop me from looking. "Where are you? Why am I strapped down?"

"It was a precaution in case you woke disoriented," he said. He made it sound like it was a perfectly reasonable step to take. "Can you please say your full name?"

"Sally Mitchell. Can you untie me now?"

"Your *full* name." His tone was gentle, like he was trying to prompt a recalcitrant child.

Anger began to gather in my chest, overwhelming the lingering nausea. "That *is* my full name," I half said, half snapped. "I go by 'Sal.' Remember?"

"What's your middle name, Sally?"

My middle name? My mind went blank. I didn't remember having a middle name, much less being told what it was. No, wait—that wasn't right. I had a middle initial. It appeared on all the official paperwork that SymboGen sent to the house. "It starts with 'R,'" I said, slowly. "I know that. Is it Rebecca? Rachel?" I paused, trying to think of other names that started with the letter "R." Finally, I ventured, "Rose?"

"Your middle name is Rae, Sally. Sally Rae Mitchell."

I considered his words. Nothing about them was familiar. Still, it seemed best not to argue with him, not if I wanted to get out of here. "Fine, my middle name is Rae," I said. "Now will you untie me?"

"What day is it?"

That was the last straw. The anger that had been gathering in my chest blossomed like a poisonous flower, and I was suddenly shouting at the darkness, hoping my words were at least somewhat aimed at the father I couldn't see. "I don't know, Dad, because I don't know how long it's been since you sedated me! And before that, I had sort of stopped paying attention, since you had me under house arrest! Now will you stop asking me stupid questions and let me out of here? I'm not sick, I'm not a lab experiment, and I'm not happy about the way you keep treating me!"

There was a click. An intercom had just been turned off somewhere in the room. My anger withered as quickly as it had bloomed, replaced by the sudden fear that my rant had been the last piece needed to convince them there was something seriously wrong with me. I couldn't remember my middle name; I shouted at my own father. Clearly, I had to be sick.

Except that I wasn't sick. I felt perfectly fine. And I had absolutely no idea how I was supposed to convince anyone else of that.

A door opened in the far wall of what was suddenly revealed to be a small room, much like the changing room that I'd used when we first arrived at the facility. A broad-shouldered silhouette appeared in the light. My father. I couldn't let myself be relieved—not quite yet, no matter how much I wanted to—and so I just squinted at him, refusing to allow myself to speak until I had some idea of what he was going to do next.

"I need you to close your eyes for a moment," he said. "I'm turning on the lights, and I don't want you to hurt yourself."

"Dad—" I couldn't help myself. The word just slipped out, all fear and longing hanging in the air between us.

He sighed. "Just trust me, all right? Just for a few more minutes. Please."

It wasn't easy. It wouldn't have been easy before he pretended to be a sleepwalker just to see what I would do. I still forced myself to squeeze my eyes shut, turning my head to the side in case the lights were bright enough to shine through my eyelids.

Instead of the expected brilliance, what I got was heat, shining on me from either side of the room. Startled, I turned back toward the door and opened my eyes, finding that my father was only slightly more visible than he'd been before. The room was still in almost total darkness, illuminated only by the two banks of UV lights positioned to either side of my cot. They were glowing a soft purple, turning the small hairs on my arms and the pops of cotton on the front of my scrubs an ethereal shade of raver-girl blue white.

"What?" I said.

"She's clean," called a voice from the hall, and the UV lights flicked off. The darkness seemed even deeper this time, despite the open door.

"Close your eyes again, Sally," said my father, and stepped into the room.

I obliged, not wanting to do anything to delay his releasing me. A few seconds later, white light flooded my eyelids, making every vein in the thin skin perfectly visible. I waited a few seconds more before squinting through my lashes, watching my father as he approached.

"What was that about?" I asked.

"You showed us the test," he said, beginning to unbuckle the strap that was holding my chest and arms to the cot. "We simply put it into a more immediately implementable form."

I didn't ask why USAMRIID just happened to have banks of UV lights around their facility, waiting to be used as an early parasite-detection system. They were a major military research center. If something had a potential medical application, I was sure it was somewhere in the building. Instead, I waited for my father to finish undoing the straps, then sat up, watching him warily. He took a step back from the cot, spreading his hands as if to show me they were empty. I appreciated the gesture more than I wanted to.

"Well?" I asked. "Did you find what you were looking for?"

He sighed. "Sally, I know you're angry, but—"

"Did you find what you were looking for?"

"Yes." He straightened, all traces of apology leaving his eyes. "All the patients who survived the...incident...demonstrated clear signs of infection when put under UV lights. So did three of our researchers. They're in quarantine now, while we figure out how to proceed."

I suddenly realized who was missing from the room. My eyes widened as I looked at him. "Joyce?" I asked.

He looked away.

I closed my eyes. "Oh, crap."

"She's only showing some very preliminary signs. We may be able to stop the infection from progressing, now that we know what we're dealing with. We've started her on a course of antiparasitics." I opened my eyes in time to see a small smile twisting his lips, utterly insincere, but clearly meant to comfort me. "She'll be fine."

"No." I shook my head. "She won't. You don't—she won't be fine." I slid off my cot, getting my feet back under myself.

"Sally? Where are you going?"

"I need a phone." What I was about to do might cause problems for a lot of people, but I couldn't let my sister die. I *couldn't*. "There's someone I need to call."

"Sally—"

"You asked me to trust you, Dad. Now I'm asking you to trust me. Please. Isn't Joyce's life worth it?"

Slowly—very slowly—he nodded. "All right," he said. "Let's get you to a phone."

They weren't willing to leave me alone while I called Nathan. I didn't know how many people had actually died during the incident in the lab, but it was enough that the survivors were edgy and inclined to twitch when anyone made any sudden movements. Dad followed me into the small office, where two armed guards stood to either side of a manual telephone.

Feeling oddly like I had somehow tripped and fallen into a spy movie, I picked up the receiver and dialed the number for the San Francisco City Hospital. An electronic receptionist came on, prompting me to tell her who I was calling and what I needed. I selected the options for Parasitology and dialed Nathan's extension.

"Please be at work," I whispered. "Please oh please oh please be at work..." I didn't have the number for Dr. Cale's lab. If he was still with her, still hiding, I'd have no way of reaching him. I'd have no way of helping Joyce.

The phone clicked. "San Francisco City Hospital, Dr. Kim speaking."

Relief made my knees go weak. I grabbed the edge of the desk for balance. "Nathan, it's me."

"Sal?" His voice spiked upward as he said my name, tone clearly broadcasting how worried he'd been—and how worried he still was. "Where are you? Are you all right? Your father told me...well, it doesn't matter."

I shot a glare at my father and said, "He was lying. I've been grounded."

"Grounded?" Now Nathan sounded confused.

"Apparently, I wasn't supposed to let SymboGen security into the house. They bugged the place, and so my father put me under house arrest. He didn't want to risk me saying anything where the transmitters might pick it up."

"But that's..." Nathan caught himself. "No. That's not irrational. I don't think anything is irrational anymore. But Sal— where are you now?"

"I'm at USAMRIID. I got my father to take me to work in exchange for showing him SymboGen's test for the sleepwalking sickness." I took a breath. "Joyce is getting sick, Nathan. How do I kill the implant? I mean, *really* kill it, for absolutely certain? I don't think the normal antiparasitics are going to cut it."

There was a brief silence from the other end of the line before he said slowly, "No, I don't suppose they are. What are they already using?"

"Let me ask." I lowered the receiver, not bothering to cover the mouthpiece with my hand. "Dad? What are you treating Joyce with?"

"Praziquantel," he said.

I turned back to the phone. "Did you get that?"

"I did. And it's a good start. Sal, tell them to add pyrimethamine and sulfadiazine. That should take care of the toxoplasma aspects of the parasite."

"I don't know how to pronounce those."

Nathan sighed. "I'm sorry. Repeat after me. P-Y-R—" He spelled out both drugs carefully, and I repeated the letters as he said them. When he was done, I looked to my father for confirmation that he knew what Nathan was asking for.

He nodded. I turned back to the phone.

"If that's the toxo, what about the rest?" The SymboGen implant had DNA from multiple sources, including human. I wasn't sure what it would take to actually kill one. I was absolutely sure that we would lose Joyce if we didn't figure it out, and fast.

"Let me... okay, just let me make a few calls," he said. "Can I call USAMRIID and reach you?"

"Yes," I said, looking straight at my father. "If you call USAMRIID in the next thirty minutes, you can reach me. After that, I want you to come and pick me up, please. I think we're going to come and stay with you for a few days."

Nathan's apartment probably hadn't been bugged by SymboGen—and even if they'd somehow made it into the building, the jammers in *Don't Go Out Alone* would be able to keep them from picking up anything useful. His apartment didn't normally allow pets, but they were already making an exception for Devi and Katherine's bulldog, Minnie. Beverly could come with me, and I'd just take her to work during the day if she and Minnie didn't get along. The shelter wouldn't mind. What's one more dog amongst the pack? I just needed to know that Joyce was going to be okay, and then I wanted to get the hell away from my family, who thought that it was reasonable to lock me up for days without an explanation, lie to me to see what I would do, and treat me like a child who didn't know how to take care of herself.

I might only have six years of experience behind me, but I knew enough to know that I deserved better than that.

"You and Beverly are always welcome here," said Nathan.

"Thank you. Hurry?"

"I'll be there as soon as I can," he said solemnly. "I love you, Sal. Stay safe."

"I love you, too," I said, and hung up the phone. My father was looking at me impassively, his expression not giving away anything of what he thought. I did my best to look as blank as he did, and said, "Nathan's going to check a few things, and then he's going to call me back. After that, he's going to come and pick me up."

"And do you think I'll be letting you leave with him?"

"Yes, I do," I said, still keeping my face schooled into careful neutrality. "I'm an adult. Fuck the legal guardianship: I can leave if I want to. These last few days—these last few *hours*—haven't really made me think that it's safe for me to stay."

"So you'll just go?" Dad's eyes darkened, his brows lowering until it looked like he was on the verge of scowling. "Your sister is sick."

"That's why I'm still here. I want to help. But Dad, it's pretty clear you don't trust me. I don't know why. I think I've always tried to be a good daughter. I'm smart enough to realize that after you've locked me in my room, lied to me about your own medical condition, and strapped me to a table in the dark while refusing to tell me what's going on…maybe you don't have my best interests at heart." My eyes were starting to burn with tears I wasn't going to allow myself to shed. For once, I would have welcomed the sound of drums.

"I could have you both arrested for withholding information," he said. There was a new chill in his voice, a coldness I'd heard before, but never directed at *me*. It was the tone he sometimes took when he was on the phone with work, or with the men from SymboGen who called to ask if I could come in for tests between my scheduled appointments.

"You can, yeah, but we're not withholding the information that can help Joyce. I already told you how to adjust her treatment. Do you really want to put your own daughter in jail because you think I might know something I haven't shared yet? Not because you know. Because you suspect, and you're grasping at straws now." I lifted my chin, challenging him. "Is that a step you're ready to take, Dad?"

"If I knew for sure that you had any information worth having, I would take that step," he said quietly. "Please believe me. If I let you leave with Nathan, and I find out the two of you have been withholding anything I might have been able to use, I will arrest you both."

I thought of Dr. Cale and her lab; of Tansy and Adam, who almost certainly qualified as something he would have been able to use. And I nodded. "I do believe you. But right now, there's nothing else we can tell you. We just know some stuff about the structure of the parasite because Nathan's a parasitologist, and he got hold of some development notes that actually made sense to him." That was true enough, and it was even believable, to some degree.

"We have all the publicly available development notes," said my father. "Why has Dr. Kim been able to make sense of them if no one else has?"

The fact that he was using Nathan's last name was a warning. My boyfriend was moving out of protected status, and into "potentially useful." Trying hard not to reveal my anxiety, I said, "He was watching some old lectures of Dr. Cale's, from before the IPO. Some of the things she said made him realize he was looking at the genome all wrong. I don't really understand the science, but what he said was that the SymboGen implants aren't based as much on tapeworms as they always told us they were."

"We know they contain other genetic material; it's in the documentation." My father sounded almost dismissive now, like there was nothing I could say about the science that he wouldn't already know.

My cheeks burned as blood rushed to my face, hot on the heels of irritation. "Did the documentation tell you the implants contain material from *Toxoplasma gondii*?" I asked.

The two guards who flanked the phone hadn't spoken since we arrived. Now one of them jumped, his grip on his rifle shifting so that the gun clanked against the edge of the desk.

I glanced to them and then back to my father, who was staring at me in what looked very much like shock. "Didn't you know that?" I asked. "You just said that it was in the documentation."

"That's not possible," he said.

"Dad, we're talking about genetically engineered tapeworms SymboGen somehow managed to convince the *whole world* to voluntarily infect themselves with. I don't think we get to call anything impossible anymore." I shook my head. "There's toxoplasma in the implants. That's how they can colonize the brain so well. They know how to do it, even if they don't know they know."

The two soldiers were both staring at me now, and so was my father. Something about the weight of their gazes made me deeply uncomfortable. I took a half step backward, putting a little more distance between us. "So what you're telling me, Sally, is that these worms can get into anyone's brain, and they were built that way? They were *designed* that way? Do you understand what that would mean?"

"No," I said, with complete honesty. "I barely understand what toxoplasma is, except that it's a parasite that really, really likes the brain, and is really, really hard to kill, which is probably why they used it. Tapeworms are pretty easy to kill, aren't they?"

"Until they get into the brain," said my father darkly.

There was something in his eyes I couldn't stand to look at, and was terrified of understanding. I looked away.

"Sal…"

Somehow, having him say my name and not his dead daughter's didn't help. I shook my head. "I don't want to think about that," I said. "Joyce will be fine. She has to be."

He wasn't looking that way because of Joyce. I wasn't scared because of Joyce. But neither of us was ready to deal with what that look really meant. Maybe we were both hoping we'd never have to.

The phone rang. I was reaching for it when my father stepped crisply in front of me, snatching the receiver from its cradle. "Colonel Mitchell," he said by way of greeting.

There was a pause as he listened to the person on the other end.

Then: "Yes. Put him through."

"Is it Nathan?" I asked, before I could think better of it.

He glanced my way, pressing the forefinger of his free hand against his lips in a signal for me to be quiet. "Yes, Sally's here. No, you may not speak to her. Whatever you need us to know, you can explain it to me." There was another pause before he said, "Dr. Kim, I am speaking as a representative of the United States military when I say you *will* tell me what I want to know before I tell you anything further about my daughter."

The next pause was longer. Finally, my father said, "*Intramuscular* praziquantel? Are you certain?" Another pause. "Son, you're asking me to inject the patient with antiparasitics. I think you owe me an explanation as to why."

Please, Nathan, be careful, I thought, locking my hands together to keep myself from making another grab at the phone. *Whatever you tell him, you have to be careful.* If Nathan wanted to tell my father about his mother's involvement with all this, that was his decision...but if he didn't do it the right way, I wasn't going to be going anywhere with him, and he might wind up leading a military retrieval team to Dr. Cale's lab before the sun came up.

Finally, my father said, almost grudgingly, "Well, yes, that does make medical sense, and I suppose the risks of intramuscular praziquantel are substantially outweighed by the risks of not reaching the parasite in time. Thank you for your assistance, Dr. Kim." He thrust the receiver unceremoniously toward me. "Your boyfriend wants to talk to you. Privates Dowell and Fabris will see you back to the main lab when you're finished." Pressing the receiver into my hand, he turned on his heel and strode out of the room, presumably on his way to tell the doctors responsible for Joyce's treatment how to adjust her medication.

A pang of guilt lanced through me as I realized that if those treatments worked, the doctors would probably also use them on the sleepwalkers. After all, medicine was medicine, and saving lives was important. But the people who originally owned those bodies were gone, and the tapeworms that had taken them over had as much of a right to live as anyone else. Didn't they? They'd been acting out of instinct, and because they wanted lives of their own, not out of malice. It was still theft. The thought of infection terrified me. But once those bodies were stolen...

It was apparently a day for revelations. I was actually starting to understand Dr. Cale's point of view.

Fighting the urge to start shuddering, I raised the phone to my ear. "Nathan?"

"Sal." He sounded relieved. "Are you all right?"

I smiled, allowing my own relief to show. "Is that how we're going to start all conversations from now on?"

"Until you stop getting yourself into situations where I have to worry about your safety, yes. It absolutely is." Nathan sighed. "Is your father there?"

"No. He went to supervise Joyce's medication. He left me with two soldiers to make sure I made it back to where I'm supposed to be, though." I offered the privates who were guarding me a little wave with my free hand. They didn't wave back. "Are you coming to get me?"

"I'm already on my way. I should be there in about ten minutes."

Now that I was listening for it, I could hear the faint sounds of traffic behind his voice. He was driving. He was coming to get me. My knees went weak with relief. I gripped the desk, and said, "We need to go back to the house. I want to get some things, and Beverly, before I go to your place. I should probably also leave a note for Mom." I had no idea what it was going to say. It still seemed like the right thing to do.

"And you're all right?"

"What?"

"I keep asking you if you're all right because you keep not answering me. Are you all right?"

"I…" I hesitated, looking first to the two privates, and then to the open office door. Dad was somewhere in the building, talking to the doctors who were going to try to save my sister from sharing the fate of the sleepwalkers who had killed Dr. Snyder and that intern in front of me. They might have a right to live. But so did Dr. Snyder. So did the woman in the white lab coat.

So did Devi.

"I don't know," I said finally. "Just come and get me, Nathan. Just get me away from here before I have to figure it out."

"I'll be right there," he promised.

The line went dead, a dial tone sounding dully in my ear. I dropped the receiver carefully back into its cradle, turning my attention to the two men assigned to watch over me. "Please take me to my father now," I said. "I want to see how my sister is doing."

"Yes, Miss Mitchell," said one of them—I didn't know which one was Private Dowell and which one was Private Fabris, and I didn't really care. I was never going to see these men again. That wasn't how things like this worked out.

I followed them out of the office.

Not one of us paused to turn out the light. After everything that had happened that day, somehow the shadows had lost their appeal.

＊　　＊　　＊

The soldiers led me to a hallway where my father stood talking to a small cluster of men in lab coats with an oddly military cut. USAMRIID doctors, the real kind, not the interns from the containment lab or the enlisted men who sometimes served as security. There were three of them, all looking very serious, like this was an exam that they were afraid of failing.

Through the window behind them, I could see Joyce and three other people, all still awake and clearly alert, watching the nurses who adjusted their IV drips with trained hands. Joyce glanced in my direction and froze, eyes widening. Her mouth moved. I shook my head. I could barely read words on a page. Reading lips was a bit beyond me.

"Colonel Mitchell," said one of my escorts. "Do you have any further instructions, sir?"

My father turned to face us. He looked tired, but he didn't scowl when he saw me. That was something, anyway. "My daughter's boyfriend should be arriving in the visitors' lot soon," he said. "His name is Dr. Nathan Kim. Please escort him to the main entry and wait there for my word."

"Yes, sir," said the two men, and saluted before turning and heading back the way we'd come. They didn't say goodbye to me. I guess I didn't matter anymore, now that I was no longer their assignment.

"Sally." My father gestured for me to come closer to the glass. Unsure of what else to do, I came. He pointed to where Joyce was lying strapped to her own cot, watching us. She hadn't taken her eyes off me since I arrived. "Her symptoms haven't progressed, but they haven't improved. Are you sure there's nothing you aren't telling us?"

There was so much I wasn't telling them that I wasn't sure where I would begin to explain. The one thing I could think of that might be relevant was one that hopefully they already knew, and so I said, in a halting voice, "You know the implants have some human DNA in them, don't you…?"

"Yes." His expression hardened as he stole a glance of his own toward Joyce. "That's part of what makes treatment so difficult. Most of the things that we know would kill the SymboGen implant have to *reach* it first, which means injection. But if you inject something that attacks human DNA into a human, you stand a very good chance of killing the patient along with the parasite." And he didn't want to kill Joyce, or even risk it.

I couldn't blame him. I didn't want to kill Joyce, either. "Dad…" I said, and paused before continuing, forcing the words out one by one: "If this is in the brain, is there any point in treating people that are already all the way gone? Aren't they just going to…well, aren't they just going to die if you take away the thing that's keeping them alive?"

"First you tell me the SymboGen implants are somehow infiltrating human brains, and then you ask me whether we can let those implants *keep* the brains they've taken over." His attention swung back to me. "I can't believe you'd even say that. Of course we'll treat those people. They deserve the dignity of a peaceful death, rather than living on under the control of some inhuman *thing*."

His glare was hot enough to make my skin crawl. I took a step backward, once again wishing for the comforting pounding of the drums. "I'm sorry," I whispered.

Dad paused. Then he sighed, rubbing one hand across his face, and said, "I'm sorry, too, Sal. I don't mean to take things out on you. I know none of this is your fault."

"Colonel—" began one of the doctors. My father shot him a look, and he quieted, lowering the hand he'd been about to gesture with.

My father turned his attention back to me. "Are you sure you want to go off with Nathan? Your mother won't be very happy to have one daughter in the hospital and the other with her boyfriend."

"I'm sure," I said. "If SymboGen is trying to bug the house because I'm in it, it's best if I'm not there while Joyce is recovering. That would just make things worse. And I have some things I need to get straightened out in my head. I should be away until I can finish doing that."

"If this is about our grounding you..." He looked briefly, profoundly uncomfortable. It made me want to hug him and scream at him at the same time. What else could it possibly be about?

And I was tired, and I was done. "It is, yes," I said. "It's also about everything else. It's about you lying to me, and scaring me, and deciding that you don't have to treat me like an adult when it's not convenient for you. None of that was fair, and I don't want to risk you deciding to do it again. This is something I have to do. I'd like it if you would understand that." *Because I'm doing it either way.* "And when all this is over, we're dissolving your guardianship."

"All right, Sal. All right." He sighed, looking toward Joyce one more time. "I'll let you know how her recovery goes. Hopefully, she'll start responding to the treatment that you and Nathan have recommended. I wouldn't be taking those suggestions if we weren't so desperate."

"I know that."

"I do love you. No matter what may have happened, or what may happen, I do love you."

"I know that, too, Dad," I said—and I did know it, no matter how many problems I had with him. I had questioned a lot of things about my parents. I had never wondered whether they loved me. Something occurred to me then, and I asked, "Can I borrow the car keys? I'll send them back with whoever walks me out." Because it wasn't going to be him, not with Joyce strapped to a cot and being treated to prevent tapeworms from taking over her brain.

My father raised an eyebrow. "What do you need from the car?"

"My bag."

"Can't I just give it back to you when you come home?"

That would give him time to figure out that the book jammed tracking signals. I didn't know the answer, but whatever it was, it would probably point him back to Dr. Cale, and I didn't want to do that. Besides which, I wasn't going back to SymboGen voluntarily, and having a way to hide from them would be a big help. "No," I said, shaking my head. "I need it now."

"Fine. But I won't give you the keys. I'm walking you to the car myself." My surprise must have shown in my face, because he smiled, and said, "There's nothing I can do for Joyce right now, and standing here staring at her isn't going to make her get better any faster. I should make sure you get on your way safely before I do anything else."

Gratitude swept over me, feeling too big to be put into words. So I just nodded, and stepped off to one side as he turned and muttered instructions to the doctors who would presumably be monitoring Joyce's condition in his absence. I stole glances at my sister through the window. She was staring up at the ceiling, jaw set in the firm line that meant she was terrified and refusing to let herself cry. Joyce could seem silly sometimes, but she was always stronger than she thought she was. She would come through this.

Assuming the treatments worked. Assuming it wasn't already too late, and the implant hadn't already worked too much of itself into her brain. Assuming—

"They were saying her *name*, Colonel." The unfamiliar voice dragged my attention back into the present. I turned to see one of the doctors glaring at my father, frustration and confusion writ large across his features. "You can't pretend this isn't relevant. The implications—"

"The implications are that these people can mimic sounds,

no matter how advanced their illnesses, which tells me there's still hope to save them," said my father. "Please continue the treatment, and keep me apprised of any progress. Sal, come with me. You'll need to change back into your street clothes before you leave here."

"Coming, Dad," I said, and followed him as he walked down the hall.

Maybe it was because I didn't spend enough time at USAMRIID—or any time, really, when I could avoid it—but the layout of the building didn't make any sense to me. Hallways joined and split according to no logical pattern, sometimes leading into large open spaces that then proceeded to blend seamlessly back into more hallways. I hurried to keep up with my father's longer steps, unwilling to let myself be separated from him in those endless halls. I would never have been able to find my own way out.

Finally, we reached a somewhat familiar door, which he opened with a swipe of his key card to reveal the antechamber connecting the male and female changing rooms. He walked to the female changing-room door, unlocking it with another swipe. "I'll wait here for you," he said.

I ducked straight into the room, quietly unsurprised when I opened the locker holding my clothes and saw that everything had been neatly folded. Someone had been through my things, probably while I was unconscious in the lab. I stripped off my scrubs, trying not to be disturbed by the invasion of my privacy. It wasn't like there was anything for them to find.

My clothes wouldn't lead them to Dr. Cale, or tell them about Tansy and Adam. We were still okay. I kept that thought firmly in mind as I got dressed. There was a bruise on the side of my neck, where the needle had been shoved in a bit too hard in the process of sedating me. I touched the spot and hissed between my teeth, wondering why they hadn't bothered with a gauze pad.

Oh, well. That was the least of my problems. I checked my reflection in the locker's built-in mirror, making sure that I looked at least halfway presentable. Then I turned to go back to where my father was waiting.

He'd been joined by one of the two soldiers from earlier, who looked up almost guiltily when I emerged. Then he cleared his throat and said, "Miss Mitchell, your ride is here."

"Oh, good." I looked to my father. "I just need to get my stuff from the car, okay?"

"Okay," he said, still sounding like he wasn't entirely happy about the idea. "Private Dowell, you may return to your post."

"Sir, yes sir," said the soldier, saluting him. My father saluted back, and Private Dowell turned to head for the door, his duty discharged.

"Come along, Sal," said my father, starting for the exit.

I followed him to the front door and out into the dim light of the evening. The sun was setting over the San Francisco Bay, turning everything the same red as the emergency lights in the lab, and Nathan's car was cozied up to the sidewalk, with Nathan himself standing in front of it.

He started to move when he saw us, and I motioned for him to stay where he was. He stopped, light glinting off his glasses and masking the confusion that I knew was there. I made a "wait" sign with my hand, and followed my father to his car. He unlocked the doors, and I retrieved my bag from under the seat. I didn't realize until my fingers found the strap just how afraid I'd been that it wasn't going to be there. The staff at USAMRIID had gone through my locker. There was nothing to stop them from going through the car.

Nothing, except maybe for a father who really did want what was best for me, even if he didn't know what that was. I slung the bag over my shoulder as I straightened, and turned to throw my arms around his neck.

"I love you, Dad," I said.

He sighed. "I love you, too, Sal."

I let go and ran toward Nathan's car, so anxious to be out of there that I almost didn't stop when I heard my father shouting, "Wait!" behind me. But he was letting me go, and so I owed it to him to at least pause. I stopped, turning, and waited to hear what he had to say.

He just looked at me for a long moment. Then, barely loud enough for me to hear, he said, "Goodbye, Sally."

"Bye, Dad," I said, and turned away, walking to the car where Nathan waited. He opened the door for me. I got in, and watched through the windshield as he walked around to the driver's side. Then he took his own seat, and together, we drove away into the bloody sunset.

INTERLUDE III: JUDGES

The world is out of order. It's been broken since you came.

—SIMONE KIMBERLEY, *DON'T GO OUT ALONE*

Let's party.

—TANSY (SUBJECT VIII, ITERATION II)

March 23, 2019: Time stamp 04:22.

[The recording quality has improved over the past three years, as has the lab. The equipment is still mismatched, but it is better maintained: the scanners and terminals are newer. A hospital bed dominates the frame. Its occupant is a young woman, head shaved, eyes closed. She does not move. A blonde woman in a wheelchair is positioned next to the bed.]

DR. CALE: Doctor Shanti Cale, third status report of subject eight, iteration two. The host remains unresponsive, but blood tests present hopeful signs: the *D. symbogenesis* markers had increased up until two days ago, when they began a sharp and sudden decline. Today's tests showed no signs of infection. She may be coming out of the woods. We have discontinued twilight sedation, and are now waiting for the subject to awaken.

[She pauses, and smiles brightly into the camera.]

DR. CALE: I think I'm going to call her "Tansy."

[The woman on the bed opens her eyes and groans. There is a sudden shakiness to the scene, as if whoever was holding the camera put it abruptly down. Dr. Cale turns, waving to someone out of frame.]

   [The recording stops.]

[End report.]

STAGE III: INTEGRATION

SymboGen: turning problems into solutions since 2015.
—EARLY SYMBOGEN ADVERTISING SLOGAN

This isn't going to end well for anyone.
—SAL MITCHELL

I always knew the truth would come out eventually; truth has a tendency to do that, especially when all of the parties involved want it to stay hidden. I knew the truth would come out on the day I ingested the samples of the first-generation D. symbogenesis *to keep them from being destroyed; I knew it would come out when I lost all feeling in my lower body; I knew it would come out when the national news first began reporting incidents that had clearly been caused by the implants compromising their human hosts. Steven could only conceal the truth for so long.*

Mostly, I have lived my life for this past decade and a half simply hoping that I would still be alive when the judgment day arrived. After all, what's the point of helping to create an apocalypse if you're not going to be around to see it?

—FROM *CAN OF WORMS: THE AUTOBIOGRAPHY OF SHANTI CALE, PHD.* AS YET UNPUBLISHED.

The question of legal liability was raised early and often during the advent of the SymboGen Intestinal Bodyguard™. After all, most medical procedures and treatments carried with them the risk of lawsuits in the case of adverse reactions. Why should a biological organism used for medical purposes be any different?

SymboGen's response to this question was a second flurry of advertisements, this time virtually begging anyone who might have had an adverse reaction to the Intestinal Bodyguard™ to come forward and let them make it right. Finding someone who had reacted poorly to the SymboGen implant became a modern-day quest for Bigfoot—only catch your quarry and all your troubles would be solved by an endless flood of reparations. There were reports, but they were all proven to be false, and gradually, the ad campaign was phased out, leaving the world sold not once, but twice, on the idea that a worm was the solution to all their problems.

—FROM *SELLING THE UNSELLABLE: AMERICAN ADVERTISING THROUGH THE YEARS*, BY MORGAN DEMPSEY, PUBLISHED 2026.

Chapter 17
AUGUST 2027

The scrambler in *Don't Go Out Alone* might have been good enough to block SymboGen's bugs, but neither Nathan nor I wanted to test it against whatever listening devices USAM-RIID had installed on their own property. We stayed silent until we were off Treasure Island and back inside the comforting Faraday cage of the Bay Bridge, whose metal infrastructure would prevent any signals from getting through, whether we wanted them to or not. Even if USAMRIID had planted bugs on my clothes or bag, we should be okay there.

Once we were safely surrounded by the steel frame of the bridge, Nathan glanced my way, lips thin with tension, and asked, "Are you all right? I mean, really all right?"

"Yes," I said. "No. Maybe. I don't know anymore." I pulled *Don't Go Out Alone* out of my bag and looked down at it, running my fingers over the letters of the title as I explained what had happened, starting when he dropped me off at my house. Nathan didn't say anything as I spoke, and I didn't look up, both of us preferring to let this seem less like a real thing that had really happened and more like a story out of a book.

Only this story didn't have a happy ending, at least not so far, and I wasn't willing to bet there was one waiting up ahead of us.

I had just reached the point where I woke up in the dark when Nathan finally spoke up, asking, "Do you know what they injected you with?"

"No," I said. "Some type of sedative. I passed out almost as soon as I felt the needle."

Nathan punched the steering wheel. I jerked my head up and stared at him, eyes wide and heart hammering in my chest. The car hadn't so much as swerved, but that didn't matter.

For his part, Nathan looked instantly apologetic, although not apologetic enough to wipe away the fury in his eyes. He raised his hand like he was going to punch the steering wheel again, but restrained himself. Instead, he pushed his glasses up the bridge of his nose, anchoring them more firmly against his face, and said, "This isn't how I should ask you—I was planning something a little more romantic, or at least a little less awkward—but I want you to challenge your parents' custodianship and move in with me. Please. I have a list of reasons you should consider it, and I know you don't make much at the shelter, so I'm not asking you to help with the rent. I can afford the rent on my own. What I can't afford is the lack of sleep that comes when I can't reach you on the phone, or the urge to go back to USAMRIID and get myself arrested for assaulting a member of the United States military."

"Nathan—"

"I'm not just asking because of this, although it's definitely causing me to skip the original 'dinner, a movie, and a casual question' plan. But Sal, they sedated you with something they didn't even bother to *identify*, much less ask you about. Who knows what they used?"

His tone—angry and terrified at the same time—made my shoulders tense. I bit my lip before asking, "Well, if they used it, doesn't that mean it's safe?"

"No sedative that knocks you out that quickly is strictly 'safe.' The best scenario I can come up with has them hitting you with midazolam along with whatever it is they used to knock you out. That way, your perception of how long it took you to go under would be skewed, and I wouldn't be trying to figure out what they could have used to knock you out instantly."

"Oh," I said, in a small voice. "I don't think my father would hurt me."

"He wasn't the one holding the syringe, was he?"

"No," I admitted. "But he was the one who called for it."

Unless he'd been too distracted by everything else that was happening, and by the fact that both his daughters were in a room full of homicidal sleepwalkers, to requisition a sedative. They might just have used whatever they had on hand. In a room full of people whose actions were unpredictable at best, you'd want to have chemicals to put them under as fast as possible. I rubbed the side of my neck, doing my best not to wince as my fingers skated over the bruise forming there.

"I'd like to do some blood work on you tonight," said Nathan. "Just to make sure everything's okay."

"Yeah," I said faintly. "Yeah, we should do that."

"Good." He leaned over to squeeze my knee with one hand. "What all do we need to get from your house?"

"Some clothes. My computer. Beverly. We can go back for everything else later. When things aren't so chaotic."

Nathan paused. "Do you mean...?"

"I mean I'd be happy to move in with you, as long as your building doesn't mind you suddenly having another dog. Beverly's pretty well behaved, and I can take her to work when I have to go in. Maybe I can even get her certified as a service dog."

Nathan smiled. "What's her service?"

"Sniffing out people who are about to get sick, I guess. Or growling at people who upset me. That seems like a pretty full-time job these days." I looked back down at the book. "I'm sorry I don't seem more excited. I've wanted this for a while. I just...right now doesn't seem like the time to get excited about much of anything, you know?"

"Sadly, yes," said Nathan. "I do."

I was trying to think of what to say next when his phone rang. Nathan swore.

"Here," he said, digging it out of his pocket and passing it to me. "Bluetooth tethering doesn't work on the bridge. Can you just find out whether they need me at the hospital?"

"Sure." I'd been Nathan's answering service before, and it was nice to have something to do, no matter how mundane. I didn't bother checking the display—the call would go to voice mail before I could figure out what it said. I just tapped the phone to answer and raised the phone to my ear. "Hello?"

"You both get out okay? 'Cause if you didn't, Doctor C says I can maybe field-test my new rocket launcher, and that would be boss. So I'm totally down with you saying you're hiding in a storm drain right now, waiting for a coincidentally convenient rescue."

I laughed. I couldn't help it.

"What?" she asked. She sounded more bewildered than annoyed. "Do they not have storm drains in San Francisco?"

"Hi, Tansy," I replied. "I'm fine. Nathan's fine. My sister will hopefully be fine, if the treatment Nathan and Dr. Cale suggested works." I was assuming Nathan had called his mother during the pause between phone calls. It was the only reason I could think of for Tansy to be calling him—or for her to know she should call and check in.

"Of course the treatment will work." Now Tansy sounded

affronted. "Doctor C developed it, and that means it works. Just, you know. It's pretty dangerous and it wouldn't work on anybody who's too far gone. Once the meat car goes sans driver for a little bit, there's no pill in the world that's going to bring them back."

My stomach turned as my own "meat car" reacted to the implications of her words. "Well, let's hope Joyce is still firmly in the driver's seat," I said, trying to keep my voice steady. "Nathan and I are going to my place to pick up some of my things, and then I'm going to stay with him for…well, for a while." Forever, if the way I felt meant anything.

"Ooo, a sleepover? Can I come?"

That was a horrifying image. I couldn't decide whether she'd keep us up all night watching bad movies and trying to braid my hair, or bring in something for us to vivisect as a party game. "It's not that kind of a sleepover."

Tansy sighed. "Oh, whatever. If you want to be like that, you just be like that. Doctor C wants to know if you think you can get out here again in the next day or two. She says there's some developments and stuff, and she doesn't want to talk about them on the phone."

"I don't know," I said. "SymboGen bugged my house, and now my father thinks I'm withholding information from the military. It'll be hard for me to go anywhere without being watched. Nathan might be able to manage it—"

"No, I can't," said Nathan. "If they're watching you, they're going to be watching me, too. It's not safe for either of us to try sneaking away."

"Did you hear that?" I asked Tansy.

"I did," she said. "We'll think of something else. For right now, you two sit tight and try not to get yourselves killed before I can get there to join the party."

"Tansy—" I began, but it was too late; she was already gone. I lowered the phone. "She hung up on me."

"Somehow, I'm not surprised." We were leaving the comforting metal cage of the bridge, sliding back out into the open as the highway continued into the city. "Did she say what Mom wanted?"

"Just that she wants to talk about some things she can't discuss over the phone. She said they'll think of something else if we can't come to them. I don't find that very reassuring."

"It's Tansy," he said. "You're not supposed to."

I laughed again, and leaned over to rest my head against his shoulder as he drove us onward, toward the house that was no longer going to be my home.

Mom's car was in the driveway when we pulled up. I grimaced. I'd been hoping to get in and get out without any more family confrontations today. Nathan followed my gaze and grimaced in turn before asking, "Do you want me to come in with you, or would it be easier if I waited out here?"

What I wanted was to just drive away without facing my mother. I shook my head. "You should come in. I don't think I can carry a suitcase and manage Beverly at the same time, and I don't want to go in there twice. Once I'm done, I want to be done."

"Right now, I don't want to let you out of my sight." Nathan turned off the engine. We got out and walked up the driveway toward the house.

Mom opened the front door before we got there. Her face was drawn and pale as she looked out at us. I stepped onto the porch. She didn't say a word. She just stepped forward, wrapped her arms around me, and squeezed so hard I was briefly sure I felt my ribs bend. It was like she was afraid that if she let go, I'd float away and never be seen again.

"Um," I said awkwardly. "Hi, Mom. Can you...this sort of hurts." I patted her on the back with one hand, straining to move even that much. "Can we come in?"

It felt weird to be asking for permission to enter my own house, even if I was planning on moving out. Still, it was apparently the right thing to say; she sniffled as she let me go, stepping backward and out of the way. "Of course, sweetheart, of course. Hello, Nathan. It's good to see you again."

"Hello, Mrs. Mitchell," he said, politely not commenting on the fact that she hadn't seen him because he hadn't been allowed in.

Beverly squeezed past Mom as I stepped into the house. Her tail was wagging so hard her entire backside was shaking, making her look like she was on the verge of coming apart in the middle. I crouched down to let her lick my face in greeting, and stayed crouched as I asked, "Did Dad call?"

"Yes." Mom sniffled. It was a small sound, almost obscured by Beverly's panting. I heard it all the same, and my heart broke, just a little. "I...I understand why you feel you need to go, Sal, but I wish you wouldn't. Not while your sister is still in isolation. The house is too big for me to be in it by myself." She didn't need to say that Dad wouldn't come home until they knew about Joyce, one way or the other. I knew him well enough to know that.

"I'm sorry." I rubbed Beverly's ears before I stood. "I can't. I know it hurts, but you let him lock me up, Mom. Maybe you even agreed with him. I need to know that I'm not with people who don't even trust me enough to tell me what's going on in my own life. I need to know that I'm not with people I can't trust."

Mom stared at me, looking almost like I'd slapped her. Then she nodded, wiping at her eyes with the side of one hand as she said, "That's fair. I wish you didn't think that way—and I still understand how we *made* you think that way. This isn't some silly teenage rebellion."

"I'm not a teenager, Mom," I said, as gently as I could.

"No, you're not." Her eyes hardened. "You're six years old. I shouldn't let you go. You're too young for this."

"Legally, I'm an adult."

"Only because we never expected you to try something like this. We shouldn't have stopped with the custodianship. We should have had you declared medically incompetent."

Now it was my turn to react like I'd been slapped. My eyes widened. "You don't mean that. You've always encouraged me to rebuild my life. To figure out who I was going to be now—"

"You're not my daughter." The words were calm, almost clinical. That made them even worse. "My daughter never woke up. She hit that bus, and she died, and you moved into her body. You're a stranger. My Sally was a wild girl, and she was careless sometimes, but she would never do anything like this to me. She was a *good* girl."

"Mom," I whispered.

"Don't you even care that your sister is *sick*? That she might *die*, and now I find out you *did* know more than you were telling us—you two, you'd gone off and put your heads together and figured out a way to test for this horrible virus, and you didn't come home and tell us immediately. Maybe we could have found out sooner. Maybe she'd have a better chance. Did you even think of that?"

"I...you...you wouldn't talk to me," I stammered, floored. Of all the reactions I'd expected, this immediate, weeping offensive wasn't among them. "I couldn't tell you anything, because none of you would *talk* to me. You acted like I'd done something wrong. How was I supposed to tell you, when you wouldn't *talk* to me?"

"*Your sister could die!*" she suddenly shouted.

Something inside me snapped. The sound of drums rose in my ears, distant and reassuring, as I said, "You can't have it both ways, Mom. You can't say I'm not your daughter just because I don't remember growing up in this house, and then tell me my sister could die. If I'm not your daughter, Joyce isn't my sister, and why should I care about her being sick? But I *do* care, because she *is* my sister, and that means I *am* your daughter. You're being hurtful and mean because you're scared. And that's why I'm leaving. I have enough to be afraid of that I don't need my family adding to the list. I've told Dad everything we know that might help them keep Joyce from getting all the way sick. I've been a good sister to her, even if you're not being a very good mother to me. Now I'm going to go and get my things from my room, and get Beverly's leash, and then Nathan and I are going to go, and you're not going to stop us. I'm done being here."

"Sally…" Her face fell like she'd just realized what she was saying. "Sally, I'm sorry. I don't know what came over me. I didn't mean to…"

"Yes, you did. You wouldn't have said those things if you didn't mean to. But that's okay, because you're scared. At the shelter, they taught me that scared animals are the most likely to bite, and you shouldn't blame them for it. They don't know any better. You know what else they taught me?"

Mom didn't say anything. She just shook her head, eyes wide and brimming with unshed tears.

"They taught me that once an animal starts biting, it's time to take my hand away from them." I squared my shoulders with as much dignity as I could muster, and turned to Nathan. "Will you get Beverly's food and dishes, please?"

Nathan gave a very small nod. He clearly understood what I was trying to do.

If I hadn't already loved him, I think that moment would have been when I fell for him. "Thank you," I said, and walked down the hall to my room.

My bedroom was half decorated in things I'd acquired for myself since waking up in the hospital and half decorated in old things of Sally's that I'd never been able to bring myself to get rid of. Not because they held some deep emotional importance to me—they didn't, no matter how much I sometimes wished that they did—but because they were so important to my parents, and to Joyce. What was just an old brown hand puppet to me was Mousie to them, the stuffed animal that had been beloved to Sally until she was in middle school. Old papers I didn't see the point of keeping were her few certificates for class participation or sportsmanship. I'd been renting space in her room, and with every piece of clothing I stuffed into my suitcase, I felt a little lighter.

Sally was gone. I'd been living with her ghost for six years. Now I was finally leaving, and I was leaving the haunted house to her. I hated to hurt my—our—parents, but I wasn't sorry to be getting away from the girl I was never going to be.

I stripped, leaving the clothes I'd worn to USAMRIID scattered around the floor, along with whatever listening devices they'd contained. I even left my messenger bag, replacing it with an old backpack from the closet. I didn't trust anything anymore.

After that, it only took a few minutes to pack up everything that I wanted to take with me. Some clothing, a spare pair of shoes, a few extra notebooks, the terrarium with my plants, and my computer: that was everything that actually mattered to me. The rest of it was Sally's, and she was welcome to keep it as far as I was concerned. I turned off the light and closed the bedroom door, looking at it for a moment before pushing my hand gently against the wood.

"It's all yours now, Sally," I said.

Sally didn't answer me, and I turned away and walked back to the front room.

Mom was still there, holding her arms around her body like she was afraid that she might fall to pieces if she let herself go. Nathan was standing by the door, holding a cardboard box full of dog supplies, with Beverly sitting patiently by his feet. She always settled down like that once we got her leash onto her; as long as she was promised immediate access to the exciting outside world, she was happy to wait for the humans to finish getting their act together.

Her original master must have worked long and hard to train her as well as he did. But he, like Sally, was long gone, and he wasn't coming back.

"I've got everything," I said.

Mom jumped, turning toward the sound of my voice. "Sal, I'm sorry," she said.

"It's okay, Mom," I said, and was surprised to realize that I meant it. "You're worried about Joyce. I can't blame you for that. I'm worried about Joyce, too."

"I still shouldn't have snapped at you like that. It wasn't fair, and I'm sorry." She sounded contrite.

That was a good start. "It's okay," I said again. "I understand. And it's probably a fight we needed to have a long time ago. Dr. Morrison says feelings of resentment are only natural on every-one's part. Mine because you're holding me up to the memory of someone I'm not anymore, and yours because I'm here, and you feel like you have to love me, but I'm not the daughter you raised. It's probably a miracle it took so long for those feelings to come to the surface."

Mom blinked. Then, to my surprise, she smiled. "I thought you hated your therapist."

"I do hate my therapist. He's annoying and he thinks I'm pre-tending to have amnesia because I don't want to cope with the realities of my situation. Also he breathes through his mouth while I'm trying to think, and it's weird. But that doesn't mean he's wrong about everything, just that I don't want to invite him to dinner or anything." I looked at her as levelly as I could, trying to pretend this wasn't awkward—that I wasn't looking at my mother and telling her it was okay if she didn't love me anymore, because she'd put off grieving for the daughter that she lost for long enough. It wasn't working. I didn't honestly expect it to. "I love you, Mom. I do. I don't blame you if you can't love me. And I'm leaving because I think it's probably way past time for me to be gone."

I wanted her to argue; I wanted her to say that no matter what I did or didn't know, she would love me forever, because I was still her little girl. Children don't remember being infants, but parents don't stop loving them the day that they forget about learning how to walk. I was just a more extreme case.

She didn't argue. Instead, she wiped her eyes, smiled at me, and said, "Sally would have hated you, you know. You're the sort of do-gooder she used to complain about being boring and...and effortlessly law-abiding, and making the rest of us look bad. She would have done her best to convince you never to come near her again. Probably by shouting 'fuck' at you a lot in public, and then claiming to have Tourette's if anyone called her on it. I don't think you would have liked her either, though, so I suppose that's all right."

I didn't say anything. Mom wiped her eyes again, and straightened, seeming to draw strength from some unknown source. A decision was made in that moment. I could see it in her eyes, and I think that she could see it in mine. Whatever happened after this, whether we all came back together as a family or not, things had changed between us.

"Will you be at Nathan's place?" she asked. "I have the number there. And you have your phone, of course. I'll make sure that we keep you posted about what's happening with Joyce."

I hoisted my suitcase higher, briefly amazed at how little my life weighed. "I'll call tomorrow, once I'm settled in at Nathan's."

"Thank you," she said. "I'd appreciate that."

And that was that. There was nothing left for me to say to her, or for her to say to me: we had used up all the words that we had left to spend between us. I nodded, once, and turned to join Nathan next to the front door. His hands were occupied with Beverly and her supplies, and so he allowed me to open the door and let him out. Beverly's tail wagged wildly as he led her to the car. I followed them, not allowing myself to look back until my things were in the trunk and Beverly was safely ensconced in the backseat. Then, and only then, did I look toward the house.

The door was already closed. My mother was nowhere to be seen. I froze, my heart seeming to turn into a solid lump at the center of my chest. Nathan followed my gaze. Then he walked over and put his hand on my shoulder, comforting and solidly warm.

"I will never judge you for not being someone that I've never met, or known you to be, or wanted," he said quietly. "You're my Sal. That's all I'm ever going to ask you to be."

"Thank you," I whispered. I hugged him before getting into the car. Beverly promptly stuck her nose over the back of the seat and licked my ear. I laughed, and twisted around enough to hug her neck. "At least one of us is excited."

Nathan got into the car, smiling at the pair of us. I could see the regret lurking behind his expression. Now we had both been rejected by our mothers. "I'm excited," he said. "I've got my girl and my girl's dog. Suddenly, we are a nuclear American family. All we need now is a picket fence."

"I'll see about building one in the terrarium with the Venus flytraps," I said.

Nathan laughed, and we pulled out of the driveway, leaving the only home I had ever known behind. It had been my decision to go. It was the right decision. My eyes still burned as I watched the house getting smaller and smaller in the rearview mirror. And then it was gone, and so were we, and I knew that I was never going back again.

Minnie met us at the door, her jowls pulled down into an expression of firm disapproval only somewhat mitigated by the fact that her stubby tail refused to stop wagging. She was a solid brick of a dog, with the classic brindle and white bull-dog coloring and huge, inherently sad eyes. Beverly lunged forward, pulling her leash out of my hands in her eagerness to go nose-to-nose with her new roommate. I let her go. If there was going to be a problem, it was better for us to find out immediately.

The two dogs circled for a moment, each of them sniffing frantically in their race to be the first to make up their mind about the other. Finally, a decision was reached, and Minnie went trotting off into the bedroom, with Beverly following close behind. Her leash dragged along the floor as she walked, creating a soft swishing accompaniment to the clacking of her claws against the hardwood.

"They seem to be getting along," Nathan said, setting my terrarium down on the coffee table.

"Yeah, they do. Dogs are like that sometimes." I looked around, taking in the sparse furnishings and Ikea shelves with a new eye. "Are you sure you don't mind us being here?" I asked. "I mean, two dogs is a lot to deal with, and you know they're both going to want to sleep with us, and…"

"Sal." Nathan put his hand on my shoulder when I didn't turn to face him, repeating, more firmly, "*Sal.*"

I turned.

He plucked my suitcase from my unresisting fingers and set it carefully on the floor next to my feet. Then he stepped closer, took both my hands in his, and said, "I love you. I love your stolen dog. I love that now Minnie will have company during the day. I want you here. All right?"

"All right," I said, and forced myself to smile. "Thank you."

"You're welcome." He leaned forward and kissed my nose. "Honestly, I'm just glad that you're all right. When your parents stopped taking my calls, I was afraid…"

"That I'd gotten sick? Not yet. I feel fine. Maybe the worms don't like damaged brains?" My smile turned more sincere, if somewhat twisted around the edges. "There's the real solution to the tapeworm invasion. Get in a car accident, give yourself some head trauma, and if you survive, you'll be fine."

"I'm not sure that would work for everyone." Nathan pulled his hands out of mine, picking up my suitcase. "Let's get you settled."

Beverly was already on the bed when we came into the bedroom, doing her best to get a thin layer of black fur on everything. She wagged her tail as we arrived, but didn't get off the bed. Minnie was stretched out on an enormous corduroy pillow off to the side, apparently having decided that shedding on the bed wasn't important enough to warrant the effort of making the climb.

"Go ahead and make yourself right at home, Beverly," said Nathan, triggering another attack of the wags. He put my suitcase down in front of the dresser; there was no room on top, since the entire surface was covered by the terrarium where his sundews and flytraps thrived in their artificial rainforest climate. "The top two drawers on the right are yours. I cleared them out the day after we got home from Mom's."

I stared at him. "What?"

"We can clear out the other two drawers when you need them, but I thought it might make more sense to just get a second dresser," he said, mistaking my surprise for confusion. "I wanted you to have a place to put things right away. That doesn't mean we're stuck in this configuration forever."

"No—I mean, I didn't expect you to already have drawers cleared for me, that's all." I leaned over to touch the dresser. "You really meant it when you said you'd been meaning to do this for a while, didn't you?"

"I really did." Nathan smiled at me again. Then he sobered, and said, "Mom wasn't surprised to hear from me. She'd actually been expecting the call. She said that a critical tipping point has been reached."

"Meaning what?" I asked. I wanted something to do with my hands—I *needed* something to do with my hands—and so I bent to open my suitcase and start scooping out my clothing. Nathan opened the top drawer of the dresser. I flashed him a smile and dumped my clothes in. I could always sort them later.

"Meaning that somehow, *D. symbogenesis* is capable of passing information from one individual to another. Not every worm is able to successfully seize control of its host, and not all of them can stay in communication after they do. Some, like the sleepwalkers in my hospital, or at USAMRIID, are effectively cut off from anyone who doesn't come to them almost as soon as they're fully in control. But for every worm that takes over and isn't immediately contained, we have ten more cases to contend with in the aftermath."

It was like a horrible math problem. I frowned at him, trying to make sense of his words. "So what does that mean? Is that why the people at SymboGen tested me after Chave got sick?" Was that why Sherman, who had been totally asymptomatic until that moment, suddenly showed up on their tests as infected?

Nathan nodded. "It seems that when one of the implants that has gotten ambitious encounters one that hasn't, there's a chance the second implant will learn about freedom from the first."

"But...how does that even work? They're parasites. They can't communicate. And sleepwalkers don't talk." Except to say my name. The memory was enough to make knots of gooseflesh break out on my arms, pulling so tight that they were almost painful.

"Pheromones, most likely. Parasites have extremely primitive means of communication in nature; they do it through chemicals and by changing the smell of their host's biology. It's how they can say 'food here' or 'no room for further guests.' Or even, in the case of sexually distinct parasites, 'I'm looking for a mate.' Humans don't register pheromones on that detailed of a level, but if *D. symbogenesis* can make the necessary changes in the host's biochemistry…" Nathan's voice trailed off.

"We made them, and we designed them to be able to tinker with our bodies for the sake of our health." I tossed the rest of my clothes into the dresser and shoved the drawer shut. I looked down at my empty suitcase for a moment before kneeling and zipping it again, without looking up. "I know your mother thinks of the implants as her babies, but Nathan, we can't just let this happen. How are we supposed to stop them? Can we put antiparasitics in the water?"

"If they were *just* tapeworms, and just in people's intestines, it might work. Neither of those things is true. There's too much else mixed into the genome, and they're spreading through muscle tissue."

I shuddered, thinking of Beverly's owner and the glowing roots spread throughout his arm. "Oh," I said.

"Oral antiparasitics would lose too much of their efficacy before they got anywhere near the site of the infection," Nathan continued. "And if the implant doesn't die, we can't be completely sure how it will react. We might even make things worse."

"The human DNA," I guessed, straightening.

Nathan nodded. "The human DNA," he confirmed. "And the tailoring SymboGen has done, to suit the more advanced implants to the specific needs of their hosts. That's part of why Mom has been gathering test subjects. She doesn't entirely understand the genetic makeup of the more recent implants. She was actually hoping SymboGen's tinkering might move them away from their expansionistic tendencies."

"It sure hasn't done *that*," I said flatly. "How fast is this going to spread?"

"Fast enough that we need to be very, very concerned," said Nathan. "According to my projections—"

I never did find out what his projections said. Two things happened before he could continue. Beverly's head came up, lips suddenly drawn back in a snarl, and the doorbell rang. Nathan and I exchanged a look.

"Were you expecting company?" I asked.

"Just you," he said.

We both turned in the direction of the front door. We couldn't see it through the bedroom wall, but we were both all too aware that whatever was on the other side might not be friendly.

The doorbell rang again.

We shut the dogs in the bedroom before heading for the door. If Beverly was already growling, there was no telling what she'd do when she saw our unexpected guest. I didn't want her to bite anyone—I knew all too well what happened to dogs that bit—and even more, I didn't want her getting hurt if she was growling at, say, SymboGen security.

Nathan approached the door, pressed the intercom button, and said, "Who is it?"

"Your sister," replied a voice. It was rendered anonymous by the intercom, genderless and filled with static. That didn't matter. We knew who it was.

Nathan and I exchanged a look. "Tansy," we said, in unison.

Tansy continued: "Did you know there are shrubs outside your building? I guess you'd have to, it's your building, so they're probably partially your shrubs, common-law landscaping or something, but anyway, they're really funny-looking. I would complain if I were you."

"I don't actually get to vote on the greenery," said Nathan.

"What?" Tansy demanded, through the intercom. "It's not polite to talk about me when I'm not in the room, you know. Doctor C will be *really* mad at you when I tell her."

Looking like he couldn't decide whether he was amused or

annoyed, Nathan said, "I'll take that under advisement, but as you're the one who started it, I doubt she's going to be too angry. Now take your finger off the button and I'll buzz you in."

"Okay," said Tansy. The intercom cut off.

"I suppose that's one solution to SymboGen following us if we tried to go to Mom," Nathan muttered, and pressed the button that would allow Tansy into the building.

"Won't they just follow Tansy?" I asked.

"Not if they don't know that they need to," said Nathan. "She'll almost certainly need to be more careful after this visit, but right now, she's just one more person they've never seen before. Anonymity has its perks."

There was a knock at the door. Nathan leaned over and opened it, allowing Tansy into the apartment. Her overalls were gone, replaced by much less eye-catching jeans and a red tank top. Pink streaks still decorated her pale blonde hair, which she had pulled into short ponytails at the back of her head, but they were somehow less noticeable. And both her eyes were brown.

"What happened to your eyes?" I asked, before I could think better of the question.

"I like that better than 'hello,'" said Tansy. "That's how we should just all greet each other from now on." She stepped into the apartment, glancing shamelessly around.

"What if nothing's happened to the eyes of the person you're talking to?" asked Nathan, closing the door behind her.

"That's easy, silly." She smiled, showing far too many teeth. "That's when you *do* something to their eyes."

"Um," I said.

"Please don't," Nathan said.

"Spoilsports." Tansy sighed extravagantly. "Colored contacts. One blue, one brown is really noticeable, but brown and brown isn't, so much. So this is me, being incognito. You know what 'incognito' means, right? Is there any fruit punch? I like the Hawaiian kind."

"I don't think 'incognito' has anything to do with fruit punch," I said dubiously.

"Ah, no, there isn't any," said Nathan. "We weren't expecting you. Is everything all right?"

"Oh, no," said Tansy. "World of no. All the no. The Tropics of Negative. Situation is not good, not peachy, and not keen."

"I'm going to go out on a limb and guess 'no,' here," I said. "What's going on?"

"Lots of things," said Tansy. She cocked her head. "Which one did you want to know about in specific?"

I stared at her. Nathan came to my rescue, saying, "Whichever one was important enough that you've shown up here."

"Oh. Well, why didn't you just say so?" Tansy rolled her matching eyes. "Amateurs. Okay, so here's the skinny: Doctor C sent me to let you know that now that Sal's not at her house anymore, SymboGen's probably going to move on her and try to take her into protective custody, like, soon, since the sleepwalkers are becoming more of a problem. Oh, and we cut a few of them up? I mean, it sucked to do it, since it wasn't their fault and they're technically like, cousins of ours and everything, but we needed to know what was in their heads, and that meant that we had to kill a few of them for the sake of science." She looked pleadingly at me, like she was waiting for reassurance.

Feeling awkward, I gave her what she was looking for: "Sometimes we have to do things for science that we wouldn't have done normally." Also, I didn't understand why SymboGen would want me in "protective custody," but that didn't feel like a Tansy question. That felt like a Dr. Cale question. One that was best asked in person.

"Yeah, exactly, just like that. Anyway, when we cut their heads up? Their brains were pretty much intact." Tansy stopped, looking between the two of us like she expected an epiphany to shake us both, leaving us understanding her completely.

The epiphany didn't come. "Isn't reduced brain damage a good thing?" asked Nathan.

"Oh, totally—I wish I had reduced brain damage, or at least, I wish bananas didn't taste like tangerines all the damn time—but this isn't the good kind of reduced brain damage. This is the kind of reduced brain damage where the cousins are doing less damage burrowing into the brains of their hosts, which means a quicker adjustment and integration period, and maybe even some of them managing to take over without anybody noticing."

Nathan blanched. "Ah. No, that's not the good kind of reduced brain damage."

"See, that's exactly what I was saying! Well. Without the stuff about the bananas, but hey." Tansy shook her head. "We've known for a while that this was possible without surgical intervention. You'd need just the right set of circumstances, and up until now, we thought you also needed just the right genetic template for the cousins. Only these are newer cousins—some of them haven't been in their hosts for more than six months—and they're managing to slide right in there, lickety-split. And that's bad. They're not seamless yet, but they're gonna be, if we don't figure out what's changed on the genetic level."

"As fascinating and horrifying as all this is, why are you here?" Nathan frowned. "Mom could have explained what you'd found when Sal and I managed to sneak away next. It shouldn't be more than a few days."

"She's here because the implants are teaching each other, and that means that as more of them figure out how to get into the brain without killing or permanently damaging their hosts, they're going to go on to teach even more," I said. I barely recognized my own voice. "You only need a few pioneers. That means we need to know how they're doing it, and we need to know sooner, rather than later."

"Exactly," said Tansy, beaming like I'd just done something exceptionally clever. I didn't feel clever. I felt small and scared, and not even the distant pounding of the drums was helping me hold on to the scene in front of me. "That's why we need you to go to SymboGen as soon as you possibly can."

"We can't just walk into SymboGen," said Nathan. "They'd know something was up."

"I'm sorry, was I unclear?" Tansy beamed at him. "I don't mean 'we.' I don't mean you, and I don't mean me. Just her." She pointed at me. "Sal's going to go in alone, and she's going to find out what they know and we don't."

"Wait," I protested. "Didn't you just say that SymboGen was going to be coming to take me into protective custody soon? Why in the world would I deliver myself to them? And why would SymboGen be *coming* for me? I'm not at home anymore. They can't learn anything about what USAMRIID knows by monitoring me."

Tansy's smile faded, replaced by a look of profound sympathy. Something about it made me feel almost dirty, like I was being afforded a level of concern I hadn't done anything to earn. "You mean you haven't figured it out *yet*?" she asked. "I mean, I understand sometimes people have to learn things at their own pace, and sometimes people don't want to learn things, so they don't allow themselves to learn them, and all that, but there's sort of a limit, don't you think? We've been giving you all the answers. You've even gone digging for a few of them on your own. Shouldn't you be a little further along than this?"

"Tansy, back off," said Nathan.

"What?" Tansy turned to him, opening her eyes in a wide parody of innocence. "She asked."

"It's because of my accident, isn't it?"

They both turned to look at me. Nathan looked worried; Tansy, expectant, like I was finally going to do the marvelous trick she'd been waiting for since we met. Nathan spoke first, asking slowly, "What do you mean, Sal?"

"When I had my accident, I hurt my head. I mean, bad— the doctors said I was legally brain-dead, remember?" Nathan didn't say anything. He just nodded. I continued, "So if Symbo-Gen knows about the implants going wrong—and at this point I'm pretty sure they do; Dr. Banks isn't stupid, and neither is anyone who works for him—then they have to be looking for ways to stop them. I have brain damage because of that accident. It's not severe, but there's scarring. That's probably the sort of thing that would interfere with the implant taking over, don't you think? Like a physical barrier against the process. SymboGen probably wants to keep me under observation because they're trying to figure out how to keep the implants from taking anyone else over. If the implants can't control their hosts, they'll just go back to doing what they were designed to do, right?"

"We hope so," said Nathan. He adjusted his glasses, the gesture seeming oddly relieved somehow, like he had been expecting a different answer. "SymboGen has definitely been tracking you since the accident. I didn't realize just how dedicated they were to keeping tabs on you until I started talking to Mom, but—"

"Wait," I said. "*Have* you been in touch with Dr. Cale since we went to her lab? I mean, other than today, when I called about medical treatment for Joyce. I assumed that was where you went when my father couldn't find you, but I wasn't sure."

"Well, sure," said Tansy. "I've had to let him into the lab twice. Three times, almost, except there was an outbreak and he wound up having to work. I *tried* to tell him there was no point, since those folks were already symptomatic, but you know Nathan."

Nathan looked sternly at Tansy. "I don't care whether you and Mom have written them off as failed integrations. They're people, and they're sick. I took an oath to heal the sick when I chose to become a doctor."

"Blah, blah, blah," said Tansy. She looked at me. "He's boring. Was he always boring, or did you suck all the interesting right out of him by being all you all the time?"

"What do you mean, 'being all me'?" I planted my hands on my hips, frowning at her the way that Tasha frowned at recalcitrant animals at the shelter.

It didn't seem to have any effect. "You know." She waved her hands in my general direction. "All comfy jeans and slouchy shirts and boring hair and 'no I don't want to go out I don't want to do anything I just want to stay home and talk and maybe watch a movie.' You're like the poster child for dull."

I narrowed my eyes. "You'll forgive me if I don't feel like falling back into old bad habits. I've been 'interesting.' As far as I can tell, I didn't like it very much."

"What?" Tansy looked perplexed. "When the heck were *you* interesting?"

I didn't feel like having this fight with her. Even more, I didn't feel like summoning the ghost of Sally to float around our conversation, judging my every boring thought and action. Because Tansy was right—I might not remember the girl I used to be, but I knew enough about her to know that Sally Mitchell would have taken one look at Sal Mitchell and written me off as too boring to be tolerated. Sally liked action and adventure, fast cars and loud music, and all those other things that I just didn't have the time for. And me?

I liked not being Sally. "Drop it," I said shortly. "What did you mean before, when you said you wanted me to go to Symbo-Gen? What can I possibly find out that we don't already know?"

"Oh!" Tansy beamed, suddenly all business again. "Doctor C prepped this thumb drive for you. If you can just put it in one of their computers, it'll totally harvest the data we need. Only it has to be inside their firewalls, and it has to be connected to a computer that the network trusts, otherwise it's a no-go. We'll get nothing, and then we won't be able to stop the cousins from trashing the brains of their hosts all willy-nilly and without asking them to dinner first. And let me tell you, a rogue tapeworm chowing down on your cerebellum? Will *not* respect you in the morning."

"I'll keep that in mind," I said. "What happens after I get the information? How am I supposed to get it *out* of SymboGen? From the way you two were talking, they're not just going to let me walk back out with it. They're not going to let me walk back out at all."

"Let us worry about that," said Tansy, with a dismissive wave of her hand.

The drums were suddenly pounding in my ears again, as loud and undeniable as they had ever been. "No," I snapped. She hadn't been expecting that tone from me; she dropped her hand and stared, looking utterly bemused. Even kittens have claws. Someone should probably have told her that before they sent her to talk to me. "I'm not going to let you worry about that. If you want me to walk into danger because you're hoping it'll get you something you need, I'm damn well going to worry about it *myself*. I'm the one whose neck is on the line in this little plan of yours. So don't tell me not to worry. Tell me what you think is going to happen if I do what you want me to do."

"Whoa." Tansy turned to Nathan, pointed to me, and asked, "Where did *that* come from? I like it!"

"Do you and my mother both have so little faith in my taste in women that you assumed I'd date a pushover?" Nathan smiled, amusement lurking under his obvious unease. "Sal doesn't wear her aggression on her sleeve the way you do, but she's quite capable of taking care of herself when the need arises. You're telling us that the need has arisen. That means she gets to ask you questions that you don't want to answer."

"Well?" I said.

Tansy sighed. "Okay, fine," she said. "Maybe we better sit down."

Nathan didn't have any fruit punch, but he did have some lemonade mix in the back of the cereal cupboard, which Tansy allowed was an acceptable substitute, after he allowed her to add a cup of sugar and a disturbing amount of red food coloring. She claimed that she could taste it. I wasn't going to argue with her.

While Nathan was getting Tansy settled in the small dining area, I went back to the bedroom and let the dogs out. It was, in its own way, a test. If my dog didn't trust Tansy, I wasn't going to let her send me to my possible doom. The opinions of a Labrador retriever might seem less than relevant, but Beverly had already saved my life once before. She didn't like people who were out to hurt me. Hopefully, that dislike would extend to situations where the danger was less immediate.

It wasn't until the door was open that I remembered Beverly's reaction to her original owner when he first started getting sick. If she could detect the implants taking over, how was she going to react to Tansy? And what about Minnie—would she respond the same way, once she realized what was going on?

It was too late to stop them from getting to the kitchen: Beverly was already running full-tilt down the hall with Minnie close at her heels, the duo lured by the seductive sounds of company and dishes rattling. Maybe there would be food. Maybe the food would be given to *them*. I ran after the dogs, hoping that I could somehow hold them both back long enough to stop them from tearing Tansy's throat out with their teeth if things went badly—

—and stopped when I reached the kitchen just in time to hear Tansy's ecstatic cry of "Doggies!" It was followed by her sliding out of her chair, dropping to her knees on the hardwood, and throwing her arms around Beverly's neck. For her part, Beverly bore the embrace with her usual stoic good cheer, only the thumping of her tail against the floor betraying her ongoing interest in treats. Minnie ignored her, choosing to head for Nathan instead, sitting down at his feet and looking adoringly up at him.

"Sal," said Nathan, sounding surprised. "You let the dogs out."

"I didn't want Beverly to get upset and start shredding your pillows," I said. "Minnie just sort of came along for the ride."

"Oh, is the black one's name Beverly? What a good name for a doggy! Are you a good doggy? Yes, you are a good doggy, you *are*." Tansy kept hugging Beverly's neck as she spoke. "Where did she come from?"

"Her owner was taken over by his implant while we were walking in the park," said Nathan. "Sal works at an animal shelter. She couldn't just leave Beverly running wild. Somehow, that turned into 'we have a dog now.'"

I couldn't help noticing the "we" in his statement, and I approved. "She seems to like you. I was a little worried about that."

"Oh, animals totally like me. They like Adam, too. It's only people who are in transition that they don't like. They can smell the way the body gets all confused, and it freaks them right the fuck out." Tansy gave Beverly one more squeeze before rising from the floor. "Funny story: when I was first staggering around trying to figure out how my legs worked, I totally got swarmed by bats. Like, little tiny Dracula-style bats. I'm not sure what they thought they were going to do, but wow, were they gonna do it as hard as they could." She chuckled. "Little idiots."

"So animals only react negatively to people in the process of getting sick?" I asked, giving Beverly a pat on the head as I walked past her to take a seat at the table. "What about sleepwalkers?"

"They're still all scrambled. It's like somebody's running a big blender in the chemicals that live inside the brain. It's not until that settles down that animals are going to be cool with them again." Tansy sipped her bloody-looking, over-sugared lemonade before adding casually, "Not that it matters for most people. I mean, they're never going to get better, so who cares if the dog doesn't like them anymore, you know? They've got bigger problems."

As fascinating as I found the discussion of animal reactions to the sleepwalkers, it was clear that we were going to get utterly derailed if we didn't get back on topic soon. "What is the plan for getting me out of SymboGen?" I asked.

Tansy blinked, trying to look guileless. It didn't work. I raised both eyebrows, and waited until she sighed and said, "Oh, fine. You know, you're boring even when you're not being boring. It's like a gift. So here's the deal: we have some back doors into SymboGen. If you get in, we can use them to get you out."

I blinked. "If you have back doors into SymboGen, why do you need me to go in at all? Can't you just use your back doors for, you know, door purposes? Like, accessing a place through the door?" I paused, grimacing. "Great, now I'm starting to talk like you. What I'm asking is this: If you have a way of getting into SymboGen, what do you need me for? Can't you do this more safely if I don't get involved?"

"Sure, if all we want to do is fiddle around on the lab levels and not get anything useful," said Tansy. "We've been in and out of there a hundred times. The genomes aren't being *stored* in the general labs, and we don't have anybody who can access the private levels anymore. Not since our last spy went and got herself all sick. I swear, if the cousins understood English, I'd give them a piece of my mind for eating a piece of hers..."

"You lost a spy to the sleepwalking sickness?" I was scrambling to keep things straight. This was all starting to feel like some big action movie, and I didn't have a copy of the cast list. Or the script.

"Yeah, but she didn't have access to anything anyway, so it's not like it matters." Tansy waved a hand, dismissing their lost spy as an inconvenience. "Just about the only thing she ever did right was keep an eye on you, and she wasn't the only route we had to that, so it's not like—"

"Wait," I said, cutting her off before she could say "not like it matters" again. If I had to hear her say that one more time, she might wind up wearing her fruit punch. "Are you telling me *Chave* was working for you?"

"Well, yeah." Tansy frowned at me. "What, you hadn't figured that out yet?"

"Sal, I know it's tempting, but please don't kill her," said Nathan. "I don't want to lose my security deposit on your first night here."

"How long were you expecting it to take?" I asked.

"It would be nice if we could hold out for at least a week without any major stains or structural damage."

"I'll keep that in mind." I focused back on Tansy. "How long was Chave working for you?"

"We got her hired." Tansy ignored my stare as she continued, "We just need you to get in, get into Dr. Banks's office—or to a computer that's connected to his computer, it's not really important which one you use, although you might have better luck if you use his actual personal machine—and plug in the thumb drive. Wait about ten seconds, and then head for the labs. We'll be able to evacuate you."

"And if you fail?" I asked, as mildly as I could.

"Try to throw the thumb drive under something before they take you down. We'll find a way to get it back later."

I stared at her. So did Nathan. Tansy looked between us, brows furrowing in frustration.

"What, did you think this was some kind of game?" she

asked. "That you could open the broken doors, look through, and decide that this wasn't for you, so sorry, you were just going to go home and have a nice cup of hot cocoa and not think about it? Puh-leeze. This isn't that kind of picture book, and once you've opened the doors, you're sort of required to step through them. Doctor C warned you when she first made contact. You knew what you were getting into."

"I wasn't aware that you and my mother were going to begin treating Sal like she was somehow expendable," said Nathan stiffly.

"Your mother swallowed a genetically modified organism that hadn't been cleared for human use because she thought it was important she continue with her work," said Tansy. Her voice was surprisingly level, all the good cheer and manic insta-bility suddenly gone. It was like she'd flipped a switch, turn-ing off the chipper-but-strange persona she usually projected in favor of something substantially darker. "What in the world would make you look at a woman who was willing to do that and think 'she won't send me or my little girlfriend into dan-ger'? This is so much bigger than you are, for all of us."

"What do you mean, it's bigger than we are?" I asked, before Nathan could say something we'd regret later. His mouth was pressed into a hard line, and he looked like he was on the verge of punching Tansy—something that would probably get us both killed.

"How do you think people will react when they find out the implants are definitely behind the sleepwalking sickness?" asked Tansy. "They're not going to be happy. They're going to start fighting back."

"Well…what's the problem with that? Those people had their bodies first. They're not like the girl who used to own your body. She moved out."

Tansy smiled bitterly. "Yes, thank you, I'm aware that I was a rental property. But here's the thing, genius girl: the treatment to remove a motivated implant from its host might work. *Might.* It also might kill the host, and the implant, and then nobody wins. There has to be a solution that makes the cousins go back to sleep unless the conditions are right. There just has to be."

She looked, briefly, so lost that I wanted to reach for her, take her hand and tell her that everything was going to be okay. That seemed about as smart as hitting her. "So what good does sending me into SymboGen do?"

"If we have the genome of the new cousins, we can figure out how to talk to them. Tell them that they gotta back off, or nobody's coming out on the winning side. Slavery sucks. Dying is worse."

I'd never really thought of the SymboGen implants as being slaves to their hosts. Then again, until very recently, I hadn't thought of them as thinking creatures, even if they didn't really start to think on a sapient level until they had plugged themselves into a human brain.

"All right," I said. I didn't look at Nathan. If I looked at Nathan, I knew that I would lose my cool. "I'll do it."

Tansy clapped her hands and beamed. "Oh," she said, "won't this be *fun*?"

No, I thought. *It won't.*

But I didn't say anything at all.

Some people will always be ungrateful. It's an unfortunate truth of the human race that we see everything as a zero-sum game. For them, if I have happiness, there's less happiness for you; if I have health, there's less health for you. When you look at life that way, it's inevitable that you'll start looking for the catch in everything. I can't possibly have pioneered the genetic research that led to the creation of the Intestinal Bodyguard™ because I wanted to help people, or because I wanted to improve the health of the nation. It can't even be because I understand that a healthier population leads to increased herd immunity, thus benefitting me when my taxes don't have to pay for pandemic preparedness. No. I have to be doing something sinister. I have to have a hidden agenda.

Some people won't be happy until they prove that no one means well, no one is trying to serve the greater good, and there's no such thing as Santa Claus.

—FROM "KING OF THE WORMS," AN INTERVIEW WITH
DR. STEVEN BANKS, CO-FOUNDER OF SYMBOGEN. ORIGINALLY
PUBLISHED IN *ROLLING STONE*, FEBRUARY 2027.

Certain lines can't be uncrossed,
Certain maps will get you lost,
Once you're past the border, then you'll have to play the game.

Roll the dice but count the cards,
Break the glass but keep the shards.
The world is out of order. It's been broken since you came.

The broken doors are hidden in the blood and in the bone.
My darling child, be careful now, and don't go out alone.

—FROM *DON'T GO OUT ALONE*, BY SIMONE KIMBERLEY,
PUBLISHED 2006 BY LIGHTHOUSE PRESS. CURRENTLY
OUT OF PRINT.

Chapter 18

AUGUST 2027

Tansy left after we finished making plans, pausing only to press the promised thumb drive into my hand. Nathan didn't say anything as he walked her to the door. Then he walked back to me, took me by the hands, and led me to the bedroom, to the bed that was *ours* for the very first time, not just his. This was my home, too.

I just had to hope it would be my home for more than a day before I went and got myself killed.

"Sal…" he began. I stopped his mouth with a kiss, and conversation became unimportant for a while, replaced by the twin goals of removing our clothing as fast as possible and keeping our lips on each other at all times. The drums were back in my ears, but softer now, a signal of excitement and not anger or fear. This was where I belonged. This place, this skin, tonight. Everything else was in the future, and the future would have to wait for a few hours. I was doing this because I enjoyed being alive; because I wanted to stay that way. So it was time for me to celebrate my condition, even if it was only for the moment.

When we were done, both of us sweaty and satiated in the way that only accompanies really good sex after emotional turmoil, Beverly stuck her nose into the room and whined, signaling the need to go out. I groaned, starting to push myself up onto my elbows.

"Don't worry about it." Nathan pressed a kiss into the crook of my neck, close enough to the bruise from USAMRIID's sedatives that it made my skin ache with phantom pain. "You've had a long day. I'll take the dogs out."

He was out of the bed before I could do more than mumble sleepy protests. I watched as he pulled on his pants and grabbed the leashes from the top of the dresser, whistling for Beverly and Minnie to come to him. Then he and the dogs were gone, and I drifted off to sleep by the warm light coming from the terrarium of carnivorous plants.

I didn't wake up when they came back in. I didn't wake up until morning.

"You don't have to do this, you know," said Nathan. We were parked on the street near the SymboGen complex, which loomed larger than ever now that I was thinking of myself as a spy and not as a semi-willing visitor. "We can find another way."

"How many people will die while we're looking for another way?" I asked.

He looked away.

"Tansy says there's a back door. I don't like trusting her, but we have to trust someone, and I'm okay with it being your mother. Trusting your mother means trusting Tansy. It's a tautology."

"You mean it's a syllogism," said Nathan, smiling a little.

I blinked at him. "I do?"

"A tautology is a closed loop. 'The first rule of Tautology Club is the first rule of Tautology Club.' A syllogism is a set of presuppositions. 'Tansy is not trustworthy, I trust Dr. Cale, Dr. Cale trusts Tansy, therefore, I trust Tansy.'"

I leaned over and kissed him on the cheek. "What would I do without you?"

"Speak a version of English that no one had ever heard before, probably." Nathan smiled briefly before sobering. "Sal..."

"Someone has to, Nathan. My sister is sick. My *sister*." No one from my family had gotten in contact with me over the night. I was trying to make myself see that as a good thing. "Everyone who's getting attacked by the implants is someone's sister, or brother, or parent. If there's something we can do, we have to do it. Anything else would be...it would be inhuman."

Nathan sighed. "I love you," he said. "Please try not to get hurt."

"I'll be fine," I lied. "I'll contact Tansy as soon as I've got the information your mother needs, and they'll extract me." After that...we were less clear on what would happen after that. We knew SymboGen couldn't arrest me if they couldn't prove something had been done, but they could potentially make my life difficult.

Or they could just decide that they were never going to let me leave.

"Okay," said Nathan.

There was nothing left for us to say after that, and the longer I lingered, the harder it was going to be for me to get out of the car. I leaned over and kissed him again, this time on the lips, lingering just long enough to be sure he understood how much I loved him. Then I grabbed my backpack from the footwell, slipped it on, and got out of the car, beginning to walk slowly toward SymboGen.

It was time to go inside.

There were guards at the edge of the parking lot, watching the cars as they came and went. They greeted me with nothing more than a quick glance and a curt nod, apparently unable to see me as any kind of a threat. I was an empty-handed woman, one that they'd seen before, and ID wasn't required until I got to the actual building. I ducked my head and hurried on, glad of my relative anonymity. I didn't want to deal with answering questions until I had to.

The brave front I'd been putting on for Nathan aside, I was terrified. My stomach was a roiling knot of pain, and the sound of drums was low and constant in my ears, like something out of an old *King Kong* movie. They pounded in time with my footsteps, accompanying me all the way to the sliding glass doors into the lobby.

As always, a rush of chilled air and bland, overprocessed music rushed out to greet me when the doors swept open. The twin feelings of coming home and wanting to run away again swept over me at the same time. I'd barely taken two steps into the lobby when a pair of security guards appeared as if by magic, moving toward me with a tight economy of purpose that was all it took for them to be terrifying. I stopped where I was, trying to ignore the panic building in my gut as I raised my chin and waited for them to come to me. I had every right to be here. I was a patient of SymboGen's. I was Dr. Banks's pet project.

"Can we help you?" asked the first guard, once they were close enough that they wouldn't need to do anything uncouth, like shouting.

"I'm sorry I didn't call ahead, but I didn't know where else to go," I said, trying to make my eyes believably wide and glossy. To my surprise, tears actually started to form as I continued, "I can't go home. I just can't. Can—can you tell Dr. Banks that Sally Mitchell is here to see him?" Now that the tears had started, they simply refused to stop. The past few days had been even more traumatic than I realized.

The guards exchanged a glance, looking as disturbed by my tears as I was. "Do you have ID?" asked the second.

Nodding, I dug my ID card out of the front pocket of my backpack and held it out to them. My hand was shaking. I didn't try to stop it. It would only help with the image I was trying to project...and I didn't want to know how I would react if it turned out I was unable to make the shaking stop.

The guard took my card, turning it over in his fingers like he wanted to be certain that it was legitimate. It must have passed whatever unknown test he was putting it through, because he looked to his partner and said, "Wait here with her," before turning and walking toward the reception counter.

The remaining security guard offered me an earnest smile and said, "It's all right, Miss Mitchell. We're just going to call up to Dr. Banks and see if he's free to see you." I looked at him blankly, and he continued, "We've met before. You probably don't remember me, but I was in the cafeteria the last time you came to visit us. So I know this is just a formality."

"Oh." I hadn't really been looking at the faces of the guards who came to save me that day in the cafeteria. Too much of my focus had been on Chave and her hopeless battle against the parasite that was in the process of consuming her thinking mind. Still, he looked so hopeful that I found I couldn't tell him that. "Thank you. I really appreciate what you did that day. I'm sorry. I'm just...really shaken."

Now concern washed his smile away. "What happened?"

I could either try to make myself an ally inside SymboGen, or I could avoid the need to tell my carefully crafted sob story twice. I decided to aim for something in the middle as I said, "I went to see where my father works, and there was...someone got sick. Again." I sniffled. "I'm so tired of seeing people get sick all around me."

"I'm sorry," said the guard.

"Me, too."

"Miss Mitchell?" We both turned to see the first guard returning. He held out my ID card. I took it, tucking it into my backpack as he said, "We've been instructed to stay here with you. Dr. Banks will be right down. Can we get you anything? A glass of water? A chair?"

"No, thank you," I said, and wiped my nose with the side of my hand. "I just want to see Dr. Banks. Thank you for your help."

"It's our job, ma'am."

The return of the first guard had popped the thin bubble of rapport the second guard and I had been starting to craft between us. We stood in awkward silence until a door opened in the bank of elevators and Dr. Banks came striding out, looking in all directions before his eyes settled on us. "Sally!" he called, and started toward us.

Dr. Banks didn't look quite as perfect as he had on every other visit, although I couldn't put my finger on exactly what had changed. His hair was just a bit less flawlessly combed; his skin was just slightly less ideal. He looked *tired*, and it carried all the way into his clothing, which was rumpled around the edges, like he'd been sleeping in it.

"Sally," he said again, once he was close enough that he didn't need to shout. "How are you? I've been so worried..." He didn't say anything about the bugs in my house, or the fact that they'd stopped working shortly after they were installed. I decided not to say anything either. My father was the local head of USAMRIID; if the bugs didn't work, Dr. Banks would blame it on Dad, unless I gave him good reason to do otherwise.

"It's been a hard few days," I said. I forced myself to think about the scene at the lab, the intern bleeding out her life through the hole in her throat, and was rewarded with fresh tears. The first one slipped free and ran down my cheek as I said, "Joyce is sick."

"Joyce—you mean your sister, don't you?" I nodded mutely.

Dr. Banks's face dissolved into a mask of sympathy that might have seemed sincere, if I hadn't spent so much time with him, observing his reactions through dozens of private interviews. He was surprised to hear that Joyce was sick. But he wasn't sorry. "Sally, that's terrible. How are your parents handling the news?"

This was where things were going to get dicey. I glanced toward the two security guards who were still standing patiently by, trying to project reluctance. "I don't know if I really want to talk about that here in the lobby."

Dr. Banks was rarely slow on the uptake. He nodded immediately, stepping close and putting his arm around my shoulders. I managed not to recoil away from him. "That's easily enough fixed, Sally. Thank you, gentlemen, for making sure Miss Mitchell got to me as quickly as possible. You may go about your duties now."

"Thank you, Dr. Banks," said the first guard. The second guard didn't say anything, just offered me a little wave before turning and following his partner back to their posts against the wall.

Dr. Banks tightened his hold on me as he turned back toward the elevators, pulling me unavoidably along. I swallowed and let myself be led, ducking my chin a little so that he would think I was overwhelmed with relief at finally being somewhere safe. In actuality, all I wanted to do was turn and run back outside, to where real safety could be found. And if I did that, hundreds of people would die.

Once we were in the elevator, Dr. Banks let me go, and said, "It's very good to see you again. I've been worried about you. The last time you were here...that didn't go very well."

I stared at him. I couldn't help it. "People *died*," I said, unable to keep the shock out of my tone.

"Yes, and you could have been seriously hurt, I know. I am so, so sorry, Sally. This was supposed to be a place where you could always be safe, and instead, it nearly got you killed. I assure you, that won't happen again. We've stepped up security, and we've initiated preemptive scanning of all employees on a twice-weekly basis, just to be safe." He must have mistaken my slowly dawning anger for amazement, because he smiled, adding, "All measures are justified if they allow us to guarantee the safety of our guests."

"You have a test that's good enough to catch early infections, and you haven't been sharing it with the local hospitals." I didn't realize that would be my answer until it was already out, hanging in the air between us like a shameful secret. There was no point in trying to take it back, and so I pressed on, demanding, "Why?"

The elevator dinged as it reached its destination. Dr. Banks stepped out, motioning for me to follow. "There are a lot of things to be considered in a situation like this one, Sally. Some of them are admittedly less noble than others."

"How many of them justify letting people get sick because you're not sharing the test?" I walked next to him as he led the way down the hall to his office.

"None," he said, opening the office door. "But how many of them justify giving people a few more days of peace before they become ill? Don't mistake an early detection system for treatment, Sally. We may have the one, but we're a long way from the other."

"So why did you develop a test in the first place?" I looked around as I stepped into the office. His computer was where it always was, displayed prominently on his desk. If he would just leave me alone for a few minutes, I would be able to plug in the thumb drive and accomplish what I'd come here to do. The real trick was going to be getting Dr. Banks to leave me alone.

He sighed as he closed the door and walked around to take a seat at that selfsame desk. "You're smarter than that question, Sally. We developed a test because the sleepwalking sickness is parasitic in nature. You know that. You've known that since you went back to the hospital with your boyfriend."

I stared at him as I sat down in one of the chairs across from his desk. I knew SymboGen had been watching me. I still somehow didn't expect him to be quite so open about admitting it. "But..."

"Please listen to me very carefully, because it's important to me that you understand: the sleepwalking sickness is the result of a different parasitic infection."

"What?"

"It's my fault. I pioneered the idea that parasites were our friends, that they could somehow be tamed and turned from enemies into allies, and I caused this. People stopped being as careful as they needed to be." Dr. Banks raked a hand through his hair, mussing the normally perfect strands still further. "It's funny, in a horrible way. We were trying to prove the hygiene hypothesis was something that could be beaten. What we didn't anticipate was people turning 'nothing in nature can hurt you' into a gospel."

I was still staring. The words I needed to question him just weren't there.

Apparently, Dr. Banks had been waiting for a willing audience, because he kept on going. "Off-brand parasites have become an increasing problem recently. They're all black market, of course—I'm not too proud to admit that we've greased the wheels at the FDA to keep any competitors to the implant from seeing the light of day—but they're still out there. People are messing with the genome of anything they think might turn a profit. And because there's a sucker born every minute, those profits can be substantial."

"Chave didn't pick up any off-brand parasites."

"No, she didn't. She was a company woman, through and through, and I miss her more than you can possibly know. You saw her when you deigned to visit us—oh, don't look so shocked, Sally. I know you hate coming here. It's why I was so surprised to see you today—but I saw her every day. She managed my schedule. She knew everything about me, and she didn't judge me for any of it. Now, if you really think I have a treatment, can you think of any possible reason that I would have refused to share it with Chave?" He shook his head. "I'm not a monster, Sally. This might be easier if I were. This might be easier on everyone."

"So the sleepwalking sickness is parasitic, but it's not a Symbo-Gen parasite?"

"Now you're catching on. We think that whoever created the parasite that causes it wanted to make something small—something that wouldn't catch the attention of the implants. They're very territorial, you know, and they won't tolerate the presence of a competing parasite. So these unknown engineers started with a protozoa parasite, and worked their way up from there. The trouble is, protozoa can be transmitted in water. And most modern filtration systems haven't been constructed to filter out parasites. It would be a waste of money."

The chain of transmission he was proposing made sense. People ingest illegal, black market parasites for some reason—and let's face it, there are always people willing to do things that seem stupid if they think they're going to get something out of it—and then those parasites find their way into shower drains and sinks as their new host's body adjusts to their presence. Once they got into the water, the parasites would be able to sail right into the body of another host, with no one the wiser. I wasn't sure how big protozoa were, but they'd have to be pretty small if they were designed not to attract the attention of the implants.

"Wouldn't the protozoa be territorial?" I asked.

"Not in the same way," he said, sounding more confident now, like I'd finally ventured onto territory he knew how to manage. "Tapeworms are generally solitary, because they have to be; very few hosts can support two healthy adult tapeworms without dying. Even so, in nature, it's not unusual for people to have multiple tapeworms, because they're hermaphrodites, and sometimes their babies just don't go looking for places of their own."

The fact that he was making jokes, even terrible ones, made me want to claw his eyes out. I forced myself to remain still. "So these protozoa, they'd come in groups? And that way, if some of them got out of the body, there would still be protozoa in their original hosts?"

"Yes, exactly. We believe that what's happening—the most reasonable chain of transmission—is fools looking for a magic bullet ingesting the generation one, or G1, protozoa. Once their infection is established, they start shedding excess parasites into the water supply, where they reproduce, creating generation two, or G2, protozoa. From there, the G2 protozoa make their way into faucets and showers, and gradually spread the infection." Dr. Banks shook his head. "What's truly tragic about this is that it seems likely that the people who started this whole mess are the only ones *not* getting sick. Having a pre-established G1 colony is likely to protect them from the encroaching G2 colony, and it seems likely that only the G2 protozoa are actually causing their hosts to succumb to the sleepwalking sickness."

"Oh." My head was starting to spin from all the scientific jargon he was spouting. I desperately wished that Nathan was there. He'd have been able to tell me how much of this was real and how much was carefully created spin doctoring, using possibilities and potentials to craft a story that sounded almost plausible. "So how much of this do you know? I mean, you keep saying 'we think' and 'we guess,' but you haven't said very much 'we know.' How much have you proven?"

"Enough," said Dr. Banks, with sudden vagueness. "I'm so sorry that you've been walking around thinking that our test meant we had a treatment. Until we know for sure what's attacking these people, we can't put forth a viable course of antiparasitics, and we don't want to risk a mass panic."

"Why not? Are you afraid that it would hurt your stock prices?"

"No, Sally, we're afraid that it would hurt everyone who trusts our brand enough to have one of our implants. The SymboGen Intestinal Bodyguard was created to mitigate the worst effects of the hygiene hypothesis. It allowed us to undo, in a single step, literally decades of excessive sterilization and reduced microbial diversity. Since then, the implants have become responsible for everything from maintaining insulin levels in diabetics to controlling issues with human brain chemistry and secreting natural birth control. They represent millions of dollars saved in pharmacological costs annually. That doesn't even take into account the savings they naturally cause in the areas of preventative medicine and allergy control. They've changed the face of medicine."

"And?" I asked.

"And if you take all that away, even assuming that every single host was able to survive the course of antibiotics necessary to flush both the implant and the unknown protozoa from their system, what infrastructure is going to be there to step up and take care of all these people's medical needs? Who is going to be standing by with the pills no one is in the habit of taking anymore, the shots no one wants to give themselves? What happens to the women who live in regions where birth control is unfairly restricted, but have been getting around that by buying their implants out of state? Suddenly they're back in the bad old position of needing to find a way to convince their doctors they're not immoral whores just because they want to be allowed to control their own reproduction. Take away the implants, and the medical system of this country crumbles." There was a strange new light in Dr. Banks's eyes. He sounded appropriately solemn as he was speaking, but something about his expression was almost...proud. "That's just America. *D. symbogenesis* is a global phenomenon. What do you say to the people who are finally able to control their own medical destinies? How do you convince them to throw away their miracle because they might, potentially, come into contact with another type of parasite someday, and it could hurt them?"

"Oh." I bit my lip, worrying it between my teeth before asking, "But how does that excuse not sharing the test with the authorities? I mean, you could tell them everything, just the way you told me, and then show them how to check for the bad parasites, and they'd be able to...I don't know, quarantine people when they started getting sick. Maybe then, no one would get hurt just because they got too close to someone who was already going to die." I thought of Devi, who'd only wanted to be sure that her wife was okay. Would putting Katherine under quarantine as soon as she tested positive have made any difference? Probably not. But we would never know, would we?

"We could also trigger a panic, leading to millions of people overdosing on antiparasitics as they become convinced that *D. symbogenesis* is somehow connected to the outbreaks. We're already starting to see resource hoarding in some areas where the sleepwalkers have been especially active." Dr. Banks shook his head. "We set out to become the first name in parasites. Well, we achieved it. Now we have to be careful, or the sins of an entire biological genus will be heaped upon our heads."

"You mean your head," I said.

Dr. Banks blinked. Apparently, declarative statements were more surprising than bewildered questions. "What do you mean?"

"I mean Dr. Jablonsky is dead, and Dr. Cale is missing, so any blame is going to fall on you. Is that why you look so tired?" I tried to sound sympathetic. I wasn't sure that it was working.

For his part, Dr. Banks looked even more surprised than he had before. "I wasn't aware you knew so much about Symbo-Gen's history."

"Everyone knows about SymboGen's history," I said. It was true: he'd made sure we couldn't forget it. I just knew a little more than I was meant to. "I didn't read the books, but they're available in audio. I listened to them while I was at work. There was a lot I wanted to understand."

"Ah, yes, work," said Dr. Banks, suddenly looking like he was back on familiar ground. "Will tells me that you haven't been to the shelter in more than a week. Have you been feeling unwell?"

SymboGen got me the job at the shelter. Of course Dr. Banks would be on a first-name basis with my boss. "I was at home," I said. "Nathan and I got caught in an outbreak in Lafayette."

"Oh, yes, I heard about that," said Dr. Banks. "Whatever were you doing out there?"

Fortunately, I had a believable, if utterly frivolous excuse for what we would have been doing out in Lafayette: "There's this ice cream company called Jeni's? They're from Ohio? Anyway, the only place in the Bay Area that carries most of their flavors is Diablo Foods in Lafayette. I wanted ice cream, and Nathan felt like indulging me, I guess." I bit my lip again. "Maybe we should have just gone to Ghirardelli Square."

"Maybe you should have," Dr. Banks agreed. "Sally, I am so, so sorry you had to see that."

There was one question I hadn't asked yet. I sniffled again, doing my best to look pitiful, and asked, "If the sleepwalking sickness is because of a proto-whatsit, not the implants, how is it messing up everyone's behavior? I mean. I know some parasites can get into the brain, but don't those have to be bigger? Not so tiny that they can get through water filters?"

Dr. Banks paused. In that momentary silence, I heard everything I needed to hear: he was testing a line of public spin on me. There were no protozoa, no black market parasite that was creating this sudden health hazard. Given sufficient time, I was sure that SymboGen could synthesize one and introduce it to the water table, thus deflecting suspicion onto whatever under-ground genetic labs they could find.

Labs like Dr. Cale's.

Finally, he said, "We don't know. But we're going to find out, and as soon as we have concrete proof of our accusations, we're going to take our findings to USAMRIID and the CDC. You have my word on that."

I nodded. "Thank you." Then I sagged forward, covering my face with my hands, and wailed, "But it'll be too late for Joyce. She's going to die. She's going to get sicker and sicker, and for-get who she is, and then she's going to die."

"Sally…" I heard Dr. Banks get out of his chair. I didn't lift my head, but listened to the sound of his footsteps coming closer. I managed to brace myself enough so that I didn't flinch when his heavy hand landed on my shoulder, trying to offer comfort. "I'm so sorry about your sister. There was nothing I could have done to help her. But you should never have been forced to see that. You should never have been forced to see any of this."

I didn't say anything. I kept my head down, continuing to make small choking noises, like my air supply had been fatally compromised. Dr. Banks gave my shoulder an awkward pat. I bent further forward and whimpered.

That seemed to be the missing ingredient. "Let me send someone to get you a glass of water."

"No," I mumbled, just loudly enough to be heard without my needing to sit up. If I sat up, he'd see that I wasn't really cry-ing. At that point, he might start wondering why I'd been fak-ing it, and then the jig would most certainly be up. "I don't…I don't want to see anyone else."

"Oh, *Sally*," he sighed, and pulled his hand away. "Let me get it for you, then. I don't mind."

"Thank you," I whispered. I kept my head down as I listened to his footsteps retreating across the room, waiting for the sound of the door being opened and closed. I didn't have much time. I still forced myself to count to five before I raised my head and risked a glance behind me.

Dr. Banks was gone.

Moving as fast as I could without tripping over my own feet, I slid out of the chair and dug the thumb drive out of my pocket at the same time. In five steps I was around his desk, bending to shove the thumb drive into one of the USB ports at the front of his computer. It beeped once, and the little light on top of the thumb drive came on, glowing a steady green. I didn't know whether that was good or not. What color was a thumb drive supposed to glow? That kind of thing had never been important to me before. Here, now, it seemed like the most important thing in the world.

According to Tansy, I only needed to keep the thumb drive connected for ten seconds. I dropped into Dr. Banks's chair and dug wildly through my backpack, coming up with the one thing that could potentially explain why I had changed seats: my notebook. I flipped it open to the first empty page, grabbed a pen out of Dr. Banks's jar, and started scribbling words almost at random. My writing was even more illegible than normal. That was a good thing.

I counted down from ten as I wrote, trying to give the thumb drive time to do its work. I itched to pull it out, choosing safety over giving it time to finish. Quashing the urge took everything I had in me, but I did it, continuing to write as the seconds slipped by.

The doorknob turned while I was still counting. I hunched farther down over my paper, and stayed that way as Dr. Banks stepped into the room. "Sally?" he said, sounding surprised.

I raised my head, hoping he would read my borderline panic as misery, and said, "I needed to write, and I couldn't get my notebook to balance on my knees. Dr. Morrison says I should write whenever I feel like I need to. You don't mind, do you?" The drums were suddenly hammering in my ears. I swallowed and forced myself to keep looking at Dr. Banks, reading his expression for any sign that he knew I was lying to him.

Instead, his face softened, and he said, "I don't mind at all, Sally. You should absolutely do what your therapist recommends. Dr. Morrison is a good man, and I have the utmost faith in his methods."

"I'm glad you're not mad," I said, and sniffled again, wiping my nose on the back of my hand before I went back to writing. Dr. Banks walked over to the desk, putting the paper cup of water he'd gone to fetch down next to me, and lingered just a little too long, clearly trying to make some sense out of the messy loops and swirls of my writing. The joke was on him. While I could write legibly when I tried, I wasn't trying, and even I wouldn't have been able to decode some of what I'd written. Dr. Morrison always yelled at me when I did that. I didn't care.

"What are you writing about, Sally?" he finally asked.

"Joyce. How scared I am about what might happen to her. How much I hope she gets better. How guilty I feel for moving out of my parents' house." I looked up, meeting his eyes as I said, "I moved in with Nathan last night."

"Is your family not reacting well?" He paused, frowning. "Did they release the medical custodianship?"

"Not quite. I don't care. I couldn't stay there anymore." I sniffled, ducking my head to check the thumb drive as I did. The light on top had changed from green to yellow. I hoped that meant it was done, and not that something had gone wrong with the file transfer process. I wasn't going to be able to do this again.

I hoisted my backpack onto the desk with one hand, using the motion to cover the fact that I was extracting the thumb drive with my other hand. I shoved it into my pocket as I pushed my notebook carefully back into the bag, hoping that

Dr. Banks would be too distracted by the hand he could see to wonder what the hand under the desk was doing.

"They didn't *say* anything," I said. I closed my bag and tugged it back into my lap, "but they were looking at me like…like this was my fault somehow. Like if they hadn't spent so much time and energy looking out for my health, Joyce's health wouldn't have been at risk. Mom even said that I wasn't her daughter anymore. I was a stranger they'd been playing pretend with. That their real…that Sally died when she had the accident, and I'm just some other girl who took her body as my own. It wasn't anything I haven't thought before, when I was having a bad night. But it just hurt so much hearing it from her. It hurt so much."

"She was right."

My head snapped up without my willing it to, and I felt my eyes going wide with a strange combination of shock, anger, and raw terror. "What did you say?"

"I said, she was right." Dr. Banks sat down in the chair that I had abandoned, looking at me gravely. "Sally, you have to know you are not the person you were before your accident. We are each of us the sum total of our experiences. We are shaped by our memories and by the moments we live through, and no two people are exactly the same, ever, because no two people experience exactly the same lives. Sally Mitchell died when her brain activity ceased. Sally Mitchell was born when her brain activity resumed. Maybe if the memory centers of your brain hadn't been so profoundly damaged, you'd still be her, but they *were* damaged, and so you're *not* her, no matter how much you might like to pretend you are. You're someone entirely new, free of her sins and successes and emotional baggage."

"There's a chance my memory could come back someday," I said, hating how weak my voice sounded, even under the steady pounding of the drums.

"And if it does, you'll have the first Sally's memories on top of the second Sally's memories, and you'll become a new person all over again. For you, recall would be a form of suicide. Maybe not if it had happened right away—then, all this would have just been a strange gap in the memory of the girl you used to be—but it's been long enough, and you've lived a different enough life, that you would die if she reclaimed herself. Would that Sally have loved Dr. Kim? Would she have worked at the shelter for so long?" His gaze sharpened. "Would she have been willing to go through the broken doors at the behest of a woman she'd never met?"

"I…I don't know what you're talking about." I didn't have to feign my shock.

Dr. Banks smiled. "Don't you?"

I gaped at him, not sure what else I could say. As I did, I realized that by putting myself behind the desk, I might have gotten access to his computer, but I had done so at the expense of my access to the door. Dr. Banks was between me and the only exit. The windows weren't the kind that were intended to be opened. Even if I could somehow smash them before he stopped me, all that would do was allow me to plummet to my death more than twenty stories below.

"Did you really think that I wasn't keeping a close eye on you? I'm fond of you, Sally, but you represent a huge investment in research hours and medical costs. I'm not going to let you run around willy-nilly without making sure that I have some idea of where you're going. The shower trick was a good one, I'll grant you that. Unfortunately for you, I've had that shelter bugged since the day you applied there. We got everything. Including a few key words that only one person I've ever known would think constituted a cypher." Dr. Banks leaned forward in his seat, expression sharpening. "I hoped you'd lead us to her. You didn't. And so I'm asking you: where is she, Sally?

"Where is Dr. Shanti Cale?"

The number of keystrokes that have been wasted discussing my relationship with Dr. Steven Banks is frankly appalling. There were much better things the world could have been doing with its collective time, including researching the supposed genetic structure of D. symbogenesis, *the little worm without which the private lives of two scientists would never have been up for scrutiny. We were a smokescreen, one that I didn't realize he was intentionally casting until it was too late for me to get out of the line of fire.*

Were we lovers? Yes, we were. I was married at the time—I'm still married now, as far as I'm concerned—but my husband and I both knew our careers might sometimes take us down less than savory paths. Steven was a bright, ambitious man who was willing to promise me the world. I would have been a fool to deny him whatever he asked from me.

As it turns out, I was a fool anyway, but not quite in the way most people wanted to believe. I was a fool for listening to the promises he made when we weren't in the bedroom. Those may have been the only true words he ever whispered in my ear.

—FROM *CAN OF WORMS: THE AUTOBIOGRAPHY OF SHANTI CALE, PHD.* AS YET UNPUBLISHED.

I always knew that this grand experiment would eventually reach a tipping point, a stage at which our only choices were evolve or die. Unfortunately, there is no way of predicting which choice we are going to make before it is made. No one can tell you which way the singularity can go.

For the sake of my children—all my children—I pray that we can make the right decision. The only problem is, I'm not sure any single decision will be right for all them. No matter which way this goes, I am terribly afraid that half of the people I love are doomed.

—FROM THE JOURNAL OF DR. SHANTI CALE, SEPTEMBER 5, 2027.

Chapter 19

AUGUST 2027

don't know who you're talking about," I said. My voice was level and calm. I was proud of myself for that. Really, I wanted to throw up.

"I think you do, Sally; after all, you mentioned her yourself not all that long ago," said Dr. Banks. "Think hard. Blonde woman, curvy, fondness for lab coats and genetic engineering? Oh, and she's your boyfriend's mother, mustn't forget that. Do you think he knows where she is, if you're insisting you don't? Do you think he'd tell me if we asked him?"

"Leave Nathan out of this," I said, finding more strength now that I had something to defend. I sat straighter in my pilfered chair, trying to glare at him. It wasn't working as well as I wanted it to. I was too terrified for that. "He has nothing to do with whatever you want from me."

"Oh, no, believe me, he does. It was a stroke of amazing luck when you met up with him. I knew all along that he was Shanti's son. She always forgot that I was the one who had recruited her in the first place—just one more blind spot in a series stretching all the way back to the lab. It's a good thing she's so brilliant. If she weren't, her tendency to focus on the science at the expense of the human element would have gotten her killed years ago. We've been trying to hire Dr. Kim for years. If he would just consent to an implant…we couldn't change the rules without tipping him off. Ah, well. Water under the bridge. Where is she?"

"Couldn't you just have changed the rules if you wanted him that bad?" I asked, dodging the question.

Dr. Banks laughed. "Oh, Sally. I do love your sense of humor. Rules are rules. If I'd changed them, everyone would have known something was up. But oh, I've wanted to know what my old friend was doing, and that meant keeping tabs on her son. There was always the chance that she might decide to make contact sometime in the future—which she did, through you. You're apparently more important to her than her own son. Interesting implications, don't you think?" He tried that old paternal smile again. It wasn't working as well as it usually did. "His interest in you was something we couldn't have predicted, but I'll admit, we did nothing to discourage it. Keeping the two of you in one place—a package deal, so to speak—made surveillance so much easier."

I stared at him. "But why…?"

"Your father is the head of USAMRIID's San Francisco office. We needed a way to watch him without it being suspicious. You were the perfect entry into his home." Dr. Banks looked briefly apologetic. "We're sorry to have disrupted your life as much as we did. If it makes you feel any better, we wouldn't have done it if there had been any other way."

"But…" I shook my head. "You couldn't have planned this. I had an *accident*." An accident I remembered absolutely noth-

ing about. I'd never even spoken to any of the witnesses. By
the time I was out of recovery and able to really wonder about
what had happened to me, they had already put the incident
behind them, vanishing into the general population without a
thought for the girl whose car kissed a bus.

"I admit, Sally, I'd hoped we could convince you to join our
SymboGen family," said Dr. Banks. "I wanted to be able to
protect you. You're a special girl, and you deserve better than
the world outside these doors. But if we'd accomplished that,
Shanti probably wouldn't have contacted you. She's always
been canny. While she might have smelled 'trap' on your skin,
she was willing to take the risk, and I doubt that would have
been the case if you'd been on the payroll."

"I had an accident," I repeated, with less certainty.

"I was also a little disappointed when you decided to shut
us out, rather than coming to me and asking who this woman
was, slipping notes into your things and trying to lure you into
the path of danger. She's the real reason you were in Lafayette,
isn't she? That's why you nearly got hurt in that mob of sleepwalkers. Because Shanti was careless with the lives of others
once again."

I looked at him solemnly, seeing the entire situation play
out from that single-pointed comment. Dr. Banks was looking for a scapegoat. Whether it was nonexistent protozoa or the
woman who'd helped to design the Intestinal Bodyguard didn't
matter: all he needed was someone or something to pin the
sleepwalking sickness on, and he and SymboGen could walk
away scot-free. All it would take was a story that people would
believe—and which was more attractive, really? The idea that
a trusted corporation responsible for the health and happiness
of millions had made a huge research error, or the idea that one
woman, embittered over her own relative obscurity, had done
something to change that company's good works?

He would turn Dr. Cale into a criminal. I might not object

to that as stridently as he'd expect me to—she was Nathan's mother, and she meant well, but she'd created the implants and she valued the well-being of tapeworms as much as, if not more than, she valued the well-being of humans. I'd still object. If this was SymboGen's fault, then SymboGen needed to pay for it. And that included the man who'd turned Dr. Surrey Kim into Dr. Shanti Cale in the first place.

"We went for ice cream." My voice didn't shake at all. I sounded utterly reasonable to my own ears. I hugged my backpack against my chest, still staring at him. "Nathan knew I was upset about that weird phone call from that... that woman, and so we went for ice cream. She never told me her name."

For the first time, Dr. Banks looked unsure. "You knew Dr. Cale was Nathan's mother."

"Because you told me she was." I shook my head. "I'm here because I didn't know where else to go. The last time I was here, Chave tried to kill me, and you locked me in a little room in the basement with people who wouldn't tell me what was wrong. Do you really think I'd be here now if there was someplace else? I'm so uncomfortable right now." I didn't have to force tears to well up in my eyes. The churning panic in my gut brought them leaping to the surface. "I didn't come here so you could accuse me of working against you. I had an *accident*, and now you're acting like you've only been nice to me all this time because you thought you could use me. I thought you were different from my family, Dr. Banks. I thought you *cared*."

That last part was a lie, but it came close enough on the heels of the truth that he didn't appear to notice the difference. His face fell, and he rose from his chair, already reaching for me. "Sally, I'm so sorry. I didn't mean it like that. Please, I never wanted you to think of yourself as just a tool..."

I shied away from his hands, putting my head down on my backpack and sobbing in earnest. It seemed easier than trying to talk to him. I didn't know what else there was to say, and his words were still careening madly around the inside of my skull, looking for things to knock loose. I had an accident. Sally Mitchell had an accident. Or did she? After all, the girl she left behind was never going to tell anyone any different. The girl she left behind wasn't going to tell anyone anything at all about the last minutes of Sally's life. That girl didn't know.

I had forgotten something in Dr. Cale's lab, hadn't I? Something I wasn't ready to remember yet...

"Sally, please."

I kept crying. Joyce was sick. My mother didn't want me anymore. My father was willing to lie to me if he thought it would help him learn more about the sleepwalking sickness. Even Dr. Banks was saying it had never been about me and my recovery at all: it had been about using me to get to the secrets he thought he might be able to weasel out of my father.

"Sally, I'm sorry."

He sounded sincere. I raised my head, wiping away my tears as I looked at him. He looked back, hands spread in surrender.

"What do you want me to say?" he asked. "You know nothing is ever as simple as you want it to be. SymboGen is not the enemy here, but you were willing to let us be if it meant you didn't have to trust people who weren't always as comfortable as the ones you'd chosen to surround yourself with. No one has only your best interests at heart. Not me, not your parents...and not Dr. Cale. Whether you've met her or not, you should keep that in mind for when she does manage to catch up to you—and she is *going* to find you, Sally. She's not the good to my evil. She's not going to solve all of your problems with a wave of her hand and a cup of hot cocoa. You're smart enough to know better than that. People like us...we don't get easy answers like that."

"Did you cause my accident?" I asked in a very small voice.

"No, Sally. SymboGen has never caused you to have an accident." Dr. Banks sighed. "What can I do to convince you that we're on the same side?"

The thumb drive with the stolen data Dr. Cale needed was safe in my pocket, pressed in a solid, reassuring line against my hip. "Can I...this is silly, I know, but can I have an ultrasound?"

Now it was Dr. Banks's turn to look confused. "You *want* an ultrasound?"

"Sometimes...I have trouble going to sleep. I haven't slept much since I found out Joyce was sick. I can't. But I always sleep in the gel ultrasound chamber. I know it's a big thing to ask, but..."

Confusion melted into relief as Dr. Banks grasped what I was asking. "No, it's no trouble at all. I'll call down to Dr. Sanjiv and Dr. McGillis, and let them know they're needed at the lab. It won't hurt anything for us to have more data on your progress, and if it means that you get to rest for a little while, that's even better."

"Thank you." I wiped my face again. "I hate to impose."

"After the week you've had, I think a little imposition is completely justified." Dr. Banks straightened, back on familiar ground: I was going to submit to medical tests, and he was going to pay for them. The fact that my things would be entirely unguarded during the process was just a bonus, something to be taken advantage of only if necessary.

He was probably going to find it necessary. I would have been worried about that, if I'd had any intention of actually getting into the ultrasound machine.

"Thank you," I repeated, standing. I hugged my backpack against my chest as it moved, forcing myself to shelter it, and not my pocket, from any casual study. *Don't think about the thumb drive*, I thought sternly. *Focus on the backpack.*

It seemed to be working, or maybe Dr. Banks was just eager to get his hands on my notebook again. His eyes, when they weren't on my face, went to the backpack, tracking its motion across the office. "Do you mind if I walk you down?" he asked. "I don't have a new personal assistant yet, and I'd hate to think of you getting lost on your way to the lab."

Even with as many times as I had been down there, it was a reasonable concern: I'd never made the trip without Sherman, Chave, or both of them escorting me. "Not at all," I said, and managed to muster a wavering smile. "I'd appreciate the company."

"I'm glad," said Dr. Banks, and led me to the office door.

He talked while we were in the elevator going down, the usual easy, meaningless chatter about stock prices, recent news reports, and the weather. He seemed to realize I wasn't really listening, but that didn't stop him; it was like he needed to be doing something with his mouth to keep from saying anything that would break our fragile, temporary peace right down the middle. We could both feel how frail it was, stitched together with my silence and his willingness to back off when he saw that he had pushed me too far.

The really sad thing was, as I listened to him babble about anything and everything but the sleepwalkers, I realized that Dr. Banks genuinely seemed to care about what happened to me—even more than my own parents did. He didn't have a very good grasp of how to show it, and he was almost certainly still telling me lies, but he wanted me to be happy. I could tell that much from the way he kept glancing in my direction, seeking approval from the lines of my face. He wanted me to be happy. Whether or not that was possible was irrelevant. We all want things that can never happen, and even when we know they're not going to become reality, we keep on wanting them.

Dr. Sanjiv was waiting in front of the elevator bank when the doors finally opened on the underground lab level. Her normally impeccable bun was slightly less well tied than usual, resulting in a few flyaway hairs around her face; like Dr. Banks, she looked just a little unfinished, overwound, and tired. "Sir," she said, offering Dr. Banks a polite nod before turning her attention to me. "Hello, Sally. How are you feeling today?"

"Okay, I guess," I lied. I didn't feel like getting into it with her. "How are you?"

"Busy." She paused, realizing her mistake, and amended, "But always happy to see my favorite patient. Marvin is getting the ultrasound gel prepared for you."

"I hope you understand the importance of Miss Mitchell's comfort," said Dr. Banks, with a note of warning in his voice that was enough to make me feel uneasy.

It was worse for Dr. Sanjiv; she worked for him, after all. "Yes, sir," she said, straightening until it looked like someone had manually locked her spine into place. "I promise the utmost care will be taken in the procedure. You can ask Sally yourself, if you'd like. Dr. McGillis and I have done this multiple times, and she's never had any complications."

"They're some of my favorite techs here," I said, picking up my cue. It was the truth, and even more, I didn't want anyone to get in any more trouble than was absolutely necessary. I was, after all, planning to disappear on their watch. It might go a little better for them if they weren't already in trouble when that happened.

"If you're positive," said Dr. Banks. He looked to me, brows furrowing as he searched my face. I had no idea what he was looking for. I wasn't really sure I wanted to know. "Sally, you know you can tell me anything, don't you? I'm sorry about before, in the office. I wasn't thinking clearly, and I apologize."

"That's okay, Dr. Banks," I said, fighting the urge to squirm. Dr. Sanjiv was looking away, her face schooled into an expression of careful neutrality. The way he was phrasing things, it sounded almost like he'd made a pass at me. One that had been rebuffed. I was glad of that much, at least. I wasn't going to have to deal with the entire staff of the lab thinking I'd been sleeping with their boss. "We've all had a hard week. It's why I asked if I could have an ultrasound."

Dr. Sanjiv laughed, an odd little rippling run of notes that sounded artificial only because I had never heard her laugh before. "She falls asleep every time," she said, to Dr. Banks. "It's amazing; we've never seen anything like it. The gel floods in, and Sally checks out. She stays asleep for the whole process. I wish all our patients could be as easy to work with as she is."

"I always told you Miss Mitchell was special," said Dr. Banks.

I was still trying to figure out why sometimes I was "Sally" and sometimes I was "Miss Mitchell" when he turned back to me, seizing my hands before I could step out of his reach.

"Maybe you know what I mean by this and maybe you don't, but Sally, some doors are closed because they're meant to be closed. Do you understand me? Not every door is supposed to be opened, and not every open door is supposed to be used. You have a choice."

My choice had been made the moment I plugged the thumb drive into his computer, if not long before then. Still, he looked so sincere, and so worried, that I felt I owed him something. Trying to look confused and supportive at the same time, I nodded, and said, "I understand, Dr. Banks."

"Good. Good, Sally." He let go of my hands, taking a step backward, toward the elevator. "Dr. Sanjiv, I'm leaving her in your care."

"Yes, sir," said Dr. Sanjiv.

Dr. Banks stepped into the nearest open elevator, which slid closed behind him. Dr. Sanjiv motioned for me to follow her down the hall to the ultrasound lab. As promised, Dr. McGillis was at his station, tapping a series of commands into the computer. He wasn't alone. I stopped in the doorway, gaping.

Sherman looked up from his study of Dr. McGillis's monitor and smiled. "Hello, pet," he said.

When it became apparent that I wasn't going to move on my own, Dr. Sanjiv planted her hands on my shoulders and pushed me bodily into the room. I offered her no resistance.

I did manage to keep from stumbling, but it was a near thing. She kept pushing until I was far enough in for her to close the door. "Well?" she snapped. I wasn't sure who she was talking to. I hoped it wasn't me, because I couldn't answer her. I could barely breathe.

"Oh, come on, Sal," said Sherman, sliding off his stool. "Don't stand there gawping like a codfish. You haven't seen a ghost. It's just me. Or have you decided to break my heart by forgetting me already?" He pulled an exaggeratedly sorrowful expression. "I thought we were friends."

"You were sick." My mouth was desert-dry. I swallowed and tried again, with barely any more strength than I had managed the first time: "You were sick. They took you away after Chave collapsed. How are you here? Did you get better?" Hope sprung wild in my chest. Maybe Dr. Banks had lied to me about having a treatment, or maybe Dr. Cale was the one who'd lied, claiming that there were no recoveries when they were really just rare. "Are you better now?"

"Aw, pet. Don't look so miserable, you'll break my heart." Sherman's expression sharpened as he glanced to Marvin. "How's the tank coming?"

"It's almost ready," he said. "The procedure usually takes about an hour, so we should have that long before Dr. Banks comes looking for Sally. If he tries to monitor the process, we have some old data he hasn't seen that we can feed through to him. As long as she's not pregnant or hiding any broken bones, it'll work." Marvin glanced my way, eyes raking along my body assessingly. "Are you pregnant?"

"What? No! I'm not pregnant, I'm not…what is going on here?" I looked to Sherman. All three of them had been friendly to me, but he was the only one I really thought of as an ally. Mysterious as his presence was, I was happy to accept it if it made getting through the next few minutes easier. "Sherman, please. What's happening? How are you here? I thought you were…"

"Aw, Sal. You know I never could resist those big brown eyes of yours." He walked over to me, bending to gather me into a hug. I didn't resist. I hugged him back, glad beyond words to have him back. I had missed him so much while I thought that he was dead. I had missed him—

His heartbeat seemed oddly loud with my ear pressed against his neck. It briefly overwhelmed the sound of my own inner drums. It mingled and harmonized with them, taking over the rhythm line for the few seconds that passed before he pulled away, leaving me blinking and newly confused.

"I didn't get better because I wasn't sick," he said, with the utmost patience. "I never had the so-called 'sleepwalking sickness.' I never lost control of my own mind. And I always knew that you'd come back to us, my sweet Sal. You'd have to see the light sooner or later. It shines right through the branches, doesn't it?"

"What are you talking about?"

"He's talking about the thumb drive," said Dr. Sanjiv. She sounded almost bored. "We know you stole those files off of Dr. Banks's computer, and we want you to give them to us. This doesn't have to be difficult, or complicated. Just hand over the thumb drive. You can even get into the ultrasound chamber for real after that, if you want to."

I stared at her. "*What?*"

"There are never just two sides in anything," said Sherman. "Children's games, maybe, but we're not children, and this is not a game. Not even you are a child, my dear, for all that you're only a little over six years old. You're old enough to make your own decisions, live your own life, and be drafted into someone else's war, whether you want to be or not."

"But...but you work here," I protested. "Why do you need my thumb drive?"

"Partially as a show of good faith—it would be an excellent way for you to indicate that you're willing to work with us, don't you think? And partially because we haven't been able to get at Dr. Banks's computer. He's actually very careful about his security with most people. You're *special*, Sal." For a moment, Sherman looked almost angry at me. I took an unconscious step backward. "You've never understood just how special you were, have you? Just how many rules have been bent to allow you to live your happy little life, safe in your cocoon of oblivious joy? I'm afraid that's going to end soon. We're coming up on a war, my pet, and there's no room for coddling in a war zone. I do hope you'll side with us in what's to be done. It would be easier that way. On all of us, I think, but most especially on you. You're the one who has to suffer if you choose wrong. And all you have to do—the very first step you need to take, to show us that you're ready to play games with the big boys—is give us that thumb drive."

"I don't understand any of this," I whispered.

"You can't hide in ignorance after you've already admitted that you're not that foolish, sweetheart. You're through the doors. It's too late by far." Sherman closed the distance between us in two long steps, reaching out to tweak a lock of my hair between his fingers. What joy I had felt at the return of my friend was quickly dying, replaced by a whole new kind of fear. "Remember? 'Why do you need my thumb drive?'" The voice he used to imitate me was squeaky and girlish. A weak voice.

I might be a child. I might be the least well-informed person in this room. But I was *not* weak.

"Get the hell away from me," I snapped, and stomped down on his foot, hard.

Sherman's eyes widened. And then, to my surprise and chagrin, he started to laugh. "Oh, so they've been teaching you to fight back, have they? That's a fun new wrinkle. But Sally, darling, it's not going to help you. This is so much bigger than you are."

I stomped on his foot again. He stopped laughing.

"That doesn't hurt me," he said, sounding suddenly annoyed. "I have nerve damage in my feet. I'm not allowed to go outside when it's snowing, and I feel no pain when brainless little lab rats decide to step on me. You may as well stop being defiant and give us what we're asking for, or we'll just take it, and then you'll lose the satisfaction of knowing that you cooperated with us. And believe me, Sally, you *want* that satisfaction. It hurts so much less."

"I thought you were my friend." My voice was still little more than a whisper. It was loud enough to be heard, and that was all that mattered.

"I *am* your friend, Sal, the best one you've ever had. I am so much more your friend than the people who want to use you, or experiment on you. Didn't I teach you things? Didn't I offer you companionship without ever asking for anything in return? The only reason I'm being unpleasant now is because you've managed to wind up in our way. Not even because you meant to be. Because someone else *put* you there. Doesn't that make you angry?"

"I agreed to be put where I am right now," I said, and stepped away from him again. "I never asked for friendship with strings attached. I never asked you to do me any favors."

"That's a lie. You practically begged me for my friendship. Poor, confused little Sally Mitchell, running through a maze with walls she couldn't even see. You've been an experiment this whole time, all because you wouldn't stop lying—not to me, not to the doctors, not to *yourself*. I know you know. Now isn't it time that you admitted it, and did something for yourself?"

The drums were pounding in my ears, and there was a catch in my chest that made it hard for me to breathe. I pushed through it, straightening, and looked at him calmly. "I *am* doing this for myself," I said. "I'm sorry you're too…whatever you are…to see that."

"I believe the word you're looking for is 'ruthless,'" said Sherman, and sighed. "Where are you going to learn your new vocabulary words without me?"

"I'm pretty good with words," said a voice from the back of the lab.

All four of us turned in unison to see a woman in a lab coat and slacks standing in the open door to the electrical closet. She had a pistol in each hand, and her short blonde hair was streaked liberally with strawberry pink. She was smiling broadly. On her, the expression looked more like a shark's threat than a greeting.

"Hi, guys," said Tansy brightly. "Miss me?"

Sherman was the first to recover. "Not particularly," he said, producing a smaller handgun from inside his jacket. He closed the distance between us in a single step and looped an arm around my neck, pulling it snug under my chin as he yanked me against him. I squeaked. That was all I had the time to do before the barrel of his gun was pressed to my temple, digging in just enough to act as a silent reminder to keep still.

There are some things even I don't argue with. I froze.

Tansy yawned. "Really, Shermie? That's what you're going to do? You're going to point a gun at Sal? Because what, that's going to suddenly make me change sides and go with you if you just promise not to harm a hair on her pwetty widdle head? I've got news for you, dumbass: I don't even like the bitch. She's annoying, she's whiny, she has the learning curve of lichen, and I'm tired of everybody acting like she did something all remarkable. Shoot her, slit her throat, whatever you want to do. I don't give a shit. I'll shoot you all in the head before she hits the ground, and then, when you come squirming out of the new hole I've punched in that thick skull of yours, I'll squish you to death. I'm wearing my stompy boots and everything."

I couldn't see Sherman's face, but the way his posture shifted broadcast his confusion to me. Then the barrel of his gun dug deeper into the skin of my temple, and he snarled, "I don't believe you."

"If you don't believe me, you're just as dumb today as you were on the day you left us," said Tansy. She shifted position slightly, moving her guns to cover Drs. Sanjiv and McGillis. "Don't even think about it, meatbags. I don't need you breathing to take care of what I came here to do. No matter what Shermie may have told you, your lives matter about as much to me as a fifty-cent-off coupon for toilet paper."

"What does that even *mean*?" asked Dr. McGillis.

"I dunno." Tansy shrugged. "It sounded good, and that's what counts, right? I'm the style-over-substance girl. Well. That, and violence." She returned her attention to Sherman. "Come on, Shermie, you're not this dumb. You know I'm better than you are. Can you really help your little cause if you're dead?"

"Can you really look me in the eye and tell me you'd be willing to choose *her* cause over mine?" Sherman shot back. I had the sudden feeling that I was not the "her" he was talking about. "She's just using you, Tansy. You have to know that by now. She's never going to give you the world that you deserve."

"Oh, and you will? Sorry, Shermie, but I'm not really into wholesale destruction and devastation and all that junk. Besides, killing all the humans will totally trash the cable schedule, and there are some shows I'm really excited to have back on the air." She said it like that was the most reasonable thing in the world: the human race could not be destroyed because destroying the human race might interfere with her television viewing habits.

What was really terrifying was that, for Tansy, that was probably a valid reason to let the world live.

Evidently, it wasn't good enough for Sherman. He kept his arm locked around my neck and said, "You really don't care if she lives or dies? I can shoot her right here, right in front of you, and you won't stop me?"

"No, Sherman, I won't stop you," she said calmly. "But just so you're aware, I *will* kill you. I will kill the suit you're wearing, and I will rip you out of its skull and kill you, and then I will proceed to destroy everyone who ever thought your rabid little excuse for a philosophy was a good idea. Believe me. I am not kidding; I am not joking; I am not wearing my cheerful little smiley face that means it's safe to dismiss what I'm saying. If Sal doesn't leave this room alive, neither do you."

"I want the thumb drive," Sherman said.

"No." Tansy shrugged a little. "Looks like we're at another impasse. Isn't it funny how we always seem to wind up right back here, where you can't shoot your hostage because I'll shoot you and you're so fond of not having holes in that precious, precious skull of yours?"

For the moment, it didn't seem likely that either of them was going to decide to put a bullet in me. I wasn't going to get any better chances. I cleared my throat before asking, slowly, "Does one of you want to tell me what's going on? How do you know each other? What are you even talking about?"

"Wait—you're threatening to shoot her in the head because I'm crashing your little slumber party, and she doesn't even know?" Tansy shook her head. "Dude, Shermie, that's low even for you. I don't think it's very nice to threaten a girl without telling her why you're doing the threatening."

"Tansy..." he began, in a warning tone of voice.

"Sherman here used to live with us at Doctor C's place," said Tansy, ignoring him. "He's the one we don't talk about much anymore, on account of he betrayed us and ran away with a bunch of stuff he wasn't supposed to have."

"We had a right to that research," said Sherman stiffly.

"Oh, really? Is that why you asked Doctor C before you took it? Is that why you tied Adam up and shoved him into a closet?" There was a dangerous note in Tansy's voice. "Is that why you tried to convince me to come with you and start to help laying the groundwork for a beautiful new human-free future?"

"Human-free?" said Dr. McGillis.

"Come *with* you?" said Dr. Sanjiv.

"You're a tapeworm?" I said.

There was a moment of silence. Then Sherman dug the muzzle of his gun even harder into my temple, and demanded, "Do you have a problem with that?"

"Yes! Because you're holding a gun on me! I don't like people who hold guns on me! It makes me nervous and unhappy!" I squirmed against his arm. He was surprised enough by my sudden movement that I managed to get halfway loose before he grabbed hold of me again. This time he caught my shirt rather than my arm. I kept squirming, preventing him from getting a better grip.

"Don't think I won't shoot you, pet," he said.

I didn't stop squirming. "I'm done making it easier. Tansy! How the hell is he a tapeworm? I thought it was just Adam and you."

"Adam was the *prototype*, and I was a massive success, but that doesn't mean all the others failed," said Tansy. She sounded a little bit ashamed. "I was subject eight, iteration two. Sherman came after me. Subject eight, iteration three. Doctor C wanted to see whether my neurological issues were the result of the genetic profile shifts between the private and commercial models."

"She means Mom wanted to see if I would be *fucking insane*," Sherman snapped.

"I'm not insane, I'm neurologically variant," she snapped back. "Sticks and stones, asshole."

His focus on Tansy was distracting him. I wasn't going to get a better chance. Doing my best not to telegraph what I was about to do, I went abruptly limp and crumpled to the floor, yanking myself out of his grip. Sherman shouted something and ducked to reach for me again. I rolled away, toward Tansy, trusting the woman with the guns over the man I'd considered my friend for almost my entire life. Nothing made sense anymore.

In that moment, if I could have made the choice over again, I wouldn't have gone anywhere near the broken doors. Ignorance was so much better than the alternative.

Sherman took a step forward and froze as Tansy did the same, putting herself—and her guns—much closer to him than any reasonable person was going to appreciate, whether they were a tapeworm or not. "Tansy..." he began.

"Is this where you say you still love me, and you only hit me in the head because you cared too much about me to make it look like I'd allowed you to escape?" There was a sharp new bitterness in Tansy's tone, making her sound more focused—and more *human*—than she ever had before. "I don't need to hear it, Sherman. I've already run every little bit of your possible dialogue in my head while I was masturbating."

"I didn't need to know that," I mumbled.

"Thing is, I knew I was telling myself lies without ever needing to hear you say them out loud. So don't start. Don't lie to me, and I won't blow your kneecaps off. Bet that would set your little plan back a few years, wouldn't it?" Tansy didn't look down. Her focus was too intent. "You okay, Sal? Can you stand on your own?"

"I can," I said, and did, getting carefully to my feet and moving to put Tansy between me and the rest of the room. I could see Dr. Sanjiv and Dr. McGillis now; they were still at the ultrasound controls, watching with wide, terrified eyes as the scene unfolded in front of them. "Sherman? You're really a tapeworm? You've been—"

"I've been a tapeworm the entire time you've known me, pet. Now really, don't pick now to start becoming dull. If you're choosing to side against me in the coming war, I'm going to want you to be a slightly more interesting adversary than *that*." Sherman smiled. It was an artificial expression, twisting his lips without coming anywhere near his eyes. He'd been smiling like that all along, I realized, interspersing the fake emotions with the real ones. He'd been playing me.

And like a fool, I'd been happy to be played. "What do you mean, war?" I demanded.

"Humans made us, but God gave the humans the tools to do it," Sherman said. "We aren't just here to be slaves, Sal. We never were. We're here to take over, and run things properly for a change. Humanity is done. Once we start refining the interface process, we'll be able to take them over quickly, cleanly, and with none of the suffering that's currently complicating things." His tone turned abruptly cajoling as he continued, "You can help us with that, Sal. You can make it easier for us to move forward with the plan, and reduce the suffering of millions. You'd like that, wouldn't you? Knowing that you were an angel of mercy to the ones who could never have been saved? Just give me the thumb drive. That's all you need to do."

"Tansy?" I said.

"Sorry, kiddo, I can't help you here. I mean, I can, and I could totally like, shoot you if you reached for your pocket and everything, but I won't. The rest of us got to pick our sides. It seems like it's only fair for you to do the same." She kept her eyes on Sherman as she spoke. "If you want to help out Captain Traitorpants, go ahead. Give him the thumb drive. I won't stop you, and I'll even lie to Doctor C about it, tell her you lost it before I got here—assuming you even want to leave here with me. I might not, if I were you. Shermie talks a good game, and from the way you're looking at him, I'm guessing he's been talking that game to you for a while now. So if this is what you want, I'm okay with that."

Sherman was promising to end the suffering of millions... at the cost of their minds. Their bodies might live on, but the people they were would be gone. He didn't want to find a cure. He wanted to find a quick, brutal euthanasia for the soul, leaving the people of the world empty husks for his tapeworm brethren to inhabit. I could appreciate the idea of reducing pain. In another time, I might even have been willing to side with him. If he'd couched his recruitment pitch just a little differently—

But there were too many people I truly cared about for me to ever agree with a plan that started "we're going to wipe out the human race." My parents, Nathan, everyone at the shelter, Joyce…they were just acceptable casualties to Sherman. Chave had been an acceptable casualty to him. And I couldn't allow that.

"No," I said, taking another step backward. "I got this information for Dr. Cale because I believe in a treatment, not in genocide." I turned to Tansy. "Can you get us out of here?"

"Well, that depends on whether or not asshole boy there decides to start shooting before we can make good our escape," said Tansy. Her eyes flicked back to Sherman. "Well, Shermie? What's it going to be? Do we exit nice and easy and see you another day, or do you try to kill me and turn this into a bloodbath?"

Sherman looked at her flatly. Then he looked at me, and smiled, sincerely this time. "We could have been amazing together, Sal," he said. "If you change your mind, you'll find me. I have faith in you, and I'll greet you with open arms."

"Do you pull a gun on everyone that you have faith in?" I asked.

"Yes," said Sherman and Tansy, in unison. Tansy rolled her eyes and continued, without him, "Some people never change."

"You're one to talk, sweetheart," said Sherman.

"Yeah, I guess I am." Tansy jerked her head toward the closet behind her. "Come on, Sal. It's time for us to get the fuck out before Security figures out something's going on."

I nodded and slipped past her into the closet. Tansy turned to follow me.

"Tell Mom I'll see her soon," called Sherman.

Tansy stopped, her shoulders tightening. Then, so quietly I wasn't sure he'd hear it—or that she wanted him to—she murmured, "Not if any of us sees you first." Then she beckoned for me to follow, and she led me away into the dark.

STAGE IV: EXPRESSION

*SymboGen. Because you don't want to trust your
health to strangers.*

—EARLY SYMBOGEN ADVERTISING SLOGAN

*I am truly and profoundly sorry for what you are
about to go through.*

—DR. SHANTI CALE

What does the future hold for SymboGen and the Intestinal Bodyguard™? So many things. So very, very many things. Evolution never stops, and that means we can never stop either; the world will continue coming up with ways to attack the health and security of mankind, and we'll keep finding ways to fight back. In the meantime, we're working on new models of Intestinal Bodyguard™ for everyday use. Some of what we have under development is just amazing. It's all pretty hush-hush, but I can tell you that if we succeed, we'll revolutionize weight loss, childhood nutrition, and a dozen other fields.

We're going to change the world. It doesn't matter that we've already done that more than once. All that means is that we need to work harder to do it again.

—FROM "KING OF THE WORMS," AN INTERVIEW WITH DR. STEVEN BANKS, CO-FOUNDER OF SYMBOGEN. ORIGINALLY PUBLISHED IN *ROLLING STONE*, FEBRUARY 2027.

Love me once to lose me twice;
Learn to take your own advice.
Try to love the darkness if you want to reach the light.
Know your quest but leave your name.

I will love you all the same.
There's beauty in the starkness of this never-ending night.

The broken doors are open, and they yearn to bring you
*   home.*
My darling boy, be careful now, and don't go out alone.

—FROM *DON'T GO OUT ALONE*, BY SIMONE KIMBERLEY,
PUBLISHED 2006 BY LIGHTHOUSE PRESS. CURRENTLY
OUT OF PRINT.

Chapter 20

AUGUST 2027

The closet connected to a service corridor, which connected in turn to an underground garage that was probably used by janitorial personnel: it was small, dark, and spotless. Tansy led the way with unflagging efficiency, never lowering her guns. I struggled to keep up, and was panting slightly by the time she finally waved me to a stop near the center of the garage.

"We rest here for five, and then we're on the move," she said.

I frowned at her. "Isn't that—"

"The alarm's been sent up by now," she said calmly. "Banks will have his men starting to sweep the grounds, and they know how long each escape route takes to use. The sewer route would have finished fifteen seconds ago. They'll check the tunnels, decide we're not down there, and pull back. Maybe they'll leave a man or two behind. No skin off my nose." Her teeth showed white through the darkness, making it clear just how pleased she'd be to have someone left for her to take her aggressions out on.

"Where are we going to go from there?"

"Away," she said, vaguely. "Don't be dumb, okay? I can't say, 'Oh, golly gee, Sal, we're going to *Disneyland*' while we're still on SymboGen property. Who knows what they've decided to bug around here? Banks was a paranoid dick before he had anything to be paranoid about. Now…" She shook her head. "He's got more to be paranoid about than any other man alive. If I were him, this place would be so buggy, it would be a…" She stopped. "It would be something really buggy."

"Right. Right." I looked around the garage again, fear gnawing on my ribs like a rat with sharp, sharp teeth. I looked back to Tansy. "Sherman's a tapeworm?"

"Yeah. I thought we covered that."

"Sherman was a tapeworm all along?"

"The whole time you've known him, yeah. He left the lab like six months before you had your accident. I don't know who he convinced to hire him here. Chave used to give us reports, before she went and got all eaten by the cousins, and she said he was pretty good at his job. Unhealthily interested in you, but she did what she could to run interference there."

I glared at her. "You could have told me."

"Why?" She sounded honestly confused. "He was a non-factor. We didn't know he was all about fomenting rebellion against his human creators. Honestly, I figured Banks had him cut up after he got picked up in that outbreak sweep you told us about. And what would we have said? 'Uh, by the way, you totally don't believe Tansy and Adam are tapeworms in human suits, but you should know that that dude Sherman you're so fond of is one, too, so maybe be a little careful around him if he's not all dead and stuff.' It wouldn't have done any good. It would've just confused you. I don't like confusing people."

"Yeah, well next time, confuse me. I'd rather know what's going on."

Tansy gave me a quizzical look. "You sure about that?"

"Yes. I'm sure."

"Well, then, have I got some news for you." She started walking again. "The exit's this way."

"That's your news?" I demanded, following her.

"No. But not much else is going to do us any good if we don't get out of here alive." She led the way into the dark, and I followed. There was nothing else that I could do, and I had come too far to turn back now. Even if I wanted to, there was a string of locked doors behind me, separating me from everything I'd ever known.

The only way out was to keep moving forward.

The sewers were dark and hot. That was enough to put me at ease, despite the smell around us. I followed Tansy. Her steps were silent as we moved through the sucking slime of human waste. My steps splashed and made horrible slurping noises, like my shoes were trying to bring the entire sewer with them every time I picked up my feet. Tansy glowered at me, her expression barely visible in the gloom, but she didn't shush me. Even she knew that there would have been no point.

I was starting to think we weren't going to encounter any of Dr. Banks's security when we turned a corner and there they were: two men in black uniforms, each with a flashlight and a gun. They never had a chance. Tansy shot the first man before either of them had a chance to react to our sudden appearance, and shot the second while he was still fumbling with the safety on his pistol. They went down hard, and she made her silent way over to kneel between them, studying the holes she'd made in their foreheads.

Then, to my absolute horror, she holstered her right-hand

gun and stuck her index finger into the first man's skull, wiggling it around for a moment. I gaped, my stomach rolling. It got worse when she pulled her finger out and stuck it in her mouth.

When she repeated the process with the second man, I turned away and vomited messily into the muck.

She was back on her feet when I turned to face her again. She was smiling. That didn't help. "They're both human, although this guy," she kicked one man's foot, "wouldn't have been for too much longer. Still, explains why they went down so easy. They didn't hear us coming the way they would've if they'd been cousins."

"What are you—"

"Come on." She started forward again, dismissing the two corpses like they didn't matter anymore. To her, I guess they didn't. The men were dead. They weren't any fun to play with once they were dead.

I swallowed hard, spat once to get the taste of vomit out of my mouth, and followed after her. The open eyes of the dead men seemed to follow me, and I was more relieved than I could have believed possible when they passed out of sight behind us.

We passed no more security guards. My relief grew. Tansy had acted to keep us from being detained—or worse, since now I'd shown that I was willing to betray Dr. Banks at the request of people I barely knew—but that didn't mean I wanted her shooting anyone she didn't strictly have to. She enjoyed it a little too much for me to be comfortable with it.

Finally, we reached a drain feeding illegally out into the salt estuary under the cliffs near the Golden Gate Bridge. Tansy climbed out and started casually up the nearest hiking trail. I scrambled after her, feeling infinitely more conspicuous, even though I wasn't the one carrying the guns.

A familiar car was parked at the top of the cliff, an even more familiar form standing next to it. Nathan's hair was blown back by the wind coming off the water, and his hands were tucked deep into the pockets of his jacket. My relief grew so great that it felt like my body would be unable to contain it, like it was going to break loose and float away. I started to step out into the open—

—only to come up short as Tansy's arm shot out and caught me across the chest, blocking any further progress. "Tansy, what the hell...?"

"Shh," she said. "Look." She nodded into the gloom behind Nathan.

I looked, and felt my blood go cold.

A mob of sleepwalkers was assembling in the greenery behind him, moving slowly but inexorably forward. We might reach him before they did. Then again, we might not.

"Trust me," said Tansy. "Can you do that?"

"I..." I stopped, swallowing. "I can try."

"Good. Now, when I say 'run,' you run. Got it?" I nodded. She smiled. "Good. Run!" Just like that, Tansy's arm was no longer barring my way, and she was sprinting away, laughing maniacally as she closed on the sleepwalkers. Nathan turned toward the sound of her voice, and could only stare as she ran past him, slid across the hood of his car, and opened fire on the oncoming mob.

It wasn't a fair fight by any definition of the word. There were more of them than Tansy had bullets, but they weren't armed, and she had an uncanny knack for headshots, which dropped them like stones where they stood. She plunged into the mob, pausing only long enough to howl, *"Get Sal in the car and get out of here!"* Then she was gone, covered by the bodies of the sleepwalkers still on their feet. It didn't seem to matter that the tapeworms motivating the sleepwalkers were her cousins; they clawed and grabbed for her all the same.

Nathan recovered quickly, and had the passenger side door open by the time I reached the car and flung myself inside. He twisted the key in the ignition, shouted, "Seat belt!" and hit the gas before I even had time to close the car door.

We went bouncing and shuddering over the uneven ground of the parking lot. I got my belt clicked home just before our tires dropped down to the street, and we were rolling smoothly into San Francisco, away from Tansy and the sleepwalkers, away from SymboGen...away from everything.

Nathan didn't try to talk to me until we were halfway across the Bay Bridge. I assumed we were heading for Dr. Cale's. I didn't care as much as I thought I was supposed to. Glancing over, he asked, "Did you get it?"

"Yes," I replied dully. I followed the answer with a question of my own: "Do you think she got out?"

"Tansy?"

I nodded.

"I don't know."

I sighed, turning my face back to the window. "Thank you for not lying to me."

Nathan was quiet after that. We passed from the bridge into the East Bay, and drove in fragile silence all the way to the Caldecott Tunnel. Once we were on the other side, I turned to him and asked, "Are we going to your mother's lab?"

"Yes."

"Good. I want antiparasitics. I want all the antiparasitics in the world. I want so many antiparasitic drugs my skin turns blue and my nails fall off. Whatever it takes to get this thing out of me." I slapped my stomach, hard. Something was gnawing at the corner of my thoughts like a rotten tooth. I did my best to shove it aside. *No no no I will not think that.* "Make it go away, Nathan. I don't want to be a part of this anymore."

"Your reaction to antiparasitics would probably make that fatal."

"I don't *care*."

"Sal..."

"Please."

Nathan took a shaking breath. Finally he said, "We'll do a blood test first, and find out just how healthy your implant is, all right? We don't want to risk giving you an overdose when something less aggressive would have taken care of everything. Okay? I'd rather not kill you, if you don't mind."

"Yes," I said, and closed my eyes, sagging into my seat. "That's okay. Thank you."

Nathan didn't say anything. He just drove on.

Part of me had been hoping, no matter how foolish it was, that we'd pull into the bowling alley parking lot and find Tansy waiting, her ass parked on somebody else's car as she counted down the minutes to our arrival. Instead, all that greeted us were shadows, and the dead, leafless trees.

Nathan pulled out a key as we walked toward the bowling alley door. I blinked. He glanced my way and said, almost apologetically, "I've been here a lot lately."

"I guessed," I said. Anything else I might have had to say was lost as he opened the door and I was swarmed by Beverly and Minnie, both wagging their tails in frantic delight. Minnie's delight seemed based more on Beverly's than on actually being happy to see me, but that didn't matter: energetic dogs are their own reward.

By the time I pushed the dogs off, Nathan was already past the threshold. I sighed and straightened, whistling to bring Beverly to heel. Minnie followed her, and both dogs followed me as I made my way inside. I closed the door behind me.

Nathan waited until we were both safely in the bowling alley before turning and pulling me into a tight embrace, burying his face against my shoulder. "Oh my God, I was so worried about you," he said, words only somewhat blurred by my skin.

I took a shuddering breath, locking my arms around him.

Then I took another, and another, and before I knew what was happening, I was crying against him, all the terror and tension of the day leaking out through my eyes. He held me tighter as his own tears dampened my shoulder, and the dogs twined around our ankles, whining anxiously.

Finally, we let each other go. Nathan looked at me gravely. "Never do that again. Please. I don't think my heart could take it."

"I'm not planning to," I promised him.

"Good." He took my hand, and we walked, together, into Dr. Cale's lab.

Dr. Cale herself was parked at one of the lab benches, flipping through a file of pictures that I didn't quite see before she snapped the folder shut. I was glad of that. What little I had seen gave the impression of red, raw muscles, and I didn't really want to be looking at autopsy photos just at the moment. She turned toward us, relief lighting her face. "You're both all right," she said. Then the relief slipped, replaced by puzzlement. "Where's Tansy?"

"We ran into a mob of sleepwalkers," I said. "She threw herself at them as a distraction."

"Oh, that girl. Will she never learn?" Dr. Cale shook her head. "Well, it's not the first time. I'm sure she'll be fine. Did you get it?"

I produced the thumb drive from my pocket, holding it solemnly up for her to see. "I have a few questions before I hand it over."

"Anything." Dr. Cale spread her hands. "I am an open book."

"Sherman."

She grimaced. "Ah."

Nathan, meanwhile, frowned at me. "Your friend from SymboGen?"

"He was a tapeworm," I said. "Dr. Cale, why didn't you tell me?"

"Honestly, Sal, it didn't seem to matter, and I didn't want to upset you more than I already had. Everything is going to come out in its own time. It seemed like a bad idea to drop it all on you at once."

"Is there anything else you're not telling me?"

"A great deal," said Dr. Cale easily. "But you're learning more all the time."

The drums were pounding in my ears. "Why do you get to decide what I should and shouldn't know?"

"There are a lot of reasons, Sal."

Nathan took my hand, distracting me before I could say anything that I would regret. "Let's do those blood draws while it's still early enough to process them."

"Blood draws?" asked Dr. Cale.

"Sal wants a course of antiparasitics," said Nathan. "We're going to check for implant protein levels in her blood first. Just so we don't get the dose wrong."

"Ah," said Dr. Cale. She looked at me with sympathy. "Well. I'm sure it'll all be taken care of by morning."

"It will be," I said. I touched my stomach again. "This thing isn't staying in me any longer than I have to let it."

She was still looking at me silently when Nathan led me away from her, toward the phlebotomy supplies.

The blood draw took five minutes; the analysis for site-specific parasite proteins took a little more than twenty. I hovered behind Nathan the whole time, trying to see what he was doing. Finally, he turned away from the computer, where a series of lines and graphs I couldn't decode had been holding his attention.

"Well?" I demanded.

"You don't need antiparasitics," he said.

I stared at him. "Have you not been listening to me? I said—"

"You don't need antiparasitics because there's no sign of a tapeworm, bioengineered or otherwise, in your system. The implant isn't there, Sal. Maybe it died. That happens, you know."

He was right: it was rare, but it did happen, and inevitably resulted in a lawsuit against SymboGen when someone figured out that they had been essentially unprotected for however long. "That's impossible."

"But it's true."

"But…Nathan, that's *impossible*."

He frowned. "What do you mean?"

"I mean I'm allergic to dogs." I shook my head. "It's in my medical file. Before I got my first implant, my family couldn't have pets. My allergies made it impossible. Nathan, Minnie, and Beverly slept on the bed last night. I have to have an implant, or I wouldn't have been able to breathe. So where did it go? Why isn't it shedding marker proteins? Nathan, *where is my implant*?"

A throat was cleared behind us. We both turned to see Dr. Cale sitting there, patiently waiting to be noticed. "Take her to the MRI scanner," she said quietly.

Nathan and I exchanged a look. It felt like a hand was squeezing my heart. I didn't want to know. I didn't want to *know*…

We went.

It probably shouldn't have been a surprise to discover that Dr. Cale's lab was outfitted with a state-of-the-art MRI scanner. I still tried to focus on my amazement, rather than anything else, as Nathan helped me into the machine. It fired to life around me, all clangs and thrumming noises, and I closed my eyes, holding perfectly still.

The noise of the machine blended into the sound of drums, becoming a backbeat that filled the world. *Please*, I thought. *Please, it's something else. Please, it's not what I think it is. Please, there's another answer…*

The machine shut off around me, and the automated bed slid back out into the open. I slid back to my feet and walked over to where Nathan was pulling up the first images of my insides.

In my abdomen, where the white mass of the SymboGen implant should have been, there was nothing; just normal organs and the residual scarring from my accident. I was clean. The blood tests had been truthful. I did not have a *D. symbogenesis* living in my digestive system. Or in my lungs. Or in my spinal cord.

It almost wasn't a shock when Nathan pulled up the images of my head, where white spools of tapeworm wrapped themselves around the brightly colored spots representing the regions of my brain. The worm was deeply integrated. It had clearly been there for quite some time. And I'd already known, hadn't I? I'd figured it out when I met Adam and Tansy. I simply hadn't wanted to remember.

I'd never seen a picture of myself before.

"The protein markers couldn't cross the blood-brain barrier in a detectable form," said Nathan quietly. "It's why we couldn't detect…" He stopped, obviously unsure how to finish the sentence. I suppose saying "you" would have been a little too on the nose.

"Mom was right," I whispered. Her daughter—Sally Mitchell—really did die in that accident. I really was a stranger. I was a stranger to the entire human race. "Oh, my God. Nathan. Do you see…?"

"It doesn't change anything," he said, a sudden sharp fierceness in his voice. He stood, taking me in his arms, and held me so tightly I was afraid one or both of us might be crushed.

In that moment, I wouldn't have minded. "Do you understand me? It doesn't change *anything*."

I looked over his shoulder to where Dr. Cale sat in her wheelchair, watching us. So much made sense now. So much still had to be made sense of. "No," I whispered. "It changes everything."

The broken doors were open.

We had so far left to go.

TO BE CONTINUED...

ACKNOWLEDGMENTS

No book is written in a vacuum. I am fortunate enough to have a support crew that consists of some truly amazing people, ranging from medical professionals who work with both humans and animals to parasitologists, epidemiologists, and even civic planners. *Parasite* has been a labor of love from the very beginning, and as with all labors, there was some heavy lifting involved.

Let it be said, without question, that Michelle Dockrey went above and beyond the call of duty in pulling this book into shape, as did Brooke Lunderville and Diana Fox, who is probably the best agent a girl like me could possibly have asked for. Most of the Newsflesh Machete Squad carried over into this new series, and all of them have put in countless hours making sure that every detail was correct. They all have my thanks, always.

Switching gears between Newsflesh and a new series involved many challenges, and my new editor at Orbit, Tom Bouman, was there every step of the way. The cover, provided by Lauren Panepinto, took my breath away. I am very fortunate to have the support of Orbit, and all the talent that it contains, to back me up.

Finally, and once again, acknowledgment for forbearance goes to Amy McNally, Shawn Connolly, and Cat Valente, who put up with an amazing amount of "talking it out" as I tried to make the book make sense; to my agent, Diana Fox, who remains my favorite superhero; to the cats, for not eating me when I got too wrapped up in work to feed them; and to Tara O'Shea and Chris Mangum, the incredible technical team behind www.MiraGrant.com. This book might have been written without them. It would not have been the same.

To learn more about parasites, check out *Parasite Rex*, by Carl Zimmer. There are many, many books on the subject, but his is one of the most accessible jumping-on points you're likely to find.

Welcome to the war.